JAMES AND THE
BAND OF FIRE

THE
BAND
OF FIRE
CHRONICLES

YE 1 AR

Dr Brandt R Gibson

JAMES AND THE BAND OF FIRE

DR BRANDT R GIBSON

AUTHOR ACADEMY elite

This is a work of fiction. All of the characters, organizations, and events portrayed in this novel are either products of the author's imagination or are used fictitiously.

Printed in the United States of America
Published by Author Academy Elite
P.O. Box 43, Powell, OH 43035

www.AuthorAcademyElite.com

Paperback ISBN-13: 978-1-64085-305-8
Hardcover ISBN-13: 978-1-64085-306-5
Ebook ISBN-13: 978-1-64085-307-2

Library of Congress Control Number: 2018943112

To my Angel Wife and my 11 Children
who daily inspire me.

CONTENTS

CHAPTER 1
THE MORNING BREAKS

He woke with a start to feel the cold, hard ground through his thin foam pad as he lay in the dark. He still felt tired from another restless night on the ground. This was not the first time he was awaken in the dark of the night, but this night was different. The usual soft hum of the nightlife was absent. He couldn't even hear the chirp of the crickets. What was going on? Why was everything so silent?

He struggled to focus his eyes in the darkness and then realized he still lay alone in his tent and couldn't hear the sounds from the other tents either. Where had everyone else gone? He felt a strong sense of foreboding and could no longer try to sleep without looking around. He had to know what was going on. He had to ensure everyone else was safe for they were his responsibility. He was their guide and had even picked this spot to camp for the night.

He carefully unzipped his sleeping bag, pulled on his jacket and clothes over the nightclothes he was wearing and crawled over to the tent door. As he looked out, the soft breeze that started just after he retired to bed was continuing to softly move the trees in the distance. But even the full moon was now covered by a dark overcast sky. Not even the stars were visible. Without light he couldn't even see the other tents that should be surrounding his. Something was wrong, but he didn't yet know what.

No lights. No ability to see. And no sounds…except a soft musical hum. He recognized the song but couldn't see where it was coming from. Just then he saw a small light appear before his eyes and the music gave way to a laugh….

James awoke still hearing the laughter, but not knowing where it had come from. He was not sure where that dream came from either, but it was just one more dream from the last four days. This was the first dream however that ended with that laugh. He felt as if he recognized the laugh, although he had never heard it before. Why was he having such weird dreams? Who was in the tent? And where was the tent located? As he thought, he realized that it was finally the morning of his 12th birthday and he was ready to spend time with friends and family celebrating. But it was only 3:00am and nobody would be moving in the house yet. He should go back to sleep, but sleep had left him after the dream, so he would spend the next several hours lost in his own thoughts.

Life had changed much over the last four years and lots of little things seemed to be happening. He had always struggled with his bow and arrow, but over the last couple years he seemed to be getting more accurate and could now always hit the target. His parents gave him a pocketknife last year and he had become a master at carving wood into small animals, cars, boats and even people. He had just recently completed an entire chess set that he was planning to give his dad for Father's Day. Many of his friends considered that a unique talent, but it seemed to come easily for him.

There were times at school where he could almost hear the thoughts of his fellow students and knew what the teachers wanted before they even asked. The strangest was when cute Sarah, the redhead that he had liked for 2 years was acting different around him. As he watched her walk past, he heard her say, "James is kinda cute. I would love to know him better."

But her mouth never moved. He would have commented, but those words made him blush a little. It was the first and last time he heard her thoughts, but he still hadn't got up the courage to talk with her.

But the weirdest thing seemed to be having animals talk to him every once in a while. He didn't dare ask others if they understood the animals, because it was just "weird" to talk with animals. Prior to his eighth birthday he never had animals talk to him. Now sometimes the dog next door will bark and other times he knows what it is saying. As of yet, however, he has never tried to talk back as he assumed he was just hearing the animal's thoughts like he did people at school. Whatever the reason, this was just one more strange thing happening in his life.

But it wasn't just those things that were different. Now even his parents have started treating him differently over the last year or so. They seemed to be very focused on teaching him about camping and living in the wild. He had known many Boy Scouts that went camping every month, but he wasn't going to have those experiences until he was at least 12 years-old. Maybe they were preparing him for Boy Scouts. They never told him why they were doing it, but they just continued to teach him to sleep in a tent, build fires, cook meals outside, and most importantly to read and use a map and compass.

They really liked him learning about maps, as his dad was a navigator and guide by profession. James had never been as good at maps as dad, but he enjoyed his dad spending time with him. His dad would show him maps and then take him outside and teach him what the map was saying in three dimensions.

"These two lines coming together show you that mountain."

"These lines here tell you there is a river. Do you see it over there?"

"And see how those two mountains come together? That is on the map here."

Dad was truly an expert at reading maps, and could take a map and know perfectly what the land looked like. This was a special gift and allowed him to read a topographic map and lead groups without a compass. He would often leave for weeks at a time with camping supplies to guide groups. Over the years James had been told many times how good his father was at leading others on these expeditions. They also usually paid large amounts for the trips and he was scheduled out months in advance. Maybe his parents were hoping that he too would be able to work as an expedition guide and join the family business. That would be an interesting thought, but in no way was he able to read maps as well as dad did. Often he couldn't even understand the topography from the map. He was very thankful that mom had also showed him how to use a compass with the map to help get it oriented and help him navigate like "normal people" do. Dad was definitely unique and everyone recognized it!

By this time, he was getting tired of lying in bed. He pulled off his covers and quickly changed his clothes so that he could start the day. He loved to watch the sunrise when he was awake and knew that his view would be amazing this morning on his 12th birthday. There were clouds in the distance, but the sky was otherwise very clear and would allow a beautiful view of the sun coming over the mountains. With mountains to his north and to his east, the sunrises were often spectacular.

He quietly opened his window and climbed onto the roof and looked towards the mountains. The full moon was still bright and allowed a perfect view of the Rocky Mountains. He loved their majesty, their beauty and the mystery they had for him. He was hoping that now he was 12 he would get opportunities to camp in those mountains and enjoy their beauty more closely. Mom and dad had never let him camp anywhere but in the backyard yet. Even when others were going camping at 11, he was told that he would need to wait for another year. That long year was finally over. Now he would be asking again for the opportunity to camp as soon as possible. Hopefully dad could take him and show him around as only he could.

The excitement filled his mind with visions of lying in a tent, hearing the sounds of the wilderness and the chirping of crickets as a soft breeze blew through the trees. He closed his eyes as he sat there on the roof and could almost feel the soft breeze passing through the tent windows and the cold ground beneath his back. He imagined the thin foam pad under his back and a warm sleeping bag surrounding him. He imagined the sounds, the smells and the feelings of camping, the long awaited camping. He could even hear the crackling of the fire and saw the flames dancing in the shadows on the side of the tent in his mind. This will be his greatest adventure, and he couldn't wait…but slowly as he thought of the wonders of the mountains, he drifted off to sleep once again. But he knew it was finally time! He would soon be camping as he had hoped for several years.

His mind began to race from the crackling of the fire to the warmth of a sleeping bag. The fire seemed to be getting brighter and he could feel the warmth on his face. His tent faded away to sounds of birds singing and he opened his eyes to see the sun above the mountain. He completely slept through the sunrise, but it was now late enough to get up. He carefully crawled back in the window, walked to the bed and pulled the covers back up and then started downstairs to see if mom was up yet.

CHAPTER 2
THE BOOK OF ADAM

James was an average size 12 year-old with an average build, light skin and thick, dark brown hair that was cut short, but slightly messy this morning since he hadn't combed it. He usually parted his hair on the left because of a slightly higher hair line there (like his father's) and a cowlick that made his hair stick up a little near the crown of his head. His ocean blue eyes radiated with excitement this morning because he was finally 12 and would get all the promised opportunities he had been waiting for since he was 8 years-old.

As he reached the bottom of the stairs, his large hands with long, thin fingers wrapped around the ball at the end of the bannister and he wondered if Dad was home yet. Although his dad traveled a great deal, he always knew his dad would be home when promised. Today was a special day and Dad had promised to not miss it.

"I am so excited for you son! You are growing up so fast and becoming a great young man. I am truly proud of who you are becoming."

"I can't wait to celebrate with you on your special day."

"After this trip, I have scheduled a couple weeks off to spend just with you. I promise I will be home in time to celebrate your birthday."

As the words trailed off in his mind, he heard his mother singing in the kitchen. He loved her voice, as it gave him great comfort. As long as he remembered his sweet mother had always sung to him. The song she sang now was "his song" that she would sing to him before he went to bed when he was younger. Now she would sing it before special events and he knew it was for his birthday at this time.

As he rounded into the kitchen, a 5-foot 6-inch shapely woman stood at the stove in the center of the kitchen cooking. She looked up with her ocean blue eyes, round face and long, black hair and smiled with love dancing in her eyes. He had always thought his mom was beautiful and loved the peace and comfort that her smile brought him.

"Hi James. Happy Birthday! I sure love you!"

"Is dad home yet? He promised he would be here."

"No. I haven't heard from him this morning, but he always comes when he promises. He will be here! Why don't you sit down at the table and I will give you some cracked wheat cereal."

James walked to the large, round wooden table in the kitchen and sat on the large chair. At the same time, his mother walked to the table with a bowl of cracked wheat cereal and milk. This was his favorite breakfast, but only the way mom made it. After a simple prayer he started eating his birthday breakfast.

Just then, the doorbell rang. James was hoping it was dad getting home, but he wasn't sure why dad would ring the door-bell. Mom walked to the front door and he then heard her talk with someone at the front door and then she returned with a small brown package with a large blue envelope attached to the front with a brown band that wrapped around the entire paper package.

"James, this is for you. It may be your first birthday present of the day. Why don't you open it?"

James took the brown package pulled off the band, tore open the brown paper wrapping and pulled out a large, heavy book.

The book had a black leather cover with gold script lettering and gold foil edged pages. As he leafed through the pages, he noticed they were very thin and of a very fine material. He was excited to find out what this book was, but he remembered the blue envelope on the cover. He closed the book and read the cover,

The Book of Adam
by Julianna G Abel

He was very excited to get to know more about this book and figure out where it came from.

With that simple thought, and with mom chuckling a little in the background, he set the book down on the table and grabbed the blue envelope and examined it. The envelope was square in shape and almost the size of the book. The blue was a deep blue, almost the color of a clear blue sky, just before dusk. The paper the envelope was made of was also very fine, similar to the envelopes his dad received from work, but of even higher quality. It had his name, James Adamson, written beautifully on the front, but contained no stamp and no address. As he turned the envelope over he saw the return address on the sealed flap of the envelope.

The Band of Fire
Campus Gaea
Rocky Mountains, USA

The Rocky Mountains are some of the mountains out his window, but he had never heard of this Campus Gaea or *The Band of Fire*. His curiosity was definitely aroused. He could hardly contain his desire to tear open the envelope and figure out what all this meant. But opening the envelope was going to prove harder than usual. The envelop was not just sealed, but had a large wax seal over the envelope seal with the script "CG" embossed.

As he struggled to find an edge to open the envelope, mom handed him his favorite pocketknife and he released the corner of the flap by cutting through the embossed seal and then lifted the flap. As he pulled out the single page letter, he began to read.

Dear James Adamson,

It is with great pleasure and great excitement that we offer to you a spot in the new class for The Band of Fire training program. On June 6th the program will start at Campus Gaea in the Rocky Mountains. You are asked to come to the Ranger Station at the base of the mountain and you will be transported for your two-month camp.

Included you have been given The Book of Adam which contains significant background of your new abilities and skills as a Titan, valuable information to help you understand the possible skills you will develop, the classes and instructions that will be provided, as well as a complete history of this program. May we recommend that you at least peruse this book for insights into who you really are.

You will also find included the list of books and supplies that will be required for the camp. Your parents have been given additional instructions on where to find these special supplies.

This is a unique invitation, but may be extended to others you know. Know that only a very small percentage of individuals in the world have been found to have Titan abilities, therefore it is recommended that you keep to yourself this invitation until June 6th when you are informed of others that will be in your company as you are all personally transported to Campus Gaea. Know that your invitation was made 12 years ago when you were born with the special skills already part of who you are. You may have already experienced some of these unique talents in your life. We are excited to help you develop these skills and abilities even further.

Sincerely,
Doc McAdams
Camp Master

James read the letter twice and then looked up to see his mother smiling at him. He felt the excitement welling up inside him because he would be camping this next month, but... What is a Titan? Why was He considered a Titan at this time and why was he being invited to the camp? None of this made any sense. Mom and Dad had never even talked about "special abilities" or his "invitation made 12 years ago." He felt a little frustration, but even more excitement.

As he looked up, it was almost like Mom understood his thoughts and concerns, as she responded, "If I were you, I would look at your book. It should give you more information. Dad said this would be coming and that any questions you have could be answered by this book."

On that, James set the letter down and opened the book to the first chapter. As he began to focus on the book, mom left the room to get back to her activities of the day. There was a lot she needed to prepare for the party they would be having later that day. And she felt she should try to contact Dad to see if he really was going to make it home.

James started reading on page one:

Over the centuries many individuals have been found to have unique skills and abilities. These skills could be simple or complex. Some were often hidden from society, while others were readily apparent. The individuals with these skills were treated very differently in different societies. In some populations and civilizations, they were considered "blessed" or were thought to have mystical or magical powers. Some were given great power and influence in societies, including some kings, the Egyptian Pharaohs, and even leaders in powerful armies.

In other societies they were thought to be wizards or witches and some were even killed for using magic as was done in the early years of the United States.

It was in this environment in the late 1800s that The Band of Fire was formed. A special band designed to train those with these abilities and skills. The purpose of the Band was to: 1) Develop and control the skills. 2) Create individuals that could function normally in society using the skills in ways that were undetected by the "Natural Born" individuals (individuals with no special skills). 3) Bring together individuals with similar skills to help them learn and help each other.

The Band chose the name of Titan to describe one with special abilities to differentiate them from those natural born, or non-skilled individuals. The term Titan was borrowed from Greek Mythology in reference to those descendants of the Gods with special powers and abilities. Since our Titans can also be described in those same terms with God given talent and skills, this term is a fitting indication of who you are.

So as a Titan, you will be invited to join The Band of Fire and will be trained in your special skill or skills by the staff at Campus Gaea in the back country of the Rocky Mountains...

As James finished the first page of the book, he felt much more comfortable and realized he finally had some possible explanations for the special powers he had been noticing since age 8. His mind wandered as he imagined himself flying on a broom through the air. He saw his mom in a witch's hat and smiled as he saw himself in long flowing wizard robes. So, was he magical? Would he need a wand or other tool to perfect his skills? Why was this training happening at a camp?

Questions and concerns started flowing to his mind and he thought he would probably need to return to the book for the answers, but he was too excited about going camping. He couldn't wait for dad to get home so that he could have his birthday party. He couldn't wait for the next couple weeks to pass so that he could go camping and find out more at Campus Gaea. Yes, he was 12 years-old, but he felt like a 5 year-old on Christmas waiting to open presents. The time couldn't pass fast enough. Campus Gaea, special powers, Titans, all would be answered on June 6th. If only he didn't have to wait.

CHAPTER 3
COUNTING TWELVE CANDLES

The hours passed slowly and Dad never made it home. Mom had told James that she was unable to get ahold of him, so that he probably would not be coming. Although that made James sad and he could tell mom was worried, he was very relieved that the time had finally arrived for him to have his birthday party. His thoughts had raced over the last several hours about the new opportunities in his life, but now he was only worried about the party and his friends that were coming. Too bad he couldn't talk to any of them about *The Band of Fire*. He was sure his very best friend would love to hear about this new adventure he was embarking on!

On that thought, the doorbell rang and he heard his mom open the front door. He heard Bekah talking at a very rapid rate. She was so excited about something and mom was hardly able to calm her down. It was always funny to listen to Bekah talk because her mood was always exhibited in the communication speed, pitch and volume. From the current talking pattern, James had never heard his best friend talk at such a great rate of speed. Whatever the cause of this great excitement, James had never heard her this animated in all his life, and he had

y were 3 years-old. He decided he needed
. was going on, so he got up from the table
just finished lunch and headed to the entryway
..ah and Mom were talking.

..ames came into the entryway, he saw his very best friend.
..ekah Solomon, or Bekah as he called her, was a very petite,
..ven tiny 12 year-old girl with small hands, small feet, shoulder
length brown hair, an olive complexion, dark brown eyes and
small facial features. She looked a lot like a geisha doll, but
without oriental eyes. She was often confused for a girl much
younger, until she started to speak. Her ability to communicate
was much better than many adults James knew. He was excited
to see her, as it was proof the party was about to start.

As soon as Bekah saw him, her dark brown eyes lit up and
she exclaimed, "Happy Birthday James. I'm so excited for you."

James ran to her, grabbed her hand and lead her into the
other room so they could talk without mom watching every
move. He knew he wasn't supposed to tell anyone about the
book, but she was his very best friend and he never kept secrets
from her. He was sure they didn't mean for him to not tell her.

As they left the entryway and mom was out of earshot, Bekah
in her excited, high pitched voice almost yelled for emphasis,
"Yes James! I am a Titan too. As you know my birthday was
4 weeks ago and I've already read the first 5 chapters of *The
Book of Adam* and I can't wait to see what my unique skill is. I
think it might be Telepathy, like my parents, and I sure hope
it is. They have been trying to teach me this skill over the
last 4 years. I hope you have telepathy too, because then we
can talk without a phone when I'm at home. I was so excited
when I saw that you received the same box for your birthday
that I did on mine. Oh, and I learned as I got close to your
house that you and your mom were excited about your first
gift. I just knew somehow that you learned you were a Titan.
But you really should read more than just the first page of the
book. There is so much information that you might need to
know before June 6th."

Suddenly she realized that James hadn't said a word and her eyes got wide with surprise that she knew as much as she did without him saying a word. James just chuckled to himself knowing that telepathy was definitely her gift. He had known that for over a year, but didn't know why she had that ability. Now knowing that she too was a Titan confirmed his suspicion that she had an uncanny ability to communicate through thought and could even read minds. As for his strength (Is he supposed to have just one or more than one?), he wasn't sure what it would be. As far as he was concerned, he had no developed special ability, but what were the abilities (besides Telepathy) that he could have? Maybe she was right. Maybe he should read more of the book.

"So, Bekah. You have read 5 chapters of the book. Do you want to point out the highlights or at least help me know what parts to focus on? I am not as studious as you are. I will probably not read the entire book before camp like you will." He then smiled at her, as her cheeks started to turn a bright shade of red.

"Well, I do think you should read it James, but I can at least help you know where stuff is." Bekah said in a soft, slow voice. She wasn't sure she should help him be lazy, but he was her very best friend.

They both walked over to the table and sat down next to *The Book of Adam* and Bekah opened the cover. As Bekah began to speak this time, her voice rose and her conversation speed accelerated. Although she didn't want to help him too much, she couldn't help being excited.

"I have only read 5 chapters, but I have looked through the book and know what the other chapters contain. I am only going to tell where you can learn things. I am NOT going to give you a synopsis of the chapters I have read. Nor will I answer questions if I feel it will allow you to skip reading the chapters. I am not going to help you be lazy. I want you to be good at what you do when you get to camp. I am hoping we will be able to be in the same classes and same patrol so that

I already have a friend at camp. So don't screw this up." she said with a smile.

She opened the book to the table of contents and pointed to the list of chapters.

"Chapter 1 is the one you read the first page of. As you can tell it gives the basic introduction to everything. You MUST read that chapter so that you understand who you are, and who you can become. I am not sure you will be ready to enter Campus Gaea if you don't at least read this chapter." She looked at him with pleading in her eyes and her usual smile. James nodded.

"Chapter 2 was amazing. It was one of my favorite chapters because it talked about the history of *The Band of Fire*. I love what I learned and can't believe all that has happened over the years, but I like this type of stuff. I know you probably won't read this chapter, but I found it extremely enlightening. I will be looking for more information when we go to buy our other supplies for camp."

"Supplies?" James thought, "I'll need to looking out that!"

"Chapter 3 gives a complete description of Campus Gaea. I can't wait to go to camp and see all the things I learned about in this chapter. The old cabins, the tents, the guardian wolves, it should be an amazing area of the world and an amazing learning experience. I can't wait to experience this portion of the book."

James realizing what she was doing, suddenly interrupted her and began to ask question, hoping she wouldn't give him a chapter by chapter description of what was there as she had hither to done. He carefully picked his words and asked, "Where do I learn about the various skills or abilities I could have as a Titan? How do you know wha you could have?"

"Well, if you'd have let me continue, I would have told you that Chapter 4 gives information about becoming a Titan, as well as all the skills, talents, strengths and abilities that can be honed and strengthened through the training provided at camp. It was in that chapter, and my skimming of chapter 8, that I learned about *The Gift of Telepathy* that I hope is my special skill."

"OK then, how will I know which skill I have? Can I have more than one." James again interrupted.

"I am not going to tell you anything more than that you should read Chapter 4! At least take the time to study this chapter and learn what skill you could have. ...Oh, and most Titans only have one well developed skill or strength. The lucky ones actually will develop a second or third skill."

James shot her a questioning look and called, "Has anyone been able to develop all the skills?"

Bekah smiled delightedly and responded, "I should have known you would ask that! Well there've been a small handful of Concordant individuals, according to the book, that have developed powerful use of all the special skills. These individuals are VERY rare! So, you should be hoping to develop one skill really well and possibly a second, but all seven would be a miracle. You are funny! You are always looking to get it all."

Her voice then increased in pitch and volume and the speed of her discussion accelerated. "The best chapters seem to start at 8-14 that talk about the gifts that could be yours. Each gift is described in great detail. I can't wait to learn as much as possible about each of these skills so that I can figure out what skill or skills I will have."

"Why didn't you SKIP to those chapters?" James asked, already knowing the answer.

"Oh no! I could never read them out of order. Then I might miss some very important information. You KNOW I would never do that!"

James began to laugh and Bekah's cheeks turned red once again. She realized he knew exactly what he was doing and she had taken the bait once again.

But she shook off the mild frustration and embarrassment and raced back to her discussion of the important chapters of *The Book of Adam.*

"I would also recommend you look at Chapter 5, as it will help you know many of the supplies you will use as a Titan.

With the additional list found in the welcome letter, you will understand what you need to purchase to be ready for the camp. ...Oh, by the way, you are not a wizard James and will not be flying on a broomstick, wearing long flowing robes or need a magic wand. Instead of imagining, may I recommend you read the book to know what is going to happen?" That last recommendation was said at a very slow and methodical pace, but with great urgency. James knew she had read his mind once again.

Before they could continue through the book, the guests started arriving, and James moved the book to his room for later perusing, and to avoid questions by others. He had over 30 friends in attendance at his birthday, but the only one that really mattered would be going with him to summer camp. He couldn't believe he was lucky enough to have his best friend join him for this new adventure.

As the day progressed, they played games, opened presents and even sang "Happy Birthday." His favorite part was the German chocolate birthday cake (his favorite) with 12 lit candles. He was finally 12 which meant he could camp, but to his surprise that morning he was informed that 12 candles in his life signified so much more. He was a Titan, which meant he had some special skill, would be attending a "secret" summer camp and would be learning more of what his parents had been teaching him. The day couldn't have ended or for that matter even started better, except maybe if his dad had made it home as he had promised.

The one big downside to the day really was the fact that his dad never made it home. He had promised and had never broken a promise before. That worried James a little, and he could tell it had worried mom much more. All she said to him was that something must have happened. As he brushed his teeth and got ready for bed, he heard his mother talking on the phone to someone with worry in her voice.

"Simon has never been late before. After his daughter left because he hadn't been in her life enough and he blamed himself for being too busy, he has never missed a special occasion. He hasn't even missed a Parent-Teacher Conference. But this was James 12th birthday. We have been planning and waiting for this day and Simon swore he wouldn't miss it. I hope he is okay. I pray that he isn't hurt, or worse. I know he isn't lost because Simon would never get lost. I just hope I can hear from him soon. Otherwise I am not sure what I will tell James. He loves his father and idolizes him. Maybe he will come home tomorrow. I just need information! Please, any information you get."

Her voice trailed off and James realized he was still brushing his teeth. He quickly finished preparing for bed and decided to go outside and look at the moon. With all that had happened this day, he really wasn't that tired. Besides the moon was still full, which would give him a great view of the Rocky Mountains. He could try to guess where in the Rocky Mountains he would find Campus Gaea.

He carefully slid open the window and climbed onto the roof and sat staring at the mountains and the bright full moon. He was reminded of his dream and the thought that the full moon was no longer visible. For that to happen with this bright moon, the clouds would need to completely cover the moon to stop the light. "I can't believe that could even happen in a single night," he thought.

As he sat on the cold roof, he heard a distinct voice overhead, a powerful, but friendly voice, "What a beautiful night. I love the feel of the wind in my wings. It is always amazing to go hunting at night. Wait, there it is. The little rabbit I was chasing last night. This time he is mine...."

The voice stopped, and James looked around hoping to see someone. But nobody appeared. Once again he was reminded of Bekah's words, "*I am not going to tell you anything more than that you should read Chapter 4. At least take the time to study that chapter and learn what skill you could have.*"

Well, she is right as usual. He should at least learn what skills he could possibly have. How else will he know why all these weird things keep happening to him ever since he turned 8. Well, tomorrow is another day and he will look into reading that chapter.

He carefully climbed back into his room, closed the window and climbed into bed. He was finally feeling tired and he knew it was time to sleep. "Thus would end his 12th birthday," he thought as he drifted off to sleep and the many sounds in the darkness faded to silence.

CHAPTER 4
ORIENTOPATHY

As he awoke, he felt ropes around his wrists and couldn't see due to a tight blindfold on his eyes and his head was pounding, but he couldn't remember why. What he did remember, however, was the slight music and laugh just before his memory went dark. He recognized that song now and knew where he had heard it last.

Years ago, that song was sung by his Aria, his ex-wife, to their beautiful daughter Camilla. Aria Thorngardner was a tall, tan beauty that he married many years ago when they were both very young. He loved her more than he thought he could ever love anyone. She was a Titan like himself and was one year younger than he. He was amazed that such a beauty would even agree to marry him. But her special skill with telepathy, the best he had ever seen, made her difficult to live with. She could read his thoughts and he was constantly trying to apologize for anything and everything that ever crossed his mind. Ultimately, he was forced to divorce from her, so they would stop fighting. After they separated, they both loved each other again and were able to continue to work together in many respects. He was even sent on multiple trips/missions with her where they were able to talk and reminisce about old times. He still loved her, but knew even then that they would never be married again.

The hardest part of their separation, however was losing a daughter. From the moment they separated, and to minimize fighting, Aria asked him to not have contact with Camilla because she felt it would be too confusing for her. That was a period of 5 years, from age 6 to 11. Some very important formative years in her life. Therefore, after the 5 years of their separation, when Aria was killed in a car crash, he realized how bad that idea really was. Camilla was forced to accept him back into her life when she was 11 years old. She didn't know him, and sometimes didn't even like him. She had good days in the home, including days when she was laughing and singing. He loved those days and thought he had his daughter back, but she always seemed to have a hard time whenever situations came up that reminded her of her mother. Those recurrent memories ultimately lead to Camilla moving out when she was sixteen years old. But the worst part was that he hadn't heard from her since. He loved her, but she never forgave him for separating from her mother. He often thought about her and worried about her, but he really hadn't seen or heard from her since that time. She didn't even return to Campus Gaea that summer.

In fact, the laugh also reminded him of that time. It was this very distinct laugh that reminded him even more of Camilla. That was definitely her laugh. It used to be a sign of great happiness in the home. He could even see her bright smile, and hear her singing and laughing with her little brother. Camilla was a tall slender girl with long curly brown hair (like her mother), dark brown eyes, a small nose and a slightly round face. Her beauty was often considered without compare, especially with her usual broad smile that lit up her entire face. She was very unique in having a great propensity for all *The Band of Fire* skills and powers and was always a powerful leader of fellow students. As a Concordant, she quickly developed many skills at camp and at home. She was always found humming simple songs and had an amazing singing voice. Her rolling laugh was often heard like a song across the room and brought happiness to all that heard it. Camilla was actually a very talented Titan, but she stopped coming to training the same year she moved out. Her greatest talent was telepathy like her mother, but she also had an abnormal ability for Hoplonosmithy, Chronopathy, and Zoonophonia. But it had been years, so he wasn't sure if she had developed any of the other talents further.

With that thought he started to wonder where he was. As an Orientopath he wasn't used to not knowing where he was. In fact, he always knew where he was. But the easiest way to know was for him to use his eyes. By looking around he could always visualize the complete map of his location anywhere in the world and localize himself better than a map or even a GPS would ever do. That is probably why he was blindfolded. What they apparently didn't know was that his other senses were also capable of localizing him.

He had gotten so good at knowing his exact location with his eyes, that he had stopped practicing the other senses. But when he was 12, 13 and 14 he used to play a game of drawing a topographic map with his eyes closed just by using the other senses. It was time to play again, but since his hands were tied he would need to try to create the map in his mind only.

He closed his eyes even though he was blindfolded, to recreate the game he used to play. He listened carefully and heard the soft breeze through the trees. Wait! Listen a little harder! Yes. The breeze is moving a forest of trees. He is surrounded by trees. Large trees, about 15 feet apart lifting into the air higher than 50 feet.

In fact, he was tied to one of those oak trees...nope not oak. He listened carefully. Wait the smell. Yes he was tied to the base of a large pine tree. Now he heard the different sound of the wind through needles instead of leaves. That means he is high in the mountains to be in a pine forest. He even felt the soft pine needles lining the ground where he sat. The bark was also consistent with pine as it rested against his back.

He took a deep breath and confirmed he was at a high 10,000-foot elevation. He listened intently and began to draw the map. He was in a large valley with a large fresh water stream 200 yards to his left. The sound of the water told him it was clean, palatable water that would allow drinking with minimal or no filtering.

The breeze was echoing off the mountains, telling him that a large peak lay to the east, another to the north and smaller peaks to the south and west. The south peak was actually hundreds of miles away.

Now it was all coming into focus. There was a lake 2 miles to the north. A sound to his right told him there was a path 50 feet from him heading north to the lake, up the mountain. In fact, he recognized the location. It was a valley where he used to camp as a kid, where he loved to fish with his dad. But how did he get here? That is hundreds of miles from where he last was.

Okay, why is he here?

Yes, he is tied to the tree, but surrounded by eight tents with a large fire pit in the center of camp. There are at least 20 individuals moving around. They must be his captors. But why?

He listened again and felt the temperature on his face. Yes, it is 10:00pm, two days after his son's birthday.

Wait...I promised him I would be there. Pain ached through his chest and near panic filled his entire body! I have never broken a promise to him. I wish I had the same talent with telepathy that Aria and Camilla had. Then I could tell James why I broke my promise and missed his birthday. Oh, and I could tell Sarah because she will be very worried....

James woke with a start. Was that dream about his dad? Where was he? He had never taken James camping or fishing! And who was Camilla? Did he really have a sister? Mom said something about that on the phone yesterday. He would need to talk with mom about this. Maybe she would know more. But would she be awake at this time? He looked around for his clock, but his eyes were still blurry from sleep.

The dream had initiated so many questions. Would mom know the answers? Was she a Titan too? How about Bekah's parents, were they also Titans? He didn't even really know anything about Aria. Camilla's mom? Where could he find all these answers?

Just then he thought of the words mom had said on his birthday when he first got *The Book of Adam.*

"Dad said this would be coming and that any questions you have could be answered by the book." he remembered her saying.

He also thought about the dream and felt he had been stupid to not read his book more. He better learn a little more about Titans and see what this dream was telling him. Maybe then he could understand a little more. Maybe the book really does have all the answers to the questions he is asking. He sat up and thought maybe it was time now to start reading.

CHAPTER 5
MOUNT OTHRYS

James pensively walked out to the car and waited for Bekah to come over. Mom was taking them to the store for their supplies because Bekah's parents were gone for a couple weeks on a work trip. Maybe the store would give him more information. He couldn't get the dream out of his mind, but hadn't told anyone about it. In fact, he wasn't sure what to tell them because he didn't know what it all meant. Since he hadn't read any more from *The Book of Adam*, he was also too embarrassed to even ask Bekah about any of it. She would just get irritated at him for not reading more.

He did, however, ask mom about Camilla. Mom's face seemed to light up about her and seemed excited to tell him about her. She didn't say much, but told him that she was his half-sister. She was a very beautiful and loving girl that moved in with them when James was just a baby. She moved out again by the time he was 5 years old. But she had always loved James.

The most interesting things she said were reminiscent of the dream. Camilla apparently loved to sing and always sang baby James a beautiful song, but mom couldn't remember how it went. She was always holding him, loved to babysit him and even taught him to talk and walk. But when she turned sixteen Camilla and James' father fought and she moved out to never return again.

Since James was 5, mom was a little surprised that he didn't remember her. She even showed him a picture of 16 year-old Camilla, but James could not remember that face. But he did remember the song and the laugh, but possibly only because he heard it in the two dreams about dad.

Bekah came running over talking so fast and in such a high pitch he almost couldn't understand her. But he didn't need to. He was just as excited to see what they were going to buy as she was. In fact, he had read over the supply list 4 or 5 times since his birthday, but had not read Chapter 5 from *The Book of Adam*. He didn't understand what everything was (the book probably would have told him), but he would soon know.

Mom came walking out and greeted both James and Bekah, "Sorry I am taking you to the store. Simon was planning on taking you, but he hasn't been able to come home yet. In fact, I haven't even talked to him since James' birthday."

James saw her try to smile, but he knew she was worried. Dad was always really good at contacting them if he was delayed for any reason. He knew that currently dad wasn't able to make contact with them. He didn't, however, feel there was any value in talking to mom about it so he just stayed quiet.

Bekah, however, was so excited that she exclaimed rapidly, "Mrs Adamson, I am glad you are able to take us. Especially since my parents are gone. I wouldn't be any more excited or happy if Mr Adamson was taking us!"

That seemed to alleviate Sarah Adamson's fears and they all loaded into the car and drove the 45 minutes to a small store in Salt Lake City on the far west side. As they drove, Bekah never stopped talking, but James was thinking about the dream and wouldn't be able to even repeat what Bekah had said throughout the whole trip. The good news was that she was so preoccupied that she had failed to read his mind as she had done so often over the last couple weeks.

They drove into a small parking lot and saw a small one room store, probably only 15 feet by 15 feet with a small sign on the outside that said *Mountain Supplies* in fading black letters. Bekah's excitement only grew, but James was very disappointed. It looked like a secondhand camping supply store. He wasn't sure why they were there.

Bekah noticed his face and started laughing.

"You didn't do your reading!" she said accusingly.

She then opened her book to Chapter 5 and showed him a picture of the store and a map to its location. She then turned the page and he saw a huge map of the inside and he was a little confused. She just smiled and took his hand and excitedly said (in her usual rapid, high pitched voice), "Come on. Let me show you."

As they walked into the store, James noted army surplus at the front of the store and mostly old second-hand camping and hiking supplies throughout the store. He even saw old backpacks near the rear of the store. Bekah, however, didn't seem to notice and raced to the shelf of backpacks. She pulled him to the side of the shelf and then walked behind it to the wall where an elevator was positioned. There was no button on that back wall. Bekah touched the door with both hands flat with fingers extended and the door opened. The three of them boarded the elevator and the doors closed again without pushing any buttons. The elevator dropped very quickly and then the opposite wall opened into a very large store that appeared to cover miles under the ground. Now James was excited again.

A large archway lead from the elevator into the store, but the immense space nearly completely distracted James from this entrance and the sign *Mount Othrys* displayed in glowing gold lettering on that same entrance. "So THIS is the store," he thought and he walked forward. Bekah started to run, her excitement now overflowing as she jabbered on. The speed and pitch of her voice now made the words impossible to understand. But James was now likewise excited, and mom walking out of the elevator just laughed at the two of them. She had been here before and was not surprised by any of it, but not since she had come with Camilla for her supplies each year before camp.

James, however, was looking at what reminded him of a very large mall, except instead of a long hallway with stores on either side, there was a long road with buildings extending as far as the eye could see. As he looked up, it appeared to be sky much bluer than the sky he saw as they drove here this morning with even a form of sunlight coming from some unseen source. If he hadn't just exited an elevator, he would have said they were outside walking on a large street, but with buildings unlike anything he had ever seen. It all seemed almost magical, and he was dizzied by all the excitement now running through his veins.

His mind was immediately drawn to a red, barn shaped building to his left with large white letters, *Mr McDonald's Mystical Creatures* and included a shop with stables behind. In the stables he noticed horses with wings, other horses with a single horn, and even a creature with the hind parts of a horse, but with a bird body, beak and wings. Inside the store he saw multiple kennels and cages containing various animals, most notably cats, dogs, mice, toads, turtles and various birds including owls. Bekah noticed the same and they started maneuvering towards this building before mom called their attention back.

"James. Bekah. We need to check-in at the desk first and get your money. Without the money you will not be able to purchase anything. Without checking in, you will not know exactly what to purchase," she said with a laugh. "The preliminary list you got on your birthday is incomplete. You will want the updated list!"

Mom was now pointing to the right, where there was a large, oak desk with a round faced, white haired, lady sitting with a smile. The desk looked a little out of place, but had a beautifully, handwritten sign that read, "New Students Please Check-in Here."

Before they knew it, mom was halfway to the desk and already talking with the lady.

"I have two new students here. James is my son and the son of Simon Adamson." To which she got a knowing nod.

"Bekah is the other and is a neighbor. She is the oldest daughter of Mark and Suzy Solomon." The lady seemed to study Bekah and decided that she must be old enough even if she looked too young since she dared not ask her for proof of age.

"Well young man and young lady, I am so excited for you. Here is your list," as she handed them each a yellow, single sheet of paper, "and may I recommend you start at the bank on my right." As James looked at the old lady, a tag attached to her shirt read *Madame Strange*, which he assumed was her name.

To her immediate right was a large building, at least two stories with white granite walls and large marble pillars surrounding a large, double wide golden door. Large gold plated letters hung just above the pillars, *Othrys First Titan Bank*.

Without looking at their lists, both Bekah and James moved towards the bank doors as Madame Strange yelled after them, "If you have any questions about your list, please feel free to ask." James looked down and noticed this list was almost the same as the list he had studied at home, but had store locations for each item and short explanations of why they were needed. He noted that list may be more useful than the one he had studied several times before coming.

As they pushed through the large double doors, they opened into a large, ornate chamber with a marble floor, large decorative woodcarvings throughout and glass walled rooms to both the right and the left. In each room were neatly dressed individuals with stacks of gold and silver coins on their desk and multiple stacks of multicolored paper money spread out on their desks. Each room seemed to have different colored bills and Bekah pointed and exclaimed rapidly, "Those are the money changers James. If we need money for different countries, they can provide it here at the best exchange rate."

Although James didn't understand why they would ever need money for different countries, he was unwilling to ask Bekah still, because he knew she would just say (again) that he should have read the book. So instead he just made a mental note for when he found out why it would be necessary to exchange money.

In front of them was a large, white granite transaction desk with multiple hurried figures moving behind the desk gathering what looked like gold and silver coins into large leather bags. Before they could even reach the desk, however, a small, thin man no more than 3 feet tall came walking from behind the desk with two leather bags. One he handed to James and the other to Bekah. He then smiled at mom and exclaimed, "Good to see you again Sarah. I hope Simon is doing well. He sent word weeks ago to have these bags ready for today. I thought he would be coming."

Mom smiled back and just retorted, "He is still away, so I got the privilege of coming to your beautiful bank again. I love the beauty and majesty. It continues to grow in beauty every time I come."

The small man just blushed and hurried back behind the desk. James was once again amazed at the kindness mom seemed to show everyone she met. He hoped that he was even half as kind as his mother was to others, and for a 12 year-old boy, that is saying something.

With the heavy leather bags in hand, they turned and left the bank and immediately crossed the street to the red, barn shaped store, for this was the one that had drawn their attention and they both wanted to go there first.

As they approached the store, James noticed a swinging door at the front and continued to be amazed at the large creatures in the stables behind. Bekah turned to him and stated matter of factly, "We can't buy any of the traveling animals yet. We are only first years. You are required to be Golden Flame rank before you can own a Pegasus, Unicorn or Hippogriff. Although I would love to have a Unicorn myself."

Again, James had no idea what she was talking about and made another mental note. I must read some of the book to make sure I at least know the basics of what is happening. He couldn't just depend on Bekah for everything.

"Young sir, the willing heart and courageous mind is needed to me have. Much waiting for you have I. Many have looked and some have asked, but to none my allegiance have gained. Much need of me have you. My flame for heat, my wings for power and my heart for courage to you. Much success together we'll have."

James suddenly looked around to see who was talking, but Bekah and mom hadn't noticed anything. He was a little startled, until they walked through the swinging door and saw Mr McDonald behind the counter with a beautiful, flame red colored, large bird that James immediately recognized as a Phoenix. He immediately knew her name to be Helia and couldn't help but want to take her home.

He walked up to Mr McDonald and asked, "How much for the Phoenix sir?"

"I would never dream of selling these magnificent creatures. I consider every creature here a special friend, but this is a most unique bird. I have only been able to find two birds of this type and therefore I don't part with them easily. I have only once before found a worthy Titan to take one home. Fogo was sold years ago to a young lady when he asked her to take him home. This young lady, however," as he pointed to the bird, "has never asked to go home with anyone."

"What if Helia has asked me?" James asked.

"So, you know her name? I have never told anyone her name."

"She is the most beautiful creature I have ever seen. I feel happier in her presence and would be stronger with her by my side."

"That may all be true, but you must prove yourself worthy to truly take her home."

James reached out his arm and Helia spread her wings and left Mr McDonald to land on James forearm. As she landed, however, James noticed that even with her large size she was light as a feather.

Mr McDonald's eyes got wide and he quickly gathered a "cage" with no bars that looked more like a firepit like nest, food and a small book on the power of the Phoenix. He handed them all to James and said "She's yours, as she has chosen you. We do not sell these creatures, but you can adopt her since she has adopted you. I do ask that you purchase the supplies I have gathered, so that I may continue to have the funds to find and protect more unique creatures from around the world."

Bekah and mom hadn't noticed this exchange, but instead were looking at various animals trying to decide what to adopt as well. The list stated that every first year student must have a pet, with whom they could practice communicating, but Bekah couldn't decide between a large green and black tortoise or a small white kitten. James knew she would pick the tortoise because it intrigued her, and as usual he was right in his judgment of his very best friend.

After adopting the Phoenix, the rest of the trip was relatively unexciting. They went from store to store purchasing the needed items. They had uniforms, and common camping supplies including tents, flashlights, pads and sleeping bags. They purchased bags and a backpack, as well as eating utensils and a small personal stove. James did enjoy the pocketknives he purchased (he bought three even though he only needed one), as well as the flint and steel that he was excited to use. Most of these supplies didn't seem abnormal at all and appeared like the supplies friends had to go camping with the Boy Scouts.

But there were several items he purchased that he didn't recognize, nor did he ask anyone what they were for. He was too proud to ask Bekah, so he just purchased what he was told and put them into his bags.

The final stop was to *Alexanders Book Shop*, that reminded James of a specialized library. But he had never really been in a book store, so he didn't know exactly what to expect. As he looked down at the list, he saw multiple books that he needed to purchase. His list included the following books:

Introduction to Camping – Preparing For The Wild – by Gibbs Crawley

Beginners Book of Fire and Fire Building – by Sandra Fuego

Alexandria's Book of Wilderness Cooking – by Alexandria Rossi

The Art of Telepathy and Other Forms of Communication
– by Aria Thorngardner

Hopolonosmithy - The Secret World of Weapons – by
Alexander Black

The Keys To Wilderness First Aid – by Daktoa Ironhorse

Introduction to Herculopathy – by Rocky Handrake

Wildlife Studies – by Amber Filtz Barde

Most of the books were self-explanatory, but James kept
looking back at the last book *The Game of Orientopathy Through
Using Your Senses* and kept wondering why he had never seen
this book before. Why had mom and dad never shown him
this book before today? He looked back down at the cover as
Bekah started to giggle:

The Game of Orientopathy Through Using Your Senses – by
Simon John Adamson

The stacks of books, however, now made him very nervous
because they looked more like school books than camping
supplies. He wasn't sure why they would take all these books
camping. Bekah, however, was already leafing through the
books with uncontrolled excitement. She even had an extra
book that he had decided to not buy since it wasn't on the list.
Greek Mythology and Other Keys To The Band of Fire by Julianna
Gaea Abel (wasn't that the same author as *The Book of* Adam?)
With her excitedly looking through the books, James figured
she would have them all read before they went to camp, and
he laughed to himself. He might even look through the pages
to see why they were so important, especially the book written
by his dad, but he couldn't help but think those books would
be of less value than his reading of *The Book of Adam.*

"Sir."

"You can call me James."

"Yes. James, sir."

"No. Just James."

"OK. James, learn from the books together we can."

"Wait. You are a bird."

"Yes, but your mind will be opened with the song of my
heart. Understand better can you and learn more quickly we

will. Become a true Titan with my you will. Only together can we learn and truly become."

James just smiled and knew that Bekah would not be the only one with knowledge when they came to camp. And he may not even need to work hard at it. "Lucky Helia picked me," he thought as he finished loading all his purchases into the trunk and Helia sat on his right shoulder. He climbed into the back seat of the car carefully moved Helia to his lap, just as Bekah placed her large tortoise, Tom on her lap.

"And so it begins!" Bekah said with James and Helia in one seat and her and Tom in the other. And the drive home was filled with thoughts of camping, beautiful phoenix song that completely relaxed everyone, and intermittent thoughts of dad out there somewhere in the darkness. This was only the beginning, but James knew much more would be coming, and with Helia as his companion he was definitely ready!

CHAPTER 6
THE CLASSIFICATION

As the room began to light up with the sun slowly flowing through his window, James closed *The Book of Adam* and placed it in his bag. He was now all packed and ready to go to camp. Helia's music softly continued in his mind and all that he had read was brought into perfect understanding. As the music continued he looked up at his beautiful bird whose fire colored feathers seemed to be getting brighter since bringing her home. He was amazed at all he had learned since Helia became his. Having not read more than the first page of the book in all the days since his birthday, since receiving help from Helia he now had finished chapters 1,3, 4 and 5. He skipped chapter 2 because he wasn't sure how history would help him. As he carefully reviewed the new information, a smile came to his face with the thought that the camping days were finally here. Mom would be taking them momentarily to the Ranger Station to be transferred to the camp as Bekah's parents were again gone for work.

Hours later and after boarding the car, Bekah was impressed at all James had learned from his reading, but she was surprised he felt chapter 2, *History of The Band of Fire*, was not a chapter he felt was important. But she was happy he read chapter 4, *Becoming a Titan,* so that they could talk about the whole process that would be happening later that day. Bekah was actually intrigued about *The Classification,* and was nervous what they would find to be her special powers. They spent the entire trip discussing this process and the more they talked the more James got excited to get it all started. Even Bekah seemed to be talking faster and at a higher pitch as they finished the short trip in the car to the Ranger Station.

Due to the great excitement they felt, they failed to realize what they didn't know about this day. What they didn't know, and hadn't really thought about, was how they would go from the Ranger Station to the camp, deep in the Rocky Mountains. As they unpacked their supplies, they finally noticed the green bus being loaded by other students. James was a little surprised because he couldn't understand how that bus could take them into the back country where *The Book of Adam* had said Campus Gaea was located. "I guess I will just have to find out!" he thought, while Bekah smiled at him apparently thinking the same thing. Even Helia seemed excited as she continued to sing in a soft, beautiful tune.

Bekah quickly stowed her bags underneath the bus and stepped in to find a seat. At that very moment, James noticed a tall, even lanky 12 year-old boy with straight, short blond almost white hair with even whiter skin. His light green eyes lit up his face underneath his round glasses that rested on his long nose. His voice came out with a slow drawl that reminded James of a farmer. He looked like someone James would like to meet.

"Hello. I am James Adamson."

"Wait, what? Are you related to Simon John Adamson?"

"Yes. He is actually my father."

"Wow. What a privilege to get to meet you! My name is Michael Peterson. I must say that your dad is my hero. I was so looking forward to meeting him this year, but was told by my older sister he won't be teaching this summer."

"He is still away on a trip. Does he usually teach at the camp? I knew he would go to camps all summer, but he never told me that he taught." James said, trying to hide the frustration in his voice.

Just then, Helia's soft music stopped. As James looked at her, she was distracted by a large brown falcon in a large cage being loaded into the bus. As Michael noticed where James was looking, he smiled and said, "Well, that is Fenwick, my best friend. I have had him since he was an egg." James a little startled turned back to Michael and pointing to Helia, "This here is Helia, my new friend of only a couple weeks." Michael laughed and they both boarded the bus.

As James looked around for Bekah, he was happy to see her seated near the middle of the bus with a midnight black 12 year-old girl, with a round face, deeply set, dark brown eyes and thick black hair reaching down the center of her back. James and Michael took the seat in front of them and James couldn't wait to get going.

The trip itself was the most unique trip James had ever taken. He had just sat down next to Michael and before they could even turn to talk with Bekah and her new friend, the bus started moving. James heard the driver close the bus door and then time seemed to stop. His mind was slowing, almost stopping and he felt almost like sleep moving through his body. It was as if life was paused, he could feel that something was happening, but had never had this feeling before. James fought the feeling and determined he would not "fall asleep" right now and he stood back up and turned to look at Bekah who seemed to be almost frozen in one place. Her talking had stopped mid-sentence (which James had never heard before) with her mouth open as if finishing the word she was saying and most the students on the bus were likewise frozen. The bus driver turned with a smile and James heard him ask very rapidly, "Can you please sit back down son." To which James quickly obliged. Then it happened.

Everything became a blur, much quicker than before. He was unable to fight this time, but it just happened. James couldn't see the bus, couldn't see the street, couldn't see the other students, just a blur over everything around him. Helia's soft music, however, continued at a normal speed, but only in his mind. She was packed somewhere below the bus and didn't seem to mind this very rapid trip to camp. James reached out to her, a little nervous about what was happening and her music just got louder in his mind until he relaxed once again. And once he relaxed, everything went back to normal and the bus stopped in a large dirt parking lot somewhere in the Rocky Mountains.

As James was trying to figure out what was happening, Bekah's conversation started right where it had left off and everyone around him acted like they had just barely started the bus. Michael exclaimed in surprise, "Wait! How did we get here?" James didn't know what to say, so he just said nothing, but similar comments happened all around him. Bekah's voice broke through the buzz of noise from the other students with her usual knowledge filled comment, "Obviously, the bus driver must be a Chronopath. He must have modified time to travel as it discusses in Chapter 12 of *The Book of Adam*." James just smiled again and made a mental note that he must ask her sometime why he had such a weird experience during that travel when apparently nobody else did…or maybe he should just read Chapter 12.

Immediately upon arriving, the bus driver stepped off the bus and walked over to an older lady that seemed to be in charge. She was a relatively thin lady with long auburn hair tied up in a bun on the top of her head, with dark eyes, tear drop spectacles and a pointy short nose. The smile in her eyes, however was almost infectious. They talked for a moment and then she walked over to the bus where James and the other students were still sitting. She stepped on the bus and called everyone's attention to her. The buzz of talking and excitement died down quickly as she spoke directly to their mind and ears together.

"Welcome Titans to Campus Gaea. I am Master Belle and will be working closely with many of you throughout your summer here and the summers to come. Before we can allow you to join the other Titans in the Great Hall, however, it is important that you undergo *The Classification*. There are three Masters outside that will join me in directing you to the various tents just past the parking lot. There are seven total tents in which you will have the opportunity to undergo the necessary procedure. Please follow the instructions very carefully. As for the process or tests you will undergo, know that you can't mess them up, nor can you trick them. Just relax and we will succeed in helping you reach the best *Classification* for you. We have been doing this for a long time and we know what we are doing.

"Once you complete the process, the examiner will give you a number and you will proceed to Camp Master McAdam's cabin for instruction on the results. Are there any questions?"

James looked up at her thin, pleasant face and couldn't help but feel an interest in learning more from her. He wasn't sure if it was her telepathic influence on his mind or the fact that she was the first instructor he had met here at the camp. He did notice, however, that the music in his mind had stopped when she started to speak. He wondered where Helia was.

"And for each of you wondering where your animal friends are, they are with your bags and have been removed from the bus. They will be placed in the appropriate tent once you are assigned. Know that they are being well taken care of while you get classified."

James smiled again, knowing she was actually answering his unasked question. "Telepathy is kind of cool, but a little scary that they can so easily be in my mind!" And he smiled again, knowing she probably "heard" that thought too.

The dismissal from the bus was very orderly and seemed to proceed quickly. James was one of the last to be assigned a tent, and was directed by Master Belle to the far right tent of the seven. Bekah had been sent earlier to tent 3, Michael went to tent 5 and Bekah's new friend was sent to tent 1. James had read about this process and knew there would be seven tents, with each tent having a specialized telepath assigned to put the young Titan through two tests. Each tent was slightly different, but the overall tests produced the same ultimate results of Classifying primary and secondary skills of each individual student. James had been excited for this process all morning, but as he approached tent 7, he now became very nervous. "Am

I really ready for this? Should I have read more?" he thought as the last student before him entered the tent.

As he stood there trying to calm his now pounding heart, Master Belle opened the door to the tent and invited him in. As soon as he was inside the tent, she started talking.

"James, the bus driver stated that you recognized how he was causing the bus to travel. Is that correct?"

"I felt my mind slowing down, but was able to fight it initially and then everything went blank. Isn't that what everyone felt?"

"You know that everyone didn't feel that. Most of them were 'frozen' as you looked at them. This is another one of your gifts that we will develop. I am excited to see who you are through these tests. I expect great things from you my boy. Great things! I also have a great love for your father and wish he was here with you for your first year at camp. Maybe he will still make it."

Although she was hoping to help calm him down, the expectations he was setting for himself and the expectations she just expressed caused his heart to start pounding more quickly. He barely noticed the interior of the cabin tent to include a small metal table with a blindfold and a small chair. He wasn't calm enough to sit, so he hoped she would allow him to stay standing.

"As you wish James. I will let you stand, but you must place the blindfold to ensure you don't cheat with your eyes throughout the examination." She then handed him the blindfold that he promptly put in place.

Once the blindfold was in place, he was whisked off to some distant area, some distant camp or maybe just a forest. He was standing by himself and could see Bekah in the distance laying on the ground as if asleep. He didn't know where he was, couldn't see very far in front of him because of the growing darkness and wasn't sure what was happening to Bekah. He heard his mother's voice in the distance, but couldn't see her either.

At that point, he began to panic even further. He didn't know what to do! "I should have read more! How can I possibly even understand what needs to be done in this test? Is this real or just in my mind? How did I get here? Did I travel again as the bus traveled? I really can't do this! I don't know how!" His mind con-tinued to race, his heart seemed to be beating out of his chest. He was probably going to fail out as a Titan and would not get the chance to stay at camp as he had hoped. Master Belle would have the privilege of telling Bekah and maybe even his father that he had failed.

Just then a beautiful music, Helia's music, began to play in his mind. This was definitely in his mind and not for anyone else to hear. His rapidly beating heart, trying to beat out of his chest, began to slow as he relaxed. That music was his secret support, his help. But that was not all...

"Don't use your mind, for betray you it will. Let your heart free while you silence your mind and dance to life your senses may be. Then peace and happiness you will find. Great gifts you have, but only if abilities set free you do."

Helia's voice became silent as her music continued, slightly louder in his mind. James was now calm and ready to start. His senses raced into action.

He took a deep breath and could feel the chill of the growing darkness. The sun must have just gone down. He heard his mother's voice in the distance...to his right. He was in a forest, a forest he had been in one other time with his parents. That means the road coming into the forest should be located behind him. It also meant the trail he was on lead to a waterfall ahead. He couldn't remember the distance, but could actually hear the water ahead if he concen-trated. But what worried him was the fact that Bekah was laying on the trail not speaking.

In the distance ahead of her he heard a wolf howl, no not howl but talk, "I smell people in the forest. Why are people in my forest?" She sounded dangerous, almost like a mother trying to protect her pups. He knew it was imperative that he help Bekah quickly. Just then he was standing next to her.

He bent down and noticed her breathing without difficulty, but her eyes were closed. He couldn't see any bleeding or any injuries at this time. As he reached down and touched her, he felt she had fallen and was unconscious from hitting her head on a rock. He examined her head and saw a small bump, but nothing more. He knew she would soon be okay, so he called Helia and she flew over and lifted Bekah up and carried her back to camp, which he now knew was to their left but he wasn't sure how far, maybe a half mile.

The voice of his mother then came back. She was tied to a tree in the area they had eaten lunch when they came years ago to this forest. He thought of the place and he was there standing next to the tree where she was tied. She wasn't bound with ropes, they looked more like thick metal cords. His simple pocketknife in his pocket would be insufficient. He reached out and grabbed the cords with all his strength, but even his strength was insufficient. Then he noticed black, glass like rocks on the ground behind the tree. He grabbed some of the larger rocks, obsidian, and took the handle of his pocketknife to chip the rocks into sharp points. He pulled cords from one of the small bushes to his left and then wove a rope that he used to tie the now sharpened rock to the end of a long stick. He was surprised at how quickly he was able to cut the stick from the surrounding tree and shape the rock, stick and rope into a dagger. When he was complete, it was quite an impressive weapon.

To his further amazement, he was able to cut the metal cords with little or no difficulty utilizing the dagger. But as the cords gave way, his mother collapsed before him. He immediately saw her thoughts and knew she was just physically exhausted and would be unable to walk back to camp. She had been out there in the forest for about 6 hours tied to the tree and she didn't know why. She was also still very nervous about Simon, his dad, who had still not contacted her or come home. So, he had one choice. He couldn't leave her here and Helia was still busy carrying Bekah. Knowing that he wasn't strong enough to break the metal cords, he decided he would need to see if he was strong enough to carry mom. He lifted her up, with one arm, and was surprised his mother was not heavy at all. He started to think about taking her home instead of camp and he was there, placing her safely back in bed. And then he knew it was time to go back...

His mind cleared and Master Belle tanding with a notebook in her hand and tears running down her face spoke directly to his mind.

"I am so sorry James that your father is still gone. I am so sorry your mother is still so worried about him. I wish we could do more to help them both."

James looked up at her in surprise and then remembered she had seen perfectly well what he had done and knew even what he thought and felt. He just wasn't sure what it all meant. Had he passed the test? Why were Bekah and his mom in his test? Why did he think about dad again? His thoughts were interrupted as Master Belle did everything she could to get her composure and then invited him to leave through the opposite door. She said nothing more, but told him that Master McAdams would give him more information. And to his surprise, she didn't give him the number she had promised on the bus. What did that mean? Did he fail to qualify for a number?

As he stepped out of the door, Helia's song came back to his mind and the calm returned throughout his entire body. "What a blessing Helia is to me! Why was I so lucky to have her choose me? "

As he took a few steps away from the tent, the warmth and brightness of the sun drew him back to now. He noticed seven cabin style tents behind him with the parking lot and 3 green buses sitting where they had been dropped off. Before him was a large wooden frame building he assumed was the Great Hall. It was about the size of a small church building and appeared to have very high ceilings. He was unable, however, to see what was happening therein, but he only saw a few students ahead of him standing in line at a table outside a separate building to the right. This building was a small log cabin with Green Letters on a sign over the front door that read *Camp Master*. On a small plaque on the door he read the words, *Doc McAdams,* in beautiful script lettering. So he joined the line to talk with the individuals at the table.

"Hi. I am the Senior Patrol Leader Marcus Regulus and this is my assistant Martha Jewel. We will be helping you this summer and can answer any questions you have. Please tell us your name?"

James thought it interesting that this was the first time someone at the camp had asked his name, but he obliged, "I am James Adamson." As he said his last name, Martha's eyes lit up and she welcomed him with a smile, "You're in the Sphinx Patrol with Master Aimee Belle. I just love her! You just met her during your *Classification*."

Marcus then looked up from the list, "Master Belle, has given strict instructions that you meet with Doc before you are *Classified*. Please wait here for a moment and he will invite you into his cabin. When you are finished, please join us in the Great Hall and we will introduce you to your Mentor, Angelica Eve."

Martha quickly jumped in, "You will like her too!"

Marcus just looked at her and they both got up and walked toward the Great Hall. As James looked around, he realized all the other students were already *Classified*, so he just waited. He wasn't sure if this was a good or a bad omen for him, but the music in his mind continued to keep him calm. Besides, he would already be meeting Master Doc McAdams, someone that Bekah was really excited to meet.

"James, please come in." came a voice as the door to the cabin opened. He couldn't yet see the speaker, however.

As he walked into the well-lit cabin, he was amazed at the simplicity of the decorations in the entry hall of this cabin. It appeared to be a one-story cabin with 3-4 rooms. He was met in the entry way by an average height gentleman, with what was once brown hair, now intermixed with multiple silver or white strands. He had distinct white streaks in his hair on either side of his head, and was cleanly shaven with short hair. Although he was older, he had broad shoulders and a muscular build, but had a slightly plump belly. He was dressed in a brown uniform with multiple colored patches over his left breast pocket and wore a leather, cowboy style brown hat with the crest of *The Band of Fire* on the front.

"Well my boy, you are a very unique individual. You have been classified by Master Belle as Concordant."

"Wait. How can I be Concordant? According to *The Book of Adam* that means I have all the skills. I don't have the telepathy expertise of Bekah. I am not even close to as talented with maps and directions as my father. And I don't even know what all the other skills even are or how they work. I tried to read about them, but I just don't understand. Bekah would be a much better Concordant!"

Doc smiled, "Patience my boy. Classification doesn't mean you are skilled at any of these skills yet. Through *The Classification* process your skills are augmented to see what tendencies you have. Many students will have multiple tendencies, some primary skills and some secondary skills. Some individuals arrive with well-developed primary skills, but often they are only rudimentarily developed. Very few if any have secondary skills developed. My job is to provide you a third test to see if this Classification is correct. This third test is a very important part of this process to ensure your safety and the safety of others."

James smiled, knowing that he would probably not be confirmed as Concordant as he again placed a blindfold on his eyes.

His eyes opened to a large pathway that he was walking down. He saw very green trees on either side of the pathway, and asphalt under his feet. He seemed to be in a very busy area, but there were no people there to be seen. To James surprise, the Phoenix music had stopped, and Master McAdams came walking up next to him. "Sorry. Helia can't help you with this one. You will need to do it on your own."

At that, James started humming her music and he began looking around. Just the thought of her music was sufficient to calm his heart and mind as that music had done previously. He continued to look around and noticed a perfectly blue sky, with a complete absence of clouds. There was no breeze, but James could feel moisture in the air. It felt as if water was splashing towards him. As he listened he could hear loud rushing water. He wasn't sure where they were, so he started to walk. The rushing water brought to his memory a story from his dad of one of his father's favorite places of all times. He realized where they were…They were on the cliffs of Iguazu Falls. These were a very large waterfall located, yes he knew exactly where they were. His mind was drawn to the picture of a globe and he noted they were in southern Brazil near the border with Argentina.

Master McAdams smiled, but made no comments. He seemed to be just observing, not necessarily helping.

James thought of his mom and realized she was safety at home and felt her relaxed with no personal fears, no personal concerns and just sitting at the breakfast table finishing up her breakfast. She did have one thought, one worry, that Simon was hurt or worse since he hadn't contacted home at all since James' birthday. James then thought of his dad and realized he was here, less than 1/2 mile ahead of them. But he knew that dad didn't feel safe. As he heard his father's thoughts he realized that dad wasn't hurt, heart and lungs were working perfectly. He was not even malnutritioned or lacking in water. And he wasn't currently tied up, but he was limited in his ability to get away. He was being held by...his mind switched from this thought almost immediately.

There was a Phoenix in the camp, singing a different song from Helia, but it was also beautiful, but it seemed to "distract" James instead of bring comfort or peace. The Phoenix was talking to someone with the name of Camilla as they were making plans to train at The Order of .... The conversation suddenly stopped, and he could tell the phoenix was blocking his participation in the conversation. He realized that the phoenix, Fogo, must be talking. He decided to try and access the other half of the conversation since Fogo wouldn't allow him to have access. He assumed Fogo must be talking to Camilla, so he reached out to talk with her, but couldn't feel her presence at all, he couldn't find her. Maybe she wasn't in the camp. Maybe it wasn't her the phoenix was talking to.

He thought very carefully about the location of his dad and then he and Master McAdams found themselves just outside a large camp similar to Campus Gaea, but without the wooden buildings. Everything was done in tents, large cabin tents like the tent of his initial Classification and a large pavilion that served as their Great Hall. He realized there were close to thirty people there in camp, with most being 15-18 years old. There were no "students" 12 years-old, but there were eight instructors, of whom he assumed

Camilla was one. Based on the conversation he witnessed she seemed to be the leader of The Order of.... He still didn't know the name of the band, but it wasn't The Band of Fire.

He realized that dad would not be able to free himself or get back to mom unless James helped him. The camp, however, would not be easy to break into. Nor would it be easy to find as it was constantly being moved. Now was his opportunity, but he needed weapons. He began to look around and noticed multiple options for preparing weapons. It was time to go save his father...

Just then he was back in the tent with a blindfold on. He felt anger well up inside him as he lost the chance to save his father...Just then he realized where he was and could still hear Master McAdams in the room, so he removed the blindfold and looked over for his *Classification*.

"My dear boy, you truly are unique in your abilities. I have only once seen an individual with such great primary skills and she's no longer a student here. She has grown too old to join our company. You are Concordant and will notice unique skills develop within you over the next several years. But it is up to you how you react to these abilities. May I give you some instruction before I excuse you to join your new patrol in the Great Hall."

He continued without James having a chance to respond, "Bordered by Israel and Palestine on the west and Jordan on the east, The Dead Sea is a large body of water located at the lowest elevation in the entire world. It has a very high salinity level and has been estimated to by almost 10 times as salty as the ocean. It has one main tributary in the River Jordan flowing into it. You may have heard of the Jordan River in Utah flowing south to north from the Utah Lake to the Great Salt Lake, but the River Jordan is flowing north to south into the Dead Sea. There are, however, no streams or rivers coming off the Dead Sea. In fact, nothing comes from the Dead Sea. The water, once it enters the Dead Sea, is considered Dead. It doesn't go anywhere, nor does it give life in any form to the borders or in the water itself. In fact, no life can flourish, not plant or animal within or around the Dead Sea. This 'Dead' environment is the reason for the name."

"At the other end the River Jordan, however, is the Sea of Galilee. Or should I say north as 'part' of the River Jordan is the Sea of Galilee. The River Jordan is the main tributary, but also the main source of outflow from the Sea of Galilee. This river is also below sea level, and is the second lowest lake in all the world (behind the Dead Sea). The difference is very apparent, however, as it is a fresh water lake and gives great life within and around its banks. It is some of the most fertile land in this area of the world and has a great variety of animal and plant growth that depend on this water to live, including human civilizations. As opposed to the Dead Sea that gives no life, this water is constantly giving and helping all around it. Yes, it receives water from the River Jordan and underground springs, but it also gives life and even gives back to the River Jordan. But because of this constant giving, instead of just receiving, it also has constantly renewing water that gives even more life and growth."

"You have a choice to make here at *Campus Gaea* as you prepare to be an active part of *The Band of Fire*, are you going to be the Dead Sea or the Sea of Galilee. Are you going to only receive or are you going to give and receive? You ultimately have the choice that will determine your destiny. Other Concordants have had the same choice and we have examples in our history that have chosen each. May I invite you to learn from the Sea of Galilee."

With that, without any further explanation or opportunity for questions, James was excused to join the others in the Great Hall. He walked from the small cabin, moving very slowly as he considered what had been determined this morning. It seemed like much more than an hour had passed since he arrived at camp, but all that had happened was only *The Classification* that took barely an hour. Apparently, they are quite efficient at administering the test to all the new students starting that day. He couldn't wait to see what had happened with Bekah and Michael. That was the first moment since starting this process that he realized Bekah may not be in his patrol. Hopefully at least one of them, preferably Bekah, was with him in the Sphinx Patrol. If he really was Concordant, he would need his very best friend to help him through the process. Now he was nervous again as he came closer to the Great Hall and prepared to enter to see where Bekah was sitting.

CHAPTER 7
THE SPHINX PATROL

As James walked toward the large wood frame building, his mind was drawn back to his mother whom he somehow now knew was home safe, to his father still not home being held somewhere by Camilla and the fact that he was Concordant. He knew what that meant based on his reading, but could he really be? Bekah had far better telepathy skills than him and orienteering couldn't be one of his strengths for his dad was never able to bring out that skill in him. But one by one, as he thought about it, he saw the skills that he was able to utilize in the two different "dreams" and realized why they would think he must have those skills. He thought of Chapter 4, "Becoming a Titan" in *The Book of Adam* and decided he needed to review the section again on what a Concordant was and hopefully get more insights now that everyone would soon know he was Concordant.

Just then he came to two large wooden doors which he opened easily with a small push in the center of both. As the doors opened, he saw a great hall stretch out before him with a ceiling probably 35 or 40 feet above him. The room was very well lit, but he saw no lights hanging from the ceiling, but light seemed to emanate from the entire ceiling. The floor had a solid oak appearance that seemed to shine as if it were wet. The room was broken into 4 large groups of round tables and a long head table up front which included all the staff and the youth leaders Marcus and Martha. To his surprise, Master McAdams was already seated at the center of the long table and didn't look surprised to see him just walking in. He looked down at him and motioned slightly with his head to the right of the hall.

To the right front corner of the hall were tables with burnt orange and black tablecloths and a large flag hanging on the wall. The patrol flag was in the same colors with a picture of a Sphinx, including the head of a human, haunches of a lion and great fire red wings of a phoenix. The picture showed the Sphinx with wings outstretched, mouth open breathing fire and the lion paws standing on a sword crossing a bow and arrow, all embossed on a large shield. At one of these tables sat Bekah, Michael and Bekah's new friend, with a chair left open obviously for him. Bekah even waved at him as he looked over and he started walking towards her. As he walked he continued to look around.

To the right rear corner of the hall were similar tables with red, white and black tablecloths and another large flag hanging on the wall. This patrol flag was with a picture of a Centaur, including the torso, head and arms of a human and the body of a horse. The picture showed the Centaur galloping with fire rising from the hooves, a head with a golden crown, a breast plate covering the chest and a bow and arrow in hand, all embossed on a large shield.

With excitement, he now turned to the left rear corner of the hall where he noticed the third set of tables, arrayed in royal purple and gold. The patrol flag was likewise on the wall with a picture of a Griffin, including the body, tail and back legs of a lion, head and wings of a great eagle and eagle talons on the front feet. The picture showed the Griffin raised up on the hind legs standing on two crossed swords, wings spread wide with lightning bolts in each front talon, all embossed on a large shield.

The final corner of the room was arrayed in navy blue and silver under a patrol flag with a picture of a Minotaur, including the head, tail and feet of a bull, body, and hands of a human. The picture showed a powerful Minotaur holding a double-sided battle axe, large metal wrist bands and anklets, and standing on a mound of broken weapons and shields, also embossed on a large shield.

At that, James noticed the front staff table with forest green tablecloths and a large American Flag on the wall over the head of the staff. Otherwise the decorations of the hall and the staff table were beautiful, but very simple. He was amazed at the majesty of each patrol flag and excited for what was ahead.

James hurried to the table and sat between Bekah and Michael just as Master Doc McAdams stood to speak. His voice was deep and loud, but also very soothing. Due to the great power with which he spoke, there was no need for a microphone and all the chatter just seemed to subside. He demanded respect, without asking for it and within seconds had everyone in the hall looking to him. His words seemed to penetrate not just their ears, but their mind and possibly even their entire being.

"Welcome all to Campus Gaea. To those *returning*, we are glad to have you back. To those here for the first time, this camp is designed to teach you of the great mother earth and all she has to offer. Through *The Band of Fire* advancement system, we will develop your skills and strengthen additional abilities that will allow you to progress and more importantly prepare you to survive in whatever circumstances you may find yourself. These skills will be invaluable to help you become a true Titan, but more importantly to be a valuable citizen of this world, a servant to build and help others, a friend and confidant, and a protector and helper for all mankind. God has blessed you with 'special gifts' or 'special abilities' for which you will have great responsibility. What will you do with those gifts? You have a choice, but you cannot choose the results of that choice."

"I am reminded of ten young men who found an old broken-down car in a field near their houses. The walls, roof and doors had long since deteriorated. There was no engine, but the wheels were intact and the frame was intact enough that the boys could all stand on the car without touching the ground. As they goofed off with the car, they realized that it would move if pushed. Since they were close to the road, they thought they would push it to the road and ride it down the hill. They figured it would be fun and if it got too dangerous they could just get off and head home."

"As the car moved to the road, two young men decided it wasn't a good idea and after trying to convince the others to not go through with it headed home. Eight boys, excited for the trip down the large hill, mounted the car with a push. The car started moving at a slow rate of speed, but the speed started to pick up near the top of the hill. Two young men knew they had made a mistake and jumped off the car just as it started down the hill. Although the car wasn't moving very fast it was not easy to keep their feet as they jumped and they rolled on the asphalt and scraped their arms and legs. Bleeding, but not seriously hurt, they headed home humbled by the simple mistake they had made."

"The speed of the car started to pick up more quickly now, and each boy could look down from where he was standing and see the road moving quickly beneath them. The boy near the back noticed the speed while watching his two friends walk away and decided he too was done. He stepped off the back of the car and due to the speed, he felt his leg crumble underneath him. He fell and scraped his face, arms and legs, but also had severe pain to his right leg. There was no question in his mind that his leg was broken, but he was happy to no longer be on the moving car."

"Now with five young men on the car, the speed continued to increase. The speed of the road under the car was now a blur and most of the young men were now getting nervous. One jumped off the right side of the vehicle, rolled across the ground and hobbled home having broken both arms and a leg from the fall. He was happy, however, to be off the now speeding car."

"The next young man attempted to jump off the left side, but slipped while jumping and fell underneath the wheels to be run over by the rear tires and being seriously hurt, but was still alive. He was, however, unable to head home and just laid on the road where he had fallen."

"At this time, the speed was so much that the last three were not sure if they could get off. They may have waited too long and would just need to ride it out. But their fear increased when they realized the road curved at the bottom of the hill and the steering wheel was not working. They all held on tight as the car bounced over the curb and headed straight for the large tree in the park. Another boy jumped from the vehicle, but the speed of the car was so much that he was unable to land normal and he fell on his head, seriously injuring his back and could no longer move his arms or even feel his feet or legs. The other two, however, stayed on the car, too scared to jump and the car hit the tree killing both young men immediately."

"Each step of the way you will have a choice. But as you get further on the road, the choices become fewer and the ultimate results of your choices can not be chosen by you. If you make the right choices at the beginning, you have much more control over the direction your life will take. Let me invite you as you go through your classes, as you progress down *The Band of Fire* advancement program and as you prepare to reach the rank of Phoenix that you take advantage of all your opportunities and learning."

"I now release you to meet with your patrols. And mentors, please take the opportunity to introduce yourself to your team and answer any questions they may have. Classes will start in 1 hour at the various campsite areas. All new Titans, your mentors will help you know where to go for classes."

He then sat down, and the roar of the hall started to pick up as everyone started to talk. James turned back to the table laughing at the method Doc McAdams used to teach his principles. This was the second story, but James knew only he had heard the first. As he turned, Bekah began to talk at her high pitched, rapid rate. She was so excited to start the learning process. He could tell she loved everything about the camp already.

"James, I can't believe we are finally starting! What's your final *Classification*? Why did it take you so long to come in?"

"They had me take an additional test before giving me my *Classification*. I'm still a little confused at why they called me Concordant. I still don't know how I could be..."

"You're Concordant?" Michael asked overhearing the conversation. "I didn't know anyone was really classified as Concordant. You'll have to tell us more about it! I was classified as a Orientopath, but I think I already suspected that."

"Yes James, I'd love to hear about your test too," Bekah exclaimed rapidly, "and I am so excited to be classified as a Telepath and to have you be classified with the same skill. I was so hoping that would be my skill. Maybe as we develop telepathy we can talk more often even when at our separate homes. I can't wait to have Master Belle teach us!"

"Congrats to both of you. I am not surprised at your skills and hope I can learn a lot from each of you." James stated with a smile. "And who is your new friend?" he asked as he turned to look.

"I'm Kari," said the midnight black girl to Bekah's left. "I'm so excited to get to know y'all. I was classified today as a Zoonophonic. Jack will be happy to hear all about it," she said with a twinkle in her eye.

Before James could even ask, he knew that Jack was the wolfdog that he saw loaded on the bus earlier that day. He would love to get to know Jack too, but he would need to talk with Kari at a later date about that he thought as a tall, slender Brazilian girl with dark blue eyes, tan skin and curly, black, long hair approached from an adjacent table.

"Hello, I am Angelica," she said with a strong accent. "I will be your mentor this summer. I is lucky enough to be assigned to you four. I hope my accent's not hard to understand."

Bekah immediately stood up and ran over to give her a big hug, which seemed to relax Angelica who had seemed nervous and almost shy.

"Where do we start?" Bekah asked in a hurry hardly even releasing the hug before she started talking.

As they continued to talk, the four new Titans walked with 14 year-old Angelica from the Great Hall towards the large lake. On the eastern shore of the lake was a large fire pit with split log benches laid out in a semi-circle. As they approached, there was a number of students separated into two distinct groups and Marcus and Martha standing next to the fire pit. They were directing all Minotaur patrol members to their left and all Sphinx patrol members to their right. Angelica therefore lead them to the right to join the other members of the Sphinx patrol.

As they arrived, Marcus started to speak and Angelica moved to the back of the group with the other older students. It appeared that each group of two - four students had a mentor assigned who was in attendance with them at this introduction.

"Hello Sphinx and Minotaur patrols. You're all new Titans this year and need some initial instruction. The Centaur and Griffin patrols will be instructed in a similar fashion here the second hour. Although we have been separated into four patrols, we will all be working together to improve our skills and grow this summer. The patrol structure is for meals, tent arrangements and competitions. Otherwise you will be expected to work together."

"As new Titans, we'll be working with you on earning the rank of *Silver Spark* this summer. If you work hard, pay attention, participate actively and help each other this summer, you'll have an opportunity to participate in the final Board of Review to earn that rank. Your goal over the next several years should be to reach the rank of Phoenix. Doc McAdams will tell you more about that in the second hour today."

"My job is to start with the basics. My job is to teach you the *Fire Sign*, the handshake and help you memorize *The Oath*. All this can be found in Chapter 15 from *The Book of Adam*. After lunch you'll be shown to your tent where you will finally have access to your books and can review it in more detail. Does anyone know the *Fire Sign?*"

Bekah's hand shot into the air as did the hand of a girl from the Minotaur patrol.

"Lizzy can you show us?" Marcus asked. Bekah looked over to see who the other girl was.

A light skinned Latin girl with short black hair, green eyes and a small nose rose from her bench. She was relatively thin and of average height for her age. As she stood, she raised her right hand to the square with the fingers close together and stood at attention.

As Marcus nodded his head and said, "That is correct," she moved her hand to a salute and said with a slight Spanish accent, "And this is the salute."

"Thank you Lizzy. You may now be seated."

"Now Bekah. Do you also know the handshake?" And he stepped forward to greet her.

Bekah jumped to her feet and grabbed his left hand with hers interlocking the little fingers and extending three fingers to his wrist, as he did the same.

"We now need all to practice the sign, salute and handshake for the next few minutes."

Everyone stood, began to shake each other's hands, salute each other and practice the *Fire Sign*. After much laughing, everyone seemed to be getting it, so Marcus called them back to attention and everyone returned to their seats.

"Now Martha will teach you the purpose of these symbols."

Martha stepped forward and began a simple explanation, "As you all may know, the right hand to the square is utilized in making commitments or promises. In *The Band of Fire* it is no different. You'll utilize this sign whenever you are making a promise or commitment to our brothers or sisters of Fire. Please consider this a binding contract and a promise you cannot break!"

After a pause for emphasis she continued, "The salute is likewise a sign of respect and support for your brothers and sisters of Fire. We utilize this symbol between us as do the military. You may likewise utilize this salute, when in uniform, when saluting the American flag or the appropriate flag of your home country. That is also a great honor afforded to the military, boy scouts and us. Please respect that right and use it appropriately."

"And lastly, I will explain the handshake using a story Master Doc McAdams likes to share."

She began to read, "In ancient times soldiers were armed with a sword and shield. The shield was held in the left hand and the right hand contained the sword. When warring armies came together in offers of peace, each general would come fully armed and place his sword on the table between them. They would then offer their right hand as a symbol of peace, but would never let down the shield in the left hand that stood between the enemy general and their heart. This therefore became the symbol of peace, but not the symbol of trust."

"When *The Band of Fire* came together, however, two formerly warring generals decided to take it to the next level. They placed not just their sword on the table, but also their shield and reached out with their left hand as a symbol of peace and trust. Instead of coming together with fear and protection between them, they committed their own life to building a better tomorrow and witnessed it by taking left hands, hand in hand. By interlocking the little finger, the bond was so much stronger and bound them together as brothers for eternity. We likewise bond as brothers and sisters with no fear, no mistrust and complete confidence between us. Only then can we work as one to make the world a better place."

With that Martha stepped back and Marcus came forward again. "Please know that I commit to you all I am and all I can be to help you succeed as my brothers and sisters of Fire. When I shake your hand from now on, you need to know that is what it means! As you shake each other's hands, it should mean the same!" He then proceeded around the group shaking each student's hand one by one.

Marcus then returned to the front and asked them to all stand again and began to teach them the oath. After nearly 25 minutes, they all had it memorized and they were released to head to the second hour of introduction. As Angelica lead them from the spot, James thought through the oath and was amazed at the significance of the words.

"I solemnly covenant before my brothers and sisters of Fire to do my Duty to God, to serve others with all my heart, to stand as a witness of faith, knowledge and strength, to use my gifts to protect freedom, happiness and independence for all, to lift the weak, to comfort the sad and to befriend the friendless. That I may by so doing stand against evil in all its various forms. To this I pledge my sacred honor."

And he knew that this was much more than just a pledge. It was his marching orders as Master Doc McAdams had instructed him earlier today. He would not just remember it, but would try to live it. Only then could he truly be a Titan, whether he was truly Concordant or not. His choice was made! Now he just needed to move forward as quickly as possible to develop the expected skills. Then maybe he could learn what really was happening to his father.

CHAPTER 8
CONCORDANT

The morning seemed to fly by and before they knew it, James, Bekah, Michael and Kari were following Angelica from the Great Hall for the second time toward their campsite. Each patrol was camped in clumps of tents on the west side of the lake. Each campsite was marked with a large fire pit in the center, and large cabin style tents creating a circle around the fire pit. The tents were colored similar to the patrol flags, meaning that this group was headed for the burnt orange and black tents.

As they approached, James noted two distinct tent colorings in their camp. The circle of tents was actually broken into two sections with a large pathway from north to south separating tents on the east and west. On the east side were black tents with burnt orange highlights. On the west side were burnt orange tents with black highlights. The girls all seemed to be migrating to the burnt orange tents and the boys were migrating to the black tents. On the path between the row of tents were two large wolves that seemed to be patrolling between the different colored tents. One of the wolves was dark gray in color, walking on the southern portion of the path and seemed older than the dark black, slightly smaller wolf patrolling the northern portion of the path.

James noticed Helia singing in the tent just to the east side of the southern path and he and Michael were directed to that tent. James was quite pleased when Bekah and Kari were directed to the southern most tent on the west side of the path. As he approached, however, he heard the dark gray wolf muttering, "Females to the west and males to the east! No crossing into the other half of camp! No exceptions! No exceptions!" He looked up to see if Michael had heard it, but apparently, he had not. He did notice Kari, however, turn to look at the wolf in surprise.

As they unzipped the door and stepped into the tent, Helia flew to James' shoulder and began to speak immediately, "The cot to the right I chose for you, for better location it is. Jacques my friend he is, but cross to the girl's side of camp you permit he will not. Know that the rules he will keep and sleep he does not, so attempt to cross I would not."

Having mentioned what she felt was most important, she switched subjects quickly, "Concordant you may be, but knowledgeable you are not. Together we learn and these skill help you they will. Only with my help can the greatest benefits you find." And she immediately flew from his shoulder to his cot where *The Book of Adam* sat ready to be examined, opened to the pages about Concordant in Chapter 4.

James sat on the cot and picked up the book and began to read with Helia's soft song ringing in his mind:

By definition, a Concordant individual has the ability to develop Titan level strengths for all seven skills including Telepathy, Chronopathy, Hippocratesense, Orientopathy, Herculopathy, and Zoonophonia. Although the capabilities may be there initially, often at an early age only some of the skills may be visualized or exercised. Therefore, the Classification of Concordant is hard to determine without very careful Classification testing.

In fact, Concordant Titans are poorly understood in all aspects because of their minimal numbers and often an erroneously classified entity. Just as only a very small percentage of living individuals are Titans as opposed to Natural Born, an even smaller, miniscule percentage are found to be Concordant. For years, this designation was often not identified at all through The Classification process until more recently in history.

In 1989, when Doc McAdams was designated as the Camp Master at Campus Gaea, the techniques were further specialized and clarified to improve The Classification process. Over the ensuing years very powerful Telepaths were employed to perform The Classification under strict guidelines. This has produced much more accurate designations for all Titans, including almost no Concordant individuals.

The accuracy of the process was improved further by Doc implementing an even more rigorous testing process including three interwoven Classification tests pulling information from the Titan's own memory and experiences. Due to the strength of the Telepath's abilities, the use of the Titan's mind can be utilized to augment any talents or strengths the individual is expected to develop throughout his or her life. Most individuals will have a single ability, but some will have two or even three skills. In the rare exception where Concordance is anticipated, an additional test, a fourth test, is performed.

The great value of the fourth test is dependent on a much more complex Classification process, through Doc McAdams utilizing his own Concordant abilities to perform a far deeper testing process. Through these highly specialized abilities, Doc is able to create a testing scenario while he is also able to be in direct attendance in the Titan's own mind throughout the entire testing process. Therefore, he is able to see and carefully evaluate the decision-making process instead of just listening to the Titan's thoughts as the Telepath does during the previous tests.

Therefore, a Classification of Concordant is now considered almost non-existent, but is very accurate when confirmed.

As the music continued in his mind, James felt himself racing through the air with Helia by his side. They were no longer in Campus Gaea but somewhere else. A place he didn't recognize but he heard the song of another phoenix ahead of them. He could feel Helia's excitement and they seemed to speed up. And they came to stop in a camp, just like Campus Gaea, but it didn't look the same. The lake was still there, but the Great Hall was missing. The fire pits were much smaller and the tents were small A frame type tents in a single green color.

As they came to the ground, Helia again landed on his shoulder and they began to walk to the growing music from a tent in the distance. Just then a 12 year-old young man came strolling from his tent with a very familiar smile, and deep blue eyes that shown with excitement. On his shoulder was a beautiful lava red phoenix singing the song they were listening to. The young man walked towards them, but didn't seem to notice them standing there. He was alone, except for the bird, but was speaking with great excitement in his voice.

"Well Felicity, they say I may be Concordant. But they seemed very confused. Nobody has been Concordant for many years, since Adonis was classified 60 years ago and was killed because he tried to walk on water and didn't have sufficient Chronopathic ability to allow this feat. I think they were scared of me, or maybe just scared for me. What do you think?"

"Docery, you must be careful! For I see danger in their eyes. For they fear the knowledge and skills unknown and already may your abilities despise. You must not show all skills at times, for if you show too much, great troubles come into your life, trying Concordant skills to crush. One skill, two skills, seldom three, and by your fruit

you will be judged, so hide your fruits whenever you can, that you still by them'll be loved. You must not act Concordant, although we know you have the skills, for Concordants have long been despised and that in full strength you'd also feel" the words sang beautifully from the phoenix and filled James with wonder.

"But how do I control them? How can I limit these abilities when we don't really even know what they are?"

"The knowledge yet you have, and have felt the abilities in mind and soul. Did you not feel power in your veins from the very day you were 8 years-old? We'll find a way in secret to develop skills unequaled still, You and I together can control and hide them all and we surely will..."

The vision quickly faded as James awoke laying on his back on the cot and heard Michael and Bekah calling for him from outside the tents. He looked over at Helia perched on the end of his bed with excitement in her eyes and he immediately knew that she too had seen the vision, but he wasn't sure what it meant. Why would they be scared of a Concordant? And who was this Adonis that tried to walk on water?

"That crazy wolf won't let Bekah close to our tent, so you will need to come out," Michael exclaimed as he burst through the tent door. "Even Kari tried to talk with him, but he would not budge. What are you doing lying there, we have class in a matter of minutes. It is our first real class, our class on Map and Compass. I am not sure who they got to teach it, because it was supposed to be your father." At that Michael ran back out of the tent with books in hand full of excitement. James remembered that this was Michael's classified skill, so he understood why he was so excited.

James looked back at Helia, who seemed to smile at him as she sang, "Worry not my James, much talking still we must do. The sun will not yet rise until the finished discussion we have had. But now is not the time even though Concordant yet you are."

Minutes later James, Bekah, Kari and Michael arrived at the fire pit only seconds before the class started. The patrol members were in attendance, but no teacher was present. As they moved to their seat, a beautiful lava red phoenix flew in and landed before them. It didn't make a noise, but seemed to be carrying papers in its right talons. Before they could even think about what was going on, she began to sing.

At the same moment, in their minds they heard the strong voice of Master McAdams, "Welcome to your introduction to map and compass. Each of you are to retrieve a map from the phoenix and pull out your compass. You will then break into patrols and use the map and compass to find where we will be holding class from now on. For the time being you will be learning from me until our usual instructor can join us. Please proceed with great speed to where the map leads you. Know that I will be tracking each of you and will help if necessary. It is very important to know where to start your individual instruction in this important topic. Only then can I guide you to greater skill and understanding."

Michael jumped to his feet and was the first to the phoenix, already with his compass in hand. "I was wondering who would be the instructor. I am so happy to be learning from Master McAdams. I have heard only great things about his abilities."

Bekah was a close second, speaking in great speed and pitch, "He's a Concordant, one of the most powerful of all times. His abilities in Orientopathy are legendary and will be of great help in our learning to find directions, even if we don't have Orientopathic abilities."

One by one, each student grabbed a map and then the phoenix went up into the air and flew back towards the Great Hall. James had been sitting back and was actually the last student to get a map, because he had tried to do this map thing for years with his dad and was worried he was not capable of truly using the map correctly. Hopefully the teachings of mom would be sufficient to let him help his patrol. As he continued to worry, Bekah smiled at him and asked him to join her. Michael, James, Kari and Bekah came together as a patrol and began to study the map.

Michael began to study the map, "I know we can do this, but I am quite worried because I have never done this with a map and compass, especially in an area I don't know very well."

Kari looked worried, "I really don't even know how to use the compass. How do you know what to do with it. All I know is that this arrow points north."

Bekah rapidly replied, "James can do this. He's Concordant, and his dad is supposed to be teaching this class and has taught him at home."

James looked at all three and took a deep breath. "Let's start with the compass. My mom taught me about compasses, not my dad!" He showed each how to hold the compass, how to orient the map using the compass, how to get directions using the numbers around the compass and even Michael was eating it up. They then started looking at the map and were trying to figure out what to do.

"This is a typical topographical map that shows the mountains over there, the lake right here and..." James continued.

"Oh, I get it." Michael said with excitement and then he closed his eyes. "I have never done this with a map, but if you continue I can create the map in my mind and help us figure out how to get there."

"Wait. I think I see it..." James voice trailed off as the map seemed to come alive. And then the music started in his ears. "Helia is helping," he thought with a smile. The mountain on the map became 3D, and the trail seemed to highlight itself on the map. As he looked around he couldn't really see the trail, but he knew where it was. He looked over at Michael and realized that the key was to get his other senses working.

"Michael, why don't you try to use your other senses. There is a trail to the north of us that winds around the lake. As it continues around the lake there will be a fork and we will take the left fork into the thick forest. From there we need to find a cave that is where the class will be held. What do you hear? What do you feel? What do you smell? I think that is the best way to do it." James finished as Bekah's eyes got bigger.

"Michael will direct us, but Bekah and Kari you should both use your compasses with the map to ensure we are going the right direction."

"I hear the water and the wind through the trees. I think there should be a path ahead behind... the clump of trees." Michael then opened his eyes and knew the path really was before them.

"Perfect. Let's look at this map together. We are here. That mountain there is here. The path should be, as you heard, ahead of us here." James closed his eyes and could see the entire map in his mind. Was the music really making that much difference or was it just that Helia helped him relax?

They started moving forward and all the sudden Michael started to talk rapidly, "Wait. We don't need to follow the path. We can move to the left here around the trees and through this other route. There should be another route, a quicker route. Can you see it on the map?"

Kari jumped into the conversation, "I see that here on the map. It looks like it might be a little steeper if these lines coming closer together mean anything."

"I say we go with Michael's recommendation." Bekah said excitedly. "I think he's found the way Master McAdams would want us to go!"

They started on the path with Michael leading. James folded the map and put it and the compass away. He could see the entire map in his mind and he knew what was ahead of them. He somehow knew where to turn before Michael lead them that way. He also knew about how many steps it would take to get to each turn. He felt as if he was his dad leading a group, but wished he had the same ability to really understand what was around them as his dad did in the dream.

Within a short 20 minutes of walking, after climbing the side of a ridge, climbing over many small boulders and ducking behind a group of fallen trees, they found the opening to a cave. The opening was only large enough for one person to enter at a time, but they all knew it was the right place because the lava red phoenix was perched just over the entrance and singing a soft song. James couldn't help but smile as Michael, Bekah and Kari each stepped into the cave. He wasn't exactly sure what just happened, but he was starting to believe he could possibly be Concordant after all.

As James ducked into the cave, he was surprised to have the small opening expand into a large round area that looked about half the size of the great hall. He noticed red, blue and green rocks at the far end pointing down from the celling or up from the floor. And past them was a more narrow passage that seemed to extend deeper into the mountain. Doc McAdams was seated on a log chair, and Michael, Bekah and Kari were sitting on the first row of long logs setup in rows. Nobody else had made it yet. "Michael was actually quite good at this," he thought as he was about to sit down.

Doc McAdams just smiled at the four of them and continued to concentrate, almost like he was staring off into the cave wall. Four by four the patrols entered the cave. Some were very excited to be there, and others came in with fear in their eyes, especially the last group. As the last group entered approximately 40 minutes after Michael walked into the cave, Doc McAdams stood.

"Well done. Many of you are seeing a map and compass for the very first time. Some of you were so worried about the map that you didn't allow your senses to lead you. Some of you actually got lost and I was forced to direct you to our cave. Know that every single one of you are able and will be capable of map use before this summer is over. In fact, by the end of this summer all of you will be able to use a compass and a map together to navigate even areas you have never been. But some of you will develop the unique ability to have the maps come to life, and hopefully over the next few years to use all your other senses to not even need a map. Only then will you truly be an Orientopath."

"For the next 20-25 minutes we will start with using a compass and how to orient your map with that compass. We will then have you meet here again tomorrow for us to continue." And he began to teach them about the compass, about the gravitational pull of the earth. He showed them magnetic and true north. He even had them move around the cave in various directions to test their ability to use a compass. Then finally he had each measure their step length to help determine distances. This distance was designed to make following a map in the Natural Born way possible for any Titan without Orientopathy. Bekah seemed to eat this up and was soon one of the best at using the compass and following the map. In fact, although her steps were short, she became the most accurate when they used coordinates to get to a location.

Michael, however, was very impressive. He soon put his compass away and with his eyes closed could move in the correct direction and although his step length and accuracy were not as good as Bekah, his motion without a compass was almost perfect.

Kari, however, seemed to get a little frustrated with several other students because they weren't getting it. No matter how she tried she was always 5 – 10 feet away from the correct ending point. This was the most common results of the first day.

James, however, seemed to be learning something entirely different. As he was starting to use his compass, he heard words in his mind that he recognized as coming from Doc McAdams, "Stop trusting tools. The compass will keep you from your full potential. Listen to the rocks. Listen to the feet hitting the ground around you. Where are the stalactites and stalagmites? (The colored rocks you saw ahead of you.) Open your mouth and feel the air temperature. Where is the opening of the cave? How far are you from it? Can you feel the breeze coming from the opening? Is it hitting the wall or the ceiling? What does all this information tell you about your location?" He wasn't moving, but everyone that looked at him saw him in great concentration, looking down at his hands like he was seeing something. Some even laughed at him not moving around.

James as he looked at his hands was seeing something. He saw the entire cave before his eyes in 3D with each individual as an "X" on the map. He could see a dial around him with the north, south, east and west all marked. He could see the numbers with 0 degrees at north and 180 degrees at the south. He really didn't need the compass! What mom had taught him about using a compass was now part of his mind creating a map of his location, and then it happened…the class was over and they were all being excused. James didn't want to go because he was finally starting to understand, but Master McAdams excused them all and sent them back towards the camp.

"James, you will have plenty of time to get better at this. Now is the time to move on!"

Michael and Bekah were talking to each other throughout the whole trip back to camp about how much they learned and how much they enjoyed that class. Kari didn't look very happy, and was almost silent until James walked up to her and began to talk with her. He explained how he had been struggling with that for years and how hard it was growing up with his dad being the master of Orientopathy. It seemed to help her relax a little more just as they arrived at their next class.

The other classes that day were less exciting and probably even less interesting, but they did learn the initial steps to building a fire, some basic cooking instructions and were given some insights on what the other days would hold in the process of "Becoming a Titan." James tried very hard to focus, but kept thinking back to the discussion he needed to still have with Helia about being or becoming Concordant. Therefore, he was very relieved when they were released to return to the Great Hall for dinner. But James wasn't very hungry and so he raced back to his tent to have the discussion he had been waiting for since leaving the tent after lunch.

As he raced into the tent, Helia was again perched on the edge of his cot and a book he didn't recognize was sitting open on the cot. He walked forward and noticed the book open to Chapter 1 – *What It Means To Be Concordant*. He then grabbed the book with excitement and turned to the front cover: *The Secret Life of a Concordant* by Doc McAdams. The name caught him by surprise, but the information in the book was too intriguing for him to even ask where it came from.

Concordant individuals used to be considered dangerous and were even sent away from camp because of the risk they were to other individuals. The classification was also very inaccurate and problematic, which increased the concern about these individuals. But the truth is that a Concordant is only seen in about 1 in every 300 Titans at most. Then depending on the training and development they receive can become a powerful resource to *The Band of Fire*. Therefore, through the careful Classification process we have created, a Concordant can be correctly classified and instructed on all that is necessary to become functional and ultimately powerful in all seven skills. Through this process, we can prevent some of the terrible accidents seen in years gone by.

In the past, there have been several notorious cases of personal injury secondary to Concordant classification, especially erroneous classification…

The pages started to blur and again he was racing through the air with Helia by his side. His mind seemed to be opening up as the surroundings started to clarify and he found himself again at what appeared to be Campus Gaea but early on. He saw green, A-frame style tents without floors and the camp had no benches, no wooden buildings and didn't even seem to have organized trails. He was not sure when he was, but then he saw a 6-foot, 4-inch boy with long blond hair, dark brown eyes and olive skin. As James looked at him, he knew immediately who he was and was wondering what year Adonis would be here at camp.

"They told me I am Concordant, but Sariah doesn't believe that I really am. I need to convince her. What should I do?" as the boy continued to talk, James notices a small rabbit hopping next to him.

"Well sir, I would recommend that you think of something amazing that would impress her. What can you think of to do with your abilities? Talking to me won't work. Maybe you can use Chronopathy and move quickly," the rabbit whispered.

"Maybe I should walk on water. No other Titan has ever walked on water before using the power of Chronopathy. If I move quick

enough I could cross the lake without sinking." And an almost evil smile came across his face and James could hear his thoughts and knew immediately that he was planning to do it the next day." And the scene faded into another scene.

Now James and Helia were standing by the lake only about 100 yards from a large group of students, but there were no teachers in the area. At the front of the group was Adonis in long billowing robes with his long hair tied into a ponytail and bragging about what he was about to do. A young lady stood to his right pleading with him to not try it. But he was adamant that it was going to happen.

Just then everything froze, but only for a couple seconds and James was reminded of his trip on the bus. As time seemed to stand still, all the students were frozen, but James was not. Adonis ran out into the water as fast as he could, but even with his rapid speed was struggling to stay on top of the water. As soon as he was about 60 feet out, he was wet to about his waist, but was currently walking with only his feet covered. Then everything happened at once. He heard the whispering voice of the rabbit screaming, "Master!" Saw the young lady cover her face. Heard gasps and screams from all the students. Saw an adult come running towards the water. And saw Adonis sink into the water and then struggle against the long, flowing robes saturated with water. He had sort of walked on water, but was not skilled enough to finish the task and he disappeared into the water and was gone.

The scene again faded and James and Helia were again flying through the air.

"Concordant all powerful is not! Strength only comes when knowledge you find. Power is not given but through wisdom is gained. Adonis knew not what true power was." Helia's song continued, but her voice grew silent as the tent began to appear again.

Adonis was never rescued from the water and was never found again. From that day for many dark years the classification of Concordant was considered too dangerous for a Titan to receive. In fact, *The Band of Fire* worked hard to only allow each Titan to develop a single skill. If a Titan was found to be developing more than one skill, he would be expelled from camp and not allowed to return.

Due to this confused and ill-informed doctrine, a counter-culture of Titans were created and developed outside *The Band of Fire*. This counter-culture has created Titans without the honor, without the standards laid out by the Oath and ultimately individuals focused on themselves and their own success. Over the ensuing years, this doctrine has been repealed and the Classification process has been updated and revised. Now only true Concordants are classified and their instruction is carefully metered and controlled to allow skill development at the proper speed.

As the skills are developed properly, many Concordants have become powerful teachers, powerful protectors and powerful instruments in *The Band of Fire* and the protection of the world as we know it. Becoming a true Concordant is more than just gaining Titan level skills in all the Titan abilities. It is actually based on the purpose for the skill development and how those skills are utilized in accordance with the *The Band of Fire Oath*.

The chapter ended, and James noticed Helia still at his side singing and he decided to look through the book for the other chapters. For he had just witnessed Adonis die because of too much pride at being a Concordant, and James wanted to gain the necessary knowledge and wisdom to find what true power really was.

Again, he notices what to him was a smile come across Helia's beak and he knew there was much to learn.

"May power come as you learn, as you study and as your mind lifted with my powerful song it is. Concordant yes, but true power you must find and help you I will."

CHAPTER 9
ORDER OF THE KRAKEN

A small group of Titans sat at a table talking as Camilla, a slender woman with long curly brown hair, dark blue eyes, a small nose and a slightly round face sat at the head of the table. To her left sat Minerva, a tiny brown skinned woman with short black hair, midnight black eyes and a small button like nose. He recognized her as Camilla's friend from years ago. To Camilla's right sat a slightly older individual that he didn't recognize with dark skin, almost brownish-yellow eyes, long brown hair down to his back and a long brown, fluffy beard and mustache. They had been calling him Zoram since sitting at the table.

As he looked around the table and strained his ears to hear, his wrists tied behind his back ached from the days of being tied up. His conversation with Camilla yesterday gave him some additional insights to what was happening and he was now trying to memorize the faces and names of all the members of the Order of the Kraken, as she called them. He thought carefully about the conversation and carefully thought through the discussion to look for any additional information he may have missed.

"Simon," she began in her melodious voice.

"I am your father."

"You haven't been my father since I was 6 years-old and even before then you were almost never home for mom or I!"

He couldn't argue, but the words still came as a dagger to him.

"And now I am ensuring that you don't hurt James as you have hurt me. Although only my half-brother, I love him far more than I ever loved you." This time her deep blue eyes twinkled and a smile came across her lips. Then she giggled at the thought of holding and playing with her little brother.

"The Band of Fire is a corrupt system that has been developed to hold Titan's back, like you strived to hold mom back from using her powers of telepathy. It is your fault she was in that car with a Natural Born and was killed as a Titan should never be. You could have protected her but were too proud to allow telepathy in your life. For this I will never forgive you. You will never know what it is like to have the very words of your mother ripped from your mind as her heart stops beating. I was talking to her, she was sharing her love as her body lay bleeding with her legs and body pinned in the passenger front seat. Her love still echoes in my mind, but the words were taken from me when her mind could no longer send that message I had known my entire life. You will never understand and can never make it up to me."

"Sarah loved you. And Doc worked really hard to help you develop your skills as a Concordant."

"Sarah never loved me as much as mom did. Only James showed me that kind of love. As for Master McAdams, he is part of the problem. He doesn't want us to truly use our skills. We are never taught the full extent of our strengths and abilities, only the extent he wants us to know. Even Master Belle was trying to get me to limit what I learned. In the Order of the Kraken I will teach all skills and all abilities. With the help of my friends we will have far more power than any Titan from The Band of Fire. As a Concordant myself, I will one day replace the limited views of Doc McAdams and help us take our proper place in the world. For the Titans were greater than the Gods in ancient mythology and we should likewise be now."

…His memories were interrupted as Camilla stood and began to instruct all in attendance.

"The Band of Fire camp has begun, and many new Titans are being instructed in the limited views of Doc McAdams. The instructors will continue, as most of you know, to teach them the limited view of what their Titan powers are and how they should be used. We have a different vision, a different plan and more importantly a very important responsibility to reach out and find them. Bring into our Order, into our camp that we can help them take their proper place in this world."

As Camilla stopped speaking, Zoram stood and began to address the group.

"Camilla is right. May we take her lead and walk the path, stand the ground and fight the fight that must be won. These Titans are my children and your children, they are men and women of unbelievable power that are being told their only job is to help and serve others. They have a right to know more. This world owes them respect and honor, for we will carry them into the 21st Century. We must infiltrate the very core of The Band of Fire and steal even the newest, and weakest of Titans. I consider it my responsibility to ensure each of them can get theirs. They deserve more than Doc will ever give them!" He then sat again in his chair with his brownish-yellow eyes burning with fire and great passion.

Then she stood, a 5'6" woman, with long, stringy, black hair and stone-cold deep green eyes. The anger and hatred in her face shown through.

"I now stand with or without you in open rebellion to the status quo! Many bands have been created over time due to The Band of Fire limiting individuals for years to one Titan ability. These secret combinations and groups have been weak because of lack of leadership. The Order of The Kraken is different. With Camilla's capable Concordant leadership we are powerful. I now stand with each of you, pushed by The Band of Fire and their limited views of Titan power. My grandmother repudiated me, degraded me and even laughed at my power. She felt a Hippocratesent was not a real Titan. Healing is not enough for her. My power is viewed by many in the Titan establishment as ignoble. But no longer shall they think that way. If healing is not enough, then I shall help all Hippocratesents to learn the power to anathematize. Only then will they be recognized as a true Titan. They shall forever remember the name, Kathryn Circe and shall fear me and fear all of the Order of the Kraken!" She broke into a smile and a simple laugh, that echoed through the hall, and made Simon's skin crawl.

Camilla, who had remained standing throughout the talks, stepped forward and a blood red phoenix flew to her shoulder as she opened her mouth again.

"Simon is our key. We must keep him separate from his family and more importantly separate from The Band of Fire. Only then can we infiltrate the Orientopathy class with Instructor Zoram Balthizar. I can shield your mind from Doc, but you must act your part well. We need an inside man. If there is any question, you will be dismissed as many of our Order have been."

"Peter." Camilla turned to look to her left where a 5'11" man rose to attention and Simon noticed his shaved head, hazel eyes and round nose. "I need you to help Zoram and Elli get to Campus Gaea." A young lady stood with a short, spiky red haircut, small build and cute freckles across her nose and cheeks. Simon had never seen her, but she was tiny and couldn't be much older than 12 years-old.

"Our goal is for them to add you Elli to their camp so that you can continue to work with Zoram in infiltrating the camp. Although you are now almost 15, they will see you as too small and probably only 12 years-old. Zoram will present himself as your father and ask if you can be admitted since he will be teaching the Orientopathy class." Elli smiled with delight and nodded in agreement.

"I then need you back Peter so that you can help me move our camp to a new location. I am thinking of moving to Brazil, where they will never think to follow us. We need to keep Simon separated from them all."

Minerva stood, but her 4'8" height made her still very short in comparison to all around her.

"Camilla, should we really be stating our plans with Simon in the room?"

"His power is Orientopathy, for which he is very capable. Even our blindfold failed to keep him from learning our location, our numbers and even the exact time and day it was. I underestimated him once, but will not blindfold him again so that I can see what he is doing, where he is looking and can continue to read his mind. He proved long ago, with my mother, that he has no power of Telepathy so he will NOT be able to send any information about our plans or our location to anyone else. Nor will he be able to stop me from reading his mind. As for Doc or anyone else reading his mind, I can sense any Telepath entering his mind! I am currently blocking his location from Doc McAdams who has looked for him. Besides, I will enjoy Simon see his complete failure as our plans come to fruition!" Camilla then smiled at Minerva in appreciation.

"May I at least request that Adam be assigned as his personal guard and travel companion?" Minerva pleaded.

"Done. Thanks for the suggestion Minnie. Adam," Camilla turned to her right. "Will you take him as your personal charge. You should know exactly what is happening with him at all times and ensure he stays in your presence. You will personally be held responsible if he escapes."

"With great pleasure!" a large, broad shouldered 6'8" man with shoulder length, white blond hair, dark brown eyes, tan skin and a large pointy nose said standing with a slight bow to Camilla. The beautifully crafted staff in his right hand appeared to be made of oak with a large hand-carved wood handle. "I will treat him as my own father…"

All began to laugh as Camilla started to hum her song, the very song Simon had heard from his tent just before all went black. "As much as I would love for you to treat him like you did your father, we need him alive…at least for now." And again, Adam bowed his head in respect as if he were Camilla's servant.

At that they were all excused and many of the Order broke into groups to make plans based on how they were instructed. And the last man at the table, a short black male, with short, curly black hair, dark brown eyes, and glasses hurried over to Camilla and asked what he was to do. She smiled at him and instructed him to prepare the camp for departure. And then his dark brown eyes seemed to light up and Simon knew they must be speaking Telepathically, because he had seen that look before when he was married to Aria.

Just then Adam walked over to Simon and picked him up and carried him from the room…

James woke, laying in his sleeping bag on his cot and he looked over at Michael who was sleeping. As he looked to Helia, she was not in her nest. His clothes were soaked and tears were running down his face. His whole body was tense and his arms and legs ached. What had he just seen? Was his dad still in the same place he was before, since they were moving to Brazil and not already there as he had witnessed in the Classification with Doc McAdams? And more importantly, what is the *Order of the Kraken*? He didn't think it would be in any of his books.

Just then he heard a voice, a very quick, high pitched but concerned voice, "Please let me by. I know that James is in trouble, I can feel it, and I don't know what it is."

"You can NOT pass young lady! That is the rule while here at camp. I don't care if he is your brother!"

"I don't have the power to understand you! Can you at least go check on him?"

"Your words mean nothing to me! And the rules will not change even if you are cute and have been kind to me. Maybe you should find a friend that can talk to me."

At that James rose and walked out of his tent to see Bekah on one side of the path with the old wolf Jacques standing before her. Bekah looked scared, but very concerned at the same time.

James walked over and Bekah seemed to relax.

James then addressed the wolf, "Jacques, why do you limit access to my tent when Bekah comes by."

The wolf then responded, "You were told the rules in *The Book of Adam*, which a good Titan has surely read. I shall not break the rules for you, for I work for Doc and He trusts me. Wolves have been deceived before by unrighteous Titans, but they didn't deceive me and I will not be tricked by you or this cute female!"

James smiled and then asked where he and Bekah could talk. Jacques pointed his nose towards the benches around the fire pit in the center of the trail. Bekah nodded and they moved to them.

As they sat, Bekah continued to look worried and began to speak in rapid succession, "What was happening to you? I could feel your anxiety in my tent! It felt as if you had traveled a great distance, but you were still sleeping in your tent. Where did you go? What happened? Please, I am not good enough at telepathy yet to read your mind. I don't even know why I felt your apprehension and anxiety, but it was strong enough that I was awaken!"

James looked at her in amazement, but before he could answer she continued. "What do you know? I can feel it, but can't quite see what you saw, where you went or what you are worried about. You're my best friend! I can help you!" Her speaking increased in speed and anxiousness. James knew she wasn't going to stop until he started to talk.

"I didn't travel at all, but in my mind I was seeing through my father's eyes again."

"Again? You have seen into his mind before?"

"Yes, but this time I saw the *Order of the Kraken*."

She looked stunned and obviously knew much more than he did about this.

"Bekah, you need to tell me everything you know. Then I will share what I have seen and we can decide what we need to do with this information."

Bekah took a deep breath and began to speak at a very slow, careful pace picking her words very carefully. "You must know that much of this information is hearsay and writings that are not common reading for a student. The biggest name of the *Order of the Kraken* is someone you should know, your sister Camilla. She was an absolutely amazing Titan and member of *The Band of Fire* until her 16th birthday when she disappeared. Nobody knows why she disappeared, but she has been seen many times since always in bad situations. She is considered the leader of the Order and has been said to direct killings, robberies and even kidnappings. Many powerful Titans have been captured by the Order and most haven't been heard of again. In fact, there are rumors that your father was captured by them."

"I don't remember Camilla from before, but she's absolutely the leader. I watched her have a meeting with many Titans. She did capture my father, for I saw it the morning of my 12th birthday and she still has him in her 'camp' right now."

"Oh…So you know where her camp is? Did you see who was in the *Order of the Kraken*? They are a secret society and the members are not known."

"I know where her camp is right now, but they are moving. I am not sure where they will be going from there, maybe Brazil or something like that. As for members of the Order, I know of Zoram something, who will be trying to infiltrate Campus Gaea. I also heard the names Minerva, Elli, Peter and Adam. There was also at least one other woman, but I don't know her name. I saw them and several others, but not sure I could describe them without seeing them again. If you were better at reading my mind, maybe you could bring it all to remembrance."

"Well, I might be able to help. I don't know who Zoram, Adam or Elli are, but Minerva is known as one of the Titans kicked out of Campus Gaea for breaking rules and hurting other Titans when she was 16 years old. She was one of Camilla's friends. Peter may actually be Peter Filtz, a Chronopath that is a nephew of Amber Barde that teaches Zoonophonic Skills. We will meet her later today."

They continued to talk for hours as James tried to remember everything he saw and explain to Bekah about his various dreams. She was very interested and interjected any information she had, but couldn't fill in very much additional information. She was carefully noting everything she could to figure out what they should do next.

As the sun came up and tents started coming to life, James and Bekah stopped talking and decided to start going back to their tents. As they walked back, Bekah quickly interjected her final idea, "James, we need to learn as much as possible from our instructors. There will come a time when you need to be as developed as possible in all your Concordant skills. We may need to go save your Dad. I will help you in every way I can."

She then ran to her tent to get ready for class and James smiled to himself as he walked back into his tent and heard Helia fly from behind him to his shoulder. It was time for breakfast, he hadn't slept hardly at all over the night and he wasn't even tired. What else will he learn or see over the next several weeks? He changed his clothes quickly, grabbed his bag and the books for the day and then walked back out of the tent toward The Great Hall for breakfast. Today was also the day he would be finally taking Helia to class for *Wildlife Studies*.

CHAPTER 10
BECOMING A TITAN

As James and Kari sat talking at the table in The Great Hall, Bekah came walking over with a large plate of breakfast. James looked down and took another bite from his plate and Bekah sat down next to him. Michael was still standing in line waiting for food and Angelica was working her way toward their table. She seemed in a hurry and had obviously already eaten.

"Where is Michael?" Angelica asked anxiously.

"He's still getting his food." Bekah responded.

"Please, when you're done eating I need to go to meet Master Julianna Gaea Abel with you. She usually has her classes with eight people usually. She likes to do fieldtrips. She loves you four to join some from the Minotaur patrol for a class about *Becoming A Titan*."

"REALLY? Right now?" Bekah was almost standing on her chair with excitement. "I don't really need to eat. We can go now. Should I go get Michael?"

"Meet me at those doors when you are DONE eating." she said chuckling a little more relaxed. "Her fieldtrips are usually very tiring and will require you want energy from breakfast." She then raced away to her table again.

As they finished eating, Bekah wouldn't leave any of them alone to do anything but eat. In fact, she seemed to inhale her food and then watched as they all tried to finish. James could tell by her excitement that this was one of the things Bekah had been waiting for.

"Do you all know that Master Julianna is a very talented Chronopath and the author of *The Book of Adam*? She is known for taking fieldtrips to the past to help us learn history more completely. I don't know how she does it, but it has something to do with Chronopathy. I read her chapter on Chronopathy 5 times this summer in hopes of learning more about this gift, but never got the inside story. I can't wait to see what she does... James, maybe you can learn how to do this from her."

Before anyone could respond to her words or ideas, Bekah noticed they were done eating and stood up. "Let's go!" and she began walking towards the great doors at the entrance of the Great Hall where Angelica was standing. James, Michael and Kari looked at each other and quickly rose to their feet and followed. James had learned a long time ago that Bekah wouldn't even look back to see if they were coming. She would just assume that they were all as excited as she was. Kari seemed to come to the same assumption as she raced ahead to join Bekah on her right side.

At the very moment they came to Angelica, she turned with a smile and began to leave. She seemed to be in even more of a rush than Bekah. They all would soon learn why as the rounded the corner and walked to a large purple tent they had never noticed before. It sat directly behind The Great Hall and had what looked like gold trimming around the door. James noted that it looked as much like what he would consider an ancient castle as any tent he had ever seen. It even seemed to have a porch with pillars made of the same purple and gold fabric as the rest of the tent. It likewise had noticeable spires at each of the corners of the tent as a castle would have, all the features were very noticeable as they came closer.

As they walked into the tent, James noticed a short, white haired, plump woman with large blue eyes, half-moon spectacles and a large broad smile standing at the front of the class. To her right were three Minotaur students, including Ryan Sampson, Emma Johnson, and Lizzy de Armas who seemed to be waiting for their arrival. The two other Minotaur students often in class were obviously absent, but before James could consider why, he noticed Master Julianna. Master Julianna got excited the moment they walked into the tent as she was obviously expecting them (which was probably why Angelica was so anxious to get them there as the mentor).

Kari's eyes immediately lit up with the view of Ryan, a tall 6 foot native American boy with brown hair, tan skin and dark brown (almost black) eyes. He had a very strong build and was easily noticed because of his enormous size although only 12 years old.

The two girls looked much smaller than Ryan, although both were average height for their ages, Emma 14 years old and Lizzy 12 years old. Of the two, Lizzy was much shorter, as a Mexican girl with light skin, short black hair, green eyes and a small nose.

Angelica moved over to Emma and greeted her quickly. It was obvious that Emma and Angelica were classmates, although different patrols. Emma was shorter than Angelica, lighter skinned and slender, with spiky bleach blonde short hair. James took a second glance at the distinct look Emma had created for herself with her hazel eyes reflecting against her white features and bleached hair.

But before he thought much more about it, a soft, soothing voice filled with excitement and oozing with southern drawl began to speak immediately as they moved closer to the group. James immediately noticed the plump woman start to bounce up and down as she talked. The excitement she had was contagious and every student turned to her with complete fascination. James felt his excitement build with every word. He wanted to know exactly what she was going to be teaching because she was more excited about her subject than he had ever seen anyone.

"Well my dear friends, I am Master Julianna and we have an amazing opportunity to learn about one of my favorite subjects and see one of my favorite locations. I want to take you on a special trip to Ancient Greece or should I say before Greece when mythology talks of the first gods, Gaea and Ouranus. We will travel to ancient Mount Othrys and introduce you to our limited knowledge about the pre-Golden Age of Greek Gods. We don't know a ton, but you will learn what I know now. I can't wait to show you into my knowledge and my learning...."

With that she had them all grab hands and close their eyes. James felt as if he was ripped through time and he opened his eyes to see a blur of light racing past him and what looked like ground and oceans racing below him. He wasn't sure if he was really traveling at an amazing speed or if it was something else entirely. All he knew was that they were no longer under the cover of the purple tent. The sky was a blur, the ground was a blur, but he could distinctly see each individual of their group without difficulty. He noticed Master Julianna with a huge smile on her face as she noticed him watching. She obviously took great pride in her ability to travel through time!

After a period of time, that was probably only seconds, James felt his feet come to the ground and Bekah took a deep breath of excitement. "Are we really here? Is that really Mount Othrys that I have read so much about?"

Master Julianna was obviously pleased and smiled and bounced with excitement as well. "Yes, we are at the base of Mount Othrys, but are not able to be seen or interrupt time in any way. As far as time is concerned, it is as if we are in a dream watching the occurrences hereof. Pay very close attention, because you will witness much information that will help you understand why we chose the term Titan to describe each of you and your powers. For the Titans were truly great...

Before she could continue, the ground began to quake and great giants began to move toward the hills of Mount Othrys. An obvious God, that Bekah quickly indicated was Ouranus, stood on the Mount with fire in his eyes and obvious loathing at the powerful giants storming the hills before him. He too was a giant and looked very powerful on the Mount. Behind him sat another great God, that James assumed must be Gaea, a very beautiful giant woman with long black hair and deep, dark eyes, but she was seated not worrying about the approaching giants. In fact, she seemed to welcome their approach and was not moving to stop them. James easily recognized the love of a mother in her eyes, similar to what he saw often in his mother's eyes.

Then James turned back to the giants storming the hill from all directions, lead by one with a large stone sickle. And Master Julianna started to speak again.

"You see before you the Titans, led by Kronus with his large stone sickle. The stone sickle was created by Mother Gaea, which is why she will not try to stop the attack. They are storming Mount Othrys because their father Ouranus has kept them and their siblings imprisoned and likewise imprisoned the people of the earth. He is a very wicked God that is not loved by the people or even by his children, the Titans. Although Gaea is a loving mother, she has been unable to personally free them and therefore created the large stone sickle for Kronus to use. His older siblings, Mnemosyne, Tethys, Theia, Phoebe, Rhea, Themis, Oceanus, Hyperion, Coeus, Crius and Iapetus are all at his side as he storms the stronghold. It is very important to watch."

The battle ensued and Ouranus, Father Sky, called down lightning from heaven and winds from the east to fight his battles. Great storm clouds rolled in, and the darkness fell. Mount Othrys was barely visible as the weather beat down from the Mount on the giants moving in from all sides. Gaea, Mother Earth, sat silently out of the flow of the battle and didn't help, but also didn't interfere. And the Titans, powerful in their own right, caught the lightning from the sky and cast it back at their father. Waves came bellowing from the ocean to the base of Mount Othrys as Oceanus called them to his aid. Tethyrs called forth the rivers to run up the Mount and block Ouranus' retreat. The other sisters rode the winds to the top of the Mount and turned back the wind and rain from blocking the path of their Titan brothers, forcing it to collapse back upon Ouranus. There was great panic in his eyes as he realized the Titans were more powerful than he.

The battle raged for hours while the students watched, but Mount Othrys was being overcome from all sides. If fact, the brothers stormed the Mount from all sides with Coeus coming up the back unseen by Ouranus and powerful Iapetus reaching the top first and capturing Ouranus before Kronus mounted the hill and used his sickle to conquer but not kill his father. The exact method of conquer was not seen, as the Titans all blocked the view of Ouranus while the battle stopped. But the rain ceased, the lightning subsided, the winds stopped after clearing the sky and the ocean and river returned to their normal routes. Just then the scene began to fade and Master Julianna's words came through the blur.

"Stay calm my friends, there is much more to come."

The blur turned to a bright blue sky with a glowing sun rising above Mount Othrys which was much brighter and housed a great building at its peak. As they looked at the great structure, powerful winged animals flew down to meet them. James recognized them as Pegasus that Bekah had shown him when they first came to *Mr McDonald's Mystical Creatures*. Bekah's excitement was contagious as each of the students and Master Julianna mounted the Pegasus that crouched at their side.

Once they were all mounted, they were carried to the top of Mount Othrys to the doors of the great palace of the Titans. The walls were of crystal white marble, that shown with light that seemed to radiate from within. The walls easily reached over 100 feet toward the sky with multiple pillars marking the entrance of such a great diameter that all nine of them together could not encircle even a single pillar. The large double doors were slightly ajar, but were likewise at least 70 – 80 feet high, made of pure gold with door handles much out of their reach.

As Bekah and the others started to move towards the door on their Pegasus, Master Julianna motioned for them to turn toward the valley at the base of the Mount. With ease, they were able to see a great people, not giant like the Titans, but great in number. They were a happy people that seemed to have no filth, no poor, and no sickness among them. In fact, they all seemed to be perfect specimens, even a perfect people.

Master Julianna's southern drawl began again, "Now these are the most ancient of people of Greece. They live in the Golden Age and were said to be free of any laws or immorality. They were a righteous, kind, loving people that put others before themselves and had no crime or wickedness among them. They even helped the sick become well, the poor earn their own keep, the weak become strong, the sad become happy, and the hungry be fed. This is what Greek Mythology would have considered the perfect society. All because of the great and benevolent rule of the Titans."

Before they could turn back to the palace, the Pegasus took off again and they were carried back to their starting place and all were invited to dismount. Immediately the Pegasus disappeared into the distance and they were asked to join hands again and close their eyes.

James felt time move much faster this time, and he was unable to even open his eyes before they were again in the purple tent, but it looked much newer and cleaner than he had noticed their first entrance. As he looked around, Angelica just smiled at him and started to nod.

A much younger, still plump and short woman, came bouncing into the room with the same half-moon spectacles, but with long brown hair to her waist. She was accompanied by a bird, a lava red phoenix that James recognized from the Orientopathy class and his dream, that was speaking to her. James could understand the bird, and as he looked around, he could tell Kari could obviously as well, but most the rest of the students could not. Master Julianna looked at James and winked with a knowing smile. Knowing how phoenix are able to speak, he assumed the Master Julianna was able to hear perfectly what she said also.

"From darkness came the light, from ignorance came the truth. For as from Greece the Gods were made, they were overthrown by Titans in their youth. The Titans were greater than Gods, and so Titans we are to now be called. So as Titans brought truth and love, we now fight for our God above."

Bekah turned to look at James and he knew from her questioning look that he must respond, "Felicity has said that we are as the Titans. We have great powers that can help us bring truth, happiness and joy into this world. That we can fight for heaven above, for our God as we help all people. As Titans overthrew the wicked Gods, we must stand against wickedness and hatred in this world."

"Well said my friend," Master Julianna continued. "Know that all y'all have powers from God. And with great power comes great responsibility. With power comes your chance to touch the heavens and produce a society much like the Golden Age of Greece. That must be our goal!"

With that they were invited to close their eyes and join hands again and they were pulled back through time to their starting place in the tent, the exact tent from where they first left. Immediately upon arriving, Kari came running up to James and started talking quickly about all that was said by the phoenix. She was talking so fast and so excited about all that he and she had both understood. She wanted James to explain more to her about how this worked and why he understood so well the limerick that had been said. James smiled and reminded her that he had a phoenix and Helia talked in a very similar fashion.

Michael and Bekah both laughed at Kari's excitement, but likewise stood and listened as they talked, hoping to get additional information about all that was said by the phoenix, since all they heard was a beautiful song from her beak.

Kari asked question after question about the conversation and James repeated almost word for word the poem sung by Felicity. He also informed all in attendance that Felicity was actually Master Doc McAdam's phoenix and that they all had seen her before in the first Orientopathy class.

As they finished speaking, Master Julianna called their attention again to her and she opened *The Book of Adam* and helped them understand how this information augmented greatly the words written in Chapter 1 (The Introduction to *The Band of Fire* and Titans) and Chapter 4 (Becoming A Titan). She then assigned them to review these chapters again to ensure they got the whole message before their next class period.

"Now we have one more trip I'd like us to take." And she invited them again to close their eyes and take hands. And James again felt them ripped through time and the blurring light shone through his closed eyelids. He didn't open them, but knew what was happening this time. He just wondered if everyone felt what he was feeling.

They were again not in a tent, but were located inside what looked like a hospital. But it was not an up-to-date hospital, but instead similar to the hospitals seen in the old westerns or old movies. There were no computers, lighting was from windows only, with what looked like old oil lamps on the wall. There was a young man sitting in the room with dark brown hair, about shoulder length, tied behind his head, and many women that looked like old fashioned nurses racing around the wooden table he was sitting on. There was a small black cat sitting in the corner that seemed to be making a great racket, but they were not yet close enough to hear. The young man looked amused at the nurses and sat there with apparently no worries at this time.

As they all moved closer, Master Julianna began to speak again in her southern drawl, "James, do you know where we are? You have felt us move through time every time and should be able to localize us with your Orientopathy skills."

James looked surprised and then knew where and when they were. "We are in Salem Village, at the time of the Salem Witch Trials!" Master Julianna smiled and nodded, as James tried to understand how he knew all this.

Bekah looked at James with pride and then they all moved closer, they could hear the young man speaking to the nurses, "So you think that I am a witch do you? Well, you need not worry as you are now. I will do you no harm, nor anyone else any harm. I am not sure why you are so worried. All I did was lift the little wagon off the Minister's son. It wasn't that big a deal. He would have died if I hadn't helped!"

"What do you mean? The wagon was fully loaded and was unable to be moved by six of our strongest men in the town. It weighted over 1500 lbs."

"Apparently, they are not the strongest," he said with a laugh.

"And how do you know what we are thinking. Nobody has the power to read our minds or know what we are worried about."

This again brought a chuckle from the young man.

"My body is perfectly healthy! My heart rate is lower than all of you. My lungs are clear, unlike the smoke you have all damaged your lungs with."

"Are you threatening us? None of us have any problems with our lungs at this time."

"What about the blood she has been coughing up since Thursday? And the great damage to her left lung?"

The small blond nurse stopped what she was doing and looked up in amazement. "How do you know that? You must be a witch! It is not yet determined what is happening with my lung or why I am coughing up blood since Thursday."

Just then a small, mousey looking man walked into the room and the nurses relieved raced from their presence. His deep black eyes looked cold and uncaring as he looked up at the young man. His high pitched almost whiney voice then rang through the room as he began to speak, "You, my boy, are not welcome here. Your dark magic has been seen before and will be destroyed if you don't leave the town immediately. You will now be escorted to the trials if you don't disappear from this town forever!"

"I told you to NOT make fun of them," the black cat purred. "Now we will have to move again."

The young man turned and looked at the cat and Bekah turned and looked at James.

"He's telling the young man that they are going to have to move again," James whispered to all within hearing distance.

"Minister Parris," the young man responded, "I saved your son. He would have died."

"That is irrelevant. The citizens don't want you here anymore and it is my job to send you away. You can leave this town and no Witch Trial will be held for you. I recommend you go to Boston. They won't notice you there! If you hadn't saved my son, I wouldn't even give you that option!" Minister Parris said with contempt in his voice.

"I will go, but you should give your son my condolences that he survived the accident. NOW he has to put up with you for the rest of his life!" the young man said with laughter in his eyes and anger in his voice.

The Minister then walked out without a response and another short, plump man in a blue suit walked in to escort him out. The nurses were nowhere to be seen as he was lead out of the hospital. The small group followed and heard the conversation start immediately when they were outside the hospital.

"You, my boy, have a gift. A special gift that the people of this town will never understand. The people fear you as the Greeks feared the Titans and the Gods. But God is on your side. I have some friends like you that will help you get better control and understanding of your powers."

"There are others like me?"

"Yes. But they are hidden in normal society and they can help you learn to do the same. But nobody can know that I helped you. I am not a Titan. In fact, you will soon learn that I am what they call Natural Born and am risking my life and that of my family to help you. Nobody must ever know or my family and I will be burned as witches as well!"

"I will never forget it! And you and your family will forever be protected. Never again will you need to fear repercussions from helping me or helping anyone else. I will personally guarantee your safety and that of your family!"

Master Julianna stepped forward and the view behind started to blur. "That young man was my great, great grand-father Cornelius Abel and is considered the first documented

Concordant in our history. As for the man in the blue suit, that is a relative of James here, Percival Owens, the great, great grandfather of your mother Sarah Owens Adamson."

James and Bekah looked at her with great surprise before she continued, "And the Titan families have continued to protect the Owens family and all offspring thereof every since. That very protection lead to the marriage of James' parents as Sarah was being protected by a group of Titans that included Simon John Adamson. You, my boy, have that same promise of protection, but probably don't need it with what I have seen of your abilities." She then winked at him before asking them to all close their eyes and take hands for the last time.

As James considered this new information, he didn't notice the quick trip back to the purple tent and Campus Gaea. His head continued to spin as they were excused by Master Julianna with a promise that she would call them to class again. And she mentioned the need to review *The Book of Adam* to be prepared for their next lesson on Campus Gaea.

They all walked out of the tent and James continued to think while Bekah was laughing and talking with Angelica, Emma, Lizzy and Michael. Kari was flirting as only a 12 year-old girl can with Ryan who talked with her but seemed absolutely oblivious to the flirtations. James didn't seem to notice anything. In fact, he was so preoccupied with all the new information that he almost forgot there were any other people around.

"Percival Owens? Maybe he should write his mother a letter and ask about him. That name just seems important! And what was this about mom and dad meeting while he was protecting her? Is that why Camilla is so angry with him?"

CHAPTER 11
HELIA COMES TO WILDLIFE STUDIES

As he walked thinking, his mind faded to black and then he was again in the past, but not like when traveling with Master Julianna, but seemed to be in a memory or maybe it was actually reading a mind. That's it, he was seeing through another's mind.

"Well, the good news is James is safe at camp, but I still don't know where Simon is. He must be in trouble. I am worried that Camilla has asked her Band of Thieves to capture him and keep him away from his family. She obviously knows that she is not yet strong enough to come after me. I know she hates me for marrying her father. I think she even blames me for the divorce that ended his marriage to Aria. But I didn't really know Aria or Simon when they were married. Neither was assigned to protect me and my family at that time. I was being protected by others, including my dear friend Aimee Belle. I truly love that woman!"

As she thought, she remembered years before, what seemed like many years ago now, when Aimee was explaining to her about the new Titan that was assigned to be head of her protection detail now that Aimee had been reassigned to help Doc McAdams in further strengthening The Classification process.

"You need to know Sarah, that Simon is one of our very best! You will never have someone that respects you more or puts your needs before his own so completely. He is injured, however, because just over one year ago his wife left with their daughter and has forbidden him from seeing her. He still loves her, but they were not compatible. He put Aria and little Camilla first and has lived this last year with his heart in pieces. He loves his daughter more than life itself, but knows the fighting was not good for her and if Aria feels it is better for Camilla to not see him, he will not interfere. He truly is a good man!"

"Is he old? They usually assign me women or old men, because they don't want me to fall in love with the Titan given my care."

"No. He is not old and if you trust me I would say he is a very handsome man. I don't know why they have assigned him to you. I do know that Doc McAdams recommended him for the job and nobody really argues with Doc."

"Yes. I have met Doc also and he is quite intimidating."

"No. He is actually an old softy, but his abilities often surprise all of us!"

Just then a 6'2" dark haired, brown eyed, pale skinned man walked into the room. That was definitely Simon John Adamson, even without Aimee introducing him. She felt her heart start to race and her hands start to get clammy. She even got weak in the knees as Aimee introduced them. Her voice cracked as she tried to greet him simply. He just smiled at her and went to work directing her protection. From that moment on she loved him, but it took her almost another year to convince him that he loved her too. But there was no doubt in her mind now that he loved her more than life itself, and not just because he told her.

"I sure love that man! He has always made me feel more special than anyone ever has. He holds me up as a princess, a queen and the greatest gift in his life. His amazing abilities are coveted by many, but he has told me time and time again that he would give it all up if that was required to stay with me. I have felt that love and KNOW that he means it!"

With that she started to relax, and the vision faded back to reality...

When James finally noticed where they were headed, he was walking into his tent to a very excited Helia who knew it was now her turn to attend class. This was actually the first real class on Wildlife Studies and they would be getting additional information on Zoonophonia so they were supposed to bring their animal companions. Helia was obviously excited to be getting out of the tent for once, because since coming to camp she only was able to sneak out once in a while at night time for a flight. James had decided earlier today that with or without this class Helia needed to be allowed to roam more freely. He figured he would ask Master Doc McAdams at Orientopathy class today if that was possible.

As James walked out of his tent with Helia, Michael joined him with Fenwick on his right arm and the girls came walking out of their tent on the other side of the path. Helia was the largest of the birds James could see, and also the only phoenix. Fenwick, Michael's beautiful brown falcon was also full grown. Bekah was holding Tom, her green and black tortoise and Kari was walking with a large wolfdog at her heels that James knew was Jack. As they walked away from the tents, James turned and waved to Jacques and thanked him for doing his job. Jacques appeared to almost smile as he roamed the path.

The walk to class was relatively quick with Helia on his shoulder. He was excited to see what they would learn in Wildlife Studies. He had looked through the book and was interested to know what they would be teaching any, like Bekah, without the ability to talk to animals. Besides, he was sure he would learn so much more about how to talk with the animals in even one class. He was also interested in meeting Amber Filtz Barde ever since his dream about the *Order of The Kraken*. Bekah seemed to sense what he was thinking and quickened her step to walk next to him.

"I think we may need to wait till the end of class to ask her about her nephew." she said as she drew close to him.

"I am debating whether we ask her at all right now or if we find her later when we have more time."

"That may be a better idea."

"My concern is that she may not want to talk about him at all."

At that they were both quiet for the final hundred yards until class.

As they entered the clearing, many students and many animals were in attendance. It appeared that all the first year students were there and James noticed every animal from a small skunk belonging to Emma, a large racoon belonging to Ryan, and a white and gray goat belonging to Lizzy. There were also frogs, toads, eagles, owls, cats, dogs and a gray rat. But once again there was no teacher. James was starting to get used to the teachers making a "grand entrance".

As they waited, James was not disappointed as Master Amber flew into class on the back of a snow-white unicorn with Pegasus wings. It was a powerful animal which landed without a sound on the hard dirt ground just behind the fire pit at the front of the class. This classroom was at the edge of a large forest and was partially shaded by the large trees but was otherwise similar to many of the other fire pit classrooms they had become accustomed to. Only a couple classes were not held outside, but this was the most wilderness like location yet. James assumed it was to add to the instruction on wildlife studies.

Master Amber, a tall, slender, woman with bright green eyes, and long blonde hair reaching down to her waist dismounted from her steed and started to walk around the class admiring all the animals. Her love and excitement at each animal was infectious and each student felt like she loved their animal, their companion the best. But when she came to James and Helia she stopped with a start.

"I didn't realize we would have a phoenix this year." she said with admiration in her eyes. "That is probably the most beautiful phoenix I have ever seen!"

She then turned directly to Helia and talked to her directly, "I would love to pick your brain a little. I have always wanted to be companion with a phoenix. Maybe you can help me learn how to make it happen."

Although James could hear her perfectly, he could tell Bekah and Michael could not understand Master Amber as she spoke with Helia.

"What did she say as she sang to Helia? Were you able to understand her? Phoenix song is so beautiful, even when spoken by a human!" Bekah looked at Master Amber with admiration and stepped forward to show her Tom.

"What a beautiful tortoise! Now you need to know that a green and black shell like this indicates a special ability to speak telepathically to his companion. Has he spoken to you?"

"Tom has not actually spoken to me," she said hesitantly, "but I haven't tried because I am not a Zoonophonic."

"But you are a telepath?"

"Yes"

"Then think what you would like to say, and Tom will understand you."

Bekah's face turned red and turned back to her tortoise. James surprised at her blushing, turned to Bekah and saw her start to bounce with excitement. James smiled and knew Bekah would be in absolute heaven with this new information. Especially since James had not even heard Tom speak since Bekah purchased him.

As Master Amber was talking to Tom, Fenwick started making a great racket and drew her attention to him.

"Oh, my beautiful bird. You like attention, do you?"

Fenwick immediately grew silent and straightened up to his full height on Michael's right arm. Michael also seemed to stand more erect.

"This is my best friend. I am not a Zoonophonic either, but we understand each other."

Master Amber looked over at Michael and smiled. "That is a gift my boy, a true blessing among friends."

Jack and Kari were the final pair in the class, and the beautiful red-haired wolfdog drew more admiration from Master Amber.

"You are unique? I have never seen a red-haired wolfdog before."

Jack stood up on all fours with great power and began to speak, "My mother was the leader of our pack, and a beautiful red wolf. My father was a large gray and black husky that joined our pack when separated from his master. Therefore, I am truly one of a kind and a prince among wolves."

Master Amber smiled and barked back, "I will consider it a great pleasure to get to know you."

Kari stood their beaming and couldn't contain her excitement at her companion Jack's revelation to the class (at least those that could understand).

Master Amber then walked to stand next to her beautiful companion and started to speak in a loud voice that everyone could easily hear, "I am Master Amber Barde. I have been teaching here for many years and love animals. You have brought some of the most beautiful companions I have ever met in one class. Since I have met your companions, I feel it is important for you to meet mine."

She then stepped forward and held her hand out to the snow-white Pegasus-unicorn mix and introduced her, "This is Medley, my unique companion of many years. She is the only Pegasus-unicorn mix in existence and loves to meet new students. As we go through this summer I recommend you all try to meet her and even speak with her if you can. Unlike the unicorn or Pegasus separate, this combination allows her to speak directly to your mind and even read your mind. To speak with her you will not need Telepathy or Zoonophonia. Her knowledge and skills may be of great value to you as a Titan."

Medley then bent her front legs in a bow and began to speak, "Young Titan friend, may wisdom come from deep within to help you stand as Titan strong."

James looked at Bekah who had obviously also heard Medley speak in her mind, but she didn't seem to understand any better than James did. James was a little disappointed in himself that he didn't know exactly what she was saying. Master Amber just smiled and continued.

"Throughout this class we will introduce you to many known animals of the wild, but we will also discuss some of the special, magical creatures that I have great pleasure introducing many of you to. We will also learn the art of animal communication, whether it is true Zoonophonia or just listening to the cues most the rest of the world will use to communicate with their pets. We will start today with this special communication."

She began by helping students understand the different types of animals and how they communicate with each other. She discussed vertebrates versus invertebrates and how a backbone changes the required environment to live. As she gave this instruction, she explained how even this simple feature may influence how an animal will speak. She then introduced amphibians, reptiles, birds and mammals and helped each student classify their companion (or pet) based on this information. She then began teaching the different forms of animal speak from hissing like a snake, singing or chirping like various birds, growling like a tiger or alligator (two different types of growl) and even purring or barking like a pet cat or dog respectively. She then began to explain that every type of cat or every type of bird has a distinct and different sound. This fact was true for all species or types of animals. Only the most developed Zoonophonic will understand and speak with all animals, some may have particular species or types of animals they are most effective speaking with, just like learning English for example, but as they develop they will gain the ability to talk with any animal in the animals native tongue.

She then explained that over the next couple years every single student should learn to speak with their individual companion, by learning that language. The Zoonophonic will just not need to learn the languages as their brain translates automatically to most as the skill becomes more developed. James could see that already happening in his own mind, as he often didn't even realize the animals were not speaking English to him.

The class continued for a quick 2 hours and then the students were released to return with their companions back to the tents before attending the next class of the day, Orientopathy with Master Doc McAdams. Bekah, Michael and Kari returned to the tents with their companions, but Helia flew off without James so that he could hurry ahead to visit with Master Doc McAdams before class. He had some questions for him and was hoping he could get some answers before the other students arrived.

As James walked into the cave ready for class, Master Doc McAdams was already there and looked up with a smile to answer his questions.

"You want to know about Percival Owens and the connection to your family? That is a question best asked your mother, for she can give you more complete information than can I."

James looked at him with surprise and Master McAdams just smiled and continued.

"You also want to know about Camilla? Well you already know some information from your dad. He is the best one to answer those questions through your telepathic connection with him that Camilla still doesn't know about. Do what you can to strengthen that connection and you will give us significantly more information on Camilla and the *Order of the Kraken*."

"But HOW do I strengthen that link?"

"You need to know that you are the strongest Concordant I have ever tested. That includes Camilla. But you don't have any confidence in your own abilities. You are still trying to convince yourself, since everyone else sees it and knows it to be true, that you are Concordant."

Master Doc McAdams then stated another story, "I once knew a young man that was born with the umbilical cord around his neck. He was diagnosed at an early age with mild Cerebral Palsy, a disease that will often limit body movement and muscle coordination. In his case, it was an impairment of muscle function, not a complete loss of function or strength. He struggled to crawl and was very slow to learn to walk until a later date because of the rigidity of his muscle motion in his legs. As he walked, his knees would remain bent towards each other and he would twist his hips and shoulders to the front to propel the legs forward. Often it looked like he was spinning his entire body. But over time with practice, the momentum of his upper body would propel the appropriate leg forward allowing motion. That motion became a slow, labored walk when he was 4 years old."

"But this boy was not happy with any limitations. In fact, he wanted to run like the other kids in the neighborhood. He therefore worked day and night with the help of his parents to walk faster and faster until he was able to slowly jog. By age 10 he could run, but not very quickly. By age 12 he was running down the street and could be seen running with friends on a football field while playing a pickup game. Because of the twisting required to run, he was often very difficult to defend in flag football and many wanted him on their team at recess."

"But even that was insufficient. When he entered High School, he was interested in competing in sports. He decided to work harder on running and wanted to run cross country. I am not going to tell you that he won state or even that he became the fastest on his team. In fact, often he was near the back of the pack in races. He did, however, compete Varsity cross country his Junior and Senior seasons because of his diligence and hard work. He actually improved his time every race he ran from joining the team as a Freshman until his final race as a Senior. He got better because he believed, his parents believed and he was not afraid to work. He had to work harder than most everyone that finished in front of him, but he worked and that was the secret."

After a short pause to let the message sink in, Master McAdams continued, "Are you willing to work? Will you improve in ALL your skills every day, whether you have class in that skill or not? It really comes down to you. What are you willing to do?"

On that note, Master Doc McAdams stood up and Felicity flew to his shoulder and began to sing, "The power of a man is known, not by what he does when he's grown. The power of a man is true, only when he's willing hard work to do."

Master McAdams smiled at James and then started setting up as the other student began to enter the cave. James was not sure he was ready for class, because he had so much to think about. Couldn't Master McAdams just tell him a simpler way? Is it all just based on hard work? He walked over to Bekah, having forgotten his other questions for Master McAdams and sat down on the wooden bench silently waiting for class to start. Bekah was excitedly talking about the next class, *The Art of Communication*, but James wasn't really listening.

CHAPTER 12
THE ART OF COMMUNICATION

Master Doc McAdams walked to the front of the class and the conversations ceased. He had a glint in his eye that James hadn't seen before.

"Since many of you learned how to use a map over the last couple classes, we will be doing a unique class today. This class will not just improve your orienteering skills, but also develop your senses to help you develop any Titan ability you have more completely. Felicity will provide each of you with a blindfold and then we will give you instruction."

The beautiful lava red phoenix flew around the cave giving each student a blindfold and then Master McAdams asked them to wear it. He then began to explain to them all that they would be utilizing their senses this time, excluding their eyes.

"What do you hear around you?"

"What do you feel?"

He continued to have them try multiple different senses and then invited them all to come forward as groups of four and join hands. As James, Kari, Bekah and Michael came forward together, he had them join hands and put their blindfolds back on. At that moment James felt them move very quickly out of the cave to some unknown location. Then they could only hear Master McAdams in their minds.

"You are now in some unknown location. You will be required to use your senses to try and determine where you are as a group. Once you have determined your location sufficiently, you will be given a map by Felicity and you will be excused to find your next class. It will take all of you to find your location, as you use all your senses you will have the best chance."

James then felt Bekah let go of his hand and start to move around.

"Okay. What do we hear around us?" she asked.

"I hear trees rustling on all sides," Kari said tentatively.

"Yes. And water, a small running water. Probably a stream ahead of us." Michael piped in.

At that very moment James knew where they were and was amazed at how complete the picture was. He could see the forest around them, with trees reaching into the air many feet up. He couldn't feel the heat of the sun, so he was sure the trees must be quite tall and dense. He knew they were surrounded by pine trees and felt pine needles under his feet. He pictured the mountains around them, the two paths that were close to them and the stream ahead of them and the lake behind them. He knew where they were headed and the quickest routes to get there. He could take over, but he waited, however, to describe their location to let the others learn through the process.

"I also hear the water, but I didn't know it was a small stream." Kari broke in again.

"Do you hear the wind?" James asked.

"I hear it and feel it," Bekah said.

"Yes. Coming from the east, passing through the branches of large trees all around us. We're in the forest." Michael was starting to get the picture.

"I feel the hard, dirt ground beneath us too. There seems to be pine needles on the ground. Yes, I smell pine," Kari said with excitement.

"Okay. Now listen harder. Do you hear the wind getting slightly louder to the west? That will be to Bekah's right and Kari's Left. Michael, I think you know."

"That is the edge of the mountains about 100 yards to our west." James continued.

"I know where we are!" Michael broke in. "We are in the forest at the base of the mountain peaks, which means the stream is in front of us and the lake is behind us. We are on the opposite side of the lake than our tents."

"Okay. We know where that is too, but don't hear the mountains." the girls both responded.

Just then the beautiful sound of a phoenix song started to ring through the trees and they all understood what was being said as Master McAdams voice rang in their minds.

"Well done. Now you can all remove your blindfolds and find the map 100 yards away at bearing 210 degrees. Please proceed to follow the map to your final destination."

The voice grew silent as the music stopped and they all removed their blindfold. Even before removing the blindfold, however, James turned to 210 degrees and pictured the tree 100 yards ahead with what he could hear as a map at the base of the trunk in a small dirt hole partially covered with leaves. He smiled and remained silent.

Kari and Bekah pulled out their compasses and likewise turned to face the correct direction. Michael began to run through the trees ahead of them, as Kari and Bekah carefully measured their steps. Michael knew exactly which tree the map was at, but was still searching the tree when Bekah arrived moments later. Kari was three trees over and had walked past the spot slightly, but was happy that she was as close as she was. They began to search for the map as James walked up and uncovered the hole at the base of the tree.

After removing the map, Michael studied it carefully and then handed it to Bekah.

"This map appears to be taking us to a tent back in the main part of camp." Kari said. "Does anyone know what tent this is?"

Michael remained silent, but seemed to be making plans to get there.

"Based on the map in Chapter 3 of *The Book of Adam*, that should be Master Aimee Belle's cabin. It's actually not a tent. In fact, according to the map in that chapter it is the classroom for 'The Art of Communication', our next class." Bekah said with excitement.

"Great. Michael, how do we get there? I think you have a plan." James asked.

Michael then began to lead them through the dense forest in what looked like the exact wrong direction. There was no path that they could see, but James knew the path was about 200 yards ahead of them and knew that a second longer path, marked on the map, was in the opposite direction.

Bekah and Kari remained silent as they walked, not wanting to distract Michael. They didn't question him, as they remembered how well he had guided them to the cave in the very first class period. They assumed that he was again taking them on a shortcut that they couldn't see on the map.

As they came out of the thick forest, a small dirt path became visible. The path was partially grown over, but was distinct and was definitely a heavily traveled trail at one time, that had fallen into disuse. They all joined the train and were turning right when James stopped them.

"Michael is correct. We need to go to the right to get to class. But we have some time still and are only a short 5-minute walk to the cabin. I recommend we go left as there appears to be another cave about 5 minutes on the trail the other direction."

Bekah's eyes got wide with excitement and they all turned left. After a short walk, they found a large hill with thick overgrowth blocking it. As they moved closer, James quickly found an opening only 3 feet high and 3 feet wide. It looked as if nobody had entered it for many years. Michael, however, didn't even hesitate and crawled into the opening with excitement. Kari hesitated and looked at Bekah who also began to enter the cave.

"Are you sure it is a good idea?" Kari asked, now sounding very nervous.

James could feel her nervousness, almost as if he was feeling it himself. He closed his eyes and began to listen. He heard her heart beating quickly, her breathing become more labored, and could hear sweat running down her cheeks while feeling her muscles start to tighten. Apparently, she was nervous about this cave for some reason.

As he continued to concentrate, his mind grew dark and then opened up to a distinct memory, not his but Kari's.

She lay in what looked like a bed in the pitch blackness. She was alone again and the darkness scared her. The sirens continued in the darkness, which only added to her nervousness. Why were there always sirens? Why was mom always so scared?

Just then she heard the phone ring and heard mom speaking. She couldn't make out her words, but could hear the anxiety in her voice. What had happened? Why wasn't daddy home? Then mom started to cry, not the usual tears she had heard mom use before, but complete and utter despair. As she heard her mother cry tears came to her eyes too and she started to cry. She had never heard mom so sad.

The vision began to blur and then cleared again with Kari looking around at the casket before her. Dad, a jet black middle-aged man, lay motionless in the casket dressed in all white with his eyes closed. He was dead and there was nothing she could do about it.

She turned to see tears streaming down mom's beautiful cheeks as one by one fully uniformed police officers came to console her and thank her for the amazing service of Captain Jack, her husband. Some even came and talked to her, but she didn't really understand when they apologized for not keeping him safe from the gang he was tracking. Apparently, they were getting 'revenge' they said for him putting many of their leaders in jail.

Everyone around her was sad! She couldn't understand why dad was dead. He was one of the good guys. And where was his dog? Was he dead too? She didn't know who to ask.

The vison faded and James found himself looking at Kari now petrified.

"I..I can't do it! I can't do it James." She took a deep breath and continued, "The dark reminds me of the night my father died. He was killed by gang members when I was only 5 years old. I," she paused again. "I later learned he was locked in a car trunk to die after they shot him." Tears started running down her cheeks as she continued with fear in her eyes, "I have always been scared of the dark, but since that time I have been very claustrophobic too."

"You do NOT have to go in. We will be out momentarily, because we need to hurry to class."

With that she relaxed, and James bent down to crawl into the cave. As he came through the opening, the cave opened up into a room 20 feet X 20 foot with a ceiling 10 feet up. The room was dark, but there was light shining from the depth of the cave. They looked at each other by the light of Bekah's flashlight that she always carried in her bag and decided they would need to come back when they had more time. Bekah looked down at the map still in her hand and she marked the location so that they could come back. They then all crawled out of the cave and hurried on down the path towards the class.

As the path broke into the clearing, the small snow-white cabin with red trim came into view. It was a perfectly cared for cabin with red and white roses growing out front. It looked almost like a yard and even had a wooden fence surrounding the cabin. James could almost feel Master Belle's personality by viewing the cabin itself. He just smiled and walked slightly faster to keep up with Bekah who couldn't even contain her excitement. From the moment she saw the cabin she couldn't stop talking about everything that would be taught in this, "her" class.

As they came to the door, it swung open and Master Belle invited them into her cabin. The interior of the cabin was beautifully decorated, with a Living Room area with 20 chairs setup in rows. The decor in the home were light and airy with a large chandelier hanging from the ceiling. On the walls were pictures of the wilderness when the wild flowers were in bloom or sunrises and sunsets. On the back wall of the Living

Room/Classroom area was a large mural of a pink, yellow and red sunset over the Rocky Mountains with a deep blue lake in front of it. James felt happy from the decorations of the house and knew it was on purpose.

Once all the first year students were seated in the classroom, Master Belle stood before them with a big smile but without her mouth moving.

"We will be teaching you today about The Art of Communication. My favorite subject." her words echoed in their minds as she continued to just smile at them. "There are multiple skills we hope to teach you about communication, and those with Telepathy skills will be taught to read minds, speak telepathically, and even block others from reading their mind. As we develop your skills you will become a powerful communicator with or without Telepathy."

Master Belle then had them break into partners to start practicing. As usual, James and Bekah were partners for this activity.

"Three tasks for this class period: 1) Tell each other your favorite memory. One should be speaking and the other should be working really hard at listening. After the memory is complete, please restate it simply back to the individual to show that you were listening. 2) Concentrate on a simple phrase that describes you and try to tell your partner the phrase without moving or speaking. 3) Try to see into your partner's mind to read their favorite memory again. Most of you will not succeed very well at tasks 2 and 3, but the process is valuable for improving your communication skills whether you are Telepathic or not."

James and Bekah started the conversation with James explaining his favorite memory. James told her about the day he got his phoenix and how his life has changed since that day. Bekah was eating up the information as James tried to describe it as completely as possible. They then switched, and Bekah started to talk.

"My favorite memory was the day that I received my invitation to Campus Gaea." Her excitement grew, and her voice became higher and the speed of speech quickened. But even more importantly, James felt her words and heard them through his ears and in his mind as her excitement grew. "I woke up early, excited for my 12th birthday. My parents had talked about this day for years and were hoping that I too had the power of Telepathy that they were both blessed with. I worried that I didn't have that skill and have been trying to work at it since I was 8 years old." She continued, and James mind was filled with her words. All the sudden he began to see it, not just hear it.

Bekah was looking in the mirror in her bathroom with her usual giant grin on her face. Her shoulder length brown hair was being brushed by her as she thought about the excitement of that day. Was she a Titan? Would she get her invitation today? Only time would tell.

The vision then faded and she was much younger sitting on her mother's lap. She looked at her mother in great excitement as she began to talk.

"You are now 8 years old. I want to talk to about a special gift that your father and I have. For years we have been working with The Band of Fire, a group of talented individuals, who have been given special gifts from God. You remember hearing my singing in your mind when you get scared at night? You remember my comfort in your mind when you are at school and feeling nervous? Your father and I have the power of Telepathy, or the ability to talk with you in your mind. We can also hear your thoughts and always know what you are thinking. This may also be your talent. Now that you are 8 years old, you can start trying to develop that skill with me."

James then heard a beautiful song, a lullaby, that rang through Bekah's mind as her mom started singing to her again. James had never heard the song before but found it very beautiful and peaceful. He felt it bring great peace and calmness to Bekah even at the age she is now.

The vision again faded, and he recognized a treehouse they had played in over the years in Bekah's back yard. It was as if he was seeing through Bekah's eyes as she climbed the ladder to the newly built house.

"This is my gift to you my little 8 year-old. I love you more than you know!" James heard a deep, powerful voice in her head. He recognized the voice to be Mark Solomon's voice, Bekah's father. The comfort this voice brought to Bekah was also unmistakable. James never knew that Mark and Bekah had built this together, but he saw the exact process of building the entire house to what he recognized race through her mind as a memory.

The vision faded again, and they were running to the door to answer the knock. As the door was opened, James recognized, the small brown paper package with a brown band wrapped around it and a large blue envelope attached to the front. As she unwrapped the book with excitement, he recognized again the large black leather covered book with gold script lettering and gold foil edged pages. She didn't even open the blue envelope at this time but immediately turned to Chapter 8 – "The Gift of Telepathy".

She began to read. James was amazed that she didn't start at page 1 as he had expected. He never knew her to start in the middle of anything. She always wanted to do things in order and correctly. But the words started to flow from the pages.

"The power of Telepathy is very unique and can be very powerful. It provides the Titan with the ability to speak at great distances to other individuals, to read the minds of individuals, to even hear the thoughts as developed more fully and ultimately provides the ability to pass strength, support and even comfort to other individuals. But this skill can also be utilized in ways to block your mind or the mind of others from Telepathic observance or sharing. A powerful Telepath can actually make themselves invisible from observance by other Telepaths."

"The connection of a Telepath is augmented by strong feelings. Love and friendship can bind minds together more deeply. Relationships, such as Father to Son, Father to Daughter, Mother to Son or Mother to Daughter are usually the most powerful connections. The support and love that a single Telepath can share through this bond is immeasurable. If both

sides of the relationship are Telepathic, the bond is unbreakable and unstoppable. It is also usually a Telepathic connection that can not be blocked by anyone outside and will often be undetectable by another Telepath. This can be a great blessing to families with even a single Telepath."

The words continued, but the vision faded, and James found himself looking with surprise at Bekah who stood there with great excitement in her eyes.   •

"Did you see all that James?"

"Yes"

"Well, I guess it is my turn."

James felt Bekah enter his mind, but she was not as success-ful as he had been at creating a vision. She raced through his thoughts and pulled out little snippets of the day James talked with Helia for the first time and heard the words she spoke to him. She was excited that she had succeeded, but James was confused at the difference her Telepathic efforts seemed to have than his. But Bekah was in his mind and knew his thoughts and responded.

"Don't worry. I am just learning to use my skills of Telepathy. Your Concordant abilities of Telepathy are more developed because of your regular visions you are having. You have been developing this ability for weeks through unknowingly entering your Father's mind. We need to further develop this ability and skill in you and I will work on my developing skill as well!

The class seemed to race by as Master Belle walked between groups and helped them move through the assignment. James was not surprised to see her skip their group as he felt her search his mind to see how they were doing. She knew that they were both succeeding, so she didn't come to their group at all. She did stop and talk with Michael and Kari who were struggling to do tasks 2 & 3. James just looked at them and wondered if there was anything he could do to help. But before he came up with an idea, they were being excused from class to head to lunch.

The morning had flown by with everything happening and the classes now being 2 hours each. The increased time allowed quicker development of the skills they were being asked to develop. James was surprised daily at his unique abilities but was even more surprised today to learn that he was "more" Telepathic at this time than Bekah. How could that be? She was amazing.

As they walked to the Great Hall, he could feel Bekah reaching into his mind and trying to read his thoughts. He kind of liked it, so he stayed silent to see what she would learn, or what she could help him remember. Nothing like having a best friend with whom he would be able to speak without words, even when she was in her tent or in her home when camp was over.

CHAPTER 13
THE WILD WORLD OF HEALING

After finishing a quick lunch in the Great Hall, James raced with the other first year students to the Medic Tent on the Southeast corner of Campus Gaea. This was a large green, military surplus style tent with a big red cross on the roof. Although it was the camp hospital, it was also the classroom for the Hippocratesense classes, including the first year *Basic First Aid* course. James was excited for this course and couldn't wait to meet Master Dakota Ironhorse, the author of *The Keys To Wilderness First Aid*. James had also become accustomed to learning an amazing amount of information about Titan skills even in the simplest of classes.

As they entered the tent, there were wooden stumps set out in rows on the east side of the tent, with cots to the west side of the tent, with curtains hung around each cot to resemble a makeshift hospital. As James moved towards the stumps, he noticed they were actually arranged into a classroom, and a large, muscular man stood at the front of the classroom with long dark black hair with brown and silver highlights throughout, tied behind his head in a ponytail. As he turned, James recognized him as Master Dakota Ironhorse from his picture on the book *The*

Keys To Wilderness First Aid. He was an older gentleman with brown skin with only a tinge of red, especially to the cheeks. His eyes were dark brown with yellowish tinge to the white part of the eyes and clearly marked dark ring surrounding the iris. Although his face looked well-worn from the wind and sun, there was a happy glow that seemed to exude from him. James liked that face and was very interested in learning about him and learning from him.

As Master Ironhorse began to speak, he had a very deep and distinct voice that sang out words that James recognized from pages he had read the other night from *The Book of Adam*, Chapter 11 – "The Gift of Hippocratesense".

"The gift of health and healing can rarely be equaled when it comes to human life. For without your health you cannot truly live. Your life, your experiences and even your interactions with others is greatly limited. For this reason, from the most ancient of times man has sought to remove sickness and restore health. From Babylon to Egypt and China to India, the practice of medicine and the art of healing were a very strong tradition. The Ancient Greeks became well known for their practice of medicine including the diagnosis and possible progression of disease."

"From these early roots come the simplest of principles such as germ theory of infection, carefully formulated herbal treatments and even medicinal treatments of disease. But Native American Medicine Men and Chinese Taoist Physicians added amazing principles of natural healing, being at one with God, one with Mother Earth and aligned with the 'way'. Although there are many distinct medicinal regimen, a very comprehensive, or integrative approach has been found to be the most successful."

"But none of these approaches reach the extent or efficacy of Hippocratesense, a Titan skill that allows evaluation and diagnosis using the natural senses of the healer and treatments utilizing an essence that seems to flow from the individual, but also inherent knowledge of all products around you (a true 'one with nature') that can facilitate healing. It is felt that Hippocrates himself may have actually been a Titan, leading to the development of his medical skills, his 'Father of Medicine' designation, and the name of this Titan skillset now."

James knew the book continued, but Master Ironhorse was not reading a book. He was quoting *The Book of Adam* from memory. James caught Bekah's eye as she leaned towards him and exclaimed with wonder in a soft whisper, "That was word for word!"

"My name is Master Dakota Ironhorse. In ancient times, I would have been a Medicine Man for my people, but today I am your teacher. This summer we will focus on Wilderness First Aid, the simplest form of healing."

He paused to let that sink in and then continued, "Today we will be discussing Chapter 1 from your textbook. We will be talking about the ABCs of First Aid. Can anyone tell me what the most important principle of First Aid is?"

Bekah's hand shot into the air, but Ryan beat her, to her dismay, and Master Ironhorse called on him.

"The first and most important principle is 'Make sure the scene is safe for you.'"

"Exactly." Master Ironhorse responded, "And the ABCs?"

This time he pointed to Bekah even before she could raise her hand.

"The ABCs are for the life-threatening problems that should be checked first. A is for airway. Without an airway, the person will die. B is for breathing. Once the airway is open it is important to ensure the individual is breathing. C is for circulation. Is there blood flow and is there any areas of bleeding that may need to be controlled."

"Perfect." Master Ironhorse said before continuing, "I also want you all to know that D has been added in the past several years because of a Natural Born technology needed to keep someone alive. D is for Defibrillation. That will not be found in our books, because with the Titan skill of Hippocratesense, defibrillation will not be necessary. We have a powerful healing skill that can restore the blood flow without the damage to the cells that electrical shock can cause."

James could almost hear Bekah memorizing every word he said, and wishing she also had the skill of Hippocratesense. She would most likely become the most adept at First Aid for all non-Hippocratesent Titans.

The class continued in this manner with Master Ironhorse discussing Natural Born CPR and the Hippocratesent method of restoring the ABCs to an injured individual. As he talked, James visualized utilizing those skills and seemed to hear more than what was said. He looked around and could hear the heart beats of the individuals. He closed his eyes and could sense Michael breathing on his left and Bekah breathing on his right. Bekah was breathing more quickly, and her heart rate was slightly elevated. Her blood pressure, however, was normal indicating a state of excitement about the subject being taught as opposed to a medical problem.

James didn't hear most the rest of the instruction, but heard a soft music in his mind, Helia's song, as his mind opened up to the health of all the individuals in the class. As the music rang through his mind, he realized that Hippocratesense was one of his skills and would need to be developed with Master Ironhorse's assistance. Just as he came to that realization, they were excused from class and he felt Bekah tapping his arm telling him it was time to go.

"Where were you?" she asked, and then continued with excitement. "That class was absolutely amazing!"

The remainder of the classes were uneventful and they were released for dinner finally with James' mind racing. He had learned so much over the last several days. He really needed to get back to Master Doc McAdam's book on Concordants, as he needed to know so much more.

They walked into the Great Hall and grabbed their food before heading to their usual table. They were having BBQ chicken and Dutch Oven potatoes, a camp favorite James was told by the cooks, and he was not disappointed in any way. The Dutch Oven Apple Crisp, however, was easily his favorite part of the meal. Michael agreed as he shoveled in his third serving of dessert and was standing to get more before they put it away.

Just then Master Doc McAdams stood and James could feel another parable coming on.

"Welcome again to the Great Hall. I pray that you enjoyed the meal, and especially the dessert." He said with a twinkle in his eye and a smile at Michael who was still enjoying his now fourth serving of dessert.

"You are now over two weeks into camp and many of you, especially the first years, are finding the work hard and the teaching difficult. Many of you were told you had Titan skills, but you have been unable to improve those skills as you have hoped to this point. Know that we are very good at developing your skills. You just need to trust us. Let me tell you a story…"

James smiled. He absolutely loved the stories Master Doc McAdams always shared. What were they supposed to learn this time?

Master McAdams continued, "There was a master of a castle, you could even call him a king, that had two sons that he gave a special assignment. There were two large stones, each measuring 10 feet tall, by 10 feet wide and 15 feet deep. The stones were rounded almost like large wheels but were very heavy and not easily moved. Both stones blocked an old path leading from the castle into the mountains. The assignment to each son was to push the rock every day for the next 90 days. It seemed like a simple task, but the master promised a great reward if the sons were diligent, each with his own rock, in completing the task."

"As the two sons talked with excitement, they were pleased that their dad had given them such an important assignment. The older of the two sons was sure they could get the stones moved quicker than 90 days but was willing to do whatever it took to finish the task. The younger son wasn't sure their dad had given them the right assignment but wanted the reward, so he was going to work hard."

"The first day the both went out, as instructed, at 6:30am and started pushing. They both pushed very hard and continued to try to move the rocks. The older son pushed with all his might and continued to push, with his back stressed, the muscles in his arms and legs constantly tight trying to get the rock to move. He pushed until lunch, broke for the hour break and then went back to pushing as hard as he could until dinner time when he was supposed to stop work for the night. When that time came, however, the rock hadn't moved. He went to bed exhausted, sure he could get it to move the next day."

"The younger son likewise pushed and wanted to ensure he worked harder than his older brother. He skipped lunch and kept pushing, finally stopping at dinner time with some frustration and his back, arms and legs all hurting from the stress. He was trying to figure out what his dad was trying to get them to do, because they were never going to move the rocks. He went to bed wishing he was doing something else."

"Day two, day three and the first entire week continued in the same fashion. The rock never moved, they both went to bed exhausted and a little frustrated. The older son trusted his dad and promised himself he would continue to push. The younger son continued to complain and try to think of another way. In fact, he wasn't sure that his dad knew what he was asking of them."

"The task continued for the first month and the older son started to notice an obvious change. He could work harder and was less tired at night, but he still couldn't document any movement of the rock. The younger son, however, had decided it was a waste of time. He had promised to work for the entire 8 hours, so he would come out on time and start pushing the rock but would take multiple breaks to use the bathroom. He was often seen pushing without real effort, sometimes only with one hand. As he watched his brother push with all his might, he would just laugh to himself and think how dumb his brother was and how much he was wasting his time. 'I promised to work, but I don't have to give it all my effort!' he was often heard telling himself."

"Month two passed in much the same fashion and the rocks continued to not move. The older son continued to give all his effort, continued to go to bed exhausted and only stopped for lunch and dinner. He was often too tired to go out on the town at night or to watch their favorite show. The younger son knew he was much smarter, as he continued to work only half-hearted, and often was seen reading a book while pushing (or should I say resting his one hand) on the rock. He also was enjoying every night after dinner, going out on the town, watching movies and staying out until late at night. He would then sleep for a couple hours and get up again to work. 'My life is so much better than the hard work my brother is doing.' he would say with a smile to himself."

"As the 90th day came, the older brother pushed as hard as he could, thinking maybe the rock would finally move. He flexed every muscle, concentrated on the task and leaned all his weight into the task. He didn't want to fail his father and was hoping at least this last time he would get a little motion. But the rock didn't move. The younger brother laughed as he pushed with his index finger on the rock that entire day, finishing his fourth novel of the week and commenting out loud about his plans for the night. He was pleased with himself as dinner was called and his rock had moved just as far as the older brothers with minimal effort on his part. They had both failed, but at least he had enjoyed the three months with friends while his brother crashed every night completely exhausted."

"As they walked into dinner that night together, they saw their dad, the king, sitting there at the table. He looked at both of them and invited them to sit at the table with him. He asked the older son to sit on his right side and the younger son to sit on his left. He then asked for an accounting of their 90 days of work."

"'My dear boys, what can you tell me about your work and diligence over the last 90 days?'"

"'Dear father, I have failed you. I was unable to move the rock from the path, although I tried every day.' the older son began. 'I spent the 10 hours each day from 6:30am to 5:30pm each night pushing on the rock as you instructed. I did everything I could and gave it all my effort. But I failed, the rock did not move.' He then lowered his head and grew silent."

"'My dear boy, I didn't tell you to move the rock. I told you to push the rock every day for 90 days. I asked you to be diligent and you would have a great reward. Well done my faithful servant! Because of your diligence, all that I have is yours.'"

"The younger son, seeing that the rock didn't need to move, jumped in as his dad promised the reward. 'Father, I too have failed to move the rock. I too worked every day and pushed on the rock from 6:30am to 5:30pm. I too was there all 90 days. Do I too get the reward?'"

"The father turned with hurt and pity in his eyes. 'My dear son, you have not been a faithful servant. You did not move the rock, but you also did not work in all diligence, trusting that I knew what I was doing. Look at your brother. See the strong, muscular back, the large powerful arms and legs. Look at his hands callused and strong. See the determination and strength in his face, the dark tan covering his body and know that his health likewise far outpaces your own. The great reward is his not because he worked every day, the great reward is his because he worked hard every day, spent all the hours exercising all his efforts. I know I can trust him with the kingdom, for he will not fail to work hard and follow the instructions that I will give him from my experience. You played at night, only partially worked during the day and failed to exercise all your effort. You have your reward! Although I will continue to love you as your father, I will not trust you with all that I own, all that I have worked for. You are a slothful and not a wise servant.'"

"The story may sound a little harsh but know that if you trust us and allow us to help you develop, your reward will be much greater than the older son, much greater than anything I can give you. In fact, the reward will be much greater than you can even imagine, for God will bless you and help you become as He would have you be. So which son are you?"

James watched in amazement as Master McAdams sat down. Was he really saying that his development as a Concordant was dependent on how hard he was working each day? Was he saying that he need not get discouraged, but should just work harder and at some point it will all come together? He looked at Kari and saw her face light up with understanding. He was excited for her because he knew she had been struggling with many of the classes. Bekah looked a little more confused and pensive, and as he looked at her he heard her thoughts. *"What does he mean? Why would he tell that story? We all know that if we work harder and study harder we will develop more quickly. I am not sure why anyone would be concerned or get depressed. It is a simple concept: If your work hard you will succeed."*

James chuckled to himself and knew she would be alright. He loved the way she thought and felt. Maybe that was why she was his best friend.

James continued to focus on what was said, and only listened slightly as everyone around him talked about the story. He couldn't help but wonder what more he should be learning, or what more he should be studying to ensure he was a "wise servant." He continued to concentrate on that thought as they were excused and walked back to their camp. He didn't even notice when they arrived at camp until he heard Jacques growling out commands.

"Males on the right and females on the left. We must follow the instructions. No exceptions."

James then noticed Helia singing from inside the tent and he raced in.

"Pensive are you? Concerned you may be, but much more to learn can we." And James looked down to see Master Doc McAdams' book *The Secret Life of Concordant* again opened on his cot to what looked like chapter two or three. He walked over and picked the book up and started to read as Helia's song filled his mind.

As he started to read at the top of the page, his mind opened up to a classroom. No, it was actually a cave. The very same cave where they had been holding Orientopathy classes. James could tell it was many years ago because it looked different, almost newer. There was a group of students seated on the ground and no teacher. A young man with a very familiar smile, and deep blue eyes was talking animatedly to all the students as a beautiful lava red phoenix sat silently on his shoulder. This was the same young man, Docery, but he was probably about 14 years old.

"There are seven skills that you must know to understand who we are. Each skill is best exercised through simple tasks and careful study. Although you are blessed with only one Titan skill, you can develop each skill to some degree as we carefully study and work. I propose that we start a study group, a secret group where we help each other develop our skills. I want to get better at each of the skills if possible, but I need your help. What do you think?"

A young man stood, and James immediately recognized him as his father when he was much younger. He began to speak, "Well, Doc, I am in. How are we going to learn and what are we going to learn each time?"

"Each of us have special skills in different abilities. The seven of us can share our skills and how we have developed them over the last 2 years."

"What should we call this group?" a beautiful, tall, dark haired girl asked in excitement.

"Aria, what do you think?" Docery asked turning to her.

"If Felicity is to be part of our band, we should use Phoenixenses or Band of the Phoenix."

"I say Phoenixenses, since that is a term that nobody will recognize as a group." another young man said from the group. James noticed a muscular young man with long, dark black hair tied in a ponytail.

Docery stood again, "All in favor of Phoenixenses?" To which they all responded unanimously.

"The vote is unanimous! Phoenixenses it is. We must ask that you don't tell anyone, especially the teachers, about this group. They

will not understand and will consider it an affront to them. You shall sign this sheet promising to keep our secret."

As all signed at Docery's request, Simon stood and began to speak. "And nobody will be invited into this group without unanimous approval of all herein. Then our secret will be sustained and our growth can progress without limitations."

To that they all cheered and the vision began to fade.

Michael stood there staring at James as he again found himself laying on his cot.

"Do you always read lying down? It may be more effective to sit at the table." he said with a smile.

James laughed and tucked the book under his pillow as he stood up. They were supposed to join Kari and Bekah tonight to look at stars for one of their classes. James stood up and Helia flew to his shoulder and they walked out. Helia loved when they were going out without heading to class.

CHAPTER 14
THE START OF A SECRET

He woke with the start lying on his back in his sleeping bag on the cot. He was surrounded by darkness and all was silent except the soft patter of wings as Helia landed in her bed. He looked up to see her flame red glow in the darkness. He had grown accustomed to her nightlight glow that reminded him of the embers of a dying fire. He loved that feature of his phoenix, her glow brought light no matter how dark it was.

As he considered her glow, Helia seemed to notice. "Asleep you should be, for still night is it now."

"I cannot sleep anymore. Something is wrong, and for once it isn't me or in my mind."

"If sleep you cannot, then maybe a walk you should do."

James smiled and watched her tuck her head under her wing and go to sleep. Her answer was always to walk or explore when she couldn't sleep. It was her way of getting out excess energy and she assumed it would help him too.

As he thought, there was growling in the darkness, outside the tents. "Jacques, all is well in Minotaur camp. I do have a simple concern to report."

"What is your concern Ralf? I thought you said all was well."

"All is well, but I am concerned about a new female student. She claims to be 12 years-old, but she is older than that. I smell the years as she passes. She must be at least 14 years-old. I am concerned that she is lying to camp and she reminds me of another student from several years ago, Minerva Madsen. That worries me, so I felt I must report to you."

"Thanks for the report. We must keep an eye on her."

The conversation came to an abrupt stop and James crawled out of bed, pulled on his clothes and his shoes and walked out to find Jacques walking more quickly than usual back and forth on the path. As James looked at him, he could hear his thoughts, surprising since Jacques was making no noise.

"Master Doc McAdams having given me a charge. He has placed the safety of this camp in my paws. I shall not let him down. I shall not let it happen again that a malevolent Titan causes harm to another. I must learn more about this new student, but he didn't know her name. Why is it always a female?"

Jacques suddenly looked up startled that James was standing there silently looking at him.

"Sir James, it is not yet morning. Should you not still be asleep?"

"Jacques, I couldn't help but hear your conversation. Can you tell me more about Minerva Madsen? I promise to be your eyes and ears around camp if you can help me understand what I am looking for."

Jacques eyes suddenly lit up and he started speaking in his soft growl to not awaken any other students.

"She was always a small, dark skinned, loner female, She had dark black hair, but her midnight black eyes made all of us nervous from day one. Her squeaky, almost mouse like voice, when she talked to us caused my hair to stand up on its end. From age 12 she was always miserable, never happy at camp, but seemed to love talking to animals. She called bats from the sky to nest on her tent. She tortured pets of fellow students by speaking directly into their minds. Her skills were unparalleled when it came to talking with animals. You, my young sir, are good, but she was a master. She even had wolves, like my good friend Ralf, doing her bidding without knowing it. The thoughts she placed in their minds would cause them to act as if under her control."

He paused, as if picking his words more carefully, and then continued. "Early on I considered her a friend. She was a master at making us feel important, an integral part of the camp. She stroked my ego and I thought I was her very best friend. Little did I know that she was using me, manipulating me to get important information. When she turned 14 and was sent away from home to foster care it got even worse. Her midnight black eyes became hard and cold. But she was my friend, so I didn't keep my guard up as I should have."

Jacques stopped walking and looked at James with a start. "I need your help to watch for this new student, but I can tell you no more. I will not make the same mistake, not even with you! Master Doc has asked me to keep this information silent. I will not share it with anyone. I have already said too much." He then turned and continued to walk the path.

James reached out to his mind but could feel his search being blocked. There would be no more information tonight. So after thanking him, he turned and walked away.

As he walked up the path toward the fire pit, his mind started racing through the weeks he had already spent at camp. What was going on? Was he learning as he should? Was he pushing on the rock as he had been instructed, or was he falling short? Was he being too distracted by these thoughts, these visions that keep coming to mind? Maybe he should focus more on what he should be learning.

As he sat down on the bench with those thoughts, his mind started to open up again. He tried to fight it and stay focused on his questions, but to no avail.

He was lying on his back, but his hands weren't tied as usual. They had allowed him to sleep lying down for the first time in many nights. They had even returned to him his sleeping bag and tent. He felt much more at home than he had for weeks. But he could hear the sentry outside his tent and knew that Adam Kane, as they called him, would kill him before he would let him escape. If only he had learned from Doc McAdams the skills of Hoplonosmithy. Then maybe he could compete with Adam in hand-to-hand combat and try to get away.

As he lay there his mind raced to when he was learning at Campus Gaea and when Doc invited him to join him in a secret cave for a special meeting. He thought of the first cave with a large opening where they started, but it was too well known. They only held their first meeting there. Years later when he came back as the Orientopathy instructor, Doc allowed him to use that cave as his classroom. But the other cave was much more secret. It was hidden along a forgotten path, but he still knew exactly where it was. It would today be located at the far end of a dirt path, partially grown over at the base of a large hill. The 3 foot by 3 foot opening was completely hidden by overgrowth and was the perfect spot for the course of the Phoenixenses to be held. He missed those times and knew the cave had not been utilized since those days long ago. In fact, the cave was blocked off for years after they were caught practicing outside of class. The leaders of The Band of Fire at the time, in our 6th year, were concerned that we were forming an army, or a group of Titans to overcome the world and take control of all others. They were punished and kept separate for the last 2 weeks of camp. Doc was even dismissed as Senior Patrol Leader as they suspected that it was his idea and that he was Concordant. That was a dangerous designation at that time.

He was called back to the present when he heard music and laughter in his mind. Camilla was coming back to talk with him. Why would she be up so early in the morning? It wasn't even light yet. "Well, I guess I will find out!"

James again found himself sprawled out on the ground. He had apparently fallen from the log he was sitting on. Jacques had moved towards him and was watching him carefully but moved away quickly when James sat up. It would take some time to get Jacques to want to talk with him again. He needed to know more about this group. Maybe the book has more information. Maybe Master Doc McAdams could give him more information. Didn't he write the book?

As he stood from his fallen position, he saw the cave again. "I know where that is! I don't even need a map to get there. But I need to go now!" He looked back at his tent and decided he didn't have time to return, and began to quickly walk out of camp. As he moved quickly, he heard short steps racing towards him. A smile came to his face as a voice popped into his mind speaking very quickly as only one person he knew could.

"You will not have an adventure without me! I don't know where you are going, but I am in." And Bekah quickly came to his side.

As he turned to look at her with excitement, a flame red glow caught his peripheral vision flying out of his tent, "I too shall by your side be." came Helia's music in his mind.

With his two best friends by his side, they hurried quickly to where James knew they were going. They raced past the snow-white cabin with red trim, up the dirt path and traveled 5 minutes to the overgrown path. Bekah's eyes filled with excitement and they continued down the overgrown path for another 5 minutes before they came to the large hill with thick overgrowth blocking access to the base of the hill. James walked right to the opening and Helia flew in. Bekah followed and James likewise crawled in.

The soft red glow of Helia lit the walls with a fire like glow. The walls seemed to reflect her light and partially illuminate the entire room but was not bright enough to truly see. Bekah smiled and pulled two flashlights from her pockets and handed one to James. As they lit the flashlights, the large room became as bright as noon day sun. It appeared that the small flashlights were being reflected off the walls and ceiling in in all directions. Each wall the light hit seemed to increase its brightness and significantly multiply the light that was being created.

This room was much larger than the great hall and had crystalline rock lining the walls and ceilings. There were no stalactites or stalagmites and no passageways coming off the large room where they stood. And there was absolutely no sound from the outside heard in that room.

James thought of his dad and closed his eyes to see if any additional information was available. Nothing happened, except he heard a sheet of paper about 60 feet in front of him on one of the walls. He quickly walked towards it just as Bekah, reading his mind, knew what he was headed for. She ran to his side and they pulled the paper off the wall and began to examine it. It was 8-inch X 10-inch sheet of yellow lined paper with beautifully written old script writing in black ink. James knew exactly what it was as they looked at it. Bekah finished the last name and looked up at James. "What are Phoenixenses?"

Felicity's Phoenixenses

- *Docery McAdams*
- *Aria Thorngardner*
- *Dakota Ironhorse*
- *Simon John Adamson*
- *Julianna Gaea Abel*
- *Zena Smith*
- *Cornelia C Sampson*
- *Jens Christensen*
- *Hans Christian Bruun*
- *Alice Magan Davenport*
- *James William Enloe*
- *Mabel J Wood*
- *Ruby Allen Seenox*
- *Logan Montgomery*

James smiled, but before he could give an answer, words seemed to echo from the walls:

"There are seven skills that you must know to understand who we are. Each skill is best exercised through simple tasks and careful study. Although you are blessed with only one Titan skill, you can develop each skill to some degree as we carefully study and work. I propose that we start a study group, a secret group where we help each other develop our skills. I want to get better at each of the skills if possible, but I need your help. What do you think?" came a strong male voice reminiscent of Master Doc McAdams.

"Each of us have special skills in different abilities. The seven of us can share our skills and how we have developed them over the last 2 years."

"What should we call this group?" a female voice questioned.

"I say Phoenixenses, since that is a term that nobody will recognize as a group." echoed a second male voice that sounded much like Master Dakota Ironhorse.

Bekah looked at James in amazement who also looked a little startled at the words but recognized them from words he had read earlier.

"I have figured out how to become a more skilled Concordant while helping each of us also become better Titans." James responded with a smile. "I want to organize a similar group, where each of us can use our unique talents to grow as a group in power and skill."

Bekah looked a little startled and hesitated for a moment before starting to talk in a low pitch, very slowly with trepidation that James had never heard in her voice.

"I heard that Master Doc McAdams was in a ton of trouble during his last year. Rumors and gossip say, since I couldn't find any documentation in the books I could find, that he and a group of students were forming an 'Army' to take over the world. Is this that group?"

"I don't know about taking over the world, but it was Master Doc McAdams only way to further develop his Concordant skills without being expelled from camp. I recommend we do the same. I need help becoming a true Concordant."

James saw fear in Bekah's eyes and then his mind went dark and he found himself in Bekah's home watching her sitting on her bed holding *The Book of Adam* with her bedroom door closed.

"*Maybe now I can live up to mom and dad's expectations. They are powerful Titans, recognized by all as talented Telepaths. But what if I'm not a Telepath? Will they still love me if I have another skill? They have always told me that they are sure I will be a Telepath. I must learn as much as I possibly can to prepare for this Camp and make sure I don't let them down.*"

The vision faded and James found himself in Bekah's kitchen looking at her mother across the table.

"*But mom, I wanted YOU to take me to get my supplies.*"

"*Sarah Adamson has offered to take you. Then you can go with James too. You always like to be with him.*" *her mom said with a smile.*

"*Can't you at least wait one more day before you and dad leave?*"

"*You know I can't. My schedule belongs to The Band of Fire. If they need us we must go. Especially since Simon Adamson is missing. Please don't argue anymore. We have already made our decision.*"

He then watched Suzy Solomon put on her jacket and walk out the door into the garage. He felt sadness flood over Bekah and the vision faded again.

Bekah sat again on her bed with her door once again closed. Grandma was downstairs since mom and dad were gone again, but she was in no mood to visit with her. She sat there holding Tom looking at him with a little wonder.

"*Master...I...want...to...help...you...be...happy.*"

Bekah's eyes got wide, because the voice came from Tom without his mouth even moving.

"*So,*" *James thought, *"*she already knew he could talk?*"

*But Bekah interrupted him, *"*I don't have the skills to talk with an animal. It has never worked when I have tried. Why can you speak to me?*"

"*I...speak...with...those...that...love...me...through...telepathy.*" *and Tom seemed to smile at her.*

"*And you are mine.*" *Bekah said with increasing speed and excitement. *"*You shall be my very best friend.*"

"No!...I...will...be...a...good...friend...but...James...will...
still...be...your...best...friend....He...will...need...your...help."

"What? Why would he need my help?"

"You...are...very...smart!...You...read...more...than...he....
Only...with...your...help...can...he...become...a...Titan....He...
has...always...needed...you!"

*The vision faded and James found himself in a tent. He knew
that they must be at camp in a tent Jacques would never let him
enter. Especially when he saw Bekah sitting on her cot holding
Tom and crying.*

*"James is Concordant. He will not need me!!" she almost screamed
in her tent. "How can I help him when he will be better at everything than me. Even his Telepathy will develop past my own skills."*

*The vision blurred and then returned to the same scene, but
Bekah was not crying. It was days later and she was talking rapidly
to Tom about the talk she just had with James.*

*"He needs me. Nobody else can help him like I can. He trusts me
and wants me to help him become Concordant. With my help he
will be able to save his dad from Camilla. Isn't that a great idea?"*

"You...don't...need...him...to...be...important....Your...
worth...comes...from...within!"

"But HE needs me. I can do it!"

The vision faded again, and James found himself looking
at a startled Bekah standing across from him.

"Did you see all that?" she asked with fear in her eyes.

"I can't do this without you!" James said immediately. "Every
step of the way I have been depending on you. That is not going
to change anytime soon."

"But the Phoenixenses will help you. You will not need me
as much."

"I want you to help me lead the Phoenixenses. Your Telepathy
skills are far more developed than mine. You can help everyone
in our group so much more because of this ability."

Bekah wanted to argue, but enjoyed the compliment, "OK,
but we must be careful. I will not be kicked out of camp our
first year. My parents would never forgive me and would pay
even less attention to me if I don't develop into a true Titan."

"Well, I can help you and you can help me. I think you will be far more powerful than your mom or dad will ever be."

Bekah smiled and nodded. "Who should we invite do you think?"

"I recommend Kari and Michael at this time. We should maybe start with just four."

Bekah looked pleased with that suggestion and James felt the fear and trepidation leave her.

Just then a song filled the cave and Helia started speaking from the walls. James knew immediately that Bekah likewise could understand.

"You shall start with two, for tonight the instruction shall start. If me you trust and listen, more powerful yet you shall be."

Bekah's eyes lit up with excitement and everything went dark.

Bekah, James and Helia were racing through the sky in the darkness and James knew the instruction was about to begin.

As Helia's music continued in the background, James and Bekah found themselves in a cabin. It was a cabin that James recognized as belonging to Master Doc McAdams, but it was decorated differently and seemed to be newer. As the view cleared, James noticed a younger Master Doc McAdams and a young woman probably around 16 years-old. She was a slender girl with long curly brown hair, dark blue eyes, a small nose and a slightly round face. James couldn't help but notice how beautiful she was, and he felt that he recognized her, but didn't know where he last saw her.

Bekah's face became a large smile, but before she could talk, the young woman started talking.

"Master McAdams, my mother told me that YOU started the secret group she was a part of. YOU organized the classes to further improve the skills of all involved. YOU are the reason it all happened. How could you also be the one blocking the organization of my group? I am also Concordant. Doesn't that count for something too?"

Master Doc McAdams stood there without even a twitch in his face as he listened, but she just kept getting more and more excited as she talked.

"You are worried I'll learn as much as you and not need you anymore! You KNOW that I'm more powerful than you were at this age and I scare you. My friends scares you."

"Camilla, you are the most talented Titan I have ever had as Head Master of camp. But you are mistaken. You have felt that by me trying to help direct your instruction I am limiting your progress and abilities. May I tell you a story?"

Before Camilla could respond, he continued, "In Greek mythology, there was a great Athenian craftsman, an inventor named Daedalus. He was asked by King Minos of Crete to build a prison for the Minotaur who was the half-man, half-bull monster offspring of King Minos' wife and the Cretan bull. Daedalus was such a great inventor, that he created a Labyrinth from which the Minotaur could not escape. It was the perfect prison. As time passed, however, King Minos became jealous of Daedalus and accused him of treason for helping his enemy Theseus survive the Labyrinth and kill the Minotaur contained therein. Therefore, Deadalus and his son, Icarus, were imprisoned in the Labyrinth."

"Now you need to know that Daedalus was truly a great craftsman and was able to develop two pairs of functional wings from a wood frame, wax and feathers. After Daedalus tried his wings first and found them to be functional, he instructed his son on how to leave the island. But the instructions were very specific:"

"'Please, my son, don't fly too close to the sea, because the spray from the water will moisten the feathers and you will be unable to continue to fly. But these instructions are only half as important as not flying too high, too close to the sun. Your wings were fashioned from wax that will melt with the heat of the sun and you will fall to your death. Please follow my path of flight and you will be safely freed.'"

"Icarus looked to his father with excitement and agreed as his father flew out from the island, positioned halfway between the sun and the sea. Icarus spread his wings and jumped out and began to flap his wings. To his amazement, he began to fly just like his father. He looked around and saw bird above him and birds below. He was really flying. As he continued to flap his wings, he saw the island moving away from him and he was filled with the exhilaration *of flight. He was like the birds and he began to rise into the air. His father called back to him to stay on the path and not lift up towards the sun, but he ignored him. His father was just trying to limit his ability to fully exercise his power, his new strengths. And he assured himself that he would be careful."*

"It was at this point that the heat of the sun began to grow and the wax on the wings started to melt. As Icarus realized what was happening, he tried to move away from the sun, but as he flapped his wings he watched the feathers fall from the wooden frame and fall toward the water. He flapped harder and called to his father, but it was too late. He fell from the sky to the sea below where he would not rise again. Deadalus watched his son fall from the sky with no ability to help him, and continued his journey with tears falling from his eyes."

"Don't think that my limiting your ability to fly near the sun or sea is to limit your powers. It is to protect you from harm, until your powers are such that you need not be limited. Please listen and please know that it is for your protection!"

Camilla started to laugh, a laugh that James now recognized very well, and then she exclaimed, "You and your stories are no use to me. I don't need your little analogies, you can't fool me by your cute stories. Don't you know WHO I AM! Very soon, you and Simon will know that The Order of The Kraken is far more powerful than your Band of Fire, because I will NOT limit their growth or their power. You will NOT see me again, but you will hear my song in your mind and when you do, you will know that it is too late! And I will laugh at your destruction!" and she finished with laughter in her voice.

With that, before Master McAdams could even respond, a blood red phoenix flew into the room and Camilla took his claw and both disappeared...

The vision faded, and Bekah and James found themselves both lying on the ground looking up at Helia, who seemed to be smiling.

"James, my boy, come a day will when see what I see you will. And weakness will not you break, and knee bend you will not!"

Bekah struggled to her feet, surprised at how tired she was, as Helia continued to speak.

"Will you as Camilla mistaken be? Or learn much more you will? As *Phoenixenses* serve yourself you will not, but to others service you shall do. Which lake will you now be."

Bekah looked at James with a start, remembering the story James was told by Master McAdams after being classified as a Concordant. They hadn't talked about that much since the first and second days of camp, but Bekah didn't forget such simple details, and apparently neither did Helia.

The discussion continued for more than an hour, until James and Bekah began to grow very drowsy and decided it was time to return to camp and get a little sleep before morning was to break. Helia seemed to smile in understanding and then agreed that it was time to go home and quickly obliged by reaching out her claws.

Bekah and James each grabbed a claw and moments later found themselves standing on the path by Jacques. They went their separate ways and James quickly fell asleep upon entering his tent. The rest of the night was quiet and uneventful, even for Helia who collapsed exhausted into your nest-like cage.

CHAPTER 15
WILDERNESS COOKING

After getting a short night's sleep, the morning was very uneventful until lunchtime. Classes contained much valuable information, but James was most excited for two new classes they would be starting that day. They weren't Titan specific classes but camping specific classes. In fact, they were talking about the process of fire building in one class and cooking in another, while having another class on camping. It was becoming more and more likely that James would be going on an extended camping trip to save his father, so he felt these classes would probably be just as important as the Titan training classes.

As he started packing his *Introduction to Camping – Preparing For The Wild*, *Beginners Book of Fire and Fire Building* and *Alexandria's Book of Wilderness Cooking*, Michael walked over to him nervously and started to talk.

"You were gone most the night. Where did you go? I heard Helia leave, but you were gone before I could follow."

"Bekah and I went to the cave. I feel that we need to learn more quickly and would like to invite you to join us."

"Wait, how are we going to learn more quickly? Aren't these classes designed to teach us at the appropriate rate?"

"Yes, but there is a Titan counterfeit that has my father."

"Are you talking about Camilla and her 'Band'. My dad says they are just troublemakers and we shouldn't worry about them!"

Just then shadows started to fall over James' eyes and he knew what was happening....

Michael sat on a couch in what looked like a Living Room. There was tan carpet, cream walls and white blinds covering the window. On the wall were family pictures, including one that included Michael with his nine siblings and parents. James counted one older sister, a very beautiful girl with long blond, almost white hair, a long nose like Michael's and bright green eyes. There were also two older brothers that could be mistaken as older versions of Michael. All the children had similar looks and the blond, white hair was from the mother of the home, who looked too young to have 9 children. James didn't realize Michael was from such a large family.

As James looked around, he noticed this same beautiful sister walk into the room.

"Michael. We are so proud of you and excited you will be joining us at camp. You have always been a Titan to us, as your ability to find directions and use Orientopathy is amazing. I can't wait to see how Master Doc McAdams develops you!"

"Don't encourage him Amanda, he needs to be like the rest of us and struggle the first year." the oldest brother walked into the room and started teasing.

"As opposed to you Matt, I love him!" Amanda said with a smile.

"You all need to leave Michael alone! Let him examine The Book of Adam and the invitation to join you at Campus Gaea. This is a moment he has been waiting for and hoping for since you each got your books." the mother from the picture entered the room with eyes filled with love and excitement for Michael.

James recognized this look as the love he felt from his own mom. He missed her, but knew she was safer away from him.

"Michael. You have a great opportunity to make your own way. Don't worry about what patrol or what skill you will have. This is your time and your opportunity. No matter what happens we will be excited for you and we are already proud of you." She walked out of the room pulling the older siblings with her.

The vision faded and the room changed. It now looked like a boy's bedroom. There was a single bed in the corner with Michael sitting on it with his legs crossed. To his left perched a large brown falcon with a cream streaking on the nape of the neck and crown of the head. It was a very large falcon and seemed to be talking with Michael.

"I am worried Fenwick. My family are well known Titans. Amanda and Matt are both Griffin patrol and have Chronopathy. Mark is Centaur patrol and has Zoonophonia. Mom is a Telepath and Dad is a Herculopath. I hope that my skills in Orientopathy are good enough to be classified with that skill."

Fenwick started squawking and James immediately understood him, and Michael did as well.

"When I was just a small bird, other falcons tried to hurt me and kill me. It was you that picked me from the ground when my own family chased me from my nest. It was you that raised me as your best friend. We don't care what they think. We don't need their approval. There will come a time when they will wish they were you. We will stand as unequaled in that camp! They will know you as all birds now know me!"

Michael looked at Fenwick in appreciation and the scene faded again and found Michael sitting alone in the tent.

"I can't believe I met Simon's son and he is sharing a tent with us...Oh Fenwick, I am excited to work with him, especially since he is Concordant."

"He will need you! He does not yet realize how powerful you truly are!" Fenwick squawked and Michael responded with a smile.

The vision then seemed to speed up and James had multiple visions of Michael's excitement from the classes, his ability to understand and perform in Orientopathy and then the visions faded...

James looked at Michael and repeated, "We need you as part of this special group! You can help me improve in my Orientopathy skills and others in the group can help us both improve in other skills."

"I am in. I would consider it a pleasure to be part of this group with you and Bekah!"

Even Fenwick seemed to stand up straighter in her cage in the corner of the tent.

"And you are invited too, Fenwick. We need a powerful bird like you!" James squawked.

"What did you say to him? I have never seen someone talk in bird like you just did."

"Oh…Sorry. I am not skilled enough with Zoonophonia yet to speak to the animal and others in the room at the same time. I just invited him to come to the classes as well. Helia would love to have him there!"

Michael smiled and got even more excited. He didn't say anything more, but pulled on his backpack and ran from the tent.

By the time, James left the tent and joined Bekah, Michael and Kari, they were all talking about the Phoenixenses (Apparently, Bekah told them the name.), and were excited about the prospect of helping each other improve in Titan skills. They grew silent, however, as other students approached. Michael was certain to ask that his siblings NOT be invited even in the future to be part of this group. They all thought that was a great idea.

As James continued to think about what had happened the last couple days, he almost ran into a short middle-aged man with a long gray and white beard, dark gray eyes and short silver, white hair. As he stopped with a start, Bekah started laughing and reached out her hand, "Master Walker. So great to meet you!"

The man smiled under his beard and took her hand with his strong right hand and arm. James immediately noticed that this 5'4" man was very strong with broad shoulders. He reminded him of what he always thought a dwarf would look like, beard and all.

"So, James. A dwarf I am?" the man asked.

James looked at him with surprise and Michael, Kari and Bekah all started giggling.

"I have a secondary Titan skill of telepathy. Often it is not very good, but your thoughts seemed to jump at me and beg to be read! I had to oblige." he said with a twinkle in his gray eyes.

As the rest of the class arrived, James quickly found a seat as did Bekah, Michael and Kari at the front of the class. Master Walker strolled to the front of the class and began to speak.

"Welcome to *Standard Fire Building*. I am Master Adam Walker and will be your instructor in this class. If I do my job right, you will be able to make a fire in any condition and have the warmth and protection that will come with that beautiful flame. It is not a Titan skill, but no Titan can function without this most important knowledge. Besides, you may need the fire for your cooking classes throughout the summer."

He had them all pull open their book, *Beginners Book of Fire and Fire Building*, and open to chapter 1.

"What are the three things a fire needs to burn?"

Bekah's hand shot into the air, but as in other classes Lizzy's hand likewise shot into the air. Master Walker smiled at both of them and turned to a tall, darkly tanned girl with long black hair pulled into two ponytails.

"Julia, do you have an answer?"

"I know fuel and oxygen, but I don't know the third thing."

Bekah's hand stayed in the air and she was almost bouncing out of her seat.

"Yes. Every fire needs fuel. The most common fuel is wood, but gas or propane are often used in stoves as well as butane. Different types of fuel will burn with different amounts of heat and may even burn with different colors."

He then made twelve piles of powder on the metal table he had and lit each individually.

The first pile burned a light blue color flame to which everyone responded with an audible gasp.

Master Walker smiled and stated, "Lead will burn light blue in color."

The second pile turned a dark orange color, much more orange than the usual fire.

"And Calcium will burn orange."

Now the class was anticipating each pile, and responding with claps as the flame color changed with each pile.

"This light green flame is Copper."

"This purple flame is Potassium."

"Sodium burns dark yellow."

"Radium burns dark red."

"Iron burns bright yellow."

"Zinc burns a pale green-blue or sometimes called colorless"

"Lithium burns a bright red or crimson."

"Tantalum burns blue."

"Potassium burns a shade of pink, called lilac."

"And finally, Barium burns a light green."

"Why would this information matter? Is this important for fire building? Is it important for Titans?"

This time he called on Bekah who was standing with both hands in the air, bouncing on her toes.

"It is not important for fire building, except it may help you understand what elements are in the earth where the fire is built, in the rocks around the fire or in the fuel being used."

"Correct. Is it important for Titans otherwise?"

"It can also be used as a protection, for example Arsenic will burn a pale blue color."

"Well done. Apparently, someone has read chapter 12 already. We also use fire color in the Patrol Challenges to identify patrols or indicate an emergency. As a Titan, a white fire will always indicate an emergency condition. And what makes a fire white?"

"Metals like Aluminum, Chromium, Cobalt, and Nickel all burn silver-white, but Magnesium metal burns an intense white." Bekah could hardly get the words out as she was talking so fast.

"Amazing! Thanks for coming prepared to class." And Master Walker pulled out a piece of metal and placed it on the table and lit it to a bright white color.

Bekah beamed with excitement as Master Walker continued. James just shook his head and made a mental note (again) that he needs Bekah on his side!

"When it comes to the most common fuel, wood, the type of wood will determine the amount of heat and how long the wood will burn. Many woods will also produce a distinct smell.

I love to burn black walnut, cherry wood and cedar. They all have strong, pleasant smells when burning."

Master Walker paused and then continued, "And all fires need oxygen. Why would that be important?"

Lizzy jumped from her seat with excitement before Bekah could respond.

"Lizzy, please."

"Without oxygen, a fire cannot burn. Therefore, a fire can be smothered with a blanket, with dirt or with rolling on the ground. That also means you can create firestarters by limiting the oxygen to them while heating them up."

"Very good. We will discuss firestarters at a later date. That is chapter 4."

"So, what is the last item needed for a fire?"

After a short pause, "Only these two ladies know? Then I will give you all an assignment to read chapter 1 before our next class and we will end early unless someone else can answer."

James all the sudden heard Bekah in his mind, "It is heat. Without heat, there is no fire. This is important to know when building a fire on cold ground, or snow. Insulating the fuel and fire from the cold surfaces will make it much easier to start a fire in these circumstances."

Before James could answer, Ryan spoke from the other side of the group. "Is it heat? I think heat is a necessary part of fire building."

"Yes. Saved by the young man over here. We will talk more about the importance of heat at a later date, but I want to help you build fires now. Everyone get into groups of 3-4 people. It is probably a good idea to stick with your patrol, as there will be competitions later this summer on fire building."

"Now, using chapter 1 as a reference, let's see who can build the first fire."

James was excited about this part, because his mom and dad had taught him to make a fire. So he grabbed Bekah's hand and said they should get Kari and Michael and build their fire. As they gathered together, Bekah started talking.

"In chapter 1 it talks about building a fire. It talks about three types of fuel, namely kindling, tinder and fuel. You need to start with the smallest, kindling, and then build around it with tinder and then fuel."

As she talked, Michael and Kari were carefully listening. James, however, was already setting out the wood to build a fire. He was following the technique his mom had indicated:

"Start with the smallest wood, especially materials like leaves, bark or very small sticks that will catch fire the easiest. Place those in the center of the area you want to build a fire. Second, put larger sticks around it in either a tepee shape or in a log cabin style. A tepee will burn higher and quicker. Last, place the wood from smaller to larger around the fire to allow it to catch fire. Those three types of wood together will quickly burn into a warm fire if laid out properly."

James carefully placed the wood as she talked. Bekah turned and noticed what he was doing and was very impressed.

"That is exactly how it says to do it in the book. Did you read this chapter before class?"

"Nope. Just following the teachings of my mom. She's really good at building fires!"

Michael started to laugh and Kari grabbed matches to help start the fire. James looked at her with a smile and pulled out his flint & steel.

"I was hoping to start it with this. Dad had showed me how to do this in a nest of leaves or bark."

He picked up the nest of leaves he had formed in the center of the fire and set it to the side. He then stated using his pocket knife on the flint to create sparks. When a small spark caught on the leaves, he quickly picked it up and started blowing. Before they knew it, it was burning and he placed it under the tinder and fuel he had stacked. Again, Bekah was impressed and just remained silent, as the fire lit into a roaring flame.

Master Walker came over very impressed and started examining the fire.

"I see you did a nest of leaves in the center. Why did you do that?"

"My dad told me it was the best way to catch a spark from flint and steel." James responded.

"That is a very good way to catch a spark, but I will teach you in another class better kindling for flint and steel." he said with a smile. "And why did you stack the tinder in a tepee?"

"I have tried multiple times at home, but the tepee seems to be the best form to catch fire from the kindling. A log cabin or lean-to has never been successful for me."

"And then you switched to a log cabin for the main fuel. What is your reasoning here?"

"My mom taught me that the warmest fires and longest burning fires are log cabins, so I always make log cabins."

"Well said. Now when you want a fire to start faster, however, and burn higher as may happen in a competition, the tepee may be a better option. For camping and cooking, I would agree that the log cabin is often the best options. Well done!"

Master Walker then went from fire to fire complementing and discussing the organization of the fires. James watched him teach at each fire and then recommend they go look at their fire as an example of a well-designed fire. Bekah, Michael and Kari just smiled as they watched this happen. They were happy to have chosen James to help them with their fire.

After Master Walker walked around to all the fires, he came to the front of the group and invited them to review chapter 1 and read chapter 2 before the next class period.

"Next time you will all be building your own fires, and I will help you make some very powerful kindling."

They were then all excused to the cooking class on the other side of the lake. Kari was very excited about this class and couldn't stop talking about how much she loved to cook. She couldn't wait to see what they would be learning in this class. James was likewise excited, but not because he was an amazing cook, but because it would help him for later. Bekah was silent and seemed to be thinking more deeply as they walked. With Kari talking constantly, James didn't notice the unusual silence from Bekah.

As they got closer, Bekah had a confused, almost worried look on her face. James had never seen this look and decided he was going to try to control his telepathy for the first time outside of class.

As he reached into her mind, he heard a soft cry and saw a 6 year-old Bekah sitting at the kitchen table in their home. In front of her was a burned tray of cookies and her mom smiling at her from across the table.

"Bekah, we learn by making mistakes. I have burned plenty of things. Next time I will help you and together we won't burn them."

The scene quickly changed to Bekah a few years older in the same kitchen, dumping a burned cake into the garbage with the smoke alarm going off in the background and mom opening windows to let the thick smoke out of the kitchen.

The scene changed from year to year and Bekah kept burning or boiling over foods with mom smiling in the background and trying to comfort her. She even burned toast multiple times to which her mom just smiled and said, "You can't be good at everything. Maybe since you are so smart you get distracted by doing something else while everything is cooking. That is probably why you burn everything."

James felt Bekah's deep sadness and fear as they got closer to the class. "I can't cook!" she said to him in his mind.

"But I can help you!" he said quickly telepathically back to her mind. "Together we are unstoppable!"

Bekah smiled and calmness started to flood over her mind, and James knew everything was going to be alright.

As they entered the clearing, there were multiple small fires burning in individual fire pits, four propane stoves were spread out through the clearing. As James looked around, he saw charcoals burning in small piles by the fires and standard 12 inch Dutch ovens spread out. In the center of the clearing was a table with stacks of egg cartons, bacon, sausage and shredded potatoes. James looked at Bekah, who's eyes were big with surprise. No teacher was in the clearing, but the area was very well organized and all the first year students were in attendance.

As James continued to look around, he noticed the patrols congregating in groups. He recognized all the other students from other classes, except one. She was a very small, white girl with a short, spiky, red haircut and freckles covering her cheeks and nose. He had never seen her before, but he recognized her from somewhere. As he continued to stare at her, Bekah also noticed her as new.

"She hasn't been here. I haven't seen her in any of our other classes. Is she part of the Minotaur Patrol?"

Just then, out of nowhere, a short, middle-aged lightly tanned and plump woman appeared in the center of the clearing. Her bleach blond hair and green eyes were very distinctive and as she began to speak with a strong accent, James knew she must be the teacher.

A thought jumped into James' mind at that very moment with Bekah's voice echoing through his mind, "That is Master Alexandria Rossi. She is from Italy." James smiled to himself as he turned to listen to Master Rossi give her initial instructions:

"Welcome to Basic Wilderness Cooking. I am Alexandria Rossi and will help you all learn to cook. We will be experiencing all types of cooking, from basic fire cooking techniques, personal and camp stove cooking, Dutch oven cooking and even some little tricks. Today we will be teaching you one of Doc McAdams' favorite meals. I invite you to all pay special attention."

"Let me start by saying that breakfast is the most important meal of the day. It has been shown to be the key to energy throughout the day, especially after sleeping through the night. Therefore, it is the first meal we will teach you to cook at this time."

"Many of you have cooked food at home, no?" She looked around waiting for confirmation and many individuals throughout the class nodded in agreement. "Perfect. When cooking on a range, you are heating with controlled heat from one side. That is similar to cooking over a personal stove or the camp stoves you see here. But camp stoves are not as controlled a heat and are usually adjusted over and over again throughout the cooking process to minimize over cooking or burning the foods being cooked."

Bekah's eyes got really big, and James just caught her eye and smiled.

"Cooking over an open fire is even more difficult to control the amount of heat, but is the easiest to prepare when cooking out in the wild without additional equipment. Therefore, I want to teach you a couple simple tricks to cooking over a fire even if you don't have a pan."

She stepped forward to the table and grabbed a paper cup, placed a large egg in the bottom of the cup and then filled it with water. She then carefully placed the cup flat on the ground in the firepit. As they watched, the top rim of the cup caught fire, but the fire stopped at the water level and slowly the water started to bubble and boil. As they watched the cup, Master Rossi continued to prepare other foods. James looked up just in time to see her grab two slices of bacon and place them in the bottom of a paper sack that she also carefully placed in the same fire pit. Portions of the paper bag burned some, but the bottom where the bacon was didn't burn.

She sat silently watching their reactions as the water started to boil and the bacon could be heard cooking in the paper bag. The egg boiled for approximately 10 minutes while the bacon continued to cook and then Master Rossi pulled out the cup and the paper bag. She pulled out the egg that was slightly brown on the shell and then cracked it to show a hardboiled egg. The bacon was also carefully removed from the bag with a fork and shown to be well cooked without the bag burning.

At this point, Kari was bouncing next to Michael and James felt the same excitement. Bekah looked intrigued, but James could feel her cautious excitement. Michael stood almost expressionless as Kari bounced in her spot.

"Now, I want each of you to get a partner that will be your partner in this class for the entire summer. Then I need you to each cook one bag of 2-4 bacon strips and 2 boiled eggs. Know that this will require 2 paper cups filled with water. I also ask that you pull out your fire gloves I had placed on your supply list to ensure we have no burns. Hippocratesense is not my talent!"

Bekah grabbed James immediately when she asked them to pick a partner, and she and he walked up to grab the appropriate supplies to cook their eggs and bacon and returned to the burning fire. James pulled is large cloth gloves out of his bag and they placed each cup and the bag into the fire. As everyone completed placing their food in the fire, the buzz of talking grew louder.

It was in this great raucous that Master Rossi called all to attention again. "Now, it is important that you track the time. The fire and the coals in the fire are very hot. The bacon will cook quickly, and the egg will boil at this altitude in a matter of 10 minutes of boiling water. Keep track so that you don't under cook or over cook."

Bekah grabbed her watch and studied the time. "How long should we cook the bacon James?"

"I can't tell you for sure, but we do need to pay attention to the sounds we are hearing. And the eggs are starting to boil."

"According to the book, in chapter 1, it says that you want the water boiling hard before you start counting the time."

"Yes. 10 minutes, and it is not possible to burn the boiled egg unless the water all boils or spills out."

Bekah smiled and nodded.

As they talked, the bacon could be heard cooking. The grease from the bacon was moistening the paper bag and it didn't burn even when burning logs fell onto the bag.

Finally, James reaching in and pulled the bacon out and Bekah used her fork to pull out the first piece.

"Congrats Bekah and James!" Master Rossi said as she walked by, "You appear to be the first ones with the bacon done and it looks almost perfect."

Bekah beamed as she realized it was the first time she hadn't participated in cooking and burned the food. That made this bacon taste extra special, especially with her boiled egg that was also not burned.

As they all started enjoying their bacon and eggs, Master Rossi started talking again, "Now for the special meal, Doc McAdams favorite wilderness cooking meal. This meal will take over 45 minutes to cook, so I will teach you how and you will have the opportunity to taste it in the Great Hall at meal time. I have yet to meet anyone that doesn't like this meal, unless there are individual components of the meal that they dislike."

She then pulled open one of the Dutch ovens. "This is a Dutch oven. This is the best way to cook if you want to maintain a constant temperature on the top and the bottom of the food being cooked. This can be done in a fire as well but is much easier if coals are prepared. I am going to give you very simple guidelines and we will review them in much greater depth when we teach Dutch oven cooking later this month."

She lifted the lid and held it up. "On this lid you will see the number 12. That states the size of the oven. It also gives you direction on the number of coal needed to produce adequate heat. A simple rule of thumb is to take the number and double it. 12 becomes 24. That gives you the number of coals required for cooking. You will put the number of coals on top to equal the size plus 2, or 14, on top. You will place the size minus 2 coals on the bottom, or 10. That will usually heat the Dutch oven to 350 degrees."

"If you turn to the back of your book, in the appendix, there is a chart that shows the temperatures for the 12-inch Dutch oven. Know that this table is not exact, but will help in determining correct cooking temperatures when cooking."

James pulled out his book and opened to the page.

Oven Temperature	Coals Top	Coals Bottom
325	12	8
350	14	10
375	17	12
400	19	12
425	21	14
450	23	14

As he looked at his book, Master Rossi explained how the chart worked and what was the usual temperature for different foods. She then reassured them that most cooking would happen at 350 degrees.

She then had them turn to page 46 and she showed them how to read the recipe and start the meal cooking.

Mountain Man Breakfast

24 eggs
1-2 pounds Sausage or Bacon
2 pounds (1 package) shredded hash browns
1 can condensed cream of mushroom soup (optional)
Bell peppers chopped or onions chopped can be added (optional)
Shredded cheese

Heat the Dutch oven to 350 degrees and brown the sausage or bacon in the bottom of the oven. Pour all the hash browns into the oven and pour the cracked eggs over the top. Add the soup if desired. Add peppers of onions if desired. Stir to ensure the bacon or sausage doesn't remain on the bottom of the Dutch oven. Then close the lid. After completed cooking, sprinkle shredded cheese over top and allow to melt. Serve.

She carefully walked them through the recipe and prepared it right before their eyes. James couldn't wait to taste it, as this sounded like something he would really like.

Once the Dutch oven was filled with food and the content was stirred, Master Rossi placed it on the 10 coals arranged in a circle, and then added 14 coals to the top lid around the outer boarder. James watched very carefully and was reminded of his father cooking Dutch oven in their backyard. He was wishing at this moment that he had been paying more attention while Dad was cooking.

At that thought, they were all released to head to the next class. James was distracted walking himself through the recipe again. This is one he wanted to remember and try. His dad had mentioned Mountain Man Breakfast before, but never cooked it for him. At meal time, he would be looking for the table at the back of the room where they could all have some.

As he walked from the class, he was still imagining what that combination would taste like.

CHAPTER 16
IF YE ARE PREPARED YE SHALL NOT FEAR

The rest of the day had been uneventful other than multiple encounters in all their classes with the new redheaded student. James wasn't sure why he knew her, but he started to definitely recognize her. His questions were answered quickly, however, when they were asked by Master Belle to concentrate on communicating with a family member in their Basic Communication class. Many students were seen writing letters, some were even making plans to make phone calls home using the phones or computers in camp. But others were sitting with their eyes closed concentrating on using their Titan skills of Telepathy.

It was at this point that James closed his eyes, forgetting about the new student and started thinking about his father...

He was blindfolded again, but Camilla was underestimating his senses once again. He had already seen everyone, recognized their voices and even knew the sound of their walk, their breathing and even their way of moving. Although he couldn't see, he knew everything about what was going on around him, who was there and where they were.

Based on the very humid climate, and the roaring waterfalls heard in the distance, he recognized their location as the eastern shores of Iguazu Falls. They were located in a large army style tent with two large central poles and doors on either side. He could hear the fabric moving slowly in the wind. There was a table by the east door, with two individuals sitting in fabric camping chairs. Camilla was not in the room at the moment, as he could hear her in the tent 100 yards away to the west, one of 6 large tents setup in the dense forested area. The two at the table were Minerva Medusa or Minnie as they liked to call her and Adam Kane, his guard over the last several weeks.

As he concentrated on the table, he noticed multiple books on the table, including The Book of Adam, with Camilla's name embossed on the front. This was the book she received when she turned 12, but the last name "Adamson" had been scratched off the leather cover. It was opened to Chapter 9 and they were reading aloud from the pages on The Gift of Orientopathy.

He absolutely loved the way Julianna had updated that chapter in the most recent edition of the book. She had interviewed him 4 years ago to write portions of it. But as he listened to Minnie read he knew they were searching for increased knowledge on his personal abilities.

"I wish Zoram was here. Simon is one of the best Orientopaths and we need to know if he has the ability to not just find our exact location but share the information with others." Minnie's voice sounded a little irritated with a hint of worry. "And can Doc McAdams access his mind?"

"Camilla has guaranteed that Doc has been unable to find him. Doc has been trying, but she has blocked his access to Simon's mind constantly since we kidnapped him." Adam reassured her, with great confidence and power in his voice. "Besides, I would love to have The Band of Fire come after us. This new bow of mine would love some practice."

Distracted by their reading and speaking, Simon had failed to feel the bow sitting on the table next to Adam. It was a large, compound style bow, mad of a composite metal and fiberglass. It was actually one of a kind in design and must have been designed

*and made by Adam. It appeared to have the ability to shoot mul-
tiple arrows at a time and based on the tension of the strings could
probably guarantee accuracy for 200 – 300 yards. If only there was
a way he could warn Doc and the others, but he has never been
successful at Telepathy, and even if he was, Camilla had John Vali
monitoring his mind.*

*It was at that point that he heard John on the opposite side of
the tent sitting in a camp chair, arms folded across his chest and
looking directly at Simon. "You are right Simon! Nobody can enter
your mind without me knowing it and your inability to communicate telepathically makes it even easier for me to block any such
communication. Nobody is strong enough to get past Camilla and
I together."*

*As his voice trailed off, Simon could feel the large smile on his
face. John was a black man, 5'4" tall with short, curly black hair,
dark brown eyes, and glasses. He had a strong build, but was not
an intimidating figure at all. His telepathic powers were not as
impressive as Simon was used to, but he was married to Aria for
several years and she was the best.*

*As he finished his thought, Camilla walked into the east door
of the tent and John stood to greet her.*

*"John, I need a report on Zoram and Elli. Are they integrated
into the camp? Does Doc suspect anything?"*

*"As I searched Doc's mind, he was relieved to have Zoram come
to teach the Orientopathy class. He feels he has more important
things to do than help with the instruction."*

*"Of course. He needs to ensure students are limited in their
development to their curriculum." Camilla said with laughter in
her voice.*

*"And Elli has been accepted into the Minataur patrol. But she
has asked about your brother. He is as camp this year."*

*"James? Oh, yes, I forgot that he is 12 now. Time flies when
your kidnapping worthless fathers to keep them from influencing
their new Titan son." she said with a smiling glance at Simon. "And
why is he blindfolded? His abilities to know where we are, who
is here, and what is happening around him is acutely developed. I
only wish Zoram was as skilled!"*

With that compliment, Simon noticed he was sitting on the hard ground, but sensed multiple chairs spread throughout the room and a cot about 2 feet to his left where he had slept last night. Yes, he knew exactly where he was with or without the blindfold. And he even knew exactly where every individual was standing in camp. There was a noticeable absence of Zoram and Elli.

Minnie immediately rose and walked toward Camilla. "I feel better with him blindfolded. I don't like seeing his eyes, don't like having him watch me. He seems to look right through me when he looks at me. But the real reason is that I recognize my father's hatred in those eyes. If you want me to not kill him, he will need to be blindfolded in my presence." the anger and hatred in her voice was unmistakable.

To that Camilla started laughing. "Oh, that makes sense. You are having pity on him. Well, there will come a time when I will remove the blindfold and allow you the privilege. For now, I want him alive."

The vision faded as James heart was beating out of his chest. He was no longer sitting on the stool he had been on in the class, but was laying on his back look up at Master Belle, Michael, Bekah and Kari.

"Are you okay James?" Master Belle asked carefully. "What were you seeing? I couldn't get into your mind. I was being blocked. What's happening? Why were you on the ground?"

"Not exactly sure ma'am." James lied. "Can I go speak with Master Doc McAdams? I have been having these fainting spells since getting to camp. I want to know if he thinks they may be related to the classification test he put me through."

Master Belle smiled suspiciously again and agreed, "That would be fine. I will let him know you are coming. He is currently in his cabin."

Bekah, Kari and Michael all looked at James, but he did not return their gaze, he just turned and walked out. He even felt Bekah trying to enter his mind to talk, but he blocked any access and was a little surprised that he could. He knew he would have to explain to her later, but it was very important that Master Belle not know any more than she now did about what he was thinking.

James walked away from the class and out of the beautiful cabin, not even looking back. He needed to talk with Master Doc McAdams and get his insights and help. James was hoping he would know what to do.

Immediately upon leaving sight of the others, he ran to Master McAdams' cabin. This was very important. As he raced to the cabin, he was hoping that Master McAdams was there and that it wouldn't be too much of a surprise for him to arrive instead of attending class. These concerns were alleviated, however, when he arrived at the cabin door and it opened without James even knocking.

"Come in my boy. I have been waiting for you. Master Belle sent ahead that you would be coming. Besides, I have been watching you since you came to camp."

As James entered, he saw the characteristic smile and deep blue eyes looking intently at him.

"So, what brings you here? We know it isn't the fainting spells you claim to be having because you know what those are." Again, he stopped with a smile.

"I missed Helia the other night on my midnight run. She is always a joy to have around and she and Felicity have become fast friends. You know that phoenix are great judges of character, right?"

"Wait. Helia is with you when she goes out at night?"

"Yes. I love those midnight runs. I learned while I was here as a student that midnight is the BEST time to be alone with your thoughts or even better, to develop your concordant skills. Especially if you can get to a cave or other specialized structure that limits the prying eyes or minds of other teachers here. It was the only way I could develop my skills when they were worried about my growing strength."

"I have wondered where she was going and when she sleeps."

"Well, you have a lot to learn about phoenix." Master McAdams said with a smile. "Phoenix thrive in night and gain strength and even rest through flight. The cool night air seems to augment the fire within and produces greater rejuvenation for the phoenix fire than any sleep could ever do. Having them with me at night seems to give me the same strength and power. As I learn to harness their healing power, I need less sleep and can accomplish more throughout the night. That is why they produce light in the darkness. That very light has rejuvenating power for the mind and body of any in their presence."

James wanted him to continue, but he stopped suddenly. "But that is not why you are here. James, my boy, what can I do for you? How can I help you this fine day?"

Immediately his mind started to race through the vision he just had, as if in fast forward. He saw Minnie and Adam sitting at the table, his father on the floor, Camilla coming into the tent and everything seemed to repeat at a very high rate of speed. Before he could start talking about what he had seen (and was seeing again very quickly), Master Doc McAdams started speaking.

"I know about the *Order of the Kraken*." he said with a slight twinkle in his deep blue eyes. "And there is more to the Camilla story than you yet know. As for Minerva Madsen, she's planning to sneak into camp this summer, something we are on the lookout for. Adam is a very talented Titan, but his parents have never forgiven me for expelling his older brother for killing the wolf separating the girl's and boy's tents in the Centaur camp. He is currently in prison for attacking a police officer that same summer when he was pulled over in a traffic stop. John has been searching my mind and is getting whatever information I want him to have. Camilla has always underestimated my abilities, but my dear friend Aria taught me well when I was a student. Even Camilla is not as talented in Telepathy as her amazing mother was."

"But Master McAdams, I am worried about Elli and Zoram. They have infiltrated the camp and think they have you fooled."

"Yes. I know about them as well. It is important that they are here right now and think they are here unrecognized. As long as they are in camp, we have a direct connection to Camilla and the Order."

"But they want to teach things in a different way and draw students to join their order instead of staying with *The Band of Fire*."

"Let me tell you a story…" as Master McAdams paused, James realized another lesson was about to be shared.

"There is a story I was told when I was just a young Titan. A farmer was getting old and was having a hard time keeping up with the farm since his children had moved away. He had worked the farm his whole life, but now the work was too much for an old man by himself. As he discussed the problem with his wife, they both felt that with the children all moved away, it was important that he find some help. So, he left his wife on the farm that morning and went into town to sell his crops, but also to find an individual to help him with the work. As he arrived at town, he was looking for help, but not many individuals were interested. As he asked around, the baker recommended he ask the young man working cleaning the street. The farmer thought he looked a little young, but decided to ask him some questions."

"'Well, young man, I am looking for help on my farm and would be interested in hiring you. Why would you be a good farmhand for me?'"

"The young man smiled and responded, 'I can sleep through the night!' The farmer looked at the boy in surprise and decided the answer didn't make any sense. He walked away and began to look for anyone else to hire. When no one was available, he decided to offer the young man a job. He could tell he was a hard worker, just a little eccentric with his answers to the questions asked. But he really needed help."

"Over the next several weeks, they never talked again about the answer the young man gave to the old farmer's question. In fact, the farmer didn't even think about it. The young man was, however, a very impressive worker and was very good at helping around the farm. After weeks of work, the farmer continued to talk to his wife about how great this young man was. 'I couldn't ask for a better worker. He is an amazing help!'"

"That very night, as the farmer was awakened from sleep with the howling wind outside. He sat up in bed with a start and knew he needed to get up. Hopefully the young man heard it too and would join him outside. There is always lots of work to do before a major storm like what was coming."

"He ran from his bed and raced outside to find the young man nowhere to be seen. He would have to talk with him in the morning, because the storm could be seen in the distance and there was no time to go get him. His biggest concern was the animals. If they got out in the storm they would be injured and probably lost to the farm. He ran to the barn to secure the animals first. As he reached the barn, he noticed all the animals were inside the barn and the barn doors were not just closed but were also secured. A wooden log was even propped against the door to ensure it didn't blow open and the gate from the pasture was tied closed with a rope.

"'That is interesting. I don't usually do that at night.'"

"He then ran around the barn to the hay. Since the animals were okay, he wanted to ensure the hay didn't blow away are get destroyed in the rain. As he reached the haystack, the hay was all carefully stacked against the back wall of the barn and a large tarp had been placed over the hay and secured in place with ropes that were staked down. The tarp was so secure, that there was no possible way for the hay to be harmed in the storm. The framer was dumbfounded."

"As he thought about what he had seen, he moved a little slower now and headed to the orchard portion of the farm. He had new small trees that they planted this year. He knew they were not yet strong enough to weather the storm. As he approached the trees, however, he noticed strong metal stakes on either side of the trees, with bands used to prop up the tree in the wind. Even these trees were already secured for the weather."

"He turned to the corn in the garden and noticed rock walls propped up to slow the wind from the east. He saw the tomato cages staked down with ropes to ensure they stayed standing. He saw the dog's home staked down and turned to protect the opening from the wind, with a small tarp covering the door to keep out the rain. He then turned to notice all the tools had been put away. The shutters on the farmhouse were even tied back to reduce the rattle in the wind. Everything really was prepared for the storm."

"He slowly walked back to his house with all worries gone. The storm could come and he would be able to sleep without a worry. Just then the young man's words returned to his mind, 'I can sleep through the night!' 'Well, yes he can. Now I will sleep through the night too.' With that he slid off his boots and changed back into his night clothes and climbed into bed. The old farmer had never slept so good through the night as he did the rest of that night."

"James, my boy, please trust me. Even with Zoram and Elli here in camp and Minerva trying to sneak in, I can sleep through the night. May I suggest you find a way so that you can sleep through the night as well!"

With that, Master McAdams recommended he return to class and promised to keep in touch. He also encouraged him to be mindful of any instruction he could get from Helia. His words echoed in James' mind throughout the rest of the day, "Trust her and let her help you become who I know you can be!"

After a few more classes that day, with James distracted throughout and Bekah a little irritated at James for his distraction, they were released to dinner in the Great Hall. James wasn't even hungry again but figured Bekah would be even more irritated with him if he skipped another meal. She was so like his mother and wanted him to eat well every day. He could even see the joy in her eyes when he agreed to go with them to dinner, since he was missing dinner almost every other day right now.

The Great Hall was bustling and the teacher were all at the head table as usual. Master McAdams, however, was not there, but was walking around the hall talking with students. Often during meals, he would go from patrol to patrol, table to table, seeing how everyone was doing at camp. He seemed to relish this interaction with the young Titans. Sometimes during meals, he would even sit with students and eat his meal while talking with them. James thought this may be one of those days. He was really surprised, however, when Master McAdams walked up to Bekah and asked if he could join them at their table.

"Well sir, it would be our pleasure." she said in a rapid, high pitched voice. Her excitement oozed from every word. Kari's eyes grew large with surprise, and James could sense almost a fear in her.

"My dear Kari," Master McAdams started, "I have been dying to talk with you. I have great respect for the work of your father. He was one of the great ones! His undercover work with gangs and his fight against gang violence is very well known."

"He was Natural Born sir. How do you know about him?"

"You don't need to be a Titan to be a hero! Your father is one of my heroes, because he stood up for truth and righteousness. I hope to help all you Titans have the same ability to stand up when the time comes." James could feel the pride rising up in Kari's heart. Master McAdams was truly a master at working with people. Why did he fail so completely with Camilla?

Doc McAdams looked over at James with a smile and continued, "And Michael, I am very impressed with your ability in Orientopathy. Rarely have I seen one so skilled at an early age. You remind me of my good friend who attended camp with me many years ago, Simon Adamson."

"You knew him when he was a student? Was he always such a good Orientopath?"

"Nobody starts out with all the skills, but he loved to play games. His ability to turn using his skills into a game became very helpful for the rest of us in at least improving our abilities in Orientopathy and other Titan skills."

James could now feel Bekah almost asking for attention, a sensation apparently not lost on Master McAdams. "Now Bekah, you are James' best friend, right?" James saw pride rise up in Bekah's eyes, but before she could answer Master McAdams continued, " I need you to help him develop his skills as a Concordant. Even though we no longer frown on the classification of Concordant, it is still a very dangerous designation if not developed properly. I need you, with your special knowledge and skills, to prepare him for a rainy day, prepare him for whatever storm may be coming in his future. We all run into storms, and I am sure James will have his share of storms coming his way."

The conversations continued for a few minutes as he asked each of them about themselves, their families and how camp was going. James noticed he focused on each of the three as they talked, but he only talked to James in passing. Although he was not sure why, he was impressed all the same with his ability to talk with and listen to the others. This was another skill James was going to need to develop if he wanted to be a successful Concordant like Master Doc McAdams!

As the meal concluded and the conversation was brought to a close, Master Doc McAdams excused himself and went to the head table again. There he stood and called everyone's attention to him and he began to speak.

"I have many responsibilities here at camp. Since camp started this year, I have been unable to be of assistance to each of you as I so desire. In fact, I have been very busy and almost distracted teaching Orientopathy classes and even map and compass classes. I love to teach! I love working so closely with each of you, but that is not where you need me. I am therefore excited to announce that we have hired a teacher for the Orientopathy class until Simon Adamson is able to return. May I introduce to you Master Zoram Balthizar."

A 5'8" dark skinned man with brownish-yellow eyes stood to Master McAdams far left. He had broad shoulders, strong arm, strong hands and long brown hair down to his back and a long brown, fluffy beard and mustache. James immediately recognized him and knew he had seen him before.

"Thank you, Master Doc McAdams. It is my privilege to be here to help train our young Titans. And a special thanks for allowing my daughter Elli to join the Minotaur Patrol without an invitation. Many of you know that we only invite 12 Titans each year, the 'cream of the crop', to join *The Band of*

Titans. Thanks for letting Elli be number 13 this year. She has enjoyed greatly already her time here. We won't let you down."

He then sat down and Master McAdams stood again to excuse each patrol table by table to return to their camps. They were given the rest of the evening off to visit as patrols, catch up on studies and prepare for the *Primary Patrol Challenge* that would be happening this next week. James didn't know much about this challenge but knew Bekah could fill him in when they got to camp.

CHAPTER 17
MIDNIGHT BREAKS

As James walked into camp, several steps behind Bekah who was still slightly angry at him, he saw the tall figure of Angelica rushing towards them. She was obviously excited and had some information to share. James liked her tan skin, dark blue eyes and curly black hair and he loved how kind she always was to them.

"James, Michael, Bekah and Kari, I've been given the task to introduce the *Primary Patrol Challenge* to you as first years. The challenges are always some of the best parts of camp but are very difficult for first years. The good news, we do most of these challenges as an entire patrol. The Primary Challenge is done by each age group and all scores added together by patrol. Our patrol has won this *Primary Challenge* the last 2 years, but a very talented Chronopath graduated. Do you know what the first challenge is?"

As she looked around, Bekah was nodding her head while the other three were looking dumbfounded.

"Well, our instruction is to help you know where to find the information and not give you all the information. The purpose of the challenges are to improve your skills more quickly by requiring you to function. Part of functioning is reading Chapter 17 from *The Book of Adam* on the challenges and what they include. Bekah, as usual, might be able to help you a little more. Please prepare, because we need you to succeed in this challenge. Our patrol is depending on your score to win again this year."

She then raced away and James turned to Bekah.

"You know what the challenge is right?"

"Oh, so now I'm your friend again? You were too important earlier today to let even me into your mind to know what was going on in *Orientopathy* class."

James' face turned a little red as he began to explain, "I couldn't risk Master Belle seeing what I was thinking or doing. I didn't even know I was able to block you from entering my mind, I just thought it might be safer."

Bekah's face softened and she turned to look at Kari and Michael, "James has visions, or should I say flashes into his father's mind and is seeing much more than what is going on here in camp. We are starting a special study group and need you two to join us. Master McAdams has challenged me to improve James' skills and in his arrogance," Bekah turned to look at James, "James will need all of us. He is Concordant, but he is not yet as skilled as he should be. Are you two interested?"

Kari looked very pleased, "You would include me? What do I have to offer?"

Michael didn't seem so sure and stayed quiet.

James interrupted, "Bekah is exactly right. This is what the Phoenixenses group is for. Each of us has our individual skills, our special talents, ways that we learn. If we work together, we will all be more skilled and more prepared for whatever may come. Can I tell you a story Master McAdams told me when I left class earlier today?" He then proceeded to share the story from Master McAdams.

As he finished the story, Bekah seemed a little more forgiving and excitement was creeping into her voice as the pitch raised slightly and the speed increased, "What exactly are we preparing for?"

"I don't exactly know. But I do know that *The Order of the Kraken* are preparing for something. Master Balthizar is a member of that order and is here to teach us as they would. Even his daughter is a member of the order and is most likely NOT 12 years-old."

"*The Order of the Kraken*?" Kari asked startled.

"That is a counterfeit *Band of Fire* that is trying to seduce Titans to fight against Master Doc McAdams and the leaders of *The Band of Fire*. My father is one tasked with keeping track of Camilla Adamson and her group." Michael mumbled almost under his breath, as he shot a glance at James.

James looked at Michael in surprise but didn't ask any additional questions. "Exactly! *The Order of the Kraken* have kidnapped my father, have sent Master Balthizar and Elli to join the camp here and are trying to sneak in with other members. Master McAdams seemed to be encouraging us to get prepared so that we don't need to fear them."

Bekah began to speak again, and her excitement was almost palpable in her high-pitched voice, rapid rate of speech and physical bouncing because she couldn't stand still. "We will do it tonight. We can go to the cave we found the other day."

"Master McAdams says he goes running at midnight because there are no prying eyes or other teachers to see what he is doing. I think we should go at that same time when all the other students and teachers are asleep. I will be bringing Helia, and you can bring your companions if so desired." James finished speaking and they all headed to their tents. James had completely forgotten to ask Bekah more about the challenges.

As James and Michael entered the tent, Michael grabbed James and urgently started speaking, "James. As much as I would like to be part of your training tonight and from here on out, I am not sure I would be of any help to you. I may be a problem for the group."

He grew silent as James looked at him. Before Michael could say more, a vision began to open to James' mind. Michael seemed relieved that he would not need to say any more.

James found himself in a green grass field, looking almost like a large garden, with a unique three-story home behind him. James quickly recognized Michael blindfolded in the field and heard voices in the distance. As he thought about the voices, he was immediately taken to a grove of trees at the far west border of the field where two tall, even lanky individuals with blond almost white hair and distinctive green eyes sat talking. They were obviously twins even with one being male and the other female. They were also obviously Michael's siblings as they both looked like him. They were talking and the girl's voice rang out first:

"I think Camilla Adamson is a very talented Titan. I consider her a friend. Why do you have a problem with her?"

"Don't you see? She has no respect for authority and seems to even question Master McAdams and all he's doing. If you allow her to influence you, we may have troubles in the future."

"She's still just a kid. She is learning so much and will be a great help to me as I strive to strengthen my Chronopathy."

"She doesn't want to help you. She wants to use you! Everything is about her since her mother died. She's even talking about how she hates her father. You have met Master Adamson and know he is definitely a good person. Do you believe everything she's saying about him?"

"I know that Camilla has treated me better than anyone else at camp! Why do you dislike her so?" She turned and started to walk away.

"I love you Sis! I'm just worried about the rumors we are hearing around camp about a new Band or should I say a 'New Order' that she's forming. Especially now that she spends most of her time with Minnie."

"I promise I will be careful." She said as she turned back to look at him. "I just don't have many friends at camp and I need help with my Chronopathy."

The vision faded and changed to a new location, a large living room with light tan carpet, family pictures on the wall and two couches. Michael was nowhere to be seen, but two adults sat on the larger couch talking. The family picture behind them was obviously

Michael's family as he saw a younger Michael in the picture. These two adults were obviously his parents.

"Doc McAdams has asked me to find out anything I can about Camilla Adamson." the man said.

"She is Amanda's friend. Should we really be spying on her?"

"I trust Doc and know there must be something going on if he wants us to watch her."

"I can't help you in this! I don't want to chase Amanda away because she feels we don't trust her."

"I understand, but you need to know that Camilla is suspected of some very dangerous and illicit activities. Minerva, her other friend, was expelled from Camp today for causing the wolves to attack students that disagreed with her in one class. They were seriously hurt, and the poor wolf was released from employ at the camp for allowing her to control him."

"I didn't hear about that. Is Amanda okay?"

"Doc said she saw it all happen, but he couldn't tell me more."

"I will contact her. Thank goodness I have Telepathy as mail and phone would be too slow."

The vision faded and Michael sat there dumbfounded at what had just happened.

"My mom is a Telepath and she has never done that to me before."

"I am so sorry. I don't yet have control of this, but it's very important information. Is your sister part of *The Order of the Kraken?*"

"No. Camilla left without inviting her, but she still considers Camilla her best friends. She keeps telling my Dad that Doc has misjudged her."

"All I know is that she has kidnapped my Dad and is making plans to disrupt us even here at camp."

"I agree that Amanda is wrong. I just worry that this connection to Camilla will hurt you if I am part of your group. If Amanda finds out, Camilla will know!"

"I need you Michael! Your knowledge will be invaluable and your abilities will just make us better. I also have a connection to Camilla. We can use these connections for our benefit."

Michael just nodded silently, and James knew the group was still four. "This will be a good place to start!" he thought.

After a period of silence, Michael walked out of the tent and was gone. James began to get nervous. He didn't know what the "meetings" were supposed to entail. The last time in the cave was handled by Helia.

"That's it! Helia." He turned to look at her and saw the beautiful phoenix fly to his bed with a book, and he immediately knew what book it was. He would read about the original meetings of the Phoenixenses and use them as his example. Maybe then he would know what to do in these meetings.

As James read, time seemed to fly by. It went so fast and he didn't even feel tired. As he finished his read and had a good idea how their first meeting would go, Michael came walking back into the tent.

"I talked with my mother and she thinks that I should help you. I consider it a privilege to be asked to join you in this group." Michael said quietly.

"Thanks. I can't do this without you!"

Just then James heard Bekah in his mind. "Are you coming or do we have to wait till exactly midnight?"

James just smiled, and he and Michael walked out of the tent to join Bekah and Kari.

They walked to the cave in silence, but Helia singing overhead kept James thinking about the pages he had just read. He barely even looked around as he headed straight for the cave. Too much had happened today and there was much to think about. This group of four was far more tied together than even he thought.

They walked down the overgrown path and again came to the large hill with thick overgrowth blocking access to the base of the hill. James walked right to the path and Helia and Fenwick both flew in the opening. Bekah and Michael followed, Bekah holding Tom, her green and black tortoise. At that moment, James noticed Kari stopped and turned to Jack, her wolfdog.

"I need to do this! Can you help me?"

Jack walked to her side and she got down on all fours, closed her eyes and grabbed a handful of hair. Jack walked through the opening with Kari crawling with him eyes still closed. Her courage was inspiring to James as he knew how hard that really was for her. Without delay, he likewise crawled in.

The soft red glow of Helia lit the walls as before, but the lantern Bekah had brought reflected the light in all directions and the large room became as bright as noon day sun. Because of the reflecting light off all the walls and ceiling, the darkness was completely dissipated in the cave. Kari and Michael were obviously impressed.

James looked around again and was again surprised that this room was much larger than the great hall and had crystalline rock lining the walls and ceilings. There were no stalactites or stalagmites and no passageways coming off the large room where they stood. And there was absolutely no sound from the outside heard in that room. Helia, however, was still singing and the sound reverberated from all sides. The peaceful sound seemed to penetrate every ounce of their beings and then everything began to fade and James knew what was happening…

They found themselves all looking at each other from one wall in the exact same cave with a propane lantern lit in the center of the cave. There were 14 other individuals in the cave, all youth dressed as if they were from many years earlier. James recognized what was happening and explained.

"We are seeing the first official meeting of the Phoenixenses when Master Doc McAdams had started it. The young man at the front is Doc McAdams. We should probably move forward and listen to the instruction."

"Welcome to our very first meeting." Doc started. "We are gathered here as 14 individuals, some of the most developed Titans here at camp this year. Each of you have been invited for one reason, because of your abilities in one of the seven Titan skills. For each skill, we have two Titans in the group with variations on the skill they have. Our goal as Phoenixenses is to develop the other 12 Titans in the particular skill you are personally best at. What tricks do you use? What games do you play using your skills? How

can each of us improve our understanding of the skill and possibly even develop our rudimentary ability in that skill. It is my belief and understanding that each of us can develop other Titan skills if given the instruction and learning necessary. Here at camp they are limiting us to developing our Primary skill only. I would like to develop the other skills that may be mine and help you do the same."

A young man stood from the right side and moved forward. He was slightly shorter than Doc and stood with blond hair and deep brown eyes. James immediately recognized him as his father, although much younger than any picture he had seen and without the distinct scar under his left eye. Simon, James' father, began to speak.

"I stand here with Doc and reaffirm our commitment as a group, as Phoenixenses, to expand our skills—All our skills—to better serve each other, the Titan community and the world. I would invite Aria, the brains behind this plan, to explain our proposed organization and processes for the meetings from here on out. I am excited about what I can learn from each of you."

A beautiful, lightly tanned, petite woman with thick, long blond hair and deep blue eyes stood and walked forward. As she began to speak in her soft, high pitched voice, the words seemed to flow through everyone in the room. James immediately recognized this as telepathic speaking or the union of oral speech and telepathy. Bekah began to bounce with excitement as she realized "who" this was.

Aria began to speak, "Thank you Simon. In organizing the Phoenixenses, each of you were carefully chosen for your special abilities and strengths. Therefore, each of you will be given a night to share your abilities and tricks in your Titan skill. That means that initially we will have two nights for every skill and then adjust the schedule as needs arise. I am so excited, for example, to learn from my Telepathy Brother, Hans. I can learn so much from you and hope I can likewise teach you."

She paused before continuing as everyone started whispering and looking around.

"We will therefore proceed in this order." And she held up an 8 X 10 yellow sheet of paper.

"Please be prepared at our nightly meetings for your instruction assignment!"

Preliminary Schedule:

- *Aria Thorngardner (Telepathy)*
- *Simon John Adamson (Orientopathy)*
- *Julianna Gaea Abel (Chronopathy)*
- *Docery McAdams (Hoplonosmithy)*
- *Dakota Ironhorse (Hippocratesense)*
- *James William Enloe (Herculopathy)*
- *Zena Smith (Zoonophonia)*
- *Hans Christian Bruun (Telepathy)*
- *Ruby Allen Seenox (Orientopathy)*
- *Jens Christensen (Chronopathy)*
- *Logan Montgomery (Hoplonosmithy)*
- *Mabel J Wood (Hippocratesense)*
- *Cornelia C Sampson (Herculopathy)*
- *Alice Magan Davenport (Zoonophonia)*

Doc then walked forward and began to speak.

"We will start as outlined tonight with Aria. We will then have three meetings a week precisely at midnight, so that we have plenty of time to receive instruction. We will then determine at the completion of the schedule what additional instruction is important or necessary. Our hope is to develop a strong team, a group that can further improve the abilities of The Band of Fire and Titans in the world. Aria, thanks for your willingness to be the first."

The vision faded, and the four students lay on the ground looking at each other. Kari appeared a little startled and Michael just looked excited. Before any of them could speak, however, a voice echoed through the cave and Bekah's eyes grew large with wonder.

"You...can...not...do...this...without...help....What... do...you...know...about...the...skills...of...Chronopathy,... Hippocratesense,...Herculopathy,... and...Hoplonosmithy?"

As the words paused, a song began to echo through the cave. "You cannot do this all alone, as others you must find. To become, together you must all be."

As the music continued, but the words stopped, James crawled to his feet and began to look around.

"This cave is most unique." Bekah said as she too arose. "But Tom and Helia are correct, we must find others to truly become Phoenixenses."

"Ryan is a Herculopath. He would be a great addition to this group." Kari said with excitement in her voice and a large smile on her face.

James chuckled to himself, wondering if Ryan would even be interested.

"I think we invite Emma and Lizzy as well." Michael broke in. "Lizzy is amazing, from what I have seen, in Hoplonosmithy and I think Emma is a Chronopath."

"The last addition should be a Hippocratesent. Maybe we should invite Angelica." Bekah said in her high pitched, rapid tone exhibiting significant excitement. "Then we will have a quorum and James can assist in all the instruction as a Concordant."

"That sounds like we all have assignments. If you recommended them, you should invite them." James said. "Our next meeting will be in two days and we need to find all the remaining members of our group by then. Bekah and I will prepare for Telepathy as the first class and then we will go in the same order as the original Phoenixenses."

The music then became words once again and the cave faded from view...

"I solemnly covenant my brothers and sisters of Fire to do my Duty to God, to serve others with all my heart, to stand as a witness of faith, knowledge and strength, to use my gifts to protect freedom, happiness and independence for all, to lift the weak, to comfort the sad and to befriend the friendless. That I may by so doing stand against evil in all its various forms. To this I pledge my sacred honor."

The words rang through the cave as they all again saw the group of 14 standing in a circle with their hands to the square finish the oath.

"And as Phoenixenses, we will uphold these values in exactness and honor. For God Himself shall hold us accountable to bless and serve others throughout our lives!"

Doc McAdams words then faded as the brightness of the cave returned.

James took the cue and invited them to all stand and together make the Oath of Fire and finish with the phrase from Doc McAdams that continued to ring through the cave as they spoke. Bekah carefully wrote the words down as they prepared to leave and placed them in her pack. It was time to return home, as there was much to do over the next two days.

CHAPTER 18
THE OTHER SIDE OF CONCORDANCE

Doc sat silently at his desk as words raced from his pen onto the page. Rarely did words flow from his hand as they did at this time. His mind was racing and his thoughts were somewhat scrambled. His furrowed brow sat over distant eyes reaching back into his memories. These thoughts were most important, but he couldn't work them out completely. And then the memory came back more quickly...

"Doc, you are giving her too much credit. She is still just a kid and doesn't have control over her Concordant abilities. Should we not be using more caution with her?"

Doc looked over at Simon as he finished speaking. "She is eleven years old. We know how powerful she already is! I want to help her develop correctly, especially with all the evil influences in the world. She may be key to The Band of Fire in the future."

A thin, petite blond woman stepped forward and began speaking, "Simon, I agree wholeheartedly with Doc here. She is not unlike us when we first organized the Phoenixenses. I know her better than anyone as her mother. In fact, I know her thoughts, her feelings and her desires. If we don't help her develop she will find another way."

At Aria's words, Doc looked startled. "What other way is she considering?"

Aria continued, "She's not considering. She doesn't yet know that other options exist, but I am worried about Ariana Stults who is seeking after young Titans around the world. She has been seeking revenge on all of us since the battle where Hans Christian Bruun defeated her husband."

"Ariana Stults hasn't been seen for many years! I don't think she is of any concern anymore to any of us now that Hans has been killed." Simon said adamantly.

"You have ALWAYS underestimated and discounted my abilities Simon! I know she is around. I hear her and feel her."

As the tensions rose, Doc jumped in. "You both have valid points, but I too am skilled in Telepathy. Although I don't have the advantage of the family connection, and Camilla is already a master, thanks to you," he looked at Aria, "at blocking unwanted intrusion into her mind, I know her desires to learn. I feel we must help her learn."

"Do I have a say in this?" Simon asked somewhat irritated.

"Well, since Aria is the legal guardian you do not. She has full authority to give permission without your approval. That being said, I want the approval from both of you if possible."

Doc found himself again at the table continuing to write. "Now what was the rest of the story?" he thought carefully.

"I must forbid this contact from continuing. She is now my responsibility with Aria dead."

Doc looked sad but didn't argue.

"I have long felt it a mistake to train her even before she is 12 years old. The Band of Fire has long felt we should wait until that age to start teaching. I likewise will not be encouraging any learning until her 12ᵗʰ birthday."

"Remember Simon. The Band of Fire didn't want any of us to learn more than a single Titan skill for many years. It was for this reason we convened the Phoenixenses and had our midnight meetings. You may not truly understand what it means to be Concordant. She needs direction and help developing. I am well equipped to help her."

"It cannot and will not happen in my home." Simon walked out of the cabin and slammed the door.

"I pray this isn't a mistake. I have seen this before and it always ends up badly." Doc said to Felicity as she sang softly in the background. "I must keep an eye on her. That shall be YOUR assignment."

Felicity bowed slightly and then spread her wings and flew off through the open window.

James again woke tangled in his sleeping bag with Helia absent from her cage. Michael was still breathing loudly across the tent and the darkness was still thick around them. James looked down at his watch and realized it was only 3am but sleep had left him. He, therefore, crawled out of his bed and lit his small lantern and grabbed the book sitting next to his bed.

"To be Concordant is not a gift and often not even a blessing. To be Concordant is often a great trial, and even a curse, for never again will individuals treat you the same. Never again will you be limited by what you see and what you hear. Never again will time matter. Never again will simple relationships develop without your interference. To be Concordant is to function almost as a God in this world. If you don't learn to control every ounce of power you have, the world will beg you to control everything outside of you. Ultimate power will corrupt you and lead to unhappiness and pain."

James paused as he read to let it sink in.

"As a Concordant, the earlier you control your Titan abilities, the more God, the True God, can use you to bless the lives of others and the world all around you. May you seek to serve God and not yourself through these unique abilities."

James set the book down and stood. "Yes, I should have started controlling these powers before now. Did Dad keep me from learning of my skills before 12 also? Is it truly his fault Camilla is on the wrong side, or is it Master McAdams as she thinks?"

James quickly changed his clothes and walked out of the tent without even thinking about where he was headed. His mind was focused on the thoughts and dreams of that night. He couldn't get the thoughts out of his mind and he just walked. No sounds were heard, no thoughts about where he was headed, not even a light to give him direction.

But as he walked and thought, he began to hear the music surrounding him. It was Helia but there was also music from another phoenix. As he realized what was happening, he stopped to find himself again at the cave located in the large hill. As he walked around the overgrowth, he was met by Helia, Felicity and Master Doc McAdams. He looked up to those deep blue eyes as Master McAdams began to speak.

"Well, my boy, you were just here, were you not?"

James nodded silently.

"So, what brings you here now? You should be sleeping in preparation for classes today."

"I can't sleep!"

"Do you have a question, or is it just the dream that is bothering you?"

James looked up startled to a large smile on Master McAdams face.

"You need to know that you are NOT behind. Your abilities are far more developed than you yet know. Your parents developed them indirectly through a new technique we have been testing since even before Camilla. Aria was not fond of the technique, but your father felt it was the ONLY way."

"Why isn't he here? I need my father to help me figure this out. He has never failed to be present when I needed him!" James said with a slight crack in his voice and water welling up in his eyes.

"He lied to me! He promised he would be home for my birthday and now months later he is still not here!"

Master McAdams remained silent.

"I need his help developing my Orientopathy! I need his help overcoming all these questions and concerns about being Concordant. How do I know if I really am, or if I just fake it really well? I can't use any of my skills as well as the other students! Why does my mom have to be Natural Born so that she can't help me?"

James collapsed and sat on the ground not even looking up. He didn't really want an answer, but he knew that one was likely coming.

Master McAdams reached down and lifted James to his feet without saying a word. He took his hand and they were gone....

James felt the time slow down and them race through space and time. He wasn't sure if they were traveling back in time as Master Julianna did or changing locations as the bus driver did. He wasn't even sure if they were just traveling in his mind as they did in The Classification. All he knew is that they were now in a different location.

As the location started to clear, he found himself standing outside his home with darkness still all around him. Master McAdams was no longer anywhere to be seen, and James was surprised to see the lights on in the house. He walked towards the front door and it opened with his mother standing there in her favorite nightgown smiling with a big smile.

"Oh, James, I have missed you!" she said as she ran to him.

"I shouldn't be here. I am supposed to be at camp with the rest of the new Titans. Everyone gets homesick, why am I being treated differently?"

"You are Concordant, like your sister before you. You will always be treated differently!"

"Did you know that I was Concordant?"

"No, but your father suspected it. You have had too many abilities since you were 8 years old."

"But, why did Master McAdams bring me here?"

"Doc asked me, almost two weeks ago, if I would help with your training."

"What? You are Natural Born. How can you help me?"

"You know so little for one so talented." Sarah said with a smile. "You still haven't read Chapter 2 from *The Book of Adam* have you?"

James just shook his head, now a little confused.

"Come inside and we can talk."

After a long hug from mom and a short discussion, James sat down on the couch in the Living Room with an old book. It was thin, probably including only about 30 pages, with no title on the cover, but leather bound in dark well-worn leather. The edges of the leather were torn and the pages were yellowed from the many years. As he opened it to the first page, James could again hear his mother's explanation of the book before handing it to him and going back to bed.

"This is my father's book and his father before him. It was given to my great, great grandfather, Percival Owens from Cornelius Abel. It is a diary of sorts but gives the most complete explanation you will ever get of Titan abilities and traits. Cornelius Abel was Concordant and wrote about it all here. This is now your book, for I have it memorized."

He began to read:

"At a very young age I was recognized as different. I could read people's thoughts, understand their deepest desires and even knew their fears. My best friends were animals, because they never tried to lie to me, tease me or fight with me. Even my parents were nervous around me. I was sent away at a young age to a Boy's Home, but it was never a home. I soon found it to be a prison, a box where I was forced to reside with individuals that despised me, stole from me, beat me (or at least tried, because it never hurt much) and often would punish me for being me. Any animals I liked having around were sent away. My one other friend was adopted out and I was not allowed to participate in any sports because they didn't want me to succeed at anything. I was different, and I never felt safe in those walls. But I knew nothing else, so I couldn't run away. The one advantage I had, was that I always knew when they were coming to be mean to me, to beat me or even to steal from me. I just stayed because I didn't know where to go. I stayed and suffered until one day, when I was sixteen years old I decided to run away forever because I had had enough. It was at that time in 1692, that I entered a town called Salem Village in Massachusetts."

"In Salem Village, I felt I could make for myself a new life. At 16 years-old, I was able to start working with the local blacksmith. He needed an apprentice, and I was very

good with working metal. At that time, I didn't understand how good I really was. Although I learned the art
of shoeing a horse, I became more proficient at making
tools, nails and weapons. Individuals began to come to the
blacksmith shop requesting my felling axe, my broad axe
and my sword. Even the blacksmith noticed my proficiency
in these items and began to raise his prices for my items.
As an apprentice, I was honored by this and didn't realize
that he was taking advantage of me. He treated me good,
compared to my entire life, so I was just happy to be in a
'normal' situation."

"In fact, my situation continued to improve. I even made
friends with some of the high society individuals. The most
notable, a good friend I thought, was Thomas Parris. His
father was basically the Minister of the village and was
content solving the various disputes in the town. That
became a good connection for me and a blessing to the
blacksmith shop where I lived and continued to learn.
That is until Betty, Thomas sister got sick at 9 years old.
Her orphaned cousin Abigail, who was also living in that
home, also got sick and the village doctor, Dr Griggs,
diagnosed them with bewitchment."

"I was very confused at this diagnosis, because I knew
exactly what the doctor was thinking. He had no idea
what was wrong with them! In fact, he was giving that
diagnosis because he didn't want to let the Minister down,
not because he really believed it. I didn't know why I knew
this, but I knew it. When I was close to Betty, I could
tell something was truly wrong. I could hear her heart
beating, could hear her confused thoughts and could sense
abnormal signals happening in her brain. She was having,
what I learned many years later, was a type of localized
seizure in the brain and some asthma that caused her to
bark like a dog. When the minister John Hale agreed with
the doctor's diagnosis, however, there was nothing I could

say to the Minister to get him to understand. He seemed to stop liking me at that time."

"It was at this time that the slave in the home and two other women were accused of witchcraft. When the slave confessed, after being beat for injuring the girls, everyone with 'different' abilities was suspect. Even my skills in the blacksmith shop were under suspicion. The business began to slow down and Master Smith began to ask me to focus on fixing wagon wheels, and similar jobs. I had been called out to an accident, where a wagon wheel had broken when my world changed once again…"

The book faded and James found himself walking down the street in a hurry. He noticed the young man from the old hospital, Cornelius Abel, walking quickly toward an accident in the street. There were several men around a wagon and another young man trapped under the cart. The two-wheeled cart had a broken wheel and was very heavily loaded. Four or five strong men tried to lift the cart off him but were unable.

As they approached, he heard Cornelius exclaim, "Thomas! We have to help him, he is being crushed by that cart! Get it off of him!"

"We have tried young man! What do you think we have been doing here?"

James then saw Cornelius run to the side of the cart and with one hand lift it off of Thomas who the men quickly pulled out from under the broken wheel. As Cornelius put the cart back down, murmuring started all around him. James could see the women talking and could hear their thoughts. They all thought he was a witch!

One of the men walked up to him yelling at him, "How did you do that? You are just a boy! What witchcraft is this? Brother Parris will want to know! Take him now!"

Many men came and tied Cornelius up and took him into a nearby building. It was a hospital of sorts, but not like any hospital James had ever seen. Just then, James recognized the building as the same one from the travel with Master Julianna. Now he knew exactly where he was and he began to look for the black cat that had followed them into the building.

As James got his bearings, he again noticed there were no computers, lighting was from windows only, with what looked like old oil lamps on the wall unlit. Cornelius was sitting on a wooden table and had many women that looked like old-fashioned nurses racing around the room. The small black cat walked over to the corner and was sitting talking to Cornelius in a rapid fashion.

"Cornelius, what have you done? Will you not ever learn? You watched Tituba be accused, beat into a confession and imprisoned. Did you think that your unique abilities would keep you safe? I like my easy life here! Even the food I am given is good in the shop!"

James could then hear Cornelius' response, although he didn't speak. "You worry too much, my friend. They cannot hurt me! They don't yet know the powers that I have. I even know their thoughts."

These words seemed to just aggravate the cat more, but Cornelius started speaking before the cat could respond, "So you think that I am a witch, do you? Well, you need not worry as you are now. I will do you no harm, nor anyone else any harm. I am not sure why you are so worried. All I did was lift the little wagon off the Minister's son. It wasn't that big a deal. He would have died if I hadn't helped!"

"What do you mean? The wagon was fully loaded and was unable to be moved by six of our strongest men in the town. It weighted over 1500 lbs."

"Apparently, they were not the strongest," Cornelius said with a laugh.

"And how do you know what we are thinking. Nobody has the power to read our minds or know what we are worried about."

This again brought a chuckle from Cornelius.

"My body is perfectly healthy! My heart rate is lower than all of you. My lungs are clear, unlike the smoke you have all damaged your lungs with."

At this, James noticed fear in the eyes of the women, but he also sensed the damaged lungs in each of them. He saw in his mind's eye each lung blackened from smoke and saw the small blond nurse with bleeding into her left lung. No, not just bleeding but something growing in her lung. Did she have cancer?

He was quickly drawn back as one of the nurses responded, "Are you threatening us? None of us have any problems with our lungs at this time."

"What about the blood she has been coughing up since Thursday? And the great damage to her left lung?"

The small blond nurse stopped what she was doing and looked up in amazement. "How do you know that? You must be a witch! It is not yet determined what is happening with my lung or why I am coughing up blood since Thursday."

Just then a small, mousey looking man walked into the room and the nurses relieved raced from their presence. His deep black eyes looked cold and uncaring as he looked up at the young man. His high pitched almost whiney voice then rang through the room as he began to speak, "You, my boy, are not welcome here. Your dark magic has been seen before and will be destroyed if you don't leave the town immediately. You will now be escorted to the trials if you don't disappear from this town forever!"

James heard fear in his voice that he didn't notice last time. Then he heard Minister Parris' thoughts, "I am losing control of my ministry. This young man is a danger! A great danger to my son and my daughters! I don't want to know how he does what he does, but I know it can't be from God!"

Just then the black cat began to speak again, "I told you to NOT make fun of them. Now we will have to move again."

Cornelius turned to look at the cat, "You are assuming they will let us leave. He is more worried than you know."

Again, James' mind was filled with the thoughts of the Minister, "First my daughter and niece were caught up in the satanic fortune telling. This, I feel, has created their illness. Then my servant, Tituba, is claiming witchcraft throughout Salem Village. I must get control. The witchcraft must end. This young man must die, or I will lose all credibility!"

"Minister Parris," Cornelius responded, "I saved your son. He would have died."

James again sensed fear in the Minister's mind, "Will God ever forgive me if this young man is killed after saving my son? Will my son ever forgive me? I will just send him away and tell the people that he escaped."

"That is irrelevant. The citizens don't want you here anymore and it is my job to send you away. You can leave this town and no Witch Trial will be held for you. I recommend you go to Boston. They won't notice you there! If you hadn't saved my son, I wouldn't even give you that option!" Minister Parris said with contempt in his voice.

"I will go, but you should give your son my condolences that he survived the accident. NOW he has to put up with you for the rest of his life!" Cornelius said with laughter in his eyes and anger in his voice.

James again heard his thoughts, "How dare this young man! I cannot send him to be killed, but Percival Owens will do what he is told. It will be his job to ensure the young man is sentenced to death at Gallows Hill. He cannot make fun of me in my town!"

The Minister then walked out without a response and another short, plump man in a blue suit walked in to escort Cornelius out. The nurses were nowhere to be seen as he was lead out of the hospital. As they exited the hospital, Percival's thoughts became very apparent.

"This young man is not evil. He is a great man and can do great things for God. As a servant of God, I must save him from the evil anger of Minister Parris. I must tell him of his gift and how to develop it. I understand that my life may be spent in so doing, but I will do the will of God, not the will of man!"

Percival then began to speak, "You, my boy, have a gift. A special gift that the people of this town will never understand. The people fear you as the Greeks feared the Titans and the Gods. But God is on your side. I have some friends like you that will help you get better control and understanding of your powers."

"There are others like me?" James recognized not just the wonder in Cornelius' voice, but the excitement rising up within him.

"Yes. But they are hidden in normal society and they can help you learn to do the same. But nobody can know that I helped you. I am not a Titan. In fact, you will soon learn that I am what they

call Natural Born and am risking my life and that of my family to help you. Nobody must ever know or my family and I will be burned as witches as well!"

"I will never forget it! And you and your family will forever be protected. Never again will you need to fear repercussions from helping me or helping anyone else. I will personally guarantee your safety and that of your family!"

Cornelius turned and gave Percival a hug and then turned to the black cat.

"You will stay with him. I need to know if there are any problems. I can talk to you and you can let me know what is happening. Will you do this for me?"

"You mean I don't need to run again? I will gladly protect the man that has protected you!"

"This is my cat. He is a powerful individual too and can speak with me no matter where I am in the world. He will hear you and share whatever you desire him to with me. Please take him as my symbol of gratitude."

"My daughter will love him. Thank you. Please go quickly and don't let anyone catch you."

The vision faded and James was again in his home, lying on his back on the couch. The book was resting across his chest with several of the pages bent from him falling asleep.

He sat back up and started to read again.

"After leaving Percival with my cat, I traveled many miles. I didn't go to Boston as the Minister had suggested, but instead went west as Percival had suggested. Percival moved away from Salem Village several months after me, but never told anyone that he had let me go. I would never forget his loyalty, and my family would never let him or his family be hurt in any way. But his greatest help to me was letting me know that I was not alone. There were other Titans, as he called them, and I needed to find them."

"The task of finding other 'Titans' was much more difficult than I thought. In fact, I didn't notice anyone for weeks, even with the knowledge that people like me really did exist. I wasn't exactly sure how to ask around, so I just started observing, trying to read thoughts, listen for animals and people communicating and even anything peculiar that might indicate a special ability. If I had fully understood my abilities at that time, it would have been much easier. But I understood very little!"

James again found himself walking next to Cornelius as he was walking down a street midday. As he began to notice he was again on location, he immediately knew he was in colonial Albany, New York. As he watched Cornelius, he noticed that a man was obviously arguing with a horse on the side of the road. Cornelius had likewise noticed and was listening intently.

"I know that you are tired. You have done an amazing job the last couple days, but my family needs your help once more. I will not ask you again."

"I have heard that before, sir. Just because you can talk with me, you think that you can demand my service. I have feelings and want to be asked, not told what needs to be done."

"I am sorry. You are absolutely correct. Will you help me bring this meat to my family? We will provide you with food upon arrival. My own horse is sick and unable to help."

Just then, James noticed a large carcass of meat lying next to the horse. The head was missing but looked like a deer or something similar. It had obviously been carried here as there was no skin, hoofs or head.

The horse then bowed slightly, and the man lifted the carcass onto the horses back and started to walk. The horse followed slowly at his heels.

Before he could get very far, Cornelius ran towards the man and remarked, "Sir, can I have a word with you?"

The many looked visibly scared and turned to see Cornelius standing there. James then heard Cornelius start to speak telepathically.

"You have a unique ability, as do I. I want to meet others like me so that they can help me understand what it means to be a Titan."

At that, the man relaxed and motioned for Cornelius to follow and lead him down a side street and pointed at a door, slightly hidden in the shadows.

"They will know if you are telling the truth and will help you if they feel it is expedient."

The man then hurried off with the loaded horse still at his heels. Cornelius looked at the door and started to knock.

The door opened and a large, white haired woman came to the door and looked at Cornelius with a slight smile on her face.

"Cornelius. We have been searching for you. You are a Titan and we want to help you become who you should be. But you left the Boy's Home before we could bring you here. We thank God that you have been lead here!"

As James began to look at Cornelius' surprised face, the vision began to fade again…but instead of finding himself asleep, he found that he was still reading the words on the page.

"…From that time, forth, I joined this small band of Titans. I was excited to know that I was not the only one with my unique abilities. I did learn, however, that my abilities were scary even to Titans. They didn't like that I was skilled in all seven Titan skills. In fact, many of the Titans refused to associate with one that was free from any discordance in ability. Not even one skill was poorly developed in me and that made most uncomfortable. I heard people call me weird and was often called the divergent or disparate Titan. Nobody else was like me and that was a problem!"

"That difference, however, did not keep them from helping me learn about and develop my various skills. In fact, I learned a great deal as the 'Disparate Titan'. What an exciting and lonely time this was for me. I often talked with Simon, my black cat, from many miles away and continued to know of Percival and his growing family. But it was a letter sent from Percival one day that made the greatest difference in how I felt about my abilities."

"Dear Cornelius,

"I have felt that you are concerned about your abilities. I am not sure if you are communicating this to me through one of your Titan abilities, or if Simon is telling me in some other way, but I do know that I seem to understand what you are going through. My daughter absolutely loves your cat and would love to meet you. That being said, I am not sure we will ever truly meet again.

As I was thinking about you, I was caring for my bees. I started keeping bees many years ago, because my family liked honey. It was this process of making honey that I felt would be most valuable to you. The bees, as a group, forage for nectar from different flowers. The greater the variety of flowers they forage from, the more delicious the honey. But it isn't the nectar that matters, but the combination of the nectar with the juices from the bee's mouth that produce a watery substance that becomes honey.

Now, the water content has to be reduced to produce honey that can be utilized by my children. I consider it a process of purifying the honey. In fairness, however, it is only the process of drying out through time and the fanning of the bee's wings. Therefore, the concordant properties of the different flower nectars, the bee's salivary juices and the desiccation process produce a very unique substance called honey. I recommend you should produce that same honey in your own life. How can you make your own talents and skills Concordant? How can you produce success in your life and in this world through bringing all those skills together as one? Only through this concordance can you become who God would have you be.

Your Friend,
Percival Abel"

"It was at this time that I determined I was a 'Concordant Titan' instead of the 'Disparate Titan' that others had labeled me. It was also at this time that I determined I should learn to use all my Titan abilities together or in a concordant fashion. Whether the other Titans felt my abilities were a good thing or a bad thing, Concordance was going to be my greatest strength!"

"The first Titan Skill I was introduced to upon reaching the home of the Titans was Telepathy. This was a skill that I easily recognized in myself. I was able to read minds of all individuals around me, except several Titans that learned a skill of Occludopathy and were able to keep me out of their minds. Not all individuals with Telepathy developed this skill, but I felt it imperative that I learn how to close my mind to others. Although it took many years to develop this skill, it has been a very valuable tool since."

"My problem with Telepathy, however, was multiple Titans who utilized this skill to manipulate individuals through placing thoughts in their minds. I found quickly that through Occludopathy I was able to protect others from this intrusion too."

"The second Titan Skill, Zoonophonia, was never taught to me, because it seemed to be inherent from the first day I began speaking with my black cat. Although I missed having a companion I could speak to regularly, I found many animals that were quick to speak with me. As I developed this skill, however, I was surprised to learn that I could manipulate animals using a specialized form of Zoonophonia that I have called Zoonoply. They were often willing to do what I asked of them through this manipulation. It became a valuable skill that is very rare. I have never met another Titan with this skill."

"I was excited to learn the third Titan Skill, that explained why I was able to lift the cart and why I was not injured when I was punished at the Boy's Home. Herculopathy, or significant strength, became a well-developed, powerful skill in my armamentarium. I was able to focus it and utilize it in many ways. The surprising aspect of this skill, however, was not just physical strength, but powerful sight allowing me to see great distances, powerful lungs that allowed me to create almost a wind, and powerful ears allowing me to hear conversations of others even at great distance. My ability to focus these inherent weaknesses of my senses and produce greater strength became known as Cyclopathize. Through Cyclopathize, I was able to not just see great distances, but also to see in the dark, not just speak loudly, but speak underwater, not just hear conversations, but recognize slight motions just as they are starting (for example knowing when someone is initiating a motion before motion has started). Just like all the other specialized skills, Cyclopathize is a rare augmentation of Herculopathy that was developed in me through careful study and learning."

"One of the most valuable skills I developed was Hippocratesense. This was the ability to treat and heal injuries and even understand what was happening inside one's own body and the body of others. This skill, although poorly developed at the time, was the reason I could see the brain malfunctioning in Salem Village, the woman's injured lung prior to leaving the town, and my own apparent health. This was a blessing throughout my life as a Titan, but also taught me that not all Titans have good intentions. One skill I was taught, I have never used, Hippocranathema, the ability to counter-heal or curse another individual. I have found no purpose for this specialized skill but have watched others utilize it. Sometimes I wish that I had never developed it!"

"Another skill that became very valuable over the years was my ability to find my way, or even more importantly localize myself on the planet. Orientopathy was a powerful and even imperative skill for my Titan lifestyle. I never again was lost, never again was unable to find my way and was even blessed again with an augmentation of this power through a specialized ability to hide locations or even myself in plain sight. The ability of Orientocclude allowed me to block people from finding my home, hide in plain sight or even hide someone else when necessary. This ability also allowed me to overcome the attempts of other Orientopaths to hide locations from me. My abilities in Orientopathy allowed me to see through the Orientocclude attempts. If I had to choose one skill, it would be this one to allow finding one's way."

"My time in the blacksmith shop, taught me of another ability that became well developed with other Titans. My ability to make weapons was never a question, but my ability to utilize them became far more developed as I strengthened my Skill of Hoplonosmithy. Through this skill, I learned to make weapons not just from metal, but also from anything. I was able to take a weapon in my hands that I had never seen and utilize it with unparalleled skills. Due to this ability, I was never again 'punished' or even 'injured' by others (except other Titans). Although I have never been an advocate of fighting or battles, this became an important aspect of fighting for this country, for my family and for Titans as a group. I even developed an augmentation of this skill, due to a dear friend that had it, called Hoplonobscure. This allowed me to not just utilize weapons well but confuse or block others (without Hoplonosmithy themselves) from remembering how to use the weapon. This often allowed me to stop battles even before they began."

"The hardest skill for me to develop of all the Titan Skills, however, was Chronopathy. This is the power to manipulate time, produce abnormal speeds through slowing time for oneself and even travel great distances by manipulating the speed the world is functioning in. It became a powerful tool as it was developed to allow me to travel outside of the constraints of time, allowing flight or even walking across unstable surfaces such as water. Once this skill was well developed, I was able to travel the world in seconds, change my location at will and even control time in many respects. My ability to manipulate time, even speed it up became known as Chronaddlize, another specialized form of this skill that no other Titan has ever developed to my knowledge."

"So, each of these seven Titan Skills became important aspects of my life, but the skills themselves were not as complete as they could be. I was amazed as each Titan Skill could become more specialized and strengthened through careful study, learning and use. The more I learned about the skill, the easier it was to develop, but until I was utilizing the skill regularly, it never truly developed. Only when I began teaching others this skill did I learn how powerful the skill really was. Often it was this act of teaching that allowed me to develop the specialized form of each Titan Skill. Therefore, my instructions to all would be to learn, act and then share. Only then will you truly develop as God would have you!"

"Although I could produce a much longer history of my life and of Titans as a whole, that is not the purpose of this record. I instead want to make an observation that is just now becoming more and more apparent in my life. Being Concordant is far more than just having all the Titan Skills. As the name implies, Concordance allows utilizing these Titan Skills together to greater value. Using two or more skills together can make them far more powerful. I am just scratching the surface at this time of the possibilities. I love jumping to locations as an observer within another's mind or memory. I am blessed to learn the skill of self-healing. And my ability to talk with my black cat, although many miles away, is through concordant use of two skills at once. There will come a time when another Concordant Titan needs to know of this to truly understand their abilities. It is for this reason that I have written this record here contained. May it be valuable when that time comes."

The book ended without another word and James sat silently on the couch after shutting the book. What did it all mean? He was sure he would be learning so much more. Before he could think much about it, however, his mother came walking back into the room.

"Well James, what did you think?"

"Has anyone else read this?"

"Your father, of course, and Doc. But I haven't shared it with anyone else and even Camilla doesn't know of its existence."

James sat there dumbfounded and wasn't sure what to say.

Sarah's eyes began to sparkle as her smile lit up her entire face, "You have all seven skills. You are Concordant as was Cornelius and as is Doc. Your skills are developing at a much faster rate than did either of those two. Doc, Master McAdams, is adamant that you be taught more quickly and develop your skills as did Cornelius. He wanted your training to start with this new knowledge, but you cannot share it at this time with anyone else. This book is yours and yours alone. If you give it, read it to or share it with anyone else, it may become a curse in your life. Your only hope is to develop the skills, even the specialized aspects of each skill, as did Cornelius. This has been my part in your training as a Natural-Born individual."

The smirk on her face at this last sentence was unmistakable and James knew she was teasing him for what he had said hours before. But that smile also reminded him how much he truly loved his mother. She, once again, was one of his greatest blessings.

CHAPTER 19
MARCHING ORDERS

James stood outside the house with his mother's smile still playing a prominent part in his mind. She really did know more about his situation than he did. James had assumed from the moment he was invited to camp that mom knew nothing. Now he knew, especially with dad not available, that she may be his greatest resource in times of need. Although he would not be visiting her again this summer, he would be talking with her whenever he got the chance.

As he continued to think about all that he had read, Master McAdams again came walking toward him from the street. James looked up realizing he didn't even hear him arrive and smiled as Master McAdams began to speak.

"Well, my boy, you now have much to think about! I was amazed the first time I read that book. Cornelius was truly an amazing Titan and has taught me a great deal even at my age. But this knowledge and this book were written for you. I believe that he saw you, saw our time and knew you would need his help."

Before James could respond, Master McAdams took his hand and they were again racing through space and time. But it was different this time. James noticed the moon moving backwards in the sky, the usual sounds of the night were absent and he felt as if he couldn't breathe. Every breath he tried to take was pushed out of his lungs as if his lungs were working backwards. His mind was getting foggy and his eyes started to black out, but before he fainted completely, his feet were again on the ground and his lungs filled with air. The influx of air seemed to awaken his mind completely and he found himself again standing next to Master McAdams.

As he realized what was happening, he found himself again at the cave located in the large hill behind the overgrowth. As he looked around, he again saw Helia and Felicity. He somehow knew that he was again back in camp at the exact time he left. He was not sure how it happened, but too much was on his mind at this time to ask. He instead looked up to those deep blue compassionate eyes as Master McAdams began to speak again.

"You are now in a unique situation my boy. No one will know of your new knowledge. No one will understand what knowledge I am needing you to develop. Many can, however, help you a great deal. I would ask that you carefully choose who will work with you to develop each skill. Let me tell you a story to help you understand."

"There was a man many years ago, located on the other side of the world, at a time when Egypt was a great power in the world. At the time, his people were slaves in Egypt and were being used to build the pyramids and many of the amazing cities for the Pharaoh. It was at this time that he was sent by God back to Egypt to ask the Pharaoh to 'let his people go.' But he was not sure he was up to the task. He was nervous about his weakness in speaking and although he agreed to attempt to free the people, he would need instructions and help from God to accomplish this great task. It was for this reason that God prepared miracles for him to perform while inviting the Pharaoh to let the people of Israel go."

"It is a few of these miracles that I wish to speak to you about. The first was a special miracle where the man's brother threw the rod to the ground and it became a great serpent. The pharaohs magicians, however, did a similar trick by throwing their rods on the ground. The pharaoh only laughed and said his musicians could do the same trick. Each time the man worked a mighty miracle from God, the magicians performed a similar miracle and the pharaoh just laughed and refused to the let the people go. It didn't matter whether he turned the river into blood, caused a great swarm of frogs, or did other miracles, the pharaoh was unwilling to recognize the hand of God."

"So how does this apply to you?"

James began to think. Then it hit him. Cornelius had talked about multiple sides to every Titan power. He also talked about special augmentation of each skill through careful training and learning. For every power that could be used for good, the same power could likewise be utilized for the bad.

"You are correct, my boy. Every Titan power can be used for good or evil. You will recognize why people are doing certain skills and then recognize if the power is from God or from some other source. You must seek to learn from and develop skills come from God. Only then can you truly be as powerful as you desire to be."

At that, a song started in the background. James recognized the song and turned to see Helia starting to open her wings. And his mind filled with words, "The time you spent to learn so much, the clock unchanged it be. For Doc you gave a special gift, the gift of time twice used."

James looked up with a start to Master McAdams who stood with a broad smile.

"Yes, I have given you back your time. Use it well!"

With that James was carried back to camp on the powerful wings of Helia. As they flew, he realized that it was as if time had stood still, for it was only 3:30am. All his learning had occurred in less than 5 minutes. He would have to ask Master McAdams how this was done, but for now he would try to get a little more sleep.

But as Helia again brought them back to camp, James no longer desired sleep, but wanted to again focus on his mother's book. As he sat on his bed, he again opened the tattered pages to the final paragraph, from which he pulled a small part, his favorite part that he still didn't completely understand.

"*Being Concordant is far more than just having all the Titan Skills. As the name implies, Concordance allows utilizing these Titan Skills together to greater value. Using two or more skills together can make them far more powerful. I am just scratching the surface at this time of the possibilities.*"

"What exactly does that mean?" he thought. Just then his mind began to race. "Concordant skills or two Titan Skills working together! So, I can use Telepathy and Chronopathy together." His minds eye was then opened to *The Classification,* he was alone in his test with Master Belle, but when Master McAdams gave him the follow-up test he was there with him in his mind. Was that the reason he keeps jumping into the books he is reading and the thoughts of his friends. Was he inadvertently using those Titan Skills together? He must learn to control that ability!

As his excitement grew, he looked over at the soft glow coming from Helia and he could feel her smile as she watched him come to this realization.

"True Powers Concordant you will have when righteous friends for each Titan Skill you learn from."

James finally understood why he was given that new book from his mother. He understood what the true purpose was of The Phoenixenses. But more importantly, he now had his marching orders from Master McAdams. There is much work to be done.

As he sat on his bed thinking of this new assignment, a deep voice was heard from outside the tent. As James began to focus on this voice, he recognized it as Jacques and it sounded like he was again talking to himself.

"That young man is always leaving at night. Does he not know the great danger that exists even here in camp? Not everyone here is good. I recognize those that are not in accordance with the teachings of *The Band of Fire* and Doc McAdams.

I cannot protect him if he is away from his tent when he is expected to be there!"

At that, James stood and decided it was time to talk with the gray wolf and request his help in determining who else should be joining The Phoenixenses. As he left the tent, Jacques turned to look at him again.

"Jacques, I need your help."

The wolf's ears perked up and he walked toward James.

"How can I help you son?"

"I have watched you and your pack since getting to camp. You have a special ability to see the good and bad in people. You know when Titans are preparing in accordance with the will of God or if they are only focused on their own success and glory. I know that you can help me find quality Titans to help me develop the skills Master McAdams wants me to learn."

"Yes James. I will pass the word. Then you might have quality students to join you and those that already travel with you."

"What?"

"Yes, the young man that shares your tent, the small little excited girl and Kari, my midnight black friend. They will be of great help to you and are some of the best I have ever met. You can trust them!"

"Yes, Bekah, Kari and Michael are all great friends. But I need those with skills in Herculopathy, Chronopathy, Hippocratesense, and Hoplonosmithy as well. Can you help me?"

"I will serve you as none others can!" Jacques then turned away from him and began to howl, but James could not understand it. Even with his Zoonophonia, he was not able to understand what was happening. Why couldn't he understand Jacques' words now?

Jacques recognized the surprise in James eyes and seemed to smile.

"When I talk with my pack, not even you, young sir, will understand. Only Doc McAdams is capable of understanding."

"Thanks. I know you can help me. Maybe someday I too will be able to understand."

On that note, being still early in the morning, James decided to try once again to get some rest before classes would start again. There was much on his mind, but sleep would be important when he had the chance, because he would be spending many nights in the cave trying to become truly Concordant.

CHAPTER 20

THE SEARCH BEGINS

James woke with a start with Michael calling his name, "James, it is time to get up. We will be late for breakfast again."

James jumped from his bed and dressed quickly and then ran from the tent with Michael racing towards breakfast. All sleep had left him, and for the moment even the happenings of the night had been forgotten. As they entered The Great Hall and heard Master McAdams addressing those already eating, he again remembered the new book resting in his backpack. A book nobody even knew he had, except for his mother and Master McAdams.

As he began to think, he stopped in the doorway of The Great Hall and his mind filled with pictures.

He stood on the edge of the hill looking down at a small village surrounded by a rock wall that was partially broken down to the west. He was looking for her now that John had recommended her to him. She was young, but a very powerful Titan and could use his Orientopathy skills. What was this Order of the Kraken? He had never been trained by The Band of Fire, as he was raised on the Reservation and the government had not allowed him to leave it because his father was a troublemaker and they were concerned he would be too. Now that he was of legal age, however, they were unable to prevent him from going anywhere. But his skills to navigate the wilderness from the age of 8 years-old made it possible for him to go anywhere and they would not be able to stop him even if they wanted to.

He closed his eyes and began to listen for voices. Yes, she was in the third house to the right. There were guards, no just one guard in the house with her. He was a large, broad shouldered 6'8" man that carried a 4-foot walking stick with a switch blade that comes out of the handle side, a removable handle that contains a complete swiss army style pocketknife, and a M15 rifle in the remaining stick. That may not be the best house to enter first.

Although they cannot sense my presence now, since I am blocking them, the best choice would be to walk into camp and then allow them to sense my presence. Maybe then they would come to me and provide me the opportunity for introduction. Hopefully John has warned them I am coming.

He reached into his pocket and removed a small note written on a small folded piece of paper:

"Dear Zoram,

"Your skills in Orientopathy are unparalleled in this world. I have watched you guide us into forbidden jungles, climb volcanos and even maneuver through great seas. I have seen you walk directly into the camps of others without even being seen. I have watched you provide food to those with you from the packs and stores of your enemies and I have been amazed at your ability to enter even the most dangerous of locations and not be seen until you stand before the face of the very individuals you are seeking. Orientopathy is a special skill, but your ability to block yourself from the view and sensing of others is unprecedented. I have never seen another Titan with this skill.

"Therefore, it is imperative that I invite you into a special order, a group that would greatly benefit from your skills and

abilities. Lead by a Concordant with steadily growing skills,
Camilla Proserpina. If you can find her in the mountain cities
long since forgotten, she will accept you as the Orientopath
capable of joining The Order of the Kraken. I commend you
to her presence.

> *"Your Friend,*
> *John Vali"*

James' eyes opened with a start to the face of the man sitting next to Master McAdams at the head table. His dark skin, almost brownish-yellow eyes, long brown hair down to his back and a long brown, fluffy beard and mustache were unmistakable. This was Zoram, the new Orientopathy teacher. So, he really was of The Order of the Kraken? That is the man Camilla sent to infiltrate and influence the camp. Why did Master McAdams allow him at camp? Maybe I will learn more in his class today.

The morning went slowly as James struggled through classes not even noticing the lessons being taught. He knew it was imperative that he study every subject to truly develop as a Concordant, but his focus was on the Orientopathy class that was second after lunch.

Bekah smiled as James inhaled his lunch and raced from the room to Herculopathy. She read the excitement from his mind and knew he wasn't excited for Herculopathy, but for Orientopathy, the following class. He told her earlier today about his vision and Master Balthizar joining The Order of the Kraken and being sent to infiltrate the camp and steal Titans. Bekah knew she needed to hurry, or James would get himself in trouble again.

As she jogged into camp, James was already seated near the front with a stool next to him being saved for her. But as she entered the room, she felt a strong anxiety in James. What was he worried about?

James smiled as she entered and knew she had just searched his mind. But she didn't see his biggest concern, a very small, white girl with a short, spiky, red haircut with freckles covering her cheeks and nose sitting across the way. She was sitting next to Ryan and talking with him in rapid fashion. James recognized her and realized she must be Zoram's partner from The Order of the Kraken. What was her name?

"That is Elli." Bekah said with great excitement. "She is Master Balthizar's daughter."

"I know she came with him, but is she truly his daughter?"

"That is what he and she are both saying."

"Yes, but she's of The Order of the Kraken too. Are we sure she isn't just someone pretending to be his daughter?"

"I don't know for sure, James, because someone is blocking my entrance into her mind."

"Yes, Camilla made sure of that."

A large, 6'10" man with broad shoulders, short black hair, hazel eyes and large hands stepped forward and began to speak. Master Rocky Handrake had been absent for the beginning of camp and was teaching his first Herculopathy class this year. All the girls in the class seemed to be stunned by his presence and James heard Bekah think about how amazing and strong he looked. James was startled by this thought and turned to look at Bekah who was already turning a bright shade of pink.

As he began to speak in a powerful, deep voice, James felt his voice reverberate through his body.

"My young Titans, Hercules was a great man in Greek and Roman mythology known for his great strength that came from the Gods. His strength was due to Zeus being his father and allowed him to perform many great tasks including killing the Nemean Lion, slaying the nine-headed Hydra, capturing the Cretan Bull and the Erymanthian Boar and many other tasks given him by the Gods. As a Titan, you too have great strengths come from our God. Some of you will develop Herculopathy, the very power Hercules wielded throughout the world, but others will learn to focus the strengths they have, including other skills to change the world. My goal is to help you develop whatever skills you may have."

Master Handrake's voice seemed to still be echoing through the camp as he stopped momentarily. James looked around and everyone was silent. Every first year Titan was there, ready and willing to learn whatever they could.

"In your classes to this point, you have been introduced to exercise, to proper nutrition to allow muscle growth and even the competitions we will be having at the end of classes. But, you have yet to truly be introduced to Herculopathy. May I invite you to open your books to page 5 and be prepared to read."

James opened *Introduction to Herculopathy* as Master Handrake began to read:

"The world has long talked about Superheroes or individuals with amazing strength. Sampson from ancient Israel was given such strength. Heracles from Greek mythology or Hercules from Roman mythology was likewise endowed with amazing strength. As time progressed, the most common name for superhuman strength became Hercules. Difficult tasks or amazing efforts we called herculean. Therefore, as Titans developed the ability to focus or utilize one's strength to perform herculean tasks, performs feats of strength with ease and even endure injury and pain without difficulty, the Titan skill of Herculopathy was born. This power or skill when developed can be of powerful assistance as *The Band of Fire* protects the earth. The true key to Herculopathy is a mind powerful enough to control the body and help it use significantly more strength than the average Titan will ever be able to exercise."

The words echoed through James mind a second time, "*The true key to Herculopathy is a mind powerful enough to control the body...*"

"But according to Cornelius, that is only the start of this great power." James thought, "He developed the ability to focus one's strength to overcome an apparent weakness. What did he call it? ... Oh, Cyclopathize."

As the class continued, and James was distracted, small little Elli seemed to be miles ahead of the entire class. Her Herculopathy talents were years ahead of others and Master Handrake continued to praise her. Ryan Sampson, a much larger young man than Elli, stood nearly 6 feet tall and exercised amazing strength that even seemed to impress Master Handrake. Elli was likewise pleased with his abilities, but Kari was constantly by his side and praising him. James knew she was truly infatuated with him.

James kept looking at Ryan and began to wonder if he was the Herculopath to join the Phoenixenses? He knew Kari would be quite excited. Elli would also, based on her Herculopathy skill, be a good addition, but she was of The Order of the Kraken and therefore would not be a good choice.

Just then, music started in James' mind and he recognized help coming from Helia. As Master Handrake tried to describe each aspect, James felt his body moving in response. And for the first time, James recognized a power he didn't know he had. James felt his heart beating with great power, and each beat sent a wave of energy from the top of his head to the tips of his toes, from his shoulders to muscles in his chest. From the spinal column to the tips of his fingers. He felt energy, powerful energy, pulsing through his body, he almost felt like he could fly, but he knew it was only the Herculopathy skills awaking in every muscle, every tendon, even every cell of his body. He even recognized his vision becoming more acute and his breathing becoming much easier. As he listened to the thoughts of those around him, he didn't notice the same happening in anyone else. Bekah seemed to be looking at him, however, with great surprise and James knew she was recognizing the change in him also. Now he would just need to develop these skills and learn to utilize them on demand.

As James continued to focus on the growing strength in his body, Master Handrake began to speak again. "Your task today will be to cross the lake. Utilize the strength you have in groups of two to canoe across the lake. Any Herculopathy skills you may have will help move the canoe more quickly, but working as a team will be just as important. Let me give you some basic instruction to help in this journey, as I will assume most of you have never captained a canoe."

He then lifted up what James recognized as a paddle.

"Here is a paddle. This will allow the canoe to move. When you grip a paddle correctly, plunge it into the water and draw backwards, the boat will move forward. The paddle is made up of four key parts. The top is the grip. This is the location where you place your top hand which will produce the strength when rowing. The other end of the paddle has a large flat piece called the blade. The blade is what is plunged into the water to produce the push on the water forcing the boat forward. The shaft is the long portion in the middle that extends from the grip to the blade. Where the shaft connects to the blade is called the neck."

Master Handrake then grabbed the paddle with his right hand on the grip and the left hand near the bottom of the shaft and began to exhibit rowing motions.

"To row, the blade is plunged in the water and the top hand is on the grip. If rowing on the left side of the canoe, the right hand is on the grip and the left hand is on the shaft. The location on the shaft determines the strength of the row using the lower hand as the fulcrum of the lever. Thus, the strength is augmented by the lever arm. The strength is also augmented by the amount of blade that comes in contact with the water. More blade, more motion."

He then put the paddle down and lifted up the life jacket.

"You will all be required to wear a life jacket, so get into partners, pick a life jacket and paddle each and come down to the lake."

Bekah and James each grabbed a life jacket and paddle and walked down to the lake.

"Each group will now choose a canoe. You will notice that all the canoes are positioned perpendicular to the shore. You will notice the bow, or front of the boat is towards the shore and the stern is away from the shore. One of you will hold the boat and the stronger individual, Herculopath if you have one, will go to the stern of the boat and then the other will get in the bow of the boat. I will assist you all in pushing off."

As James latched his life jacket and climbed into the boat, he looked around and noticed Elli and Michael climbing into a single boat and Kari and Ryan climbing into another. Kari must have migrated quickly to Ryan's side and Michael was left looking for a partner. What was interesting was that Elli was climbing to the stern of the boat. Michael must have noticed also that she was a Herculopath.

"Now that you are all in your boats, listen carefully to my instructions so that you may succeed in crossing the lake."

James looked around and noticed there was not a canoe for Master Handrake. That seemed strange as he was not sure how they would continue to hear him as they were crossing the lake, but the strength of his voice seemed to be increasing.

"To move the canoe, you must push water the opposite of the direction you hope to move. Push toward the shore to move away from it. Push toward the stern of the boat, the back if you don't remember, to move forward or the bow of the boat to move backward. To slow or stop, you can either place the blade in the water and hold it still or row against the direction you are going. To maintain a straight course, you will need to row on both sides of the canoe at the same strength, or when the stronger individual is at the stern, they may need to switch sides to maintain rectus motion. The boat will turn away from the stronger rowing side. Are there any questions?"

With no questions, Master Handrake quickly moved down the shore and pushed each boat into the lake.

James began to row hard on the left side of the boat away from the shore and the boat spun in the water to the left. Bekah looked back and just smiled.

"So, you have found your strength? Now how am I supposed to row with you?" she said in a rapid, high pitched voice.

"You stay on the right side, and I will do all the adjustments here at the stern of the boat. I will row on whatever side is necessary."

They began to row quickly and leave most of the class behind as they were trying to learn to move the canoe and turn the canoe. But Kari's laughter could be heard from their right as she sat in the bow of the boat just holding on and Ryan rowed quickly from side to side. The speed of their motion was impressive.

To the left came another boat moving quickly through the water. Michael and Elli were both rowing hard, but Elli kept switching sides as they rowed. She was carefully giving instructions from the back.

Bekah looked up with excitement in her eyes and a broad smile pursed her lips. "We need to be first! Tell me what to do!"

James smiled and then stuck his blade deep into the water on the left side of the canoe with his left hand partially buried in the water. "Put your blade as deep as you can and row hard. Stay on the right side and row. I will follow your lead and adjust as necessary to stay straight. We will win!"

The race was on. No other boats were even close. Just the three boats were racing towards the opposite shore. Each boat was working as hard as they could, but Kari was still not rowing and Elli's commands were becoming more angry. As she became more commanding, the excitement left Michael's face and he just continued to work hard without the joy that was on his face earlier. Ryan rowed hard and drops of sweat began to fall from his forehead. James, however, felt increased strength with each row. His body seemed to be thriving on the push. As he worked harder, he gained more and more strength. James quickly realized that Bekah could not keep up, although she continued to row hard and was starting to sweat and breath hard, so he switched sides of the canoe with each row. The speed of all three boats continued to increase.

They continued to hear commands from Master Handrake coming from behind them, but the voice seemed to be moving closer and closer.

As James started to pull ahead due to the speed of each row increasing, Master Handrake came swimming to the side of the boat and was cheering them on.

"Bekah and James, you are doing great. You might even be able to beat me to the other shore." he said with a smile. And then he sped past them swimming with ease towards the other shore. Bekah just looked back with a smile and they kept rowing, but no matter how hard they rowed, Master Handrake was increasing the distance between him and them.

Just then, Michael and Elli came rowing past with great speed. Elli was now quiet and Michael was giving the directions. Elli was burying her paddle in the water and with each row the boat was jumping forward. She was working so hard, however, that she was unable to speak. Kari and Ryan were still back about two boat lengths, but were keeping close.

James watched Elli push their boat into the lead and began to hear a familiar voice in his head. James had to smile when Bekah's pitch and speed was even noticeable when she spoke telepathically.

"Watch her carefully James! Follow her technique exactly and we can push ahead again!"

James looked again at how deep Elli was burying the paddle and he began to do the same. As he pushed, he felt every ounce of his body tighten. Muscles he didn't even know existed seemed to ripple with each stroke. He knelt in the bottom of the canoe, to allow more force and began to flex his legs, back, shoulders and arms with each motion. Slowly they started to catch Michael and Elli's boat.

Just then, Bekah looked to her right as Kari's laughter had stopped. She was rowing with all her heart as Ryan was likewise burying his paddle in the lake and catching the other boats. At that, Bekah likewise began to row harder. The boats were all three even and only about 100 yards from the shore. Master Handrake was on the shore cheering them on, and he was somehow completely dry.

"Row, row, row! You can all do it!"

Just then, music came into James' mind and words from Master Handrake's instructions came back to his mind.

"Utilize the strength you have in groups of two to canoe across the lake. Any Herculopathy skills you may have will help move the canoe more quickly but working as a team will be just as important."

"Working as a team…" James thought, and Bekah heard him. She quickly looked back.

"Bekah, move your paddle to the other side to use your arm that is not as tired! You will then call out each stroke. You can use telepathy if that is easier. As we row together, the motion will be even quicker!"

Bekah quickly switched to the left side of the boat and the command "Row!" began to echo in James' mind. With each command, they inched ahead, and water sprayed up around them. First one stroke, and then two stokes and then half a canoe length lead. By the time they hit the shore at full speed and stopped with two-thirds of the boat on dry ground, they were a whole canoe length ahead of Michael and Elli and a little more ahead of Ryan and Kari.

Master Handrake was jumping up and down and cheering. "I knew you would do it! Team work ALWAYS wins!!"

Bekah crawled from the boat and collapsed exhausted. James just felt invigorated and his whole body was tight with excitement. He had never felt like this before and Master Handrake could tell that something had happened.

"So my young James, you have found your Herculopathy? Only Concordants have it present as yours did. I have only taught one other student that this happened to. She is actually your sister. Your dad would truly be proud!"

"Well done James," a voice said from his left. "I have wanted to meet you since I came to camp."

James looked down to his left to see very small, white girl with a short, spiky, red haircut with freckles covering her cheeks and nose smiling up at him. She was slightly taller than Bekah, but still very small.

"I haven't lost a competition of strength since I was 8 years-old!" she said with admiration in her eyes. "How'd you do it?"

James turned and pointed to Bekah still lying on the beach. "It was teamwork. She ensured we were rowing together, so I could use every ounce of her strength to add to my efforts."

"Interesting. I have never thought I needed anyone else to win. Maybe you can teach me more things."

Alarm bells went off in James head, but the flattery was working.

"You are an impressive Herculopath. Maybe I can learn from you as well. We will have to talk."

The conversation quickly ended, however, as Master Handrake grabbed James and Elli and walked them over to Ryan who had just finished helping Kari out of the canoe because she was "too tired" to move. Master Handrake wanted to ensure the three most skilled Herculopaths in his class knew each other.

"James and Elli, this is Ryan. He almost beat both of you too."

Ryan looked up with a smile, but said nothing.

James reached out his hand to the much larger Ryan, and they shook hands without a word. Elli just looked up at Ryan without offering a hand. Master Handrake didn't seem to notice.

"The three of you should work together! You will find much greater strength if you learn with another Titan with similar abilities. I will get permission from Doc to see if I can hold a special class to help you all develop even more. I would love to see you competing in other areas. It was the most impressive race I have ever had with first year Titans. I almost want to do it again, but it is time to head to Orientopathy and Elli's father won't allow me to hold you any longer."

Just then, James noticed most of the canoes were now reaching shore, an impressive 15-20 minutes after their canoes had arrived. Were there not any more Herculopaths in the group? Before he could look around, Bekah came walking over and grabbed James' hand.

"Let's go to the next class. Michael is waiting for us over there."

Kari quickly stood and joined them, leaving Ryan and Elli standing where they were. James mind was still racing. "A special class? Is that a good idea? Master Handrake would be a great resource for truly developing his skills. But should he invite Elli or Ryan to join the Phoenixenses? He would need to talk with the other three."

CHAPTER 21

THE OTHER SIDE OF ORIENTOPATHY

As they walked to the Orientopathy Class, Bekah was reading James mind and began to speak.

"You must agree to that class! You know that he can help you develop your Herculopathy skills much quicker than any of us can. Master Handrake is an amazing teacher and your abilities started to blossom as soon as he started pushing you." her voice was filled with excitement and it was just as high pitched as ever.

"As for our study sessions…" her voice faded and she continued to talk directly into his mind, "Elli is too dangerous. She is a direct connection to Camilla."

"I know! We need all the help we can get to help me to become a Concordant. She's not a first year Herculopath and may be able to give me some additional insights." he said out loud.

The thoughts continued, "That is why you MUST do the class. Then you can get the protected instruction and learn from her as well."

As they walked into the campsite, many students were already sitting and Michael was just looking at James and Bekah in surprise.

"You really shouldn't talk in front of me without letting me hear the whole conversation." and he sat down near the back of the class.

Bekah's face started to turn a bright shade of red, but James didn't even seem to notice. He was already studying the teacher at the front of the class. The dark-skinned man with almost brownish-yellow eyes, long brown hair down to his back and a long brown, fluffy beard and mustache stood at the front of the group with his powerful arms and hands extended to the class. As James sat down staring at Master Balthizar, a vision opened for him again…

Camilla stood at the front of a group of individuals with anger on her face, even her deep blue eyes seemed to have a fire behind them. Her hands were clenched and her breathing was slightly labored. Master Zoram Balthizar stood in front of her to her right and she seemed to be looking directly at him.

As she began to speak, a soft, haunting phoenix song began to play in the background, but blood red Fogo was nowhere to be seen. As James looked around, he recognized many of the individuals from previous visions.

"Doc McAdams and Simon Adamson have crossed the line this time. I will no longer associate myself or any of us in the Order of the Kraken with The Band of Fire. As Titans, we will stand apart from them for the good of all Titans and to ensure we are not held down or limited. Now that Zoram is one among us, we can disappear. Never again will The Band of Fire be able to track us. Never again will our names be recognized among them. From this time forward my old life and my old name will be changed. I shall now be known as Camilla Proserpina!"

Many nodded in agreement as she continued to speak. "Proserpina is the goddess that was commonly associated with rebirth or renewal in Ancient Greek and Roman mythology. I am being reborn! We are all Titans being renewed. Titans will never again be the same. Thus shall my name change forever."

"And I too shall change my name!" said a small dark-skinned woman to Camilla's left with short black hair. *"I shall be called Minerva Medusa as I have long desired to be free of my Natural Born parent's name. The name of Medusa in Greek mythology brought fear and dread to all, even the Titans. They shall likewise fear me and the Order of the Kraken!"* and she began to laugh a laugh that made James' skin crawl.

The vision faded and Master Balthizar was speaking to the class. Bekah was just looking at James in surprise and he could hear her thoughts. *"Where are you? Your mind seems to be far from here and I can't get in."*

James just smiled and turned back to Master Balthizar as he finished his instructions.

"So, Mister Adamson, are you too good for my instructions on Orientopathy because your father was such a great teacher? Why do you feel that you don't need to pay attention to me?"

"Oh...Master Balthizar, I am trying to pay attention. My father taught me nothing."

"No surprise there. Maybe you just think as a Concordant you don't need me. Especially with all the special help you are getting from Doc McAdams."

The whole class seemed to turn and look at him. James could feel his face turning red.

"He hasn't helped me. I don't know what you are talking about."

"Then where do you go at night? I know you keep leaving your camp. Sometimes alone and sometimes with this little know it all." as he pointed at Bekah who was now standing with anger welling up insider her.

When she began to speak, her voice was very high pitched and the speed very rapid. But she was very careful to ensure he heard every word.

"How dare you! You are a guest teacher here because Master McAdams has allowed it. Everything we know about Orientopathy this year is because of Him! The only reason you even have a job is because Master Adamson is not here. His Orientopathy skills far outweigh the skills you have. Maybe there is nothing you can teach us. Maybe you aren't as good a teacher as you think you are. Maybe we are all wasting our time with a teacher that has to pick on students instead of teaching..."

As her voice trailed off and she started to sit down, Master Balthizar began to smile and began to speak again to the entire class.

"Well, Miss Solomon gives Doc and Simon much more credit than they deserve. For my instruction will continue to be truly different than they would provide. It is not that I couldn't teach as they would, but I want to ensure that we are not limiting your ability to learn. As Titans, you deserve to learn all that can be done through Orientopathy. You must become even more skilled, more talented than they would ever allow you to become."

As he spoke, he walked around the small class and handed out blindfolds to all the individuals.

"Please place these on and then listen carefully."

As James looked around, he noticed everyone placing their blindfolds and he did the same.

But everything changed once the blindfold was in place. He began to hear music, Helia's music in his mind, and the whole world opened up. He could "see" everything. Without the interference of his eyes, he knew much more about what was happening around him.

There were seventeen students in the class. He could see each one, hear their breathing, knew where they were sitting in the class. In the front center, without a blindfold, stood Master Balthizar, but he was not alone. A shadowy figure was next to him....no not really, but someone was influencing the class from a great distance. A black figure, with curly black hair, dark brown eyes and glasses. Was this John protecting Master Balthizar from outside the camp through Telepathy? Why was he seeing him as a figure in the class?

Just then, Master Balthizar started to speak again.

"Now that the interference of vision has been removed, I am asking you to use all your senses. What do you hear? Do you hear the people around you? What do you feel? Which direction is the breeze coming from? Are there any sounds that would tell you about things in your presence? Open your mouth and taste the air. What does it tell you?"

James began to focus on what he was saying. Yes, he could hear and feel a breeze coming from the northwest. It was coming through trees, tall trees, from that direction and hitting trees behind them. But there was more. He could hear Bekah breathing to his left, Michael to his right and Kari just past him. Bekah was very nervous, as he could hear her struggling to understand. Kari was relaxed, but not sure what was happening and Michael's world was coming together and he was so excited.

"Many of you are struggling I am sure. If you don't consider yourself skilled in Orientopathy, what are you skilled at? Use your skills together. What can Telepathy tell you about your surroundings? What animals are speaking in the distance and influencing what you know for those with Zoonophonia? For you with Hippocratesense, listen to the health of those around you. Every voice should be used to help you determine your location. All the Titan Skills can work as one!"

James began to hear Bekah's excitement as she realized she could "hear" everyone in the area. As he focused on her thoughts, he began to see what she was seeing while blindfolded.

Nellie Lamberson was on the far side of the room sitting with Mabel Enloe on her left and Julia Salamander to her right. Each of the girls were concentrating on the sound of Master Balthizar's voice, but only Nellie was starting to recognize the trees around her. Mabel was, however, localizing animals in the surrounding areas, but struggling to get location information from them. Julia Salamander, however, just seemed lost. Jens Albertson and Roland Cushman were behind Mabel Enloe and were likewise currently lost and unable to picture anything. Jens was a little annoyed and kept repeating in his mind that he could only hear the wind.

As she continued around the room, see found Julia Salamander again, who's mind was now filled with significant information. Julia was monitoring the heartbeats of all 17 individual Titan students in the room and knew their various locations. She recognized the asthma in Adlebert Evans two individuals away from her and the anxiety that Elli Ferrimore was feeling. Bekah found this information interesting and decided to continue around the circle to Elli who was closer to her.

Melvina Hoguel was next to her and was still searching for sounds, sights or indications that would help localize them all. Bekah knew her as a Telepath, but Melvina had not yet figured out what Bekah was doing to find her location.

Donald Barton English and Adlebert Evans were standing next to each other and both concentrating with no success on finding their location. Donald's mind, however, kept coming back to items in close proximity to them that he could use to make weapons. He was obviously one skilled in Hoplonosmithy.

Next were Sidonia Maple and Alexander Black, but Alexander's mind seemed to draw her in. He seemed to know a great deal about almost every individual in the class and where they were standing. He knew every student's primary skill:

- *James Adamson is difficult to determine but seems to have multiple Titan Skills.*
- *Rebekah Solomon was a Telepath and was quite excited at the moment as her heart was racing.*
- *Michael Peterson was an Orientopath and was calm as a summer's morning with this exercise.*
- *Kari Gabriel was a Zoonophonic and also seemed to be calm.*
- *Nellie Lamberson was an Orientopath and was just starting to calm down.*
- *Roland Cushman was a Chronopath.*
- *Jens Albertson was a Herculopath.*
- *Mabel Enloe was Zoonophonic.*
- *Adlebert Evans was a Hoplonosmith.*
- *Donald Barton English was a Chronopath.*
- *Melvina Hoguel was a Telepath, but not as excited as Bekah.*
- *Julia Salamander was a Hippocratesent, but he already knew that from other classes.*
- *Ryan Sampson was a powerful Herculopath, but slightly nervous about his lack of sight while blindfolded.*
- *Elisabeth de Armas was a Hoplonosmith.*

- *Sidonia Maple was a Chronopath.*
- *Elli Ferrimore was a very developed Herculopath.*

With Elli being brought up again, Bekah turned her mind to her, but was blocked from entering her mind. Only James was able to stop her as a first year, but there was no question she would not be entering Elli's mind at this time.

"Please remove the blindfolds at this time." Master Balthizar called out drawing everyone back.

As they removed the blindfolds, James looked around in surprise at how much information he truly had through this exercise. Bekah's eyes were wide with excitement as she likewise looked around. Michael had a smile that couldn't be mistaken, as this was one of his favorite classes so far!

Master Balthizar continued, "Look around carefully. What were you able to determine without your eyes? Many of you were frustrated, but many of you found new eyes, deeper eyes that will guide you to much more information. I am therefore giving you an assignment, homework per say, to use the blindfold at least once more to try and develop your Titan skill. Even Chronopathy can be developed in this manner! You will bring to me a one-page report on how this helped develop your skills and how you will never see the world the same because of it."

He then turned with a smile to James, "Even YOU can learn something from this activity! Maybe even something about how your father has limited you throughout your life."

Turning back to the class, he continued, "If you ever want to learn more quickly or become more powerful in your Titan abilities, I can help. If you want to know how I can help you, please come talk with me. You are all excused."

James turned to Bekah, Michael and Kari and they began to walk from class around the lake.

"James, please wait." came a voice with a strong Spanish accent. James recognized the voice as coming from Lizzy who other than her accent spoke very good English. "Ryan and I want to speak with you all."

Kari spun around with excitement and Bekah chuckled under her breath.

Ryan began to speak as they approached, "We know that we are from the 'wrong' patrol, but we need your help. Your Herculopathy seems to be more developed than mine. Can you work with me so I can become a more powerful Titan?"

Lizzy continued, "And I want to learn anything and everything I can from each of you. I am very impressed by Michael's abilities in Orientopathy. I struggled in class today and will need all the help I can get. And Bekah, were you in my mind today? Maybe you can help me too."

Before James could even answer, his mind was drawn to the recent vision in Bekah's mind:

"Ryan Sampson was a powerful Herculopath… Elli Ferrimore was a very developed Herculopath"

"Elisabeth de Armas was a Hoplonosmith…"

"Actually, I have a proposition…Although I haven't talked with these three yet about it." James looked at Bekah who was smiling with approval.

"We have a special opportunity to learn together, because we need you as much as you need us. I cannot give you more information now, but it happens again tomorrow night at midnight. Meet us outside our camp, and we will show you the way. Once we are in the cave, we will be able to tell you more. If you don't come, we will assume you are not interested, which would be fine."

"We will be there!" both Ryan and Lizzy said together.

"You can bring your animal companion, if desired, but don't invite anyone else at this time." Bekah said in her high pitched excited voice.

Michael and Bekah stood silent, but both had broad smiles on their faces.

"And so it is," James thought "the Phoenixenses are now six!"

CHAPTER 22
THE PRIMARY PATROL CHALLENGE

Bekah was almost skipping as they hurried to the large castle-like purple tent with gold trim around the door immediately behind The Great Hall. She had been so excited for *The Primary Patrol Challenge* all morning, but even got more excited when the first year Titans were assigned to Master Julianna. Bekah loved her classes and figured this Challenge would be similar.

James kept going over in his mind what Bekah had told them about the Challenges.

"Each summer there are three challenges in growing difficulty as you progress in Titan abilities."

After getting mad at him again for not reading more in *The Book of Adam*, she couldn't hold back her excitement.

"The Primary Patrol Challenge has each year competing against themselves. Patrol by patrol, first year Titans will compete only against first years. But any Titan skills developed to this point are fair game."

James began to review...4 Sphinx, 4 Centaur, 4 Griffin and 5 Minotaur, since Elli is extra for them.

Bekah's explanation continued:

"The location will be chosen by one of the Teachers. In this location, each patrol will be given a flag that they are to hide and protect. While protecting their flag, they are also to capture as many of the other flags as possible. When time runs out, an eight-hour competition, the patrol with the most flags will be the winner. When your patrol has no flags, you are eliminated. As long as you have control of at least one flag, your patrol remains in the game, even if you lose your original flag. Once captured, each flag must be hidden in a new location before searching for another flag. Rarely does any patrol get all four flags or get control of three flags while maintaining control of their own. If this feat is accomplished, the game is complete and the winning patrol will be recognized before the entire camp."

Michael and James had already decided that the Sphinx patrol was going to win with all four flags. Maybe then they could spend some additional time with Master Julianna and have more Chronopathy experiences…At that thought, James reached the gold trimmed door with Michael right behind him.

Everything had been moved in the tent this time and it appeared much larger than the last time they were there. The Centaur patrol entered right behind Michael and all four patrols were now present.

Master Julianna bounced into the room with her half-moon spectacles falling down her nose. She didn't seem to notice because she was too excited.

"Doc McAdams has given me a great privilege today!" she could hardly contain her excitement, "The first year challenge has been given to me. Therefore, we will be traveling to another location, maybe even another time, to participate in this game. I have found the perfect place…"

She then paused and looked around carefully counting all the individuals.

"Listen carefully for the rules, such that you may all enjoy this challenge:"

"Every Patrol is invited to utilize the Titan skills you have developed thus far in camp. If your skills are more developed because you have been focused or working hard, it will be to your advantage. Each patrol will be placed in locations to best utilize your patrol skills. Expect every individual in your patrol to be required to exercise a Titan skill through the challenge. Doc McAdams will ensure that is the case."

She again paused with a smile, but the bouncing as she stood there never stopped. James loved her excitement and was almost begging for her to continue.

"Your patrol will be given a Patrol Flag that must be hidden and protected, for the other three patrols will be seeking it out. Your job is to get as many of the flags as possible, while protecting your flag. When your patrol has no flags, you are eliminated. As long as you have control of at least one flag, your patrol remains in the game, even if you lose your original flag."

James chuckled to himself, as he recognized the words Bekah had used to explain the game as word for word from Master Julianna. Most likely it was written that way in *The Book of Adam.*

"Once captured, each flag must be hidden in a new location before searching for another flag. May I recommend that you find ways to protect each flag. Although we will protect you from serious injuries, injuries will most likely occur during this task. Dakota Ironhorse will be available as necessary."

"I didn't realize there would be injuries and danger. That makes me a little nervous." Bekah's voice rang in James head. Kari and Michael, however, also looked over in surprise. So obviously, she had spoken to all three of them.

"You can invite our companions to attend but cannot return home to get them. As a patrol, you can summon them to your location once you are positioned, and I will ensure they all arrive. Amber Barde will be assisting me in this task."

"The competition will continue for 8 hours, or until one patrol controls all 4 flags, which I have seen happen only once. The patrol with the most flags will be the winner."

"Are there any questions?"

Bekah's hand shot up, to which Master Julianna nodded with a grin.

"How will we know when a flag has been captured?"

"Great question. Doc McAdams will tell all participating in your mind at the capture of each flag. For example, if the Sphinx flag is captured, all will hear 'The Sphinx flag is now controlled by _____.' So that everyone will know. You will also know if a patrol has been eliminated in a similar fashion. Any other questions?"

When nobody responded, Master Julianna began to smile and took one step towards the Centaur patrol. But at that very moment, everything started to get fuzzy and James saw Master Julianna simultaneously step to all four patrols at the same time and invite them to all hold hands and hold her hand. And they were suddenly ripped through time and space as commonly happened in Master Julianna's presence...

James, Michael, Bekah and Kari found themselves standing at the opening of a mine. The mine seemed to still be functioning, so when and where were they.

Michael looked up, "How'd we get here? I am always amazed at what she's able to do!"

"Where are we?" Bekah asked looking at Michael and James.

"I haven't learned how to localize us on the world yet, but this is definitely still Utah." Michael quickly answered.

"Let's get our companions here! They may be a great help." Kari said, as she looked frightened at the mine.

"Good idea," Bekah said. "What do we need to do?"

At that very moment, a snow-white Unicorn-Pegasus mix appeared with Master Barde on her back with Helia, Tom, Fenwick and Jack all appearing at the same time. And a moment later, Master Barde and Medley disappeared again.

Tom didn't move, but Helia and Fenwick flew to their companions and Jack walked quickly to Kari's side. Helia began to sing and Fenwick swayed from side to side from the music. Bekah stepped forward and lifted Tom from the ground where he had scarcely moved.

"We must first hide the flag, and then make a plan. How will we find the other flags?" James was already walking toward Bekah who was holding the flag in one hand and Tom in the other.

"My recommendation is that Tom and Jack guard the flag." Kari said quickly. "But where should we hide it?"

"That is a great idea, Tom can tell me if anyone is coming close to the flag. He is small enough that nobody will see him."

"Fenwick has great eyes, we should have him fly up and give us any information he can about location of the other flags." Michael jumped in. "As for our flag, I can take it into the mine and hide it there if we want."

"Another great idea!" Bekah jumped in, "And we should split up to find the other flags."

At that, Fenwick lifted into the air and began to fly and Kari began to bark and growl her discussion with Jack. James, of course, understood every word.

"They would like you to guard the flag. They recommended hiding it in the mine."

"That is where they would expect it to be. I will gladly do it, but would recommend another location."

Helia's song became louder and all four heard her voice in their minds, "The mine is far too easy a spot. But Jack guard the mine he will. Then when they come a searching, find the flag they never will."

"Tom says he has an idea." Bekah said smiling.

"See…the…tree…over…there?…We…can…hide…it…there…. And…then…I….can…sit…under…the…bush." James heard Tom speak to Bekah's mind.

"He says to hide it under the tree over there. Then he can hide under the bush nearby and they will never find him. I will know, since he can telepathically tell me anywhere, if they are getting close."

"I like that idea. Michael, did you bring your blindfold?" James asked.

"What? No, why would I do that?"

"Here, take mine. Put it on and let me know where everyone else is!"

"Oh, yeah. Great idea. Thanks." Michael said as he grabbed the blindfold and put it on.

James looked up and saw Fenwick circling high above. He looked like a small spec in the bright blue sky. It was only about 8:00am, they were in Utah near a small mining town called... Frisco. He could see it now. But the town was now mostly abandoned, and the year was 1915. He wanted Michael to find all the patrols, but he needed to find the flags. He closed his eyes and began searching.

Donald was speaking to Melvina, as James stood next to Julia Salamander. He thought she, Julia, was very pretty, but that was not his purpose right now. He was seeing what she saw now. Adelbert was using a shovel he had made from a rock that he split and a branch he cut off a tree. It was very impressive and was making quick work of digging a hole behind a red one-room school house. The royal purple and gold flag was behind him ready to be buried.

"Melvina, can you try to find the other patrols? Master Balthizar thought you would be able to figure out our location and the location of others through your Telepathy."

"I was just starting to get the hang of it, but I don't have the blindfold right now."

"I have my blindfold, let me try a little first." the voice came from Julia standing next to James and the vision became dark momentarily as she placed the blindfold on.

James was back with his patrol as Kari was again barking at Jack, *"What do you think about behind the tree, with you as a decoy in the mine?"*

"Yes. I will dig you a hole quickly, as none of you are equipped to do it." Jack seemed to smile as he leapt to the tree and began digging a deep hole at its base.

Bekah knew immediately what was happening and walked over with the flag and Tom to the tree and placed Tom next to the bush where he would be hiding and placed the flag into the hole that was quickly buried by Jack. Jack then jogged into the mine with a quick howl.

"I am ready. Now you all get to work."

"James, you and I can speak from anywhere, so we should probably separate." Bekah said very cautiously and slowly. James could tell this made her very nervous.

"I have a report." Michael said removing his blindfold. "The Griffin patrol is approximately two thousand yards to the southwest. They are close to a small building, maybe a schoolhouse. All four are currently behind the building at this time."

James nodded and smiled, and Michael continued, "The Centaur patrol is to the southeast over three thousand yards surrounded by round dome buildings that look a lot like large beehives. The four of them have already hidden their flag most likely, because they are all in a circle.

"The Minotaur patrol is five thousand yards to the south. They seem to be close to a mine or other hole in the ground. I didn't find any buildings or other recognizable areas here. All five are there, but Elli seems to be moving away from the others in a southerly direction. The other four are already moving north."

"I think we must stay close together, initially. We don't yet know what to expect. This will not be a simple Steal The Flag exercise, so we must be prepared to help each other. And Helia and Fenwick can be of assistance as well." James paused as they all stayed silent looking at him.

"It worries me that I don't know how we might get hurt. There must be more to this."

"I was hoping it was just a scare tactic!" Bekah said rapidly, but at a very low pitch.

"Jack is doing his job; shouldn't we get moving?" Kari said nervously

At that moment, a large snake came slithering from above the mine. It moved slowly, but separated them from the mine and stopped to curl at the entrance. It raised its head, to be 3 feet above the ground and started to shake its rattled tail.

Bekah backed away slowly and grabbed James' arm. "We need to get going! We can worry about the snake later!"

"But Jack is in the mine!"

"Bekah is right! We need to move southwest toward the town. I know where the flag is buried!"

Michael then looked up with a start, "Wait! What? How do you know?"

"My Orientopathy skills are still developing, but I do have other skills we can use! I saw them bury the flag behind the schoolhouse. That is why they were all there when you found them. Oh, and we are in Frisco, an old mining town in Beaver County, Utah. The year is around 1915, so it should be basically abandoned."

"Frisco?" Bekah said with a start. "That is the town well known for a Titan killing many years ago."

As everyone looked at her in surprise. "I read it in *The Forgotten History of The Titan* from Master McAdams library. Master Julianna recommended I read it."

Kari started to laugh. "You are ridiculous!"

"What? I like to read. Oh, and if this is really a different time, according to *The Book of Adam*, Chapter 12, when Chronopathy is utilized for a different time then it is not true time travel, but an image of the location. Animals and people may not truly be there. That snake may not be really a threat!"

"Yes, but we have already dug into the ground. There is something different about this location. We should treat everything as if it is real. I have seen multiple 'visions' but this is different." James stopped and looked back at the snake. "If you are concerned, Helia and I can take care of it while you three start traveling toward the Griffin patrol!"

They agreed and started moving as Michael directed, and James turned back to the snake. Helia immediately flew into the air and caught the eyes of the snake. Red eyes shown from the opening of the mine and James began to bark a command.

"Jack. Helia and I will keep it distracted. Can you help us kill it?"

As he barked, the snake turned back to him. James looked carefully into the darkness and Jack didn't say a word.

"I am ready when you are!" James read Jack's mind and responded to him again in a bark.

"Now!"

Helia flew at full speed directly toward the head of the snake, as the rattling became louder. James stepped forward to just out of the reach of the snake's strike and Jack stepped from the dark mine and crushed the snake's head with his powerful jaws before it even knew he was there. The snake was too focused on Helia and James to hear Jack strike from behind.

As the snake fell limp to the ground, James pulled a pocket knife from his pocket and cut off the rattle from the tail, skinned the snake and then using a branch from the nearby tree created an arrow that he laced with the venom from the snake and a club to which he affixed the rattle. He carefully placed these two items in his bag and they turned toward the others.

With the excitement of the battle over, James felt great power coursing through his body and he began to run to catchup with the others. Within minutes he was by their side and although sweating a little was very energized and ready for more.

As they continued to move slowly toward the town, they got close enough to be within eyeshot of the schoolhouse. It was definitely a red one-roomed schoolhouse that was slightly broken down from disuse. The building appeared unguarded, but something didn't seem right to James.

Michael began to direct them around the building, but James sensed something wrong.

"There's a moat around the building. We will need to go 200 yards to the west to get around it. There is only a small 1 foot path available on that side."

"The owls on the roof won't talk to me. I am assuming they are prepared to attack." Kari said as she continued to hoot to the owls.

"Bekah and Michael. I will give you the map of where to go. Michael, it is imperative that you lead her to the flag. Kari, keep distracting them as much as you can."

James then leapt into the air and Helia caught him and started to soar up into the air. Fenwick flew lower to join James & Helia in the air over the schoolhouse. The owls took the bait and Kari began to shout directions to Fenwick and Helia as the battle began. James dropped to the top of the schoolhouse and pulled the club from his bag. As he shook it, the rattle sounded and distracted the owls just enough to allow Michael and Bekah to run across the moat on the small path to the schoolhouse. Once they reached the back wall of the schoolhouse, they were hidden from view.

At that moment, James heard what must be a great battle happening to the east. James wanted to focus on the other battle, but he felt it important to focus on the current battle at this time.

The birds and owls fought in midair, but the poor owls, three of them, were no match for the powerful wings of Helia and the speed and agility of Fenwick. The battle raged on, but the owls were losing at every turn.

At that very moment, sounds echoed through the sky, *"The Centaur have been eliminated! The Centaur Flag is now controlled by the Minotaur!"* James quickly recognized the voice as coming from Master McAdams.

The air was then filled again with the powerful cry of Jens from the Centaur patrol, "NO!" And then all was quiet again.

James looked up and the owls were nowhere to be seen. Helia and Fenwick flew down to the roof where James still stood.

"We need a shovel." Michael called out as Bekah was trying to dig with her hands. "We will never make it."

Helia lifted James to the ground and then James quickly shaped the other half of the rock (that Adelbert had used for his shovel) into a small hand shovel. It was not as impressive, but it would work. As Bekah and Kari dug for what seemed like hours, James began to search for the other flags and Michael replaced the blindfold to search for the other teams.

At that very moment, an arrow came whirring through the air and hit Kari in the shoulder. She dropped the shovel and Bekah screamed. Michael tore off the blindfold and began to point to Adelbert about 100 yards away raising his bow to shoot again. Bekah had stopped digging and was holding Kari with fear in her eyes. Kari was panting and cringing with pain. James just looked over at Michael and began to yell commands.

"We need to protect the girls, so they can continue to dig. If we get the flag, the battle is over. Can you get Fenwick to attack?"

As he spoke, he quickly removed his backpack and began to remove the single arrow he had, but he had no bow. What was he going to do? Then he looked at Kari, who was now crying and anger began to course through his entire body. Nobody was supposed to get hurt. How could Master Julianna and Master McAdams allow this to happen?

As he continued to think of options, Adelbert was joined by Julia, Melvina and Donald. All were carrying what looked like guns and were running forward to join the fight.

On their side, however, Bekah was still holding Kari and Michael was staring at James still wondering what to do. As the anger increased in James, however, time seemed to completely stop. Nobody was moving, even all sound had completely stopped, every sound except Helia's music. She seemed to be moving as normal and seemed to be smiling at him. This gave him courage and he began to search his backpack for options. He looked around and everything changed…

He wasn't standing next to Michael anymore, but was standing by a large tree. The willow tree had a large, straight branch that he easily removed with his pocketknife. As he was cutting the branch, some of the bark fell to the ground, and he placed it into his backpack. With minimal effort, he formed the branch into a bow. He then quickly formed a string using a combination of roots and willow stems he was able to find around him. He also quickly cut three additional arrows and sharpened them to a point. If he was going to fight, he was going to be prepared. He looked around again and noticed a large fallen tree to his left and quickly shaped a portion of it to a club and another portion into a shield. The shield when complete was about 4 feet wide and 4 feet tall. This would be perfect to protect the girls as they continued to dig. He also quickly formed a second shovel and decided it was time to return.

Moments later he was standing next to Michael again and he noticed everyone was still stopped. He wasn't exactly sure how it all happened, but he was excited to see he was now ready for the battle. So, he placed the shield covering the girls and placed the second shovel next to them. Everything then started to return to normal speed. He could hear Donald yelling:

"Where did that shield come from? We need to get James! We must stop him before they find our flag!"

Michael's voice also broke in, "James, what can we do?"

James handed him the club and then readied the first arrow in his new bow. The spring of the arrow felt very powerful as the branch bent. The elasticity was truly coming from the bow itself, and not from the string, but it appeared it would work really well. He pulled back the string and aimed it at Adelbert. If he could hit his right arm, he would be unable to shoot anymore. The arrow jumped from his bow as he let the string go and it ripped through the sky and found its mark in Adelbert's right bicep muscle. Adelbert's right arm fell to his side and he fell to his knees, but not before he had released the next arrow.

The arrow whirred through the air and James noticed it was coming directly at him. It was coming very strait and directly at his chest. Due to his shooting his own arrow, he would not have sufficient time to dodge or stop the arrow. But then time slowed again.

The arrow seemed to almost stop in midair and slowly moved towards him. James eyes got really big as he could see the arrow slowly rotating and barreling towards him. As it got closer, he reached out his hand and grabbed it from the air, turned it around and placed it in his own bow. The motion was quick and fluid, and actually quite easy with time moving so slowly. The moment the arrow landed in his bow, the time returned to regular speed and he heard a terrible scream from Julia.

"Did you see that? He just caught your arrow in midair!"

Michael's eyes were also large in surprise, but a smile started to move across his lips as James shot it back at Donald. As the arrow flew through the air, Donald dived to the ground and it missed. Julia and Melvina ran to Adelbert as Julia was quickly removing her backpack and searching for bandages. James and Michael ran to Kari, behind the shield, and James began to examine her wound. The battle had been paused, due to the injuries, but it wouldn't be long before the attack continued.

As James walked towards Kari, Master Julianna and Master Ironhorse appeared standing next to her.

"Do you know how to help her James?" Master Ironhorse asked.

James looked carefully at her and began to shake his head. "I have not yet figured out Hippocratesense. I do know that the injury is not serious, that we can remove the arrow and just bandage it, but because of the pain and swelling that will start, her right arm will be hard to use."

"Very good! If we help you, she will no longer be allowed to participate."

"Please James," Kari pleaded. "I can deal with the pain."

As James looked at the tears in her eyes, and the pleading look from Bekah, he looked very carefully at the arrow and the associated wound. The arrow was not very deep. It missed the nerves and blood vessels to the shoulder and was stuck in the deltoid muscle as it attaches to the scapula at the back of the shoulder. The damage was minimal, but the location would directly interfere with the movement of the shoulder.

James carefully removed his backpack again, pulled out the small bandages he had packed that morning, looking for the larger ABD pad that he remembered removing from his home first aid kit before coming to camp. He then grabbed the shaft of the arrow and thought, *"Bekah, I need you to hold her tight. This is going to hurt!"* Bekah eyes got bigger again and she hugged Kari immediately. At the exact same moment, James pulled the arrow and it released from the deltoid muscle fibers and Kari screamed, tears pouring down her face. James then placed the ABD pad to her shoulder and pulled the elastic bandage from his bag and wrapped her shoulder to hold the pad in place.

Kari's face turned white and eyes seemed to roll back into her head and she went limp.

"What happened? Is she dead?" Bekah screamed at a high pitched, rapid pace. "Please Master Ironhorse…"

James just continued to move quickly. "Please lay her flat Bekah and raise her feet 12 inches. She is in shock."

Michael looked up as he continued to dig. "I have the flag. Here it is!" And he lifted the royal purple and gold flag above his head.

As he lifted it from the hole, a voice filled the air. *"The Griffin have been eliminated! The Griffin Flag is now controlled by the Sphinx!"* Master Julianna then disappeared.

"Master Julianna, do we really have to be done? Can't we at least try to get another flag." James heard Donald pleading, but the sound soon stopped as the Griffin patrol were returned to Campus Gaea.

"Well done James," Master Ironhorse said. "You did well in treating shock. Ensure they are laying down, raise the feet 12 inches and keep them warm. She will be awake in the next few minutes and will be able to continue to work with you."

At that very moment, Master Julianna reappeared and both she and Master Ironhorse were gone.

Michael took a deep breath and sat down. "I think I need a snack." he said with a laugh. "That was more intense than I was expecting. Where did you get all this equipment James?"

"I seemed to jump to where everything was and then jumped back while time stood still." James responded.

"Chronopathy! I didn't know you had if figured out." Bekah said, now with excitement back in her high-pitched voice.

"Wait. I didn't do it on purpose. Nor do I think I could do it on demand. It just happened."

"Too bad," Michael said. "It would be much easier to get to the other flags if we could jump there!"

Kari said nothing, but just sat there with a bit of a grimace on her face.

"Are you sure you shouldn't have gone back with Master Ironhorse Kari?" Bekah asked.

"I will not…leave my team," she groaned, obviously in pain. "But the pain is getting worse!"

James looked at her in concern and then his mind started racing. He grabbed a cotton sweatshirt from his backpack and his canteen. He also noticed the bark sitting in his backpack. Good thing he brought two canteens to this trip. He took a quick swig of water from the canteen to reduce the water amount in it and then ground up the bark and placed it into the metal canteen. He broke up one of the arrows he made and created a small fire, using flint and steel and his bow string for kindling. With the small fire, he placed the metal canteen in the fire and started to heat it up. As it heated, he continued to stoke the fire with pieces from the shield he had brought to protect Kari and Bekah. In no time at all, the canteen water was bubbling, and James put the fire out.

Everyone else were just watching, not sure what he was doing. He then cut the sweatshirt into strips and began to soak them with the willow tea. He also poured a small cup and handed it to Kari.

"Drink this. It will decrease your pain."

He then immediately went to work unwrapping the wound on her shoulder and placing the wet strips over the wound and replacing the elastic bandage to keep them in place. Almost immediately, Kari started to relax as her pain began to subside.

As they all started to relax, Bekah prepared a snack for everyone and Michael started looking again for the final patrol by replacing the blindfold. *"Where were the Minotaur?"* as he began to search.

James closed his eyes and began his search for the other two flags.

Elli stood by a dome shaped building with anger in her face and looking with almost hatred at Lizzy.

"Why should I listen to you? We must move away from all our flags or James will be able to find us."

"How do you know that?" Lizzy asked.

"I have my ways. He has been searching and can read your mind, see your location and even review our past. Why are we still here?"

"You are giving him more credit than he deserves!" Alexander shot back.

"I agree with her. He seems to be getting stronger every day. I fear even his strength is greater than mine." Ryan said quickly. "We must set a trap, for they may already be coming here."

Michael pulled his blindfold. "They have obviously just hid the Centaur flag again. They are where the Centaur started over there." He pointed to the east.

Kari stood with a smile on her face. "I am ready. Let's go."

Bekah handed each a snack, and they began moving to the east after carefully crossing the moat again. The speed of travel accelerated as they followed Michael as their guide. James knew it was a trap, but also knew it was their best chance to get the next flag. As they approached, however, he began to worry that another one of them would get hurt. He needed to find the flag.

The dome building was one of four buildings, and Ryan stood behind the third one from the left. He was carefully placing the flag in the hole and then using his hands quickly covered it. With his great strength, he easily filled up the hole without a shovel. He then quickly looked around and the vision stopped.

"Charcoal kilns? I forgot that they had these here in Frisco."

Everyone looked at Bekah as she pointed to the four dome shaped buildings.

"They were used as smelters to prepare the Silver ore." Bekah continued.

"The flag is buried behind one of the kilns." James said quickly.

"Four kilns, each of us should search behind one." Michael jumped in. "Why don't you take the second one from the right James."

James smiled, knowing that was the location of the flag and the likely trap.

"Be careful! I fear there is a trap." James whispered.

As he finished his statement and moved around to the back of the kiln, from the left side James heard a goat just moments before he was caught under his right side ribs and was butted 10 feet away from the kiln.

"To scared to come at me face to face?" James bleated at Beliza.

"I have watched you since coming to camp. I am not dumb enough to face you head on!"

All the sudden Kari bleated from the left, "Senhora Cabra, did you think he was the only one that you needed to surprise?"

As Beliza turned to look at Kari, Michael came from behind and knocked her out with the club James had given him. He then quickly tied up the dazed goat and started digging behind the second kiln.

James quickly stood, laughing and he and Bekah walked over to likewise start digging. If that was the only trap, they were in good shape.

With three of them digging, Kari still not able to use her arm very well, they quickly found the red, white and black flag of the Centaur. As they lifted it from the hole, a voice again rang out, "*The Centaur Flag is now controlled by the Sphinx!*"

The Sphinx patrol looked at each other with excitement. "We must stay one step ahead of the Minotaur patrol and we have this one." Bekah almost screamed in her rapid, high-pitched excited voice.

James mind broke into vision:

Elli was looking angrily at Lizzy and berating her for the failure of Beliza. "Was that the best she could do? They didn't even need to try very hard to beat her."

"You have no right to blame all this on her!" Ryan jumped in. "We have all failed so far!"

Alexander Black walked up and began to speak more quietly, "If we fight, we have already lost. We need to go get one of the flags. I suggest we go get their flag."

"Great idea. Do we have any idea where they would have started?" Ryan asked.

"I have my sources...and they were by the mine north of here." Elli jumped in.

"Let's see if I can get us there quickly." Sidonia Maple chimed in.

James then saw them take hands and time start to slow down. Was this from the past, or was it happening now. Were they already by the mine?

The vision cleared and Bekah seemed to be reading his mind this time.

"I agree, we need to split up."

"How should we separate? Should we do what Bekah suggested at the beginning?" Michael jumped in.

"Yes. Kari with me and Michael with Bekah." James chimed in. "Helia will get you back to camp quickly because the Minotaur may already be there. She can also help you fight."

Before James could say more, Bekah was already running towards where they came from and Michael joined her. Helia swooped down and each grabbed her feet and they were gone, quickly being carried into the sky.

James then walked toward Kari, who was now very nervous.

"You will travel with me. We are going to try Chronopathy if you are willing."

"I am ready. Will it hurt?"

"Not if I do it correctly. But I have never tried to do it myself. Every other time it has just happened."

James grabbed her hand and time stood still. He knew right where the flag was and before he could even concentrate on going there, they were standing over the packed dirt where the hole was. He could even see how it was folded. This was too easy, James was wondering what was going to happen.

Suddenly, James saw a cage falling from above and he rolled out of the way to stay free of it. Kari, however, was not so lucky and the cage caught her. Arrows then flew from all sides, several catching him, as he tried to stop time and catch them. Kari in the cage was protected from the arrows. But neither of them was protected from the ring of fire that immediately surrounded them. As James struggled to his feet, pain searing into his left thigh and right arm from the arrows deeply embedded there, rocks began to fly again from all directions. The rocks didn't seem to stop and seemed to be being shot from all directions.

James dodged the rocks as he hurried back to the cage. This was impressive protections, but lucky for him the rocks didn't hurt at all because of the growing strength in his body. Even the pain from the arrows was subsiding. They needed to get the flag before the Minotaur got their flag.

He jumped to the cage and with one quick motion, he disarmed the cage and threw it off Kari. They then began to dig. Kari seemed to be feeling much better as she realized they were just moments away from completing the challenge. Both dug with all their hearts, using the shovels James made earlier that day. And all of the sudden, they saw it. The flag was there, folded as James had known, the navy blue and silver colors shown bright. Kari reached down with her right hand and through the pain lifted the flag into the air.

The sky seemed to erupt with light as they were all ripped back to Campus Gaea as the words rang out. *The Minotaur have been eliminated! The Minotaur Flag and ALL FOUR FLAGS are now controlled by the Sphinx! The challenge is over! The Sphinx have won."*

As James and Kari found themselves back in Master Julianna's tent, Bekah and Michael were also there. The Minotaur patrol was also there but were not happy. Elli was again berating everyone in her patrol and blaming them for being incompetent. She was obviously very unhappy that she had lost.

At this point, James didn't care! He grabbed Kari's hand and ran to join Michael and Bekah.

"You did it!" Bekah screamed in excitement.

"No, we did it. It took every one of us to succeed." James responded.

"Well said my boy." James turned with a start to see Master Doc McAdams walking towards them.

"It has been years since anyone has retrieved all the flags. No patrol has ever done it as a first year and even in later years have never done it so quickly. You shall all be rewarded, but first we must treat your wounds."

It wasn't until that moment that James remembered he still had arrows stuck in his arm and leg. But before he could say anything, Master Dakota Ironhorse was treating each of the injured Titans and the wounds and pain were gone. James wasn't sure exactly what was done, but he was not just treated, but completely healed. Even Kari's wound was gone. He would definitely need to learn that skill.

CHAPTER 23
PATROLS NO MORE

James sat on his bed staring off into space and could hardly focus on the book laying open on his lap. His mind kept being drawn back to the Patrol Challenge and the dinner after. His wounds were gone thanks to Master Ironhorse and he didn't even have pain. But he kept hearing the words of Master Doc McAdams during dinner.

"Never before has a first year patrol succeeded in completing the Primary Patrol Challenge with ALL the flags. Well done! Just know that you now have targets on your back for every other challenge this year."

Was it really true? Nobody had done that? How did they do it as four learning Titans? Why were his skills presenting themselves when necessary even before he had knowledge how to use them? They would not be underestimated again, and the Secondary and Final Challenges will include students from higher years. He looked down at the gold medal in his hand and knew that everything was going to change now. Angelica said at dinner that all the courses get harder now (after the Primary Challenge) and they will be expected to finish the requirements for their rank advancement before summer was over. He would need to ask Bekah when he got a chance what was still needed to finish the *Silver Spark* award.

As he continued to think, he realized that the next class for the Phoenixenses was happening tonight and he wasn't sure how to proceed. It would need to get more organized as more individuals were joining them. With that thought, he looked down at the now wrinkled page of *The Secret Life of a Concordant* and read the words again:

"Learn, Do, Show, Go"

So that was how they were supposed to learn. They were supposed to learn how to do something first. At that point, they would strive to do it based on what they learned. The next step would be to show someone else how to do it. Go was then to help the individual taught to do it themselves. Then let them go and do. That was how Master McAdams was running the Phoenixenses classes all those years ago. Maybe they should strive to do that as part of their classes as well. So, using that as their method, what should they be teaching tonight?

At that moment, he heard an excited Bekah in his mind.

"She wants to take us again!"

Before James could ask for more information Michael came running into the tent.

"Let's go James, Master Julianna is taking the entire first year Titans on a field trip. She is teaching us again!"

He too sounded very excited, and James could completely understand because her classes were usually the best. He quickly closed the book on his lap and tossed it on the bed and jumped toward the door to just miss Michael as he ran out. As the two raced out of the tent, they saw Kari and Bekah already running toward Master Julianna's tent.

James ran next to Michael as they caught up to the two girls easily and James heard Bekah's thoughts again.

"I wonder where she will be taking us this time. Maybe we will go to another historical site. I wish I was a Chronopath!"

As they ran to the large purple ancient castle-like tent and through the gold trimmed door, the room was already full with the Griffin and Centaur patrols. Senior Patrol leader Marcus

Regulus and Assistant Martha Jewel were also there as was Angelica Eve who was excited to see them. Master Julianna was bouncing at the front of the class and kept counting the students waiting for the entire class to be present.

As Emma Johnson and the Minotaur patrol entered the tent, Master Julianna called out with excitement.

"We are all here. I have one of my all time favorite trips planned for you today! Please move closer so that we can all take hands. This is always the largest group I ever take on a Field Trip, but this is only effective if you all are present."

Her voice rang through the tent as if she was screaming, although she was just speaking. All the first year Titans were looking at each other in excitement. Master Julianna's excitement was so contagious, even James felt excitement similar to how Bekah usually was with a new class.

"Where is this favorite place?" James thought as Master Julianna looked on with excitement shinning through her half-moon spectacles.

The tent began to fade and they were off...James, however, was getting more accustomed to this form of travel and although everyone else was frozen could see Master Julianna still bouncing up and down with everyone linked hand-to-hand in a circle. As she smiled at him, he immediately knew where they were going. *Gettysburg, Pennsylvania, here we come!*

As the surroundings came back into view, Bekah looked up at James with surprise.

"Gettysburg?" she thought with excitement. "Why are we here?"

"Cemetery Hill, to be exact." he thought.

But before he could continue, Master Julianna started speaking.

"As some of you have already determined, we are on Cemetery Hill near Gettysburg, Pennsylvania. And here was fought one of the greatest battles of all time when it comes to freedom. The year is 1863 and the date is November 19th. In the beginning of July, a three-day battle was fought and close to 51,000 soldiers were killed on both sides. Bodies of brother fighting against brother, father fighting against son and neighbor fighting against neighbor fell to never rise again. Hot lead ripped through their bodies and swords beat against swords. Artillery and rifle fire could be heard echoing through this great valley and the future of a nation lay in the balance. This battle was much more than a simple battle in the Civil War of the United States. This battle changed the course of history and changed a nation forever. What can we learn as Titans from the herculean battle that ended on the 3rd of July 1863?"

As her voice rang in the wind, another voice could be heard in the distance. James could see a great gathering of people in the distance and heard a voice ringing out a well recognized speech.

"Four score and seven years ago our forefathers brought forth on this continent, a new nation, conceived in Liberty, and dedicated to the proposition that all men are created equal.

"Now we are engaged in a great civil war, testing whether that nation, or any nation so conceived and so dedicated, can long endure. We are met on a great battlefield of that war. We have come to dedicate a portion of that field, as a final resting place for those who here gave their lives that that nation might live. It is altogether fitting and proper that we should do this.

"But, in a larger sense, we can not dedicate—we can not consecrate—we can not hallow—this ground. The brave men, living and dead, who struggled here, have consecrated it, far above our poor power to add or detract. The world will little note, nor long remember what we say here, but it can never forget what they did here. It is for us the living, rather, to be dedicated here to the unfinished work which they who fought here have thus far so nobly advanced. It is rather for us to be here dedicated to the great task remaining before us—that from these honored dead we take increased devotion to that cause for which they gave the last full measure of devotion—that we here highly resolve that these dead shall not have died in vain—that this nation, under God, shall have a new birth of freedom—and that government of the people, by the people, for the people, shall not perish from the earth."

Bekah turned with excitement. "That was President Abraham Lincoln! Are we really here?"

Master Julianna again began to speak.

"With the help of Master Belle, I was able to make it possible for you to hear what is happening below us in that large gathering. That speech changed the course of the war. That speech reiterates what I would like all of you to learn. We have just completed a very competitive Primary Patrol Challenge and only one team was able to win. But as Titans, our battle is far bigger than competing one patrol against another. We need not fight brother against brother, sister against sister or neighbor against neighbor. Instead we should stand up as a group and stand for freedom throughout the world. You are TITANS first and members of a patrol second. Please join with your sisters and brothers and be one!"

As James looked around he could hear the thoughts of many.

"She's right. We should work together and we'd be so much more!"

"Wait...why are we working as patrols then?"

"Aren't there other Patrol Challenges? What are they trying to teach us?"

"Ha. Does she really think this speech will change any of us?"

James looked up with a start. That last one was coming from Elli, who seems almost annoyed at this fieldtrip. But the rest of the First Years may be buying in! As he continued to think, they returned to the tent and were excused to return to their camps.

As he walked back towards camp with Bekah, Michael and Kari all talking with excitement, he couldn't help but hear the words again in his head.

"...Does she really think this speech will change any of us?"

Is that how Camilla felt while she was here at camp? He felt sadness that she never enjoyed the excitement and joy of learning and growing together with fellow Titans. She never experienced the happiness that could come from this new opportunity and this new learning. Did her anger and frustration at life keep her from seeing these great blessings that

God had given her? Did the death of her mother keep her from recognizing a loving father? Did her Concordant abilities cause her to discount the teaching and learning that she could receive from the teachers here at camp? He felt sorry for her and wished he could help her in some way.

"James, I was told there is a special meeting tonight. Can we join you?" he looked up to see Angelica and Emma standing next to him.

"Master Julianna wants us to work together! We want to learn with you and help you learn. Master McAdams suggested we join you as well." Emma added.

"Your skills and learning would be greatly appreciated. There is much we can learn from each of you!" James felt relieved to have two additional skilled Titans joining them that night. He looked at Bekah and smiled as he realized the Phoenixenses were actually becoming a mini-Band of Fire.

The rest of the evening flew by to the moment James found himself walking down the overgrown path and again came to the large hill with thick overgrowth blocking access to the base of the hill. The moon was full and lit the sky signifying midnight and James heard each of the individuals entering the cave behind the overgrowth. Helia immediately followed, and James crawled in last of all.

The soft red glow of Helia again lit the walls and Bekah's soon lit lantern reflected off all the walls and ceiling creating a large room as bright as noon day sun. With all eight individuals in the room, it still was obviously much larger than the great hall and had crystalline rock lining the walls and ceilings. There were no stalactites or stalagmites and no passageways coming off the large room where they stood. And there was absolutely no sound from the outside heard in that room. Even their talking seemed to be muffled as James entered the room. But the walls seemed to come to life immediately upon his standing and voices from the past seemed to echo through the hall.

"I solemnly covenant, my brothers and sisters of Fire, to do my Duty to God, to serve others with all my heart, to stand as a witness of faith, knowledge and strength, to use my gifts to protect

freedom, happiness and independence for all, to lift the weak, to comfort the sad and to befriend the friendless. That I may by so doing stand against evil in all its various forms. To this I pledge my sacred honor."

James looked up with a smile and each of the eight stood with their right arm to the square repeating the words as they echoed through the hall.

James then added as the room again grew silent, "And as Phoenixenses, we will uphold these values in exactness and honor. For God Himself shall hold us accountable to bless and serve others throughout our lives!"

Everyone repeated after him.

"Tonight, we will be improving our skills in Chronopathy. For this reason, I am excited to have Emma with us. But we are going to learn in a unique way. The process is called *Learn, Do, Show, Go.* We will all learn from Emma how Chronopathy works and then she will use this skill that she has taught us. We will attempt to follow through with what she has taught us with her help and then try doing it without her help. The hope is that we can all gain at least some abilities in Chronopathy by the end of the night."

As James stopped talking, Emma stepped forward with excitement.

"Master Julianna has never let me teach but has only allowed me to help. I don't know how to go back in time but have gotten good at changing location. We will start with the basic principles of how Chronopathy works."

Emma paused for a moment, and then continued. "Chronopathy is actually the manipulation of time. By changing the speed at which time is progressing, travel can be done outside of time. Or in other words, in a matter of seconds, I can move distances that would usually take hours. As the ability is improved, however, even the world is constrained by time and a Chronopath can fly through the air, walk on water or jump over mountains. James has asked me to teach each of you, so I will show you how this works. I am not sure how much each of you can do not being Chronopaths."

Helia then began to sing, *"Titan skills more than one have you may, and in this cave power much greater shall be."*

Although James was not exactly sure what she was saying, he smiled and stepped forward.

"The purpose of the Phoenixenses is to improve our Primary Titan power but is also to help us develop additional Titan powers and strengths if possible. Master Doc McAdams used this process years ago to help many develop additional skills. Even Master Julianna has developed two additional skills that she uses with her Chronopathy to have greater abilities. I don't know how it happens, but this cave is supposed to help."

Bekah stepped forward in excitement, "I have read that using skills together in a Concordant fashion—two skills together—makes both skills more powerful. There are stories of self-healing, jumping to an exact time and place and even jumping to location of a memory as an observer. I would love to learn Chronopathy if possible to use with my Telepathy." The speed and pitch of her speaking just increased as she spoke.

Angelica looked impressed and stepped forward. "Where did you read that? I didn't know that was even a thing."

"I think it was in *The Forgotten History of The Titan*." Bekah responded.

"Master Julianna has told me the same!" Emma jumped in. "That is how she's able to jump through time and space to and exact time and place. I think she said it was Orientopathy and Chronopathy together."

At that, everyone was interested and Emma began to show how Chronopathy worked.

The initial task was very simple, as small circles were drawn on the ground and Emma jumped from one circle to the next. Her explanation was very simple, "Focus on the location and then move there. The key is to concentrate on moving there faster than you can physically move. If you do it right, you will be there immediately. Moving to a location you can see is easier than moving to a location you cannot see."

She then had each individual try to move, as she explained and instructed them. Each tried. Some would walk from circle to circle and then laugh. Kari and Lizzy couldn't stop laughing after trying multiple times and always ending up walking to the circles instead of jumping from one to the other. Michael, however, didn't find it funny that he was unable to accomplish this task and was getting visibly frustrated. As Michael got more and more frustrated, Ryan wasn't sure he even wanted to try. After several tries, Bekah found herself jumping from circle to circle on command. Angelica was also able to jump, sometimes, from circle to circle, but was often seen just standing in the circle concentrating. James and Emma were encouraging everyone as they attempted. James, himself, didn't even try to jump between the circles.

The second task, however, James did do. This task was jumping from the cave to the lake and back. Emma did it with ease and was actually even surprised herself at how easy it was. James likewise did it with ease. As he returned, he could hear Helia's voice again, *"In the cave, easy it will be. Practice you must to elsewhere it do."*

Bekah and Angelica were visibly disappointed when they were unable to jump to the lake. But with James and Emma working together, the group was easily able to jump as a whole to the lake and back. Bekah was surprised at how it felt to make that jump. James had previously told her what it felt like, but she had never felt it herself until that night.

Everyone began to talk about what it felt like.

"I felt the time seem to slow down and everything fade. Then we were at the lake. Does it always feel that way?" Ryan was asking.

"For me it felt like I was being ripped through space and then my feet again touched the ground. Are we sure this isn't actually magic or teleporting?" Kari said with a grin.

"From what I have read, it is the principle behind teleporting. Time is slowed to a crawl, while the speed of your body is increasing in speed and the particles of your body move through the particles around you at such a great speed you seem to fly or teleport. I understand the principle from *The Book of Adam*, but have never felt it before. It must be the cave." the

slow, meticulous speed with which Bekah spoke was almost a
reverence for what she had just discovered.

James remained silent, as he had felt this many times before.
He thought back to the first time he traveled this way, in the
bus and knew he still had much more to learn.

Emma finished her lesson, "You are correct Bekah, as usual.
You are actually manipulating time in two directions. Speeding
up every atom of your body while slowing every atom around
you. Often when someone else transports you, your brain is
slowed with the elements around you and it appears as if you
moved in the blinking of an eye. I LOVE that!"

Angelica then stepped up again, "Next lesson it is my turn.
I am excited to teach you the healing powers. Hopefully it is
as helpful as Emma's lesson today. Thanks again, Emma!"

Each Titan then left after a similar expression of appreciation
and James and Bekah stood in the now empty cave with Helia
and Tom by their sides. It was now 2:30am and it was probably
a good idea to return to their tents for sleep, but neither James
nor Bekah were ready for that.

"James, I know what you are thinking."

"Yes, you do." he said with a smile. "Will you go with me?"

"Do you think you can really do it?" she asked slowly and
in a low, almost nervous pitch.

"Only one way to find out."

With a cautious nod by Bekah, James took her hand and
the world started to fade.

*They flew through the air and found themselves in a hospital
waiting room. It was 12 years before and James quickly recognized
a beautiful young girl sitting in the waiting room with a beautiful,
lightly tanned, petite woman with thick, long blond hair and deep
blue eyes. The girl, although excited, was visibly anxious.*

"He is your half-brother. Are you sure you don't want to see him?"

"But HE is here. He left US and I don't want to see him!"

"He left ME, not you. It is MY fault that he isn't still with us."

"But SHE is also here. How could he marry her, a natural born?"

"But don't you want to see James?"

The girls face started to light up. "Can we see him in the nursery without dad being around?"

"I am sure it can be arranged."

The lady then started speaking without moving her mouth. "Simon. Camilla wants to see the baby but doesn't want to see you. Can you have the baby returned to the nursery for a few minutes?"

Bekah smiled, and James knew she had also heard the telepathic voice.

"Okay Camilla, James is in the nursery."

"How does she know that?" Bekah asked. "I didn't hear a response."

"My father isn't telepathic. She just reads his mind, which is why I think they got divorced."

They then followed Camilla and Aria to the Nursery where a small child was lying in a little bed. No other babies were in the nursery at this time, so there was no question which baby James was.

His full head of hair, blue eyes and a chubby little baby face made him cute. Bekah couldn't hold back her gasp.

"I didn't know you were such a cute baby." she said with a smile.

Before James could respond, however, Camilla stepped forward and fell in love.

"That is my brother? Can I hold him, please?"

The nurse reached down and lifted James from the bed and handed Camilla the little bundle. No words were spoken, but tears fell from her eyes and she cuddled the little baby next to her heart.

Camilla's thoughts were easy to read as Bekah and James heard her, "Oh my dear James. I so wish I could hold you more, could watch you grow and help you learn of the great things of this world. I can't believe that life is so unfair to not allow me to be with you as your sister." Her tears continued to flow, "Although I may not be in your life much, I will always love you and protect you. I will not allow Simon to hurt you or leave you as he did me and my mother. I love you my dear brother and I will always love you!" She then bent down and kissed him as tears continued to fall from her cheeks and she handed the infant back to the nurse and turned away.

As James looked up, he saw tears welling up in Aria's eyes as well that she carefully tried to conceal. She looked up to the far corner of the hall and James noticed his father hidden around the corner, *likewise with tears in his eyes. Through his confusion at all that was happening, James too began to tear up. Camilla loves him? What does that mean for the Order of the Kraken? He had to turn and look away, and Bekah grabbed his hand.*

"Should we go?"

"Yes"

And in that moment, they were back in the cave and tears were still in James eyes and he turned away from Bekah again.

"Why did we go there?" Bekah asked carefully.

"I wanted to see if I could and it was an easy time and place to think about." He then choked back a tear and continued, "I didn't know Camilla was there when I was a newborn. Why haven't my parents ever told me?"

Bekah remained quiet and just stood there in the cave in silence. There was nothing she could say, and truthfully James didn't really want an answer. The night air and the silence thereof was all the answer he felt he deserved at this time.

CHAPTER 24
THE FOURTH OF JULY

As James lay on his cot, he couldn't get the vision of his first day as an infant in the hospital out of his head. What did all of it mean? Why didn't he ever know that Camilla was at the hospital when he was born? Why hadn't he seen her since she was sixteen? He hadn't slept much since coming back from the cave, but he wasn't tired. In fact, he was wondering if he should just get up and start the day.

As he continued to lie there and think, he started to feel almost an anger at his dad. He saw dad there in the shadows and he never told James about Camilla being there. Not even when Camilla lived with them for those years. All those years he felt like dad had always been honest with him and never let him down, but actually when he didn't show at his 12th Birthday, it was just one more time that dad had let him down...

He sat in a small tent, it was very dark. No blindfold this time and the sound of Iguazu Falls still in the distance. He could hear Adam breathing from outside the tent door and could tell he was sitting on a chair. Camilla was in a nearby tent with several other people. By this time, Simon recognized each of them. Minerva Medusa was there to Camilla's left, while Kathryn Circe, Peter

Ulnar and John Vali were to her right. Zoram Balthizar and Elli Ferrimore have been missing from all these discussions for a long time. They haven't been around since....

Oh yes, I remember a meeting that they didn't know I was listening to. Let me think though the meeting again.

"So, do you understand your direction?" Camilla asked. "Doc McAdams will not be easy to fool."

"I don't know that I trust he can do it." Minnie said quickly.

"I understand and will do this. But what about your brother?" Zoram asked with a smile toward Minnie.

"And will you ensure that Doc can't read my mind?" he said turning to John.

"I can block anyone. As long as you don't spend too much time alone with him it will not be a problem."

"Don't underestimate Doc McAdams. He is a powerful Titan." Minnie said with fire in her eyes.

"Don't give him too much credit either." Camilla jumped in. "I have been hiding my thought from him for many years."

"I am more worried about Elli!" Katie said with her deep green, stony cold eyes focused on Zoram. "Can you promise us she's ready too?"

"What worries you about her?"

"You know what we are worried about!" Katie said without blinking. "And it isn't just her age. She will want to make friends. She will want to WIN in competitions. She will try to be liked by the teachers. And her temper, her anger, will be an important obstacle to her keeping her mind from being read by others with Telepathic abilities. Doc McAdams will have no problem entering that mind if she gets angry!"

"You are personally responsible for her, Zoram. I trust you and know you can do it. It is your job to ensure she keeps her anger in check." Camilla said slowly, while looking straight at Katie.

"And I will stay close to camp, in the shadows, so that she will not have an opportunity to mess up. If she gets too competitive, or starts to get angry, I will remind her what she has promised to do." Minnie said with her slightly crooked smile. "I will ensure that she does what she has promised!"

"And if I get the chance," Minnie said again with a smile, "I will find James and take him from the camp."

"You will not hurt him!" Camila said with the first sign of anger in her eyes. "There will come a time when we can help him understand, but for now you CANNOT hurt him. I will NOT allow it!"

The vision faded and Simon sat silently listening carefully to the silence around him.

So, she still cares for James? I was wondering if she had forgotten her promises she made to him those many years ago. But I didn't think about what the meeting was saying. Zoram and Elli are at Doc's camp. I wonder if Doc knows who they really are. And Minnie is also there close to the camp. I don't trust her. Even with Camilla threatening her, she can't control her. Is James in trouble at camp? I wish I had worked harder on my Telepathy back in the days of the Phoenixenses. It might have helped my marriage to Aria too... but I couldn't be happier than I am with Sarah.

The vision faded with James again lying on his cot in the darkness. I need to talk with mom. Maybe she can give me more information. Minnie, or Minerva as Master McAdams calls her, is outside of camp. Is that where Elli was going during the Challenge? What about Camilla? What does this information tell me about Zoram and Elli? Why do I keep having visions of my dad? Too many questions and no answer. I am going to need some help. Maybe mom knows more than she taught me last time. Good thing I get to go home today for the Fourth of July.

The day seemed to pass uneventful from that early morning until James found himself walking toward the cave at the recommendation of Master McAdams. As usual, Bekah was bouncing along side him talking at a fast rate. She seemed to understand why they were headed to the cave, but James was still wondering. Master McAdams said he would meet them there. But why were Kari and Michael sent with the other students to the bus to return home for the day? Were they not going home today? What additional instruction was going to be provided?

As the questions continued, they found themselves coming face to face with Master Julianna and Master McAdams as they came close to the cave. Master Julianna could hardly control her excitement and seemed to be bouncing as they approached. As Bekah saw her there too, she squealed with excitement.

"We are going somewhere, or Master Julianna wouldn't be here!"

"You are correct, but we must enter the cave first." Master McAdams responded.

James looked up with a start as his mind continued to focus on the morning visions. He needed answers and wasn't sure he was excited about this new "trip". He wanted to talk with mom!

As James crawled into the cave, the light from behind him faded and he found himself alone in a dark cave. Although Master McAdams, Master Julianna and Bekah had all crawled in before him, this was not the cave he was used to. In fact, he knew immediately that he was in another time and another place. He was in the dark without a light and was all alone.

"You're not alone James, we are all where we can see you. But this must be you alone that completes this task. Nobody can do it for you."

Anger grew inside him as he listened to the voice that he recognized. What was Master McAdams doing now? Don't they realize that he's not yet a well-developed Titan? Don't they know that he's only 12 years-old?

Then a soft voice, in a slow almost anxious tone rang through his mind, "James, please…you need to trust them. I don't yet understand, but we must trust them."

"Trust them? I can't even see them! Why couldn't they give me more information? Everyone expects me to just understand!"

He even surprised himself as his yell echoed through the cave. Although he had telepathic powers, he had no desire to think his anger and yelled it at the top of his lungs.

"I need to know NOW! What am I supposed to do?"

The cave started to fade and he was whirling through the air. This felt different, however, as he couldn't breathe, couldn't see and couldn't hear anything. His mind was a fog, but every inch of his body ached from his toenails to the hair on his head. He was sure that he was going to die...

As his eyes finally cleared, he sat on the floor in a room he recognized. He was home, but the walls were different, the carpet was newer and mom looked much younger. Then he heard the laugh from behind him. As he turned his heavy head, he could feel his heavy body falling over. Just then a hand, a soft hand, caught him and lifted him from the floor. He knew that hand. He knew that laugh. It was Camilla, but she was much younger.

"Careful Camilla, he has just eaten." Mom's voice rang out.

Camilla was humming a simple song and bouncing him up and down. His head still felt heavy and he struggled to control the motion of his hands and feet. He wanted to yell out and ask what was happening, but the words came out all jumbled. He was just babbling nonsense, not the words he was trying to say.

"I know your thoughts my little man." Camilla whispered in his ear. "I know that you understand far more than we give you credit for. But I also feel your fear. I have felt that fear when my mother died. You will never be left alone! I won't let anyone hurt you! I promise to keep you safe, even if dad fails to protect you as he has often failed me!"

As her words started to trail off, James felt his eyes getting heavy and his head start to droop onto Camilla's soft shoulder. He loved her! He felt safe in her arms. As sleep started to come, he felt her place him in a small bed and then he was asleep.

...He moved restlessly in his small bed and fought to open his eyes. He could still hear Camilla in the distance, but she was not as happy and loving.

"Don't you know that you have blocked me from progressing as a Titan? What are you afraid of? I know your thoughts! I know you don't want me to become powerful! How dare you try to limit my progression. How dare you think you know more than my mom did about what is best for me. You haven't been around at all and now you want to keep me from progressing. I will be a much more powerful Titan than you will ever know. Not even Doc McAdams can stop me from becoming who I am meant to be! If it weren't

for James, I wouldn't be here at all. If you had protected mom as you should have, instead of being selfish, she would still be alive."

"Camilla, we love you." a soft voice said that James recognized as his mother.

"You are not my mother. My mother is dead because of you and dad!"

James then heard a door slam and knew she had once again left the house alone.

"Simon, don't worry. She's just a teenager and is going through a hard time."

"I can't have her talk to you that way."

"It doesn't bother me. I just hope that she understands someday how much we really love her."

The vision faded and James again found himself in the now well-lit cave with the other three.

"Very interesting Doc. I have never seen anything like it. How did you know it would work?"

"This cave has special characteristics. It expands the abilities of individual Titans and helps them do much more than they could do themselves."

"Going that deep into someone's mind to infancy? Even I have never been able to travel like that!"

"It was imperative that we have all four of us to make that happen. James was the key piece because it was his memory. Your ability to travel through time with Chronopathy was key to augmenting his abilities. And Bekah's telepathy, and special connection with James," Master McAdams said with a smile, "allowed us all to hear and see all as it happened."

"What? You needed me here for this?" Bekah said in a rapid, high pitched sound.

"Absolutely, my dear, your telepathic abilities are far more developed than you realize for a first year. There are many in their fifth and sixth years that would love to have your abilities."

"But you could have done it yourself as a Concordant!" Master Julianna said suspiciously.

"Maybe. But Titans are far more powerful when working together, especially when love is involved."

Bekah's face turned a pink, but James didn't notice. In fact, he was more angry than he was when he first entered the cave.

"I keep having these visions. Many are instigated and caused by you!" James shot Master McAdams an angry look. "But I have no answers. Everything causes more questions. Where am I to get the answers?"

Bekah looked at James with fear in her eyes, but Master McAdams smiled with a slight twinkle in his eyes and waited for James to finish. Master Julianna stepped forward to hug James, but Master McAdams raised his hand to stop her.

"Are you done my boy?"

James nodded with tears streaming down his cheeks. His anger seemed to be melting away as the tears dropped onto his now wet shirt.

"Then we shall work on those questions. Know that I can't give you all the answers, but I can help you find the answers. Master Julianna will be an important resource as will Master Belle and your Phoenixenses."

At that last word, Master Julianna shot him a startled glance.

"Yes, Julianna. The Phoenixenses are back. The time is now!"

At that word, Master Belle came through the cave opening and stood.

"You called Doc? Can I help you?"

"Bekah will need some individual attention for the remainder of the summer. We need to develop her Telepathy more quickly. She will be the key to James getting the answers he seeks."

"Oh?" she said with a look at Bekah who couldn't contain her excitement. "If we are not careful Doc, she will far exceed my abilities."

"That is my hope!" he said with a twinkle in his eyes. "For James will far outpace any Titan we have ever known."

Master McAdams then stepped forward and took James and Bekah by the arms and stated walking towards Master Julianna.

"Please help them go home for the holidays."

Then turning to James, he continued, "We will talk tomorrow and start answering your questions. But first you must see your mother. She's expecting you!"

CHAPTER 25
HERCULOPATHY AMONG FRIENDS

James walked out of the Great Hall wondering why Master McAdams wasn't there. Everyone came back this morning from the 4th of July vacation and he was hoping to talk with Master McAdams as soon as possible. In fact, the entire time he was there he kept thinking about the promise that his questions would be answered when he got back. Bekah kept telling him to not worry, but after all these questions and visions, it would be nice to have at least some answers.

The vacation trip was fun, but from the moment he learned he was a Titan, he hasn't been able to release the great pressure he was feeling. Mom recognized it! Bekah recognized it. Even Helia kept telling him to trust God and allow things to happen as they should. Even now he could hear her comforting music in his mind with simple words.

"You think too much, and trust too little. For God from you can do what is great!"

He couldn't help but be comforted by those words as a smile grew on his face. Without Helia and her wisdom this would be much harder.

"We have a free period this morning. What are your planes James?" Bekah asked with excitement in her voice. "I was thinking you should talk with Master McAdams."

"I was told he was gone until this afternoon. They recommended I try and talk with him then."

"So are you heading to camp or to the cave then?" Michael jumped in.

"Neither. Master Handrake has asked me to come meet with him, Ryan and Elli for a special class."

"Wait!" Kari broke in. "Isn't Elli the one from The Order of the Kraken? Is she dangerous?"

"Master McAdams has recommended we use her and learn from her." James said almost non-chalantly.

"But does he know the whole story? Does he know who is here in camp and who is close to camp?" Bekah asked in a nervous high-pitched voice. "You may be in danger!"

"Right now I need to just act on his words. Until I have more answers I have no choice!" James said as he turned and started walking to Master Handrake's class area. "I am not scared of Elli, now Minnie may be another story."

As he walked away, Michael, Kari and Bekah all looked at each other with fear in their eyes.

"Does he know something we don't know?" Kari asked, but none of them had the answer.

James heard those words and smiled as he entered the camp where Elli and Master Handrake were already waiting. Ryan was jogging up from the opposite direction.

"It looks like we are all here. Elli has been asking me questions about what we will be doing, but I made her wait until everyone was here." his hazel eyes seemed to sparkle as Master Handrake spoke.

"I know you have all been taught to talk to us with respect, but for these lessons you should leave off the 'Master' and just call me Rocky. We will be progressing really fast, as I have never been able to do with first years and I need to treat you more like equals, as friends, than a Teacher-Student relationship. Do any of you have a problem with that?"

Elli smiled with a crooked, almost evil smile and readily agreed. Ryan looked excited and James just nodded.

But Rocky didn't even wait to see the answers and had already turned and started walking quickly.

"Follow me and do what I do. We will see how progressed your abilities truly are."

Rocky then broke into a run, full speed and raced toward the lake. Ryan was quickly by his side and Elli was too with that same smile on her face. James hesitated a moment and then raced up to join them. As they came do the lake, Rocky continued around the lake and towards the mountainside. He wasn't slowing and wasn't breathing hard. James was startled to find he wasn't breathing hard either. Even as they raced up the side of he mountain in a full run, his legs and lungs just seemed to be gaining strength. His muscles seemed to thrive on the activity and were just getting stronger.

Rocky seemed to be enjoying this even more than they were as all the muscles quivered in his 6'10" frame. He even seemed to be trying to speed up as they ran and was pleased as each of them stayed with him.

Trees raced by and birds took flight as they ran. Campus Gaea seemed to disappear far below them and James' mind was free of concerns for the first time in many days. The adrenaline of running seemed to give him a high unlike anything he had ever felt. His mind seemed to be opening up and everything was "perfect". He even felt himself chuckle, a deep, powerful chuckle from deep within. He hadn't laughed like that for a very long time! But nothing mattered now except the run.

They jumped from rock to rock, climbing higher and higher and then James saw it out in front of them, a large drop off, a cliff that was probably ten feet across. But Rocky wasn't slowing, but seemed to be speeding towards the cliff with reckless abandon. Elli, Ryan and James looked at each other and started to slow.

"Trust your abilities! You are ready! Just follow me!"

And he jumped, sailing up into the air and landing 15 feet from where he started, easily clearing the ravine just past the cliff. He then stopped and waited for them.

Ryan saw the results of Rocky's jump and decided he would do the same and with a smile sailed across the ravine and landed approximately 2 feet past the end of the ravine.

James felt Elli's nervousness, but heard her thoughts, "If he can do it, then I have to." and she sailed across, just clearing the ravine.

"I could probably get across with Chronopathy, but I think I will try jumping." he thought after only a slight hesitation.

He raced to the edge and then jumped. As he pushed off with his right foot, he felt wind seem to lift him from the ground. He soared through the air feeling as if he was flying. He looked down to see a small river miles below him and a smile crossed his lips. He could get used to this flying thing. He looked up at the sky and dared the birds to try and compete with him. Nobody or nothing would be able to fly with such ease. He could feel the strength flowing through his body and then his feet touched the ground. As he turned to look, Rocky came running to meet him.

"That was amazing! You looked like you were a superhero flying through the air. You traveled nearly 30 feet further than me."

"How'd you do that?" Ryan asked with admiration.

"I don't know. It just felt like the wind was carrying me."

"Really?" Rocky asked. "I have only read about that. It is a special form of Herculopathy where a level of physical flight is involved. The book called it Volariopathy and said it is considered a combination of Herculopathy and Chronopathy. As a Concordant, it is possible for you to have those abilities together."

"Volariopathy? Is that Latin? Bekah would know."

Elli looked a little irritated and couldn't believe she had the worst jump but tried to not show it. She instead walked up to Rocky and started talking.

"Are we doing more? We still have over one hour of free time."

"Yes. Let's go over to that hill right there. See that pile of rocks? Underneath them is a mine. Let's go in the mine." Rocky then turned to James and continued, "I know you could get inside without moving the rocks, but this is actually a Herculopathy class, so use strength only." He then smiled and walked over to the large rock pile and started grabbing rocks and tossing them out of the way.

As he started, Ryan ran over and started too. Elli, after shooting James an irritated look, joined the other two. James, after a short pause to think about what was happening, ran over and excitedly started moving rocks too.

With the four of them competing with each other, the rock pile disintegrated and they found a deep hole in front of them. It was very dark within, but at this point James wasn't worried about anything. Nothing could hurt him right now!

"As much as I would like to take you into the mine, that is NOT our next task. We will cover up the mine and then head back to camp a different way. But covering the mine will need to be done by the three of you working together. I will not be helping."

Elli immediately started taking control and offering suggestions. She didn't even look towards James but seemed to be talking to Ryan only.

"We will need to gather the rocks again and get the mine covered. It is important that we build the mound around the outside first."

"I think we should all be involved in the decision. James, do you have any ideas?"

"I think we are focusing too simply. We have forgotten that we have superhuman strength. How would a superhero do it?"

"I think we could cause an avalanche and it would cover the mine...or maybe we cause the mine to collapse."

Elli's eyes began to light up as she realized they were much better together. "Can we cause the sides to collapse on itself?" she asked now more carefully.

"Perfect." James said. "What do you think would be the best way to do it?" he asked turning to Elli.

As the three formulated a plan and executed, the plan worked perfectly and the opening of the mine collapsed on itself, creating a large pile of rocks. As it collapsed itself, Elli hugged James in excitement.

"We did it!" she screamed and then pulled away quickly as she realized what she was doing.

"Yes. Thanks for the idea. It worked perfectly." James said with a smile, not reacting at all to the hug.

The rest of the special class, they continued as friends. They learned how to further work together. They gained greater control of their abilities, and even swam down the river back to camp. A friendship had been forged. The three of them now understood each other. As they came back into camp and said bye to Rocky, the three of them were different. James even thought differently about Elli than he did before the class. He wondered how he would explain all that had happened to Bekah and the others.

CHAPTER 26
MEDUSA IN THE CAMP

James walked to the cave slowly, trying to determine what to tell him about the "new" Elli and all that had happened that day. He was going to go talk with Master McAdams just after lunch, when Felicity appeared and invited James to meet Doc (as she called him) in the cave. James knew what cave, because it had become a common occurrence to enter the cave to learn and be taught. Master McAdams had taken him there or met him there on several important occasions this summer. Apparently, it was there, he was told, where they could start working on the answers. But what were the questions? After everything that had happened today, he wasn't sure he could even know where to start.

As he crawled through the door, he came into the brightly lit cave and heard Helia and Felicity singing as it echoed through the cave. Helia's song always seemed to relax him and his mind started to clear. He could feel the excitement building within him as he prepared to ask the questions he was most worried about.

As he came to his feet inside the cave, he looked over to Master McAdams deep blue eyes and infectious smile. This too brought him to ease.

"Well James, I am excited to search with you for answers to your deepest questions. But first we must solve a simple problem that you are already worried about."

James looked at him in surprise. What was he worried about that Master McAdams already knew about?

"We have a very important instructor here for you from the Order of the Kraken." James started to speak, but Master McAdams raised his hand for silence and continued. "Master Zoram Balthizar is a key to helping you learn Orientopathy more completely. And I know you have already met Elli, who is NOT his daughter. I am hoping we are helping her by having her interact with you and others at Campus Gaea! But the concern is another individual. We go to meet her now!"

Master McAdams stepped forward and took James' hand and he felt himself pulled through space at a very rapid rate. Chronopathic travel was becoming more normal to him, but the pull was still a little strange and sometimes even concerning.

As the travel stopped, James and Master McAdams found themselves standing outside camp near a large clump of trees. In the distance was a black dome style tent, surrounded by trees where it couldn't be seen easily. There was a small fire-pit approximately two feet in front of the tent, but no fire. Nobody seemed to be moving within the camp, but James could sense something.

"Now is the next step in your training my boy. Using Orientopathy, I need you to tell me about that camp and find Minerva Madsen."

"They call her Minnie, and she has changed her last name to Medusa."

Master McAdams smiled and continued to speak. "Minerva has always had the flare for the dramatic, but we need not fear her, as she hopes we would by calling herself Medusa! Please find her."

Master McAdams then went silent and waited as James began to search. James even closed his eyes, as he had seen his dad do in the visions. As he focused his mind, the whole camp seemed to come to life.

"I see a small 2-man dome tent, with a foam pad and sleeping bag inside. There is no cot, but the floor has markings as if there usually is one. There are no other bags in the tent, because they are actually 40 feet deeper into the forest, buried in the stump of a large fallen tree. There are two wolves surrounding the camp, with a large covered trench on all sides, except one small path behind the tent measuring four feet wide. This path was recently traveled with footprints I can't recognize. There are also human footprints there, so Minnie has been here very recently."

He continued to search his mind, while using all five senses to take in as much information as possible.

"The wolves I recognize, but I have never met them before. Why do I recognize them?"

"The wolves are siblings of Jacques, who is guarding your Patrol site. They are known to be helping the Order of the Kraken. Minerva is very good at Zoonophonia and has complete control over these poor wolves... Please continue my boy."

"I see small footsteps coming from Campus Gaea, Elli's prints leading to the tent. But they are at least a day old, which means she has not visited the tent for several days."

"Wait, there is another tent or dwelling off to the right about 100 yards. It is mostly buried with a single opening along the back wall. It also has a sleeping bag, but it is resting on a cot with a foam pad. There are no guards and two individuals are within the tent, one is Elli and the other is Minnie, I mean Minerva."

Suddenly his mind broke into a vision...

"You shouldn't be here. I have been told that James is suspecting something is different about you."

"He doesn't suspect anything! I think he would consider me a friend."

"You think you are better than you are? You trust your Titan skills more than you understand them."

Elli looked visibly angry.

"How dare you! You are forgetting that Camilla gave me this job."

"And I tried to convince her not to! Wait…Someone is in my mind. We need to stop talking now."

The vision went black and James turned back to a smiling Master McAdams.

"So, we have found her. It is time to go talk with her."

Master McAdams grabbed James and they were standing at the door of a small black dome tent. The zipper started to zip open and Master McAdams stepped forward.

"Minerva, what are you doing here at camp?"

The zipper came open with a start and Elli and Minnie were both standing there. The anger was unquestionable in Minnie's eyes. The fear in Elli's was also unmistakable.

"I can be anywhere I want. You are no longer my teacher!"

The shout startled James, but Master McAdams continued to smile. Even the two wolves running toward them didn't seem to phase him.

"Minerva, you have no power here. You will NOT threaten my students, especially James."

"I am not threatening them, I am threatening you."

As the two wolves came close, Minnie turned to address them.

James heard her speak in her mind with great power that he never recognized before from Zoonophonic individuals.

"He is our enemy. You can attack him now."

Just them Jacques came into the clearing as well and began to bark at the other wolves.

"You shall not hurt my friends! You weak minded young pups, why do you let a human female control your minds? Can you not think for yourselves?"

The wolves paused for a moment as Minnie turned to Jacques but before she could speak the barking continued.

"You poor, stupid female. You have no power over me. We have met before and you failed even then! Never again will I be fooled by your friendship!"

The anger grew in Minnie's eyes and fire seemed to dance behind them. Her face was bright red and she pulled from her tent a large crossbow.

"Then I shall kill you."

She turned to Master McAdams who still stood with a smile on his face and laughter in his eyes, but he didn't say a word.

Jacques began to run at Minnie as the two other wolves jumped on him.

James began to step forward, but Master McAdams put his arm out and stopped him.

"Do you think you can hit me?" he said quietly to Minnie and then words filled James mind.

"So my boy, here is lesson number two. What is her weakness? How can you beat the crossbow? Use your Herculopathy and Hoplonosmithy together." and he continued to smile.

James began to concentrate. What could he know? He thought a response to Master McAdams mind directly.

The weapon is not optimized. Although her finger is on the trigger and the mechanism is properly engaged to fire, there will be a 3/8 of a second delay from trigger pull. But an even bigger problem is the slight quiver in her hand, not visible to the naked eye, showing her hesitancy to fire. Her aim is also slightly off center, meaning she may miss to the right if she hesitates.

"You will not kill me, and you will leave camp and all my students now!" Master McAdams' voice rang through the forest and even the wolves stopped fighting. The smile still rested on his face, but even James was nervous.

James saw Minnie's finger start to squeeze the trigger and at that very moment, Master McAdams had the crossbow in his hand, and the arrow shot off to his right and fell to the ground. The speed at which he moved was amazing for anyone, but especially for an "older man" James thought. For the first time, Minnie's face flashed for a moment with fear and then she was gone.

Again, Master McAdams stood with a smile on his face and turned to Elli as James noticed the two wolves running from a victorious Jacques. They were whimpering as they ran, looking for their master.

"Elli my dear," Master McAdams began to speak, "You are welcome to stay at camp if you would like. But you will need to follow the rules and stop sneaking out of camp."

Elli said nothing, but just nodded her head as she was visibly shaken.

"Jacques." Master McAdams barked, "Can you please take Elli back to camp?" And the wolf turned and walked back to their side.

As Jacques and Elli walked back towards camp, Master McAdams turned back to James.

"So my boy, what have you learned? What new skills do you now know?" Before James could respond, he continued, "James, we need to gather up the tents and the gear and see what we can learn about The Order from them."

Master McAdams was already inside the tent and folding the cot, pad and sleeping bag. The tent was otherwise empty, as they already knew the bags were hidden elsewhere. Instead of putting down the tent, or carrying anything out of the tent, however, he just placed them on the floor and stepped out.

"I will have Master Walker gather the tents and bring them to my office. I would like us to go examine the bags in the stump."

As they moved to the stump, however, everything was gone. It was empty, except for a large green and black pocket knife. Master McAdams smiled, "Apparently she had more help than we thought. But you my boy will want to take that knife. May I suggest that you examine it when we get you back to camp. You may be surprised at what information it may hold for you."

James carefully picked up the knife and placed it in his pocket. Master McAdams then took his arm and they were momentarily back in the cave. Nothing else was said at that moment as Master McAdams left the cave without a word. James stood there in the well-lit cave wondering what had just happened.

James carefully reviewed the happenings in the forest and wondered why Master McAdams had run off so quickly. Was there nor more he needed to learn? He was hoping to ask him some additional questions, but as usual the questions would have to wait.

As he stood there in the silence, a familiar voice could be heard outside the entrance. Not just one voice, but several voices. His friends had been sent to find him. He walked out of the cave and back into "normal life"…

CHAPTER 27
CAMPUS GAEA

The rest of the day was uneventful and almost boring after James' little adventure with Master McAdams. He tried to act normal, but the heavy pocket knife in his pocket seemed to be begging him for examination. He didn't want to pull it out with others around and definitely wanted to pay close attention to it when the time came, but every class just became an obstacle to his personal time examining this new object. He was so distracted, that he tripped entering Master Julianna's tent and fell to the floor. The roar of laughter filled the room and James felt his face turning bright red. But, before anyone could tease him, Master Julianna with her half-moon spectacles came bouncing into the room.

"James," she said with excitement, "will you please join us for our next adventure?"

James jumped to his feet and jogged to join Michael, Bekah and Kari standing on the left side of the group.

"Today your history lesson is on Campus Gaea. I think we should go on another field trip." she said with her excited smile and before they could respond they were again zooming through time. They found themselves standing in a heavily wooded area, with a man walking from 20 yards ahead of them and seemingly talking to himself.

Bekah began to squeal with excitement in her rapid, high pitched voice, "That is Cornelius Abel!"

"Right you are Miss Solomon! Do you know where we are?" Master Julianna said with equal excitement.

James knew immediately, as he had been in this exact location only hours before, but…this was many years ago!

Master Julianna saw the recollection in James eyes and smiled broadly at him. But Michael jumped in quickly with the answer. "The question is WHEN are we. We are located just outside Campus Gaea."

"Correct Mr Peterson. So, when are we?"

"I am not yet good at localizing time." Michael said without hesitation.

"Well, Cornelius Abel lived from 1670 to 1776. He looks much older than the last time we saw him, but this part of North America was still not owned or even explored during that time. Since we know he is Concordant, we can assume that traveling here was not a problem. Based on his appearance, and from what I have read, he would be about 80 years-old. That would mean around 1750."

James was again amazed at Bekah's knowledge and started looking closer at Cornelius. Was he really 80 years-old?

"Well done Miss Solomon! Now let me increase the volume of him talking to himself."

"We have a problem here. The Titans are not learning of their skills as they should! The Titans are not working together! In fact, we have many being killed as witches or being put into Asylums because they are 'hearing voices' or talking with animals. I have seen many in circuses or being used as anomalies to make others money. We need to get them out of the civilized world and teach them from an early age who they are."

Cornelius Abel went silent as he continued to walk towards them, and then James began to hear his thoughts as if they were being broadcast to him directly.

They will never trust me with this new endeavor. In fact, they will consider it an affront to the Titan Creed to consider gathering the young to teach them. As a Concordant I cannot recommend this location, but I can implant it in their minds. How long will it take before they decide to follow on the idea? I will probably long be dead before they create this camp. Someday it will be of value to our youth!

Master Julianna seemed to pause for the thought to be completed, but James knew quickly that nobody else had heard it. Not even Bekah was quick enough to read his mind as he was listening.

"This is the outskirts of where Campus Gaea will be, but Cornelius did not originally get credit for finding the location until many years later."

"When she wrote it in *The Book of Adam*." Bekah whispered with a smile.

"So, let's continue…" Master Julianna stated and they were speeding through time again.

This time they found themselves in a large building, almost like a warehouse, with windows at least 10 feet off the ground, many wooden chairs aligned in rows and a large table with 15 men seated facing the audience. James was quick to recognize the complete absence of women at the table but noticed many in the audience. At the center was a tall, gray skinned individual with a long, billowing white beard that reached well below his belt. He was the only individual standing, in the center of the 15, with all others looking at him.

Bekah immediately spoke with a start, "That is Lafeyette Hogmire, the once powerful leader of the Titan Coalition."

"Right you are again, young lady, but do you know why we are here?"

"In *The Book of Adam* it talks about Master Hogmire pushing for a unification of the Titans around the world and talks about his recommendation for *The Band of Fire*. But I don't remember any years associated or any additional information on who Lafeyette Hogmire is in that chapter. He is mentioned again, however, in *The Forgotten History of The Titans*, chapter

16 as the founder of *The Band of Fire* and he 'invented' the advancement program we now use. But I don't know what meeting this is."

"So there is something you don't know?" Master Julianna said with a smile. "Well in chapter 20 you will read about this meeting, a very important meeting for Titan education as a whole. Does anyone know what year it is?"

James knew immediately and couldn't keep himself silent. "It is April 6, 1910."

Bekah looked at him in surprise. "How do you know that?"

"I am an Orientopath, and time is one thing I am able to determine."

"Yes, April 6th. It is very important that you recognize that as the founding of *The Band of Fire*, as it will be an important date for the rest of your training. And more importantly, it is part of your advancement this first year to *Silver Spark*."

As she finished speaking, Master Hogmire began speaking with a strong stutter. Often as he spoke, there were long pauses, but nobody seemed to mind because of the great intelligence and power with which he spoke. James personally was impressed with his confidence and strength through what to him seemed like a major disability.

"My fellow...Titan Council Members. I..I..I come to you today with a prop...osition. A very im..im..portant opportunity...to..to train up our Titan Youth. M..M..Many years have we been trying to unify our Titans. M..M..Many years have we struggled to find...and...and teach new Titans of their skills. I...I...I have been work...working for...for the last year to.. to..to help organize a pro...gram of education for the Titans."

As he continued to speak in a stuttering tone, James began to hear his thoughts, words without the stutter, a mind perfectly clear, brilliant and as powerful as was his confidence.

These Titans, our very youth, will be invited in small groups of the most well-developed of Titan Youth to join The Band of Fire. A new group, a youth group specializing in survival skills, Titan instruction and team development following the military style of Troops, Patrols and rank advancement. The key to advancement and organization will be to develop well-developed, skilled Titans that can help protect this world from evil, while learning to utilize their Titan abilities without becoming 'witches' in society that are troublemakers. If we develop our skills correctly, they will become well integrated members of society with skills that can be utilized for the greater good. This greater good must be our Titan Creed from this time forward.

The thoughts paused and James was back with the rest of the group as Master Hogmire struggled to finish his thoughts for the group.

"...must be...be our Titan Creed f...f...from this time forward."

A short bald, black man stood with a strong English accent, "And how will this be taught to our youth?"

Master Hogmire smiled and continued...and James was back in his mind.

Exactly, Sir Gallahad. We shall teach as you were taught in the army, through skill classes and instruction by developed adult Titans. We should find our best Titans, our best examples, our most valiant examples of service, kindness and love of God to teach them through a Summer Camp. The location was recommended yesterday by Thais Abel in the mountains of Utah. This area is still well wooded, hard to find and can be protected through careful use of our Titan skills.

The Council seemed interested, so Master Hogmire continued...

As with any organization, there will be promises, signs and symbols that indicate participation in the group. Uniforms will be a key piece of the puzzle and are still being developed. May I present the Oath or Promise, the Fire Sign, Salute and Handshake as determined by the committee you all designated:

Master Hogmire then stood at attention and made the Fire Sign by raising his right arm to the square, palm to the front and all fingers close together.

This is the sign. And the salute is a standard solute to the right side of the forehead, with the fingers close together.

He then proceeded to salute with his right hand.

He then turned to the individual to his right and took his left hand in a handshake, interlocking the little fingers and extending the middle three fingers to the center of the wrist.

This is the handshake, utilized to indicate trust and respect one for the other. It is imperative that the left hand be utilized to indicate a much closer brotherhood and sisterhood than the standard handshake. We are asking The Band of Fire to trust each other completely, to defend each other through life and death, to stand together against any evil that may arise.

Before he could continue, another individual stood with dark black eyes, deep wrinkles around the eyes and long white hair pulled back into a long ponytail. "I have a serious concern Lafeyette! You talk as if we are NOT different from the rest of the world. You stammer about with your promises, your high-minded ideals, about a society that wants our help and will value our skills and abilities. You know as well as I do that we are still being killed, still being hunted throughout the world. We are being seen as mutants, part-humans and monsters. Why should we train our youth to serve and help them? Why shouldn't we not prepare them for battle so that one day we can overcome and rule them?"

The audience became restless and all began to speak. Murmurs filled the hall and Bekah grabbed James arm with concern in her eyes. "He is right you know," she said in a whisper. "The killing didn't stop for nearly 50 years. Even now there are rumors of 'crazy' individuals that may actually be Titans being locked up in prisons or in mental hospitals."

A man to the far right made movement to stand but seemed to be shorter once he climbed from his chair. His height, under four feet tall, was mostly blocked by the table, so he walked from behind it. He had thick, brown hair with a short, well-trimmed beard and mustache. He began to speak with great power, and the whole room grew silent.

"I believe in God with all my heart! I recognize evil for what it is and refuse to be party to it! I shall not stand here and allow our future to be bound by fear! I shall not stand here and watch this noble council get distracted by a society that fears what it doesn't understand. God has long sent noble men, great men and women, to this earth to stand against evil, to 'do good to them that hate you', to 'pray for them that hurt you' and to 'serve them that oppress you.' Are not we blessed with great spiritual gifts, even physical gifts for which we are held even more accountable. Are not we asked to be even better, to serve even more fully, to stand even more carefully because of the gifts and skills God has given us? Would not a mother, with her nurturing skills, not nurture her neighbor's child if in need as one of her own? Would not a physician be expected to help the sick whether they had ability to pay or not? How much more then are we not expected to stand for good, to rise against the evil and not join their pettiness, their weakness, their hate. Happiness can never be ours without looking to others and forgetting about ourselves. Happiness is serving outside oneself! I choose to be truly happy!"

The room grew silent as Master Julianna whispered to the group, "That is Apollo Leviathon, considered the most intelligent and well respected of all the Titan Council members. Don't let his size surprise you, for he's considered a giant among the Titans of any age!"

James quickly turned to Bekah and whispered, "He is a Telepath! That is why his speech is so powerful, he is speaking vocally and to their minds at the same time."

"Really? How do you know that?"

"I just feel it. Maybe that is part of being Concordant."

Master Julianna continued to speak, "Many of you may recognize the power with which he speaks. He is a Telepath, but the power of his conviction is the real reason he touched a chord with all those in attendance."

As the silence continued, Master Hogmire began to speak again and once again James could hear his thoughts.

I agree with my well-respected friend Apollo. We must NOT fight anger with anger and hate with hate. I choose instead to use fire, The Band of Fire, to create a Titan that works miracles in the world. We will try to designate their standards based on the following oath:

I solemnly covenant my brothers and sisters of Fire to do my Duty to God, to serve others with all my heart, to stand as a witness of faith, knowledge and strength, to use my gifts to protect freedom, happiness and independence for all, to lift the weak, to comfort the sad and to befriend the friendless. That I may by so doing stand against evil in all its various forms. To this I pledge my sacred honor.

May we help them not just pledge, but live according to this pledge. We will then have them work on a series of rank advancements to show their "Fire" Abilities. This should correlate with their progress in Titan development and allow a well-developed Titan to reach the rank of The Phoenix by the end of Year 6. The rank advancements earned if active participation and learning is undertaken throughout the summer camp year as follows:

- *Year One → Silver Spark*
- *Year Two → Midnight Coal*
- *Year Three → Golden Flame*
- *Year Four → Lightning Brand*
- *Year Five → Thunderbird*
- *Year Six → The Phoenix*

As James heard these thoughts, he also saw a picture of each rank and couldn't help but be excited to earn *The Phoenix*, especially as he thought of Helia.

Each rank advancement will include basic survival skills, basic life skills and Titan Skills training. The more well-rounded the program, the better integrated and more powerful our Titan students will become. Only then can we have a unified Band of Fire!

James heard the stuttering come to an end and watched as the Titan Council took a vote to implement the program and designate a committee, led by Master Hogmire and Thais Abel to implement the program over the next year to start in the Utah mountains the following summer (two months away). The smile on Master Hogmire's face was unmistakable! But when a young brown haired, plump woman with large blue eyes, and a large broad smile stood from the audience measuring only about 5 feet tall, James could swear it was a young Master Julianna. Even the excitement with which she bounced up to join Master Hogmire as she was designated to help was reminiscent of their teacher. There was no question that she was absolutely an ancestor!

Master Julianna smiled at James and just nodded, as she took their hands again and they were racing once more through time...

As the racing through time cleared again, James found himself at the edge of the forest, near where the camp is now and he could see many individuals putting up tents and arranging the camp very different than the camp they now attend. The year was still 1910, but the date was May 28th, and they were preparing for the first Titan Camp.

Master Julianna began to speak, "This is the Titan Camp. Notice that the name has not yet been chosen. We are here to witness this discussion."

As they stood at the edge of the camp, Master Thais Abel came walking towards them with sweat and dirt on her face. Her brown hair was lifted in a bun on top of her head and her clothes were filthy with dirt and grime. She was carrying a small brown bag in one hand and wore a beaming smile on her face. Master Hogmire came walking out of the woods from behind them, with a perfectly white beard, but dirt on his face. His beard didn't seem to have any of the dust or sweat that was plastering his face. He had a concerned look on his face as he walked toward Thais.

"I..I..I have tried to name our camp! It m...m...must be the per...fect name. H..H..H...How do we f...f...find the correct one?"

"You worry too much Lafeyette." Master Abel said with a smile. "Mother Earth will give us a name. Yes, Mother Earth or Gaea. May I recommend Campus Gaea? Gaea for God's great earth, after the Greek Mother Earth, for we are training up the stewards, the protectors, the Titans of the earth. And in recognition of the complete knowledge we are asking them to partake, may we use the ancient Latin language of Campus instead of camp?"

As she continued to describe the camp, James noticed a relief fill the mind of Master Hogmire. "Tha..Tha..Thank You!"

With that the trip ended, and they found themselves back in Master Julianna's tent. Everyone was looking at each other and wondering what had just happened, but Master Julianna couldn't contain her excitement.

"Doc McAdams has asked me specifically this year to take you on this trip. I usually don't take first years to the Titan Council meeting. That is often reserved for 5th years students after they have grown more skilled and are better able to understand Master Lafeyette Hogmire. His stuttering is slow and methodical, but you will find if you carefully consider his words as a whole he is truly a brilliant man. Often 5th years are able to understand more quickly and some are even able to hear his thoughts. My concern is many of you will discount this trip because of the hardness of the speech he has been blessed with. Do you have any questions?"

The class remained silent, and Bekah looked slightly disappointed that she had not been able to hear Master Hogmire's thoughts. "With my Telepathy, why couldn't I hear his thoughts?" she thought to James. But James was unable to give an adequate response, so he stayed silent.

Master Julianna smiled again and continued, "Please review the chapter in *The Book of Adam* on the origin of *The Band of Fire* and you will understand what just happened. Review the rank advancements and you will know what he was discussing. Review the information on *Campus Gaea* and you will understand, as Miss Solomon already knows, what the final stop of our trip was. Campus Gaea now is laid out as Master Doc McAdams has designated it. You are all really blessed to have quality tents, classrooms and firepits designated, cots to sleep on and buildings to eat in. All these are the doing of Master McAdams and his vision for you. Even your education and progress toward your first year rank of *Silver Spark* is under his careful direction. You are truly blessed. I invite you to study carefully what you have learned this day. Master Doc McAdams wanted you to know it now, and only he knows why. Consider it a great blessing!"

They were excused from class and Bekah couldn't stop talking about that trip. James could feel and hear the excitement in her voice as she recapped everything that happened and explained where the information was in *The Book of Adam* and *The Forgotten History of The Titan*. She was even pulling the book from her bag as they walked and turning quickly to chapter 20 to see what was said about the meeting and her excitement couldn't be contained as she began to read out loud about the meeting they had just attended. As she read, James could again see each individual at the table, the discussion happening and heard the thoughts of Master Hogmire at each part. Kari and Michael were eating up every word, as they now understood more completely the happenings of the meeting. But James just wondered why he was so blessed to have the God given skills he had? Why was he the only one that "heard" the thoughts, that knew every aspect of the training they were receiving? And was there anything more he should have learned from their meeting today?

CHAPTER 28
ELLI'S LITTLE SECRET

As others went to dinner that evening, James returned to his tent and quickly found himself sitting on the cot examining the green and black knife. As he rolled it over in his hands, he reviewed the adventure of the day and couldn't get Minnie's face out of his mind. He could feel her hatred and saw the fear in her face as Master McAdams confronted her. Although she tried to portray power, he recognized her fear and knew it was that which caused her to flee from them. But what would Camilla think of it? It was with this thought that James found his mind fading into darkness...

The sky was still dark as he lay on his back alone in the small tent. The camp was silent, but the happening of that day were still very apparent in his thoughts. Camilla had been very angry. Even as her father he had only seen her that mad one other time, the last time she lived with them. But this was different! He saw a hatred in her eyes that almost scared him. He even wished at that time that he still had a blindfold on. He never knew his daughter had that anger, that hatred in her. He often hoped she would come back and return to her happy, laughing and singing self. He loved her, but those eyes scared him! He couldn't get it out of his mind...but the discussion, the words she said now filled his mind and he tried to understand them more completely.

"You were NOT sent to Campus Gaea! You have done us a great disservice!"

"I am sorry Camilla! But I did what I felt was necessary. I did not think I needed your permission to protect The Order that you and I BOTH helped develop. I think Master McAdams has more power than you give him credit for."

The laugh echoed from her as she looked with anger at Minnie. It was not her usual happy laugh he had grown to love, but a maniacal, almost demonic laugh.

"You fear him, as you always have. He is not as powerful as me! He is weak and gets his power by limiting the power of those he teaches. He even speaks in stories to make himself seem smarter. And now you have told him what is going on in camp under his very nose. How dare you make decisions for The Order of The Kraken without discussing it with me. Both Zoram and Elli are in danger now that he knows!"

And then there was silence as Camilla walked from the room. Minnie looked around and saw everyone looking at her. Was she really scared of Doc McAdams? Was her respect and "fear" of him, as Camilla describes it, the reason he was able to chase her from Campus Gaea? Or was he really more powerful and more knowledgeable than Camilla gives him credit?

With that another cold voice echoed through the tent. "Minnie, I am with Camilla on this. You are a powerful Titan, but still don't believe we are more powerful than The Band of Fire. You still respect Doc and possibly even fear him. I know too much. Alice Abertine Stults, who once was my grandmother, talked of the great power of Master McAdams. When I had respect for her, when she still loved me and helped me learn about Titan skills, I believed he was powerful. But when I felt of her disappointment in me and he failed to correct her, I knew that he remains in power only because of that 'respect' for an assumed power. You could have easily defeated him if only you had believed. Do you really believe in your power, in our power? Camilla believes and for this we must allow her to guide us and direct us. Camilla has powers that I have never seen, strength that makes us better. Don't be angry with her, be angry with Doc and help us all figure out how to get more of these students to join us. I am especially interested in Camilla's brother who was there with him. Isn't he just a first year? Why was he there with Doc at such a dangerous time?

...As those words echoed again through his memory, Simon felt a little anger himself. Was Doc McAdams really putting James in danger in his first year as a Titan? Why would he take James to meet Minnie in the trees? But I trust Doc! He had always been really good at protecting the Titans at camp. Or were Katie and Minnie both right? Was Doc more concerned with his reputation and needed someone there to "see" him defeat Minnie?

James looked up from the knife with a start and felt the silence around him and recognized he was still sitting alone in the tent. They were likely still eating dinner, so Bekah would be coming soon to ask him why he skipped dinner again. But the questions asked were important.

"Why did Master McAdams take him to the forest if it was truly dangerous?"

"Was he still teaching him?"

"What was he supposed to learn from this?"

As he thought, Helia again began to sing and the song filled his mind but no words came. And then his mind was filled again...

A small 6 year-old girl sat crying in a small room with no pictures on the wall and white paint peeling in the corner. She sat on a thin mattress on a metal framed bed that sat in the corner. There were no blankets and no sheets on the bed, but only a small bumpy pillow at one end. The mattress was stained and filthy, with small tears at the opposite end of the pillow. There was a small sink in the corner with a one burner stove on the small wooden table next to it and a broken armoire with the door half hanging off in the other corner. The armoire was almost empty with no clothes and no food visible in the room. A small window sat on the east wall with bars on the outside and cracked glass in the pane with a small breeze whistling under the almost closed frame. The window was slightly crooked and appeared to be unable to close. Dust covered the floor and seemed to swirl a little with the breeze through the broken glass.

As he continued to look around the room, his mind was drawn back to the little girl. She was dressed in an oversized dress and her hands and feet were black with dirt. Even her face was streaked from the tears falling down her dirty face. She was very tiny, but James recognized her face, but he wasn't exactly sure why.

"Mommy, please come back!" she cried as she sat there alone. But nobody came, no comfort was offered. In fact, she appeared to be completely alone. James hurt for her and wondered who she was.

... The vision faded and James saw the same girl much cleaner now, in the same oversized dress, sitting in a court room. She sat alone behind a large table as two adults were talking to the judge. He couldn't hear them, but he knew they were discussing where she was to live. And then the adults left the bench and the judge started to speak to her.

"Elli, we are happy to say we have a place for you to live. We have been unable to find your father, and your mother has disappeared since we last talked with her. But this young lady," he pointed to a short, plump dark-haired woman near the other table, "has promised to take good care of you. She runs a house for girls and will help you grow up with enough food and good clothes until you are 18 years old."

Elli began to cry again, and James looked over at the woman and began to feel very uncomfortable. There was something wrong with this women, even though she looked very kind and loving at the moment. Something wasn't right!

... The vision faded again and James saw this same short, plump woman but without the kind and loving look in her eyes. She had a hatred in her eyes and she dragged Elli to the corner and threw her on the bed. Elli was obviously older now, but still very tiny.

"You, young lady, shall not eat again tonight! You will do what I say, right when I say it."

"Madam, I was trying to. I have never cleaned a toilet before."

"Don't talk back to me!" she said as she slapped her across the face. "You are lucky to be here. I could have let them send you away."

"*I know I am lucky to be here! I just don't know where my mother is.*" *She said with tears again in her eyes.*

"*Don't you start crying. I will not feel sorry for you!*" *she said with hatred in her eyes.*

"*Your mother is never coming back! She doesn't want you! Don't you get it, she ran away and wanted us to take care of you! If it weren't for the money I am being paid to have you here, even I wouldn't want you. Why would anyone want such a naughty girl?*"

As the lady walked away, Elli again began to cry and she whispered to herself, "*Somebody wants me, I know it!*"

…The vision faded again and James saw Elli in the same room older still. But she didn't look sad at this time and looked much more like he knew her. But she sat now almost defiant on her bed. It was at this time that the door opened and the short, plump lady came walking into the room with another tall, silver-haired woman by her side.

"*Are you sure you want this one? She scares the other children and has a demon or something within her because even with her small size she has scary strength. She may be too dangerous to bring into your home. I have other, more beautiful and friendly girls that would love to be adopted into your family.*"

"*I want this one. She needs me as much as I need her.*"

"*Suit yourself, but know that the state will not allow us to take her back. Oh, and the cost of adopting her is not any cheaper.*"

"*You will get your money!*" *the silver-haired lady said with disgust in her eyes,* "*And we will not be bringing her back here ever!*"

With that the short, plump lady walked out quickly without looking back.

"*Elli, you are very special. I want to bring you into my family. Do you want to go with me?*"

"*You want me?*" *Elli said with surprise in her voice.* "*Nobody has ever wanted me, not even my mother.*"

"*Your mother did want you, but she was very sick and couldn't take care of you. She died almost two years ago now. She was my youngest daughter.*"

"*What? You are my grandma?*"

"Yes, and I would be glad to have you in my home. I have been looking for you for two years! You are now 8 years-old, right?"

"Yes. I had my birthday three months ago."

"Did you know that your mother was a Titan?"

"What is a Titan?"

"Titans are very special. From what I have heard, you are a Titan too."

"There is nothing special about me."

"But there is. Have you not noticed increasing strength?"

"Well, the bigger kids can't hurt me anymore."

"You have a special Titan skill called Herculopathy. I can help you learn to control and use your strength. It would bring me great pleasure. I have a cousin of yours that is also a Titan."

James again found himself alone in his tent. The knife had fallen from his hand and was sitting on the floor. But Elli was now on his mind. She had a very hard life. But why did she leave her grandma to join the Order of The Kraken? Maybe Master McAdams will know. James stood and started walking from his tent when he heard crying again in his mind. It was the same cry he had seen in the vision. He walked quickly and found a crying Elli sitting alone just outside his camp, but she didn't notice him. As he watched, her face covered with tears, he again began to see her thoughts.

"You are a great Titan, my dear, but your cousin says you are being underestimated and degraded at home. Is that true?"

"I don't know. I love my grandma, but I still miss my father."

"Well, I can be your father and would consider it a great privilege to help you develop your Titan skills at a much more rapid rate." a man with dark skin and brownish-yellow eyes with a long brown beard, fluffy mustache and long brown hair down his back. *"You will be the daughter I have never had."*

James felt her intrigue and excitement at the idea and she quickly agreed. He also realized that she never again returned to her grandma after that fateful night. But as he searched her mind, he found the reason in the form of words being inserted into her mind.

"You are much more powerful than anyone lets you be! You are a Titan that has received no respect! In fact, you were treated with

disrespect by your mother, and by the girls' home. Do you remember that?"

James saw tears coming to Elli's eyes.

"Grandma Stultz treated you good, so you were excited to enter her home, but have you noticed how she treated your cousin? Katie has been unable to develop her Titan skills while in that home. Grandma has felt that only certain Titan skills should be developed. Campus Gaea, to which you may be invited this year, will also limit your ability to develop. If you stay at home, you will be limited as you were by the orphanage. Is that what you are looking for?"

James could feel her excitement at the opportunity to grow and develop her skills, but he sensed a great deal of confusion and worry. Her biggest fear since leaving the orphanage was returning to the same circumstances and Grandma was getting older. Would grandma truly limit her abilities as she had been doing for Katie? She couldn't have this happen again!

Then her mind was filled with pictures of powerful Titans and all turned to look at a 5'6" slender woman with long curly brown hair, dark blue eyes, a small nose and a slightly round face. James immediately recognized her as Camilla and Elli's mind again became blank…

"What are you doing here?" Elli asked, looking up at James.

"I heard you crying. You loved your grandmother! Why did you choose to leave her?"

"I thought they were blocking my mind from everyone."

"I don't know what you mean, but your mind was not blocked from me."

"Camilla made many promises, but I am confused after Doc McAdams treated me so good."

"Master McAdams has been nothing but helpful to me in developing my skills."

"But you are different! He doesn't treat anyone else here like he treats you."

"He treated you that way when he didn't make you leave with Minnie."

"She's my friend. She has helped me fit in here at camp. I don't know how I will survive without her here."

"What about Master Balthizar?"

"He has been a great friend, almost a father to me. I have needed him, but he can't help me now. He is too busy trying to not get kicked out of camp too because of Minnie being caught." as she finished, she looked embarrassed and wished she hadn't said anything.

"I already knew he wasn't your father. Camilla is the leader of the Order of the Kraken and she sent both of you to infiltrate here."

"I don't know what you are talking about. I just want to be a Titan."

Before James could respond, Master Doc McAdams came walking around the tents and into the same clearing where they stood.

"James and Elli, you didn't make it to dinner."

"I apologize Master McAdams, but I was too busy thinking today." James quickly replied.

"Yes, I know. And Elli here has been likewise thinking. She has wondered how I could be the monster Camilla has said I am and still be kind to an orphan with poorly developed Herculopathy. She has wondered why I didn't know she was 14 years-old when she came. She has wondered how Camilla and her 'Order' are tricking me if I am such a powerful Titan. She's even wondering if her grandmother is right in trusting me."

Elli looked up with wonder and fear in her eyes but said nothing and didn't move.

"I could answer all these questions, but I would rather tell you a story and let you answer them yourselves."

"Many years ago, while growing up in a farming community in Utah, I had a neighbor that grew the most amazing cantaloupe I had ever tasted. Every year they just seemed to get more sweet and always were even beautiful on the outside. I figured they were sure lucky to have such amazing seeds from which to grow the fruit. Since they were good seeds, they were blessed with the best fruit. But years later as I have considered this, I started to realize how much work goes into this process. Seeds are important as only good seeds will produce good fruit, but careful selection of the fruit over

time can produce even greater seeds for the following year. In fact, there are three principles that help produce a good crop:

1. *Proper amounts of water are necessary for producing good fruit. Too much or too little water and the plant will die. Did you know that too much water can also kill a plant?*

2. *Careful thinning and pruning is necessary to get the best fruit. Each plant can produce a certain amount of growth. Therefore, a good farmer will often ensure only a portion of the fruit will grow to maturity, limiting the production but creating the best fruit by allowing the limited resources to be utilized by a finite number of fruit.*

3. *Every fruit is carefully monitored and allowed to grow under careful direction. Some will be moved or turned to allow progression under the careful eye of a skilled farmer. This is the same technique utilized by farmers growing the largest pumpkin for example.*

The interesting point I have learned over the years is that uncontrolled growth is unable to produce the best fruit. Do I control the growth of Titans? Yes, but only to allow them to develop more complete and powerfully in the right way. When I evaluate another individual, I strive to evaluate them based on the fruit they are producing. What kind of fruit am I producing? What kind of fruit are you producing? What kind of fruit is Camilla producing?"

With that, Master McAdams winked at them with his deep blue eyes and turned and walked away. Elli just starred without a word as James, hearing the others coming back to the tents, wished Elli good luck and walked back to his tent.

CHAPTER 29
FOLLOWING A STAR

As James walked back into the tent, Michael looked at him excitedly.

"We are going to the cave tonight, right?"

"Yes. We are supposed to do Hippocratesense, but I think we should do Orientopathy instead. What do you think?"

"I love night orienteering. Should we focus on following the stars tonight?" he asked excitedly.

"Are you ready to teach it?"

"Please...I have been waiting for this opportunity."

As they both laughed, James felt Bekah in his mind. *"Are you two ready yet?"*

And with that, they raced out to join Bekah, Kari and Angelica as they walked to the cave, only to be joined momentarily by Emma, Lizzy and Ryan. Helia flew ahead as they approached the cave and all entered with their companions ready for the next meeting of the Phoenixenses.

As the cave lit up, James stepped forward and began to explain the plans for the night. Angelica, although slightly disappointed with the revelation that she was not the next teacher, got excited with the prospect of learning more about

Orientopathy. That was one skill she hoped to improve more easily than Chronopathy.

Michael then stepped forward and began to teach. Each Titan studied and learned the constellations of the night sky, how they could be utilized to orient and then were invited to go view the night sky outside the cave. But as they started to discuss leaving the cave, James made another suggestion.

"Emma, can you help me transport everyone to the top of the mountain? I think we can do it."

"What?" Emma asked with a start. "Why the top of the mountain?"

"The view of the night sky will be much greater there, without the light pollution that comes from the nearby cities." Michael said before James could answer with excitement in his voice. "Then I can really show you how it works."

They all carefully grabbed hands and closed their eyes. James just looked up at Emma and smiled as time began to slow and immediately their feet were touching the firm ground outside the cave at the peak of the mountain. A breeze was easily felt as they looked around. The night was dark and the night sky seemed to open to them.

As James looked to the sky, he quickly found Ursa Major with the seven stars that make up the Big Dipper. Bekah became animated as she found the same grouping of stars and pointed out Polaris or the North Star. As she pointed, Michael began to teach again.

"The Big Dipper is made up of the seven brightest stars of the constellation Ursa Major or the Bear. And, as Bekah is showing us, the edge of the cup portion of the Big Dipper points to the North Star or Polaris. Extend a line from the edge of the cup and you will encounter Polaris. Does everyone see that?"

Ryan was carefully showing Kari where Polaris was, and Angelica was starting to discuss the Little Dipper.

"Know that the North Star is often also called the Pole Star because the other stars in the heavens rotate around it. Therefore, we always know north from the location of the star." Michael continued. "Polaris also makes up the tip of the handle of the Little Dipper or Ursa Minor."

Lizzy then began to speak, "I don't think I have ever seen the stars so beautifully. I am so impressed with the Milky Way." she said as she pointed to the white grouping of the stars of the Solar System. "I don't think I have ever seen it more clearly.

"Can you believe that is all the stars of our Solar System?" Michael asked again with excitement. "Do you all know how to utilize this information?"

James then began to talk, "So, we will all use Polaris to direct us in orienting our compasses and our maps. We can then pick coordinates based on the 360-degree coordinate system as seen on a compass."

Bekah was standing there bouncing with excitement as they continued to practice directions, coordinates and finding the constellations in the sky. She completely understood and couldn't believe how easy the coordinates were to her even without the compass.

Michael was likewise excited as everyone was quickly catching on, but he wasn't sure what to do next. James then took over.

"Now, you know how this would be useful with a map or a compass, but we want to discuss Orientopathy as an extension of orienteering. True Orientopathy requires you to picture your surroundings, use all your senses to localize yourself and then 'Follow The Star' in this case or move based on the information you are receiving from your senses. Maps should be useful, but unnecessary as you develop this skill. Compass should be likewise unnecessary."

Over the next hour, Michael and James worked with each individual to understand how to use their senses, how to develop a picture of their location and how this could help them get oriented and even find directions. As they continued to work, Michael took a special interest in Emma and helping her succeed. Lizzy likewise seemed to be getting better at it. Bekah, however, could never get past not having the map. The more she tried to picture a map, the more frustrated she got.

"My mind is blank! I can't see even the mountain we are on. I know north based on Polaris, but how would I travel 20-degrees, 80-degrees or something similar? I need something concrete I can look at."

As James and Bekah discussed the process, they realized that her Telepathic mind was limited in its ability to "imagine" the surroundings based on the senses. Her mind just didn't work that way. In fact, her concentration or focus on learning information from various books was her way of getting sufficient information to be able to understand it completely in her mind. Orientopathy for her would require her to memorize the map or use a physical map.

Emma, however, with Michael's focused instruction was understanding a great deal and seemed to be improving minute by minute. Although she was still unable to picture a map, finding directions, even coordinates were becoming easier. The excitement she was feeling became infectious as even Bekah was excited that she was succeeding.

The most impressive non-Orientopath, however, was Ryan. Due to his Herculopathy, his senses were also heightened. He could hear the stream to the west of their location. (James knew it to be 300 yards west of them.) He could smell the pines around them and could create a rudimentary picture of their location. Localizing where they were in the world was not possible with this information, but he could describe perfectly with the information he had how they would be able to hike back to camp. Nobody else was able to develop that much control outside of Michael and James.

At this point, James gave each Phoenixense a map and he and Michael helped them localize on the map. For the next hour, they worked to orient in the local area utilizing the map. By the end of the next hour, all were able to use basic Orientopathy skills with the map and the surroundings, including Polaris. This seemed to be much more useful to Bekah especially as her senses seemed to augment the map but could not replace it. Even Kari, for the first time, wasn't frustrated holding and utilizing the map.

Time continued to speed on as they worked and began to succeed at various aspect of the new skill. It was at this time that Angelica caught everyone's attention.

"I think it is time to return to camp. We can't be so tired in the morning because the rest of the week will be spent in Titan's Camp."

"You are right." Emma added. "Master McAdams would not want us unable to participate because we are sick."

Bekah began to jump up and down. "It is Titan Camp time?" she said in her high pitched, rapid, excited voice. James couldn't help but smile.

"What is Titan's Camp?" Michael asked.

"Let's get back to the cave and we can discuss it for a moment before going to bed." James said with a grin. "I need to know what it is too!"

Bekah just shook her head at James and Michael as several others were shaking their head in agreement.

With the improving skills of Emma and James, the trip back to the cave was easy and the other Phoenixenses were feeling less and less as they traveled.

"Why didn't I feel it that time James?" Bekah asked. "I didn't notice time slowing down this time."

James just smiled and she knew he couldn't give her an answer.

The quick discussion of Titan's Camp didn't help much for their understanding but alleviated some fears. The big lesson from this discussion, however, was that only Lizzy and Bekah had read about the camp in *The Book of Adam*, although Emma and Angelica knew about it from their previous camp experiences.

As they returned to their tents and James lay on his cot, visions of Titan's Camp seemed to race through his mind. This was Patrol Challenge 2 and would include the entire patrol competing not against each other, but against three tasks. James was excited to interact and learn from the Titan's with upper year skills in the Sphinx Patrol.

CHAPTER 30
EMBARKING ON TITAN'S CAMP

As Doc McAdams sat at his desk, a 6'6" woman with white, blond hair, light green eyes and a very thin build continued to talk to him.

"Doc, I am not sure Titan's Camp will be fair this year. The Sphinx Patrol has a Concordant that seems to be developing much quicker than a usual first year student."

Master McAdams just smiled and looked to the other three individuals in the room. Master Belle stood next to her with two other adults, a short middle age man with a long gray and white beard, dark gray eyes and short silver, white hair and a 5'8" dark skinned woman with curly, black hair cut short.

All looked very animated and involved in the conversation.

Master Belle spoke next, "We have never limited the powers of students during the patrol challenges."

"Yes, but the purpose of the patrol challenges are to have the entire patrol learn to work together and depend on each other's skills." the short middle age man said while twirling his long gray and white beard in his hand. "Will the Sphinx Patrol members ALL get experience?"

"Master Walker, you are not worried about the Sphinx Patrol! You are worried about the Griffin Patrol." Doc McAdams said

with a smile. "You have always focused more on the competition than the learning."

With that, Master Walker blushed and remained silent.

"You are all giving James more credit than you should. He is still developing his Concordant abilities and doesn't have complete control of those skills. Often he even doubts his abilities."

"But his skills are unmistakable!" the dark skinned woman retorted.

"Okay." Master McAdams said with a smile. "Master Walker, Master Lindsley and Master Savage, you are asking me to limit just James in this challenge?"

They all nodded and Master McAdams raised his hand as Master Belle started to speak.

"You have all forgotten the dangers we face. The Order of the Kraken have infiltrated our camp. They are seeking to steal our students and corrupt their teaching. They feel we are 'limiting' the Titan growth by placing rules and limitations on their abilities. And now you ask me to limit the progression of our best hope for stopping Camilla and the Order?"

The four teachers looked at each other with concern and didn't say anything.

"The rules cannot change just for one student. I fear we cannot put more restraints either on the students in general. Therefore, the rules will not change from Titan Camps previously. I will monitor the Sphinx Patrol and ensure James isn't the only one learning and growing in this task. When the Sphinx Patrol wins this challenge again, it will not be because of one Titan." and Master McAdams smiled and turned back to his book lying before him on the table.

James woke with a start, wondering why he had a vision that seemed to be happening in real-time. Were the other teachers really worried about his abilities? Was he that good as a Titan? As a Concordant? He knew he wasn't, but the challenge must be a big deal. And what did Master McAdams mean by him being the best hope for stopping Camilla and the Order?

These thoughts were still percolating in his mind as he entered the Great Hall that morning with Bekah, Michael and Kari. The buzz of excitement in the hall was infectious and

Bekah was bouncing as she moved to the Sphinx table. James just couldn't get the words out of his mind, "*I will monitor the Sphinx Patrol and ensure James isn't the only one learning and growing in this task.*" He was so distracted, that he ran right into Ryan who was getting his food.

"Sorry I am so small you didn't see me." Ryan said with a grin and Kari started to laugh.

"Oh. I guess I am a little worried about the Patrol Challenge."

Ryan just smiled and nodded, "Good luck then!"

"And you! I wish we were on the same team."

"Yeah."

James carefully grabbed his eggs, two slices of bacon and orange juice and headed back to his table. He was feeling a little sick and wasn't real hungry, but Bekah would never let him skip breakfast this morning.

Breakfast was uneventful, until Master McAdams stood and began to speak.

"The Advisors to your patrols and I have spoken this morning and want to ensure you all understand the rules. Rules are often considered 'suggestions' in this task but are designed to protect you and ensure all receive the experience and learning we desire to be gained from the assigned tasks. No one patrol member can succeed in this task without the others. But I invite you to think of the rules we will share similar to the string helping a kite to fly. Let me explain with a story."

"There was a young man who loved the wind and was amazed at its great power. He watched it move the trees and even blow shingles off roofs or break fences when blowing strong. He was so intrigued with the power of the wind that his dad purchased him a beautiful kite and took him outside to learn to fly it. As he learned to fly the kite, he was amazed at how the wind would lift the kite into the air, how the kite could dive and spin as he pulled on the string. But he felt the kite's pull on the string and wondered if it would fly much higher without the limitations, without the string holding it down. He thought for days about this string and realized he was keeping the kite from really flying by pulling the string and holding the kite down. He decided he really wanted to see the kite fly and see what the wind could do with it. So, on a very windy day he made a decision to free the kite and let the kite and wind work together to much greater heights. He was so excited about this opportunity, so as the kite lifted into the air higher and higher, he was sitting there with great anticipation. What would the kite do once it wasn't tied to the ground? At that moment, he cut the string waiting to see what happened. But to his surprise, the kite fell from the sky and crashed into the ground breaking into pieces. As he carefully gathered the pieces and headed into the house, he wasn't sure what had happened. Why didn't the kite fly even higher without the restrictions of the string?"

"As he explained what had happened to his father, the father just smiled and said, 'My dear boy, you saw the string as a limitation, as an obstacle to be overcome. But the string created a limitation that instead of holding the kite down allowed it to fly higher and higher. Without the pull of the string from the ground, the kite was unable to maintain the correct orientation and alignment to the wind and it fell from the sky. As opposed to a limitation, it allowed the kite to fly much higher than it could on its own.'"

"I likewise warn that any limitations or rules we place on you at this time are NOT designed to keep you from succeeding. We want you all to be more powerful than us. We determine our success by how much more skill you each have than us. The best teachers will always be surpassed in knowledge, skills and abilities by their students! With that, I turn the time to Master Belle for explanation of the rules."

Master Belle stood and began to speak.

"For Patrol Challenge 2, each patrol is competing in their entirety, all ages. It is imperative that every Titan in your patrol be involved and participate. No Titan should be left out, even the first years. A well-functioning patrol will determine what skills each individual can utilize for the group and plan the challenge based on these determinations. As this is a timed challenge, the quickest patrol done wins, but time will be added

308 JAMES AND THE BAND OF FIRE

for each individual from the patrol that was not involved in helping. If a majority of the challenge is done by a single Titan, the patrol will be disqualified."

With that, many of the patrols gasped. James heard Angelica behind him say to her friend, "That wasn't a rule last year. Why did that change?" James just smiled, knowing why.

Master Belle continued, "This is a multi-day activity and will include carrying your own backpack, tent and food. You will need sleeping bags as well, but your cot will not travel with you. When you are traveling as a member of *The Band of Fire* as an adult, you will travel in this fashion. You will also be cooking and camping as patrols and will be given a specific fire color, to facilitate us following you on your travels. Each Titan will be given a small satchel of elements that will burn in the specified colors. Sphinx Patrol will have a bright orange flame, Centaur Patrol dark red, Griffin Patrol purple, and Minotaur Patrol blue fire. We will also be giving each Titan a small piece of Magnesium for emergencies. Don't burn this unless you are in danger or ready to quit the Challenge!"

James looked over at Bekah who was already answering in his mind, "Magnesium burns intense white, and our element will be Calcium to burn orange!" Even in his mind he could hear her excitement.

"Each Patrol will be given a map and be required to travel to the starting spot based on that map. From that starting point, you will be required to travel to three distinct locations and gather the flag of your patrol color. Each flag will have the next map attached. If you fail to find a flag, you will be unable to continue. Therefore, the basic rules are:

1) Following each map, find each flag and collect it.

2) Bring all flags back to camp quicker than every other patrol.

3) Don't get hurt or distracted.

4) All patrol members must participate."

Master McAdams then stood and began to give instructions as Master Belle stepped away, "Please go gather your individual backpacks and ensure everything is packed based on the list placed inside your tents. Food has already been transported to your tents for your portion of the Patrol food and should also be packed. Each patrol will then return here for your satchels and initial maps. Your time will start from the moment your entire patrol leaves here. Any questions?"

When nobody responded, they were all dismissed.

As everyone walked from the Great Hall, James was amazed at how excited he was to participate in this Patrol Challenge. He looked at the older Sphinx members and was so excited to learn from them and participate in this task without needing to lead. He was especially interested in learning from the sixth year Lafeyette Wilcox, who he considered a very talented Hoplonosmith.

Bekah walked up to James talking very quickly, but he was so distracted in his own mind that he didn't even hear a word she was saying. He just smiled and nodded, and she seemed to accept that as the expected response. James figured he would need to find out later what she really said.

As James looked up, Michael was running ahead towards the tent. He was obviously also very excited. Then he stopped running next to another Sphinx Patrol members that were obviously his brother as he looked like an older version of Michael. James even recognized him from the picture he had seen on their wall when he was inside Michael's mind. Michael had also told him that Mark was a 5th year and was skilled in Herculopathy. James walked a little faster, hoping to be introduced to Mark before the Patrol Challenge started.

CHAPTER 31
BACKPACKING THROUGH TITAN'S CAMP

Yesterday was still a blur from the moment he first met Mark, Michael's brother, to the Chronopathic travel to the Uinta mountains where the map started. Michael was in absolute heaven, Gracey B Smith, the Sphinx patrol leader and many of the other older Titans were having him guide them with a little assistance from Ward Whitlow and Richard Hinde, the older Orientopaths in the Sphinx patrol. James was okay staying out of the spotlight, but Bekah kept telling him to get more involved. She, Bekah, however, was struggling to carry her little backpack. As excited as she was to start, the backpack was a hard test for her tiny body. The instructions were to keep your pack to less than 1/3 your body weight, but Bekah weighs almost nothing. As they tried to get her pack to 1/3 her body weight, she wasn't even able to carry any food in her pack without making it too heavy. James volunteered to carry her portion of food, but now James was carrying the dome tent that she was sharing with Kari, her sleeping bag that he just added to his pack a few moments ago and all her food. Good thing having his pack weigh more than ½ his body weight wasn't a problem as a Herculopath.

Bekah looked over at James, breathing heavily, and thanked him again for taking the sleeping bag.

"I am so sorry you have to carry everything! I should at least do my part!"

"Remember, I am Concordant, so it is not a big deal."

"I need to find a way to participate, or I will be the cause for us to lose. Apparently, it will not be helping carry anything extra." Bekah tried to smile, but James sensed the pain in her eyes at that thought.

A 5'7" 18 year-old girl with curly blonde hair and soft green eyes came walking back with a smile on her face. "How are you doing Bekah? Are we going too fast? We are going to need you later today, most likely. Every year the first flag requires us to get through some obstacles. Last year it required Telepathy, because the area was too loud to allow talking. Sarah Jean, Rose, Cole and yourself are the only Telepaths we have."

"Gracey, James is also a Telepath."

"Yes." Gracey looked at James and smiled, "And we may need him too, but there will most likely be other skills we require of him."

"Are you sure mate that we can't travel more quickly?" came words from a large black girl walking back towards Gracey. James quickly recognized her as Nora Perrin, the 6th year Chronopath that along with Adam Simon, the 5th year Chronopath had brought the whole group to the mountains.

"I am not sure that is a great idea. We don't know what we are going to get ourselves into, nor what obstacles are coming."

"Can't we at least get us closer?"

"I still think we need to hike in. We are relatively close according to Ward."

James began to think of Ward Whitlow, a 6'3" boy in his 6th year at camp that was the expert of the Sphinx Patrol at Orientopathy. He would love to learn from him more about the skill of Orientopathy. With that thought, his mind started to fade, he felt a vision coming on, but he had never had a vision while hiking…

A burnt orange flag was tied to the back of a dark cave at the top of the next peak over 1 mile away. The cave was covered by water falling from the peak....Yes, a fast flowing waterfall covered the opening. But there was something outside the cave. A very large creature that was covered in shadow, almost blurry. Why couldn't he see it clearly?

In his mind, he then began to run down the mountain towards their current location. Was there anything else? Yes, there was a bridge, a broken bridge, over the large ravine about ½ mile ahead. Chronopathy may not succeed in crossing that bridge, without the abilities of a very talented Chronopath. They may need to fix the bridge to cross....

Suddenly James tripped over a rock and fell flat on his face. Apparently, he could walk and have a vision at the same time, just not very well.

Bekah looked down at him in concern and he felt her search his mind and she knew everything.

"James has found the flag!"

Gracey came running back from the 100 yards ahead where she had resumed her position near the lead.

"What? The flag is still over one mile ahead!"

"Yes, but he has seen it. Remember that he's Concordant and has very unique Orientopathic abilities. You may remember the speed and ease with which we finished Patrol Challenge 1."

"Ward, Lafeyette and Nora" Gracey called out, "Will you join us back here with these first years?"

James face began to change a bright shade of red as all four 6th years were walking quickly towards him as he crawled up from the ground with his heavy pack on his back. The tall Gracey was soon joined by the even taller Ward Whitlow with his dark brown hair, brown eyes and freckles covering most of his face. Ward reached down and lifted James to his feet as the 5'11" Nora also joined them and the short but muscular Lafeyette Wilcox with his curly red hair and pale white skin came back as well. They all looked at he and Bekah with questioning eyes and James couldn't help but be a little intimidated, even by the 5'3" Lafeyette. But before they could ask any questions, Gracey started speaking.

"Bekah here," as she pointed to a very excited Bekah, "has shared with me a vision that James had. I am still a little confused, but she told me she would share it with you three as well. As the presiding council of the Sphinx Patrol, we need to make a decision on how to proceed."

Lafeyette looked over at James with understanding in his eyes and began to speak, "I believe James will need to tell us more. The vision seems incomplete. What more can you tell us?"

"The vision was incomplete. I saw a waterfall at the top of this hill, about 1 mile away. The cave is covered by that waterfall, but something large is guarding the cave. I only saw a shadowed creature that was very large, but I don't know what it was. I am not sure why I couldn't see it fully. That has never happened to me before. The flag, however, sits at the back of the cave, tied to a wall in the darkness."

"Your vision was being blocked." a short, lightly tanned girl said walking from behind the 6th year students. "A very talented telepath can block another's mind. It is through the power of Occludopathy. I have been learning this ability from Master Belle. She says only Master McAdams is fully capable of controlling visions happening in someone's mind. That is why he ran the final test that James took to confirm Concordant abilities."

Bekah ran over to this girl speaking in great excitement, "I have read about that ability. Do you really have it?"

The short girl started to chuckle, "Not me! I am just trying to learn it. Hopefully by my sixth year I will have it figured out."

"Thanks Sarah, but what does that mean? Who would be blocking him?" Gracey asked with a little concern.

"I have felt a great deal of concern from many of the teachers and older Titan students about James here. They feel he is an unfair advantage to our patrol because of his abilities."

"Isn't that the purpose of the Patrol Challenges? I have read that the Patrol Challenges were instituted to force all the patrol members to improve their abilities and fully exercise their various skills and abilities. Why would they want to limit his growth and abilities just because he is Concordant?" Bekah said in her irritated speed and pitch.

"Concordants are still considered dangerous by many of *The Band of Fire*, including many of the masters in camp." Gracey said as she turned back to Sarah.

"How will we know what he saw?"

"We can't. He can try to look again, but he will probably be blocked again."

"I don't know how to look again. Sometimes it works, other times it doesn't. I am just learning." James said quickly. "But I will try if you would like."

"Please," Sarah said quickly. "And let me in your mind so I can try to see it too."

"I can help. We have a friendship that gives me a stronger connection." Bekah said in a high-pitched excitement as she stepped forward.

"Okay!" James said almost silently and he closed his eyes.

His mind came to the flag, still tied to the dark wall of the cave and he expanded the vision to the waterfall....

The vision stopped abruptly and his mind was empty. He shook his head a little frustrated and concentrated harder.

His mind again opened to the flag....

The vision stopped again, as sounds of wind blowing and water flowing seemed to fill his mind. Why couldn't he see it again? Then he began to play the Orientopathy game his dad had taught him so many years before.

He could hear the trees around him and counted each of the 23 additional people in the Sphinx Patrol around him. He saw the path moving ahead of him and counted the steps to the bridge. Oh yes, he had forgotten about the broken bridge half-mile ahead. He saw the ravine, measuring 40 feet across and 300 yards down to a small river deep below. The river was actually filled with rainbow trout... What? Why does that matter?

Back to the trail past the bridge. The ground was much steeper and covered with shale and broken rocks. The climb would be very difficult for the next half-mile with the 40% incline. This may be too steep for many of the Sphinx Patrol to climb without assistance. Then at the top was a large body of water, probably a lake, with a waterfall at the far end. Covering a cave. But there was something very large. Much larger than a bus, but animal in form. It has a large body, walks on four legs, and....

Again, his mind was blocked.

Bekah started laughing and Sarah turned in great surprise as she looked at James.

"How in the world did you do that?"

"Do what?"

"Walk the path to the cave in your mind? I have never seen any Orientopath do that before."

"Thanks for pointing out that I am not as talented an Orientopath as a first year." Ward said with a smile. "That is actually the skill Master Simon John Adamson has been teaching me the last two years. Nobody does it as well as him, except maybe his son." He then bowed to James as if to show him respect.

Everyone started laughing.

"Well, Sarah, what did you see if he walked the whole path."

"Half-mile ahead, James can probably give you the exact location, is a bridge that crosses a 40-foot ravine. It is much too deep to climb down and the bridge is broken. That is the first task we must overcome. Then we have a 40% incline we must climb to the lake where we have a creature guarding a cave where the flag can be located. It is larger than a bus, but we don't know anything more."

"It's a dragon!" Bekah said with excitement. "I would say a very large dragon, as I saw the wings before the vision was stopped!"

"Finally, some tasks that me and my Hoplonosmiths can handle. We will start on the bridge." Lafeyette said with excitement and ran off to the rest of the Titan group.

"Maybe we don't need to fight or kill the dragon. Maybe we can talk with it. I will get the Zoonophonics discussing an option. I am not sure any of us speak dragonese yet. Hopefully my skills are sufficient to make it work." Gracey said as Lafeyette was running up ahead. "Nora...."

"I am on it. We will get us to the base of the bridge! James can you give me exact coordinates, so we are within 100 feet of this side of the bridge?"

"Yes. I can tell you exactly where."

The group was in a great amount of excitement as everyone realized the first task was finally at hand and they would be at the flag before they knew it. Every Titan was trying to help. Each skill group was discussing what was happening and what the possible outcomes would be. Even those with Hippocratesense abilities were gathering supplies and discussing possible injuries and treatment options for a battle with a dragon, swimming through a cold lake, falling on the rocks from such a steep climb and how to help maintain the health of every individual in the next mile or so trip. Even Bekah seemed to have a new bounce in her step now that she was considered a hero because she recognized the dragon. She kept telling people about where she had read about the dragon in her many books of reading. The Zoonophonics seemed to be the most interested, with many of them looking through *Wildlife Studies* for some of the pages she had talked about. They were obviously hoping for some language help in talking to dragons.

James just stood back, observing and thinking carefully. Was Master McAdams stopping him from seeing the whole vision? Was there a piece of the puzzle he was missing? Was there another way he could examine the road ahead and get there before Master McAdams could stop him. Just then music filled his mind, but it was not Helia's music. It was different, but very familiar. Yes, it was Felicity's music. And then a voice he likewise recognized:

"The mind is but a simple thing, but blocking can be done, unless you become a powerful king, and protect your mind from everyone!"

James just shook his head. Well, at least I know it is Master McAdams blocking my visions. Now I need to figure out what Felicity was telling me.

Before he could think anymore, or even mention the thought to Bekah, they were all gathering for the quick trip to the bridge. James was a little excited, because every time they traveled by Chronopathy, he learned more. He made sure he was standing next to Nora as they prepared to move the first group. He was excited to hear her thoughts and know exactly how they were traveling:

"Careful now…Okay, James said to travel just under one-half mile to the north-east. If I concentrate very carefully, we will be there in one, two, three."

As James saw the location come into view in her mind, they were there. He looked at her and was amazed that as skilled as she was she was still very careful about the travel. Everyone had arrived safely and she was gone before he could grab her hand and do it again. She was only traveling with 6 Titans at a time, so several more trips brought the remainder of the group, including Gracey. She immediately walked the 50 feet to the bridge and observed what they could see.

"Patrol Leader, madam," LaFeyette said with a smirk and a bow. "The ravine is too deep to climb down, even Chronopathy in this size group would be too dangerous. I think we need to fix the bridge, unless you know how to fly."

"What about the broken bridge hanging on the far cliff edge? Can we retrieve it?"

"Yes, with the right archer it shouldn't be a problem. But we are still working on making the appropriate bow and arrow."

"Do you have a better idea?"

"Well, I can get someone down into the ravine, but blimey, not sure I can get them back up. Would that help anyone? Oh, and we would need a solution to getting me back up." Nora said quickly.

James had forgotten the Chronopathy was not teleportation or flying, but actually following the laws of travel, just at a more rapid rate (and expending less energy of course). But then he realized he had the answer in his pack.

As he removed his backpack and began searching, he removed the bow and a single arrow that he had made while participating in the Primary Patrol Challenge. Lafeyette got really excited and ran over to James to examine the bow.

"What an amazing design. How did you know that this particular branch would work this well to add spring to the non-elastic string you were using?"

"I did it without thinking! I didn't have much time to consider it."

"Can you shoot it?"

"He is very accurate. He has been practicing for years, even before he knew he was a Titan." Bekah jumped in with excitement.

As Lafeyette carefully attached a rope to the arrow, he turned back to James, "Then you shall shoot it. It is important that you hit the last rung of the bridge, so we can pull it back to us."

"That should not be a problem. But I have never tried to shoot that distance with this bow."

"Pull hard my boy, and hopefully the branch is strong enough to not break."

Gracey, who had been standing there without saying a word quickly agreed to the plan and James was off to shoot.

James stood at the edge of the ravine, bow firmly in his left hand and the arrow with a rope tied to it, carefully being placed with his right. The rope from the arrow hung by his left leg as he prepared to shoot. He carefully looked down the shaft through the sharpened edge. He pulled and the bow seemed to bend almost to breaking point as he focused his right eye through the arrow and pointed his left shoulder (aligning the rest of his body) and touched the string to the right corner of his mouth. He dropped his left hand to point directly at the location where he wanted the arrow to land. At that point, he felt something come over his mind....

A perfect red X seemed to float from the tip of his arrow to the location he was shooting. His eyes seemed to zoom in and the last rung of the bridge came into perfect view. The strings on either side were slightly frayed and the last rung was not firmly attached to the rest of the bridge. The second from last rung would be better. As he examined that rung, a small weak area in the wood was obvious. He focused more carefully on that spot and then let the arrow fly….

His vision returned to normal as he watched the arrow catch the second rung and bury itself into the wood. It was firmly attached.

Lafeyette groaned, "I hope that will work. I was hoping for the last rung."

"It is not firmly attached to the rest of the bridge."

"How do you know that?"

"I looked saw a weak point on the rope."

"I saw it too. I was running to tell you but was unable to get here before he shot the arrow." a 5th year large boy with black goatee and short black hair said.

"What do you mean Mark?" Lafeyette asked.

"Because of my Herculopathy, I was able to see the rope weakness by zooming in on the bridge."

Mark Peterson then grabbed the edge of the rope and started to pull. Grace Harrell, and Perry Smith also grabbed to help. Before James could assist, after stowing his bow again, the bridge was pulled within a few feet of the edge of the ravine.

"It is too short." Gracey said with a start. "Now what Lafeyette?"

But even as she talked, Lafeyette was already fastening ropes to the edge of the bridge and attaching it.

"With a bridge, we can now use Chronopathy to get closer to the lake and the dragon." Nora said in excitement.

"Perfect. Please take James in the first group and I will come at the last." Gracey said, gathering individuals quickly. Kari stepped up and grabbed James hand, hoping she could also be in the first group.

With location instructions again from James, all the Sphinx were quickly transported to about 100 yards from the dragon. They didn't dare get any closer. James, Bekah and Kari walked closer and could hear the beast making a great racquet. As they got closer, a large black dragon stood menacing in front of the lake and waterfall. The view was impressive.

Bekah was almost bouncing with excitement, "Look at that amazing animal!"

James carefully examined it. Large black scales, similar to that of a crocodile, but much larger covered its entire body. It had large bat-like wings folded on its back. Large plate like crests ran down the neck and back onto the large serpentine tail with large spikes on the end. It had strong legs, the size of trees that supported its enormous body. At the top of its neck sat a large wedge-shaped head with curved horns and long sharp fangs in its mouth. Steam or maybe smoke bellowed from its nostrils and fire belched from its mouth.

As individuals approached, all the Zoonophonics started to attempt to speak with the dragon, but none succeeded, until Kari did something unique. She stepped forward from the group and dropped to her knees, prostrating herself on the ground. And she began to grunt...

"We come before you, your greatness, to seek access to the cave for a short moment. We know it is your cave, and seek your gracious permission."

Although James understood her, even Gracey was struggling. But the dragon understood, but didn't speak out loud. It just looked at Kari and she nodded. James searched her mind, but it was blocked.

"He says we can enter the cave."

Many stepped forward and the air filled with fire. Gracey and LaFeyette jumped back, but several fourth year Titans were burned. The Hippocotesents immediately started treating them as Kari jumped forward.

"He said it must be me. Only me." She said with terror in her voice.

"Who's blocking her mind?" Bekah asked with a start as she tried to reach out to Kari.

"I don't know, but it could be Master McAdams or the dragon."

Gracey stepped forward and started to grunt and growl. James heard the words perfectly, "She's a young one. Can not one of us go instead?"

This time the voice of the dragon rang out like thunder and many of the Titan seemed to step back in fear at the powerful thundering voice. Bekah turned and looked at James, not understanding, but James understood again perfectly.

"I am Androf, the son of Petrof, the son of Edenof, the powerful son of Adamof. I have been unmolested and uninterrupted by the weak race of humans for more than 200 years. You dare threaten my cave and my privacy by attempting to enter my cave? You dare dictate the method of entering therein? How dare you! I shall not permit the entry therein. Even this young lady, who showed me great respect, shall not be permitted to enter now because I have once again been disrespected by those she considers her friends. You, young lady, are no leader here!"

As the words ended, the sky filled with fire and all the Sphinx were diving for cover. James felt the anger rising up within him and he began to speak with a power he had not hitherto known.

"You speak as if you deserve respect, but you are not a noble and great dragon as was your father. You bend to the will of weaker men than me. You cower at the sight of knights in armor. You even watched your father die because you dared not fight. And now you threaten our small band of children. I myself could destroy you! I know every weakness you now have! And I know that this is NOT your cave! You were brought here by Master Doc McAdams for this game. Don't pretend you are more than you really are!"

Everyone looked at James, understanding his grunts and growls perfectly, even as they knew he had spoken in dragonese. Somehow James was speaking dragonese to the beast while telepathically broadcasting his words into their minds. But the words that followed were not understood, until the fire came again and everyone knew the dragon was even angrier still.

"You must stay out of my mind!" the growls came. "How dare you see my history and interpret for your own benefit. How dare you talk of my father and his death at the hands of wicked men. I will not trust you or anyone else to enter this cave. I was promised by Doc McAdams that no harm would befall me or my children if I served my purpose well. Did you see my family when you searched my mind? Did you assume I was only thinking about me, as you obviously are thinking only of yourself and your desire to win! The rules are exact, the options are not any other. I have chosen who can enter this cave and you shall have no other option to enter this cave. You cannot fight me, for no weapons you wield can penetrate my scales. You cannot withstand my fire, because no clothes you wear will prevent a burn. You cannot hear my voice, unless I permit it, as I have more power of telepathy than anyone here. So, if Kari, chosen by me for the great respect and kindness she showed unto me, is not willing or able to enter the cave, nobody shall enter and your progress is stunted. Will you not do as I have said?"

"I will go!" Kari growled to the dragon as she walked forward. "Please, permit me to enter your cave." Then she looked at James with a concerned look and he knew what she was asking.

As Kari walked forward, Androf seemed to bow and allow her to walk past, as he continued to look menacing at everyone else. James concentrated and felt his mind breakthrough the wall and enter Kari's mind, he could see her thoughts and even see through her eyes…

As Kari walked forward, she could feel her heart beating faster. She had to go into a cave. She hates dark, confined spaces, but will do it for her friends! She thought of the great bravery of her father and hoped he would be proud of her as she stepped to the cave door. She carefully removed her pack and pulled out the gift Bekah gave her as they were packing. A small yellow flashlight that was bright and powerful. Hopefully it would be enough light to limit the darkness. She walked to the left of the dragon and followed the small path that ran behind the waterfall. The waterfall got louder as she walked behind it and then she couldn't see the Sphinx Patrol or the dragon anymore. Her nervousness was getting worse as she got closer to the cave, but she could feel James in her mind and she found great comfort in that knowledge.

She could feel the mist as the waterfall fell past her and she felt a small breeze coming from the cave. As she entered the cave, she heard the dragon voice echo through the cave.

"Don't touch anything in the cave except the flag. If you touch anything else, I will remove you from the cave!"

Kari smiled to herself and turned on the flashlight. The darkness seemed to flee from before her and the cave opened to a large cavern. The walls were lined with gold, everything from gold coins and goblets to large gold statues. This reminded Kari of movies she had seen of ancient artifacts found in ancient caverns. Her flashlight reflected around the room and she was amazed at how full the cave was. There was a small pathway down the center of the cave with every other inch of the cave covered. As she walked through the cave, she thought of her mother and how much this money, even one goblet would help her family since her father's death. Couldn't she at least take one thing? But the words of Androf seemed to echo through the cave, "Don't touch anything…" So, she just continued to walk towards the back of the cave.

As she reached the rear of the cave, a large Sphinx flag sat attached to the back wall. She walked toward it in excitement and reached out and grabbed it.

Every Sphinx member heard Master McAdams' voice echo in their heads.

"You have just retrieved Flag #1. You are currently in 3rd place. Please proceed to follow the next map and continue the Challenge. Well Done Sphinx Patrol."

CHAPTER 32
TITAN'S CAMP CONTINUES

The sky was dark with only a sliver of the moon visible as James sat outside the tent looking up at the stars. The camp was asleep after traveling to the oceanside area to start the trek for the next map. But James couldn't get out of his mind the view he saw of the cave with all its treasures, the dragon and the damage and injuries inflicted on the Sphinx patrol. He couldn't get out of his mind the courage and power with which Kari acted for them. And he couldn't forget the words, "You are in 3rd." All are worried about him as a Concordant, but he hasn't been a great help to them. Why didn't he help them travel more quickly? Why didn't he have his vision earlier? Why couldn't he block his mind from Master McAdams or even from the dragon? He just didn't believe that him being Concordant was any advantage to them. He was a little frustrated that he wasn't as functional a Concordant as he had wanted to be. As he sat there thinking, his mind started to fade into a new vision...

"I have been given a new assignment Doc. They are asking me to protect the Owens family. I am not sure that I should take that responsibility. I am an Orientopath and don't have any major skills for protecting them."

"Have you met Sarah?"

"No sir. But that is the individual I have been assigned."

"She's a beautiful young lady."

"But I still love Aria. I don't believe I could even look upon another as beautiful now that I have lost my family completely."

"God often works in mysterious ways. You shouldn't keep your heart locked, because God may be carefully orchestrating your life at this time."

"But what if my responsibility Is to just protect the family and her? What if nothing comes of this?"

"Then she will be greatly protected! But if you are to fall in love, she will be even more greatly protected than Percival Owens could have ever dreamed."

Simon sat up from his thin pad on the ground, the tent still dark. He really did love her, but Sarah and James were not protected now that he was captured by the Order of the Kraken. They were both in grave danger and there was nothing he could do. If he could talk to James he would tell him that he had always been proud of him, that he loved him more than life itself and that he would do anything to protect him. But there was nothing he could do now. If only he had learned this before losing his first wife. He truly loved Aria as well, but Camilla would never believe him. What had she been told about him? Why did she dislike him so? Was there anything he could do there as well?

The vision faded and James, lying on his back, was looking at the Big Dipper and the North Star. He loved the consistency of those two structures in the sky, they gave him courage and confidence that life was not out-of-control as it sometimes felt. He closed his eyes again and wished he could see his mother again and share his father's great love with her.

Sarah sat on her bed with tears in her eyes. She knew James was safe, but knew nothing of Simon. He had never gone even a week without contacting her and Doc had said he felt Camilla's group had captured him. But why didn't Simon fight? She watched him fight in great fury when her family had been attacked many years ago. That was the day she knew she loved him more than anything or anyone else in this world. It was that battle that confirmed to her that she would never again need to worry. But the worry she has now couldn't be greater. There was no way for her to find him or rescue him and Doc wasn't exactly sure where he was. He said something about Brazil, but didn't seem to know more.

As she continued to cry, sitting on her bed, she closed her eyes and begged heaven to protect him. For she knew completely that he loved her and loved James. She knew that he loved Camilla as well and ached for her almost daily. She hoped James knew this, for she felt it would give him great strength as he strived to become fully functional as a Concordant. And a small smile came over her face as she thought of James and how excited Percival Owens would have been to have a Concordant descendant. How blessed they truly are.

"James, are you okay?" Gracey said as she walked toward him. "Shouldn't you go to bed? We have a busy day tomorrow."

"I don't sleep very well. My mind is constantly filled with visions of my father."

"Do you know where he is?"

"Yes, but there is nothing that I can do to go help him. I am not talented enough as a Titan."

"You may be underestimating your own abilities. I have never seen a first year as skilled as you in even one of the Titan abilities. You seem to have abilities that 6th year Titans don't have. I am sure there will come a time when you will need to go after him. We as the Sphinx patrol will help you in any way we can."

"Thank you. Hopefully you are right and I can bring my family back together. My mother needs that!"

"Family is very important! My father and mother are both gone. I lost them last year in a car accident. Often, I ache for them when the sounds of the day give way to the darkness. Know that you can come talk to me anytime, if you need." with that, Gracey walked away leaving James still resting against the outside of his tent.

James was surprised to learn that Gracey had also lost her parents in a car accident. Why was she stable and Camilla was not? Why did Gracey continue as a Titan in *The Band of Fire* and Camilla run away and form her own band. Was

Concordance the difference? Was it the corruptibility of power? Was he too at the great risk of corruption?

He unzipped the tent on that thought and crawled inside. He didn't want to sleep but knew Gracey was right. As he closed his eyes, the darkness seemed to give way to great light...

"James, wake up. It is time to get going!" Michael was shaking him. "Why are you still asleep? Most of the tents are already packing up. You still need to eat breakfast."

James woke with a start and crawled from the tent. He turned and started packing up the tent and Michael just looked at him with a smile.

"Aren't you going to eat?"

"I don't want to slow us down too much. Let's pack the tent up first."

"Did you have another dream last night?"

"Not that I can remember. But did you know Gracey lost both her parents last year?"

"Yes, my brother told me about the accident. She's amazing isn't she."

James smiled, "You like any girl older than you."

Michael blushed, but said nothing.

As they continued to pack up the tent, Bekah came walking up with a plate of food in her hand.

"James," she said in her motherly tone, "you will not skip breakfast today. We have a hard trip ahead of us. Gracey says we will need to be using boats this time."

As James looked at Bekah with a smile, he noticed several Titans moving toward the beach area with large logs that they had carved into canoes. James saw others carving paddles, while Gracey was talking with the 6th years Sphinx about the plans. Maybe he should have awakened earlier and he could have helped carve, but apparently they weren't needing him to help with that.

As he continued thinking, Gracey came walking forward and started talking. "So James, we need you to find the flag. Here is the map."

Before he even saw the map, Ward walked forward and started explaining where he thought the flag was. "The map seems to describe a cave somewhere out in the ocean as marked by the map. It is about 60 feet under the water, but we don't have any scuba equipment. I can't completely visualize the cave because of the interference of the water. Mark Peterson thinks he will be able to dive down, but we need at least one other person to join him."

Sarah came walking forward and asked if she could enter his mind again.

"That shouldn't be a problem."

As Bekah got more excited, he realized she was going to do the same, so James closed his eyes and asked Ward to start his description again. Without looking at the map, James started to move along the path as it was being described in his mind....

He was moving across the water at a great speed as if he was flying. He noticed the waves moving quickly against him and was able to sense the depth of the water. When he was ½ mile from shore, the slowly deepening water dropped off in a hurry. Then he saw it, a cave 60 feet down facing away from the shore. The opening to the cave was about 10 feet X 10 feet. There were fish of all kinds swimming around, but there appeared to be no guard for the cave. As James entered the cave, his mind became blurry and he was unable to localize the flag directly. He could see it resting against a deep wall in a water filled cavern but was unable to see the pathway into the cave. He attempted to turn around and look, but again the pathway was blurry until he was back at the cave opening.

James opened his eyes and looked frustrated at Gracey, Ward and Sarah. "Why are they blocking me again. Shouldn't it all work? There is no 'creature' they are blocking from my view this time."

As he continued to just stare at them, Bekah entered his mind and started speaking in a rapid, excited tone. "It is being blocked because that is the obstacle. Inside the cave is the secret, the obstacle that must be overcome. I can help you here. We just need to come up with a plan. Think about what the options must be. Think about a solution!"

His mind started to race and then he understood completely. He looked at Gracey, Ward and Sarah and then he looked at Michael, Bekah and Kari. Michael was the key, but how could he utilize him? And then he heard her voice again.

"You can speak to him directly without anyone else hearing. Maybe you can use his mind to search the cave. Maybe together you and he can see the whole picture."

"What are you thinking James? We need to figure out the cave." Gracey said in concern. "Ward doesn't know if he can get himself into the cave like you do in your mind. And Sarah is as confused as you are."

"Bekah and I have an idea, but I have to use my friends because I know them."

"Great idea!" Sarah said from behind them. "Bekah is a strong enough telepath that she can help. I will stay out of your mind this time in hopes of not interfering."

Michael was already walking forward and Kari was looking at Bekah in concern.

"Is there anything I can do to help?" Kari asked quickly.

"We may need you too, but I need to start with Michael." James said quickly.

"Bekah has already told me what we need to do. I am not as good at this as your father is, but I think I can do it if we get close to the water." Michael said with obvious excitement in his voice.

As Michael, James, Emma and Bekah walked toward the beach, all the Sphinx watched in excitement. Gracey was pacing back and forth and Sarah was sitting on a rock covering her eyes. Lafeyette continued to twirl the hatchet he had in his hand as he stood next to the newly completed canoes. He was obviously nervous, but was trying to act relaxed.

As they reached the water, the Sphinx patrol became completely silent with all looking on. James turned to Michael and Michael pulled a blindfold from his pack and covered his eyes. As James concentrated, he felt Michael's mind open up and....

The cave was located quickly and Michael was surprised at the size. The entrance seemed to be carved out of rock, not cut as a water formed cave usually was, but carved as if with manmade tools. The edges were smooth and a small step was located just inside. The opening became a large cavern with three pathways just inside. Three paths, but only one would get into the correct path for the flag. Michael stepped forward and the pathway started to blur.

"What do you hear? What do you see? What do you feel?" James voice was echoing in his mind. Michael knew it was up to him as James was being blocked from seeing anything more than he was seeing. But he had never seen it this clearly. Was this always how James saw his maps?

"Please. Concentrate. I can place you in the location but can only act based on your mind and your senses. What do you hear, see and feel? Concentrate on each pathway individually!"

Michael tightened his eyes and concentrated. He was no longer on the beach. He was deep in the ocean, walking into the cave with the ability to see in the dark. His lungs didn't hurt, in fact he could breathe completely like he was standing on the beach…which he was, but he knew what was happening in the cave. He began walking towards the first path on the left. He looked down the path, but it was completely black. He walked to the middle path with the same results. He couldn't hear anything in the water, couldn't see into the pathway. Then he felt a breeze coming down the center pathway and the smell of…trees. The center path goes up to the shore. So, it must be either the left or right pathway.

"Remember the game? Try to draw the map of the cave with all the pathways. If we do it right you will be able to find the flag." James thought into his mind.

He looked down at his hand in his mind and began to draw a map. As the pathways came into more perfect view, he saw a maze of intertwining paths. Some pathways diving deeper into the cave. Some pathways ending in dead ends. Some pathways turning back on themselves. He drew all the paths and was able to localize exactly where the center path opens up (in a cave 300 yards to the northeast of their current location). And the flag was located in the right pathway at the rearmost part of the maze. As he completed the maze, he looked down at the picture and tried to memorize it….then the cave was gone.

James finished drawing the map on a small paper and then walked to Ward and Gracey and handed them the map.

"There are two ways to enter the cave. One is located 300 yards to the northeast in a cave. I am not sure if that entrance is being guarded, as I haven't looked yet. But the entrance in the water can be reached by a Herculopath without too much trouble. This is the map to the flag. I recommend we use that pathway."

"May I recommend that you join the Herculopaths on this trek into the ocean?" Gracey asked James quickly. "I am not sure why, but something is wrong here and I am not sure what."

She then turned to Ward, Sarah and Lafeyette, "Sarah can you invite Mark Peterson to join us?"

Without a word, Sarah just smiled and the 6'8" Mark came walking to the group.

"I am asking you to lead this expedition. Here is the map drawn by James....Oh, and he will be joining you."

"With pleasure. Sarah said you will want all the Herculopaths to be involved. Grace Harrell and Perry Smith are both young, but I think they can do it."

"May I suggest that several of us go find the other entrance just in case." Ward asked.

"Great idea. And Sarah, can you keep contact with James during the whole process?"

"I think the connection will be stronger if we use Bekah." Sarah said quickly.

"Are you sure?" Gracey asked. "She is just a first year."

"But the connection of friendship or family is usually much stronger when it comes to Telepathy. I will remain close if it becomes a problem, but I am sure she can do it."

"Okay. This is a big endeavor. Let's pull everyone together and ensure everyone is involved in some way, and that we are ready."

James looked at Gracey, once again impressed with her abilities to lead and felt confident they could accomplish this task. He knew, however, that they were missing something and he sent his concerns to Bekah for reassurance. She always felt he had much stronger abilities than he believed, and right now he needed her reassurance. And a smile came to his face as he felt her arm around his shoulder and a quick thought come into his mind, *"You are concordant. This task was designed for you..."*

The discussion and organization took another 45 minutes as Gracey ensured every piece and every team was ready and designated for their exact task. Mark, James and all the Herculopaths changed into swimsuits as the divers for the flag. Ward, Michael and Lafeyette were to take a group of Hoplonosmiths to find the cave and locate the other entrance into the maze. Sarah and Bekah were discussing the plan to stay in contact with both the groups to ensure the divers and the spelunkers could coordinate if necessary. Gracey was organizing a group to head to the beach to launch with the Herculopaths so someone could bring the canoes back. Adam Simon, Earl Stanton, William Trussel, Lillie Jane Smoke, Richard Hinde, Cole Puett, Arsula Brinkley and Rose Hamilton were assigned to run the four canoes with a diver in each one. Nora was asked to organize the remaining Sphinx to setup camp and prepare to spend the night at this location after retrieving the second flag. Kari was excited to be participating in this important task under Nora's direction and was following her around asking questions about the assignment.

James looked at the canoes and was amazed at the carved-out logs that looked like perfect canoes. He thought of the canoes back at camp and was amazed at how similar these appeared. The Sphinx Hoplonosmiths were quite amazing. As he examined the second canoe, Mark climbed into the first canoe with Earl Stanton and Cole Puett. Perry Smith climbed into the third canoe with William Trussel and Arsula Brinkley. And Grace Harrell climbed into the forth canoe with Richard Hinde and Lillie Jane Smoke.

As they all pushed off, with Rose Hamilton and Adam Simon rowing his canoe, the waves seemed to push hard towards the shore and he saw their muscles aching as they attempted to row against the current. Rose and Adam, although rowing hard, couldn't seem to get away from the shore.

James heard Mark's voice echo over the waves, "Herculopaths, take an oar and get us where we need to go. Then the rowers can bring the boats back after we dive!"

James smiled as Rose handed him an oar and all the canoes quickly started moving through the water. After just a moment, even Adam stopped helping because he couldn't keep up with James' powerful strokes. James felt his muscles ripple, felt the water give way to each stroke and seemed to see the water almost part as he pushed the wooden canoe quickly toward the dive point. Mark was already there and the other two canoes were quickly approaching. But James felt alive. He loved the power flowing through his hands. Loved the damp salt air flowing in and out of his lungs and the spray of salt water on his face. Even the shine of the sun on the ocean seemed to bring all his senses to life. He couldn't believe how much he loved to canoe!

But even as he was thinking, Mark reached over and grabbed his canoe and pulled him next to his. Grace and Perry both similarly arrived and came to a stop as the waves continued to push them towards shore.

"Please get in the water quickly!" Mark said. "We will need to let the canoes travel back now. Please head back to shore as quickly as possible and help setup camp. But stay in contact with Sarah and Bekah so that we can have the canoes back when the time comes."

As they each jumped into the water, with the cold water lapping over their bodies, the canoes raced towards shore with the rowers and the waves pushing together now. James began to breathe deeply and fill his lungs as Mark gave final instructions.

"You don't have much time. Please fill your lungs as we discussed and head straight down about 60 feet. You will not be able to breathe at all, so hold your breath. We will enter the cave on the wall facing away from the shore and then we will see what our options are."

James knew there wouldn't be air until they were about 30 feet or more into the cave and then some air available at the top of the cave. But could they hold their breath long enough? He was hoping they could.

As Mark and Grace took a deep breath and dove, James looked over at Perry and took a deep breath himself and began to dive down.

As he began to dive deeper and swim with great power downward, he felt the air in his lungs start to compress. But his body didn't seem to mind. His heart was beating slowly, his eyes were completely clear. The deep blue ocean stretched for miles and he could see fish in all directions. Deeper below them he could see the cave opening, a 10' by 10' opening. He saw Mark, Grace and Perry swimming quickly, as if they were in a hurry, but he felt completely relaxed. Mark was making hand signals and then James felt a unique desire to breath. But breathing underwater didn't make any sense. But his mind was calm and clear and without hesitation, he knew he could breathe. So, he took a deep breath and his lungs filled with water.

As he took a deep breath, Mark was shaking his head vigorously with his eyes wide open. He grabbed at James, but it was too late. He was drowning as his lungs filled completely with water and then James felt his chest tighten and he saw every alveolus of the lung contract in great strength, almost like a grape being squeezed for juice, but instead of juice oxygen was released into the blood stream from the water. He was breathing without difficulty under the water. And James just smiled as Mark's eyes got even wider. Grace and Perry likewise looked at each other in great excitement but continued to hold their breath with Mark.

"Wait, how is he breathing?" he heard Mark think. *"I have never heard of anyone with that ability. Can he speak underwater too? I can't breathe, but at least I can speak."*

With that, Mark opened his mouth, still holding his breath in his right lung and part of his left. He then began to speak. "I am not sure how James is able to breathe, but we don't have time to think about it. We have approximately 30 minutes to find the flag or we will run out of air even as Herculopaths!"

As the words vibrated through the water, Grace and Perry nodded their heads and swam the other 5 feet to the cave opening and then entered, missing the step in. Mark followed close behind and James entered amazed at how accurate Michael's vision was of the carved opening to the cave.

"We will need to go 30 feet in and then we can swim to the top of the cave and you can each get another breath. The air is coming down through the center pathway that leads to the beach." James said easily through the water.

Mark smiled and just shook his head. *"Concordants are truly weird individuals, but we are lucky he is on our side. But what I don't understand is why he as a first year has the skill of Cyclopathize while it has taken me years to develop."*

"Mark," James thought quickly, "I don't know either. It just seems to jump out of me. That worries me a great deal. What if I can't ever learn to control it?"

Mark again smiled, as they swam up to the top of the large cavern and the three took a deep breath. James had no desire to breath air, as he was amazed and intrigued by his ability to breathe under water. He had read about Scuba Diving, but this was much different. He felt as if he was breathing normally, as if he was on the beach, except if he paid attention he could feel his lungs wringing the air out of the water and expelling the hydrogen.

As they caught their breath, they moved to the Right pathway and started to enter. As they entered, James saw a small wire crossing the entrance. It was tiny, almost invisible, but he swam over it with ease, but Grace didn't see it and upon touching it with her hand, the cave entrance exploded. The pressure collapsed the opening completely and all the water was pushed up and out of the center pathway and the water level dropped to less than a foot of water in the cave. Luckily, they were just barely entering the right pathway and the great flow of water out the center pathway protected them from injury form the blast. Grace, Mark and Perry all took a deep breath and James spit out large amounts of water from his lungs and likewise started breathing normal again. But James was distracted...

Michael approached the cave with caution. They had finally found it, but they didn't know if it was dangerous or not. He turned to Ward who was looking around suspiciously. Lafeyette continued to sharpen his spear and was turning and looking in all directions. They were here. Now someone would need to be the first to enter the cave. Judson Stratton, a 5'10" boy with wavy, auburn hair, freckles and blue eyes stepped forward.

"I will volunteer to enter."

"What protection do you have?" Ward asked him.

"His staff in his hand is a long sword, a spear and a rod all in one. I have fought that sword and had to be careful to not allow a 4th year student to beat me." Lafeyette said with a smile. "I would let him go if he is interested."

"Then go ahead." Ward said nodding his head.

As Judson walked into the cave, the ground began to shake and water shot out of the cave, propelling Judson about 15 feet into the air and then to the ground with a thud. Michael saw his head hit the ground first and he fell to the ground limp and didn't get up…

James came to himself, lying on his back with Ward and Perry standing over him.

"Are you okay?" Mark asked quickly.

"Yes, just slipped."

"Well, let me help you up. It may be the stress of going from breathing in water to breathing air again."

"Maybe…" James agreed, not wanting to frighten them by talking about Judson at this time.

"Let's continue through the maze. Your map should allow us to move very quickly, especially now that we don't need to hold our breath."

The group began to walk down the right pathway that headed deeper under the ground. It traveled approximately 300 yards and then had paths going right, left and strait. From the previous vision of the map, they knew they needed to go to the right again, so they followed that pathway. They turned right, and left and right again. They climbed over walls and through small holes. They continued until they came to the final obstacle, another 65-feet drop to the final cave that led to the flag. Mark turned and looked at them and then began to speak.

"James and I are going to dive down and find the flag. The 65-feet drop will take us approximately another 2 atmospheres and it will be very difficult to hold your breath. I am the most experienced and James can breathe underwater, so please wait here."

James and Mark dove into the water and James immediately felt his lungs fill with water and he was breathing again. He was amazed at how alive he felt, but as he watched Mark, he could tell it was very difficult for him to hold his breath at that depth. So, James began to swim more quickly and forgot about the ease he had breathing in the water. Within seconds they found the cave and followed it back 5 feet to the wall and grabbed the flag. Mark tucked it into his pocket and they raced back up. As Mark was racing to the surface, James began to look around. This was a true water formed cavern, as opposed to the man carved opening that was now collapsed. As he began to leave the cavern, he saw another cavern 25 feet to his right. He felt a strong urge to examine it.

As he swam to the other cavern, he noticed what looked like a light coming from the cave. It was almost a florescent blue light, but the glow was almost eerie. He turned into the cave, but a large metal grate was blocking it. He looked deep into the cave and saw the glow from about 15 yards back. In his swimsuit he didn't have any way to get into the grate, so he decided to just pull on it. As he grabbed with both hands and pulled, he felt his muscle tighten throughout his whole body. He placed his feet firmly on the ground and pushed with all his might. The grate didn't seem to move or even give at all. As he continued to pull, however, his mind began to hear instructions from a voice he recognized the voice of Master Doc McAdams.

"You are more advanced that I had hoped at this time. Your Concordant abilities are advancing very quickly. I was not expecting to have anyone find this cave today. But if you focus your strength, even into one hand, the grate can be broken. Do you have the focus to make it happen?"

James removed his left hand from the grate and placed his right hand in the center of the grate and closed his eyes. How would he focus? Carefully he thought about the center of the grate, the very center covered by his right hand. He pulled, every inch of his strength was coursing through his right hand. He pulled, but nothing happened. He locked his legs against the wall and pulled harder. The grate began to give way and the cave walls started to crumble. As he pulled even harder, the grate collapsed into his hand and the cave was open.

Just then he heard Mark's voice ring through the water, "James, what are you doing down there? Do you need help?"

"I am fine Mark," James called through the water. "I will be up soon! There is another cave that I need to examine."

"Hurry! We still need to find a way out of this cave now that the entrance collapsed."

As James swam toward the glow, his mind was clouded again…

"Bekah, can you speak with him? I have lost contact."

Bekah looked extremely nervous as she turned to Sarah. "I haven't been able to speak with him or see into his mind since he and Mark dove into the water."

"Yes, but Mark has come out and I can speak with him again."

"So, does that mean something has happened to James?" Bekah said in a high pitched, rapid voice.

"Mark has said no, but he is going into another cave. Why would he do that?"

"James is just that way! I wish I could see what he was doing."

The vision faded and James was holding a baseball size stone in his hand. It was that very stone that was glowing. He had no idea what it was, but knew he needed to take it. He carefully placed it into his pocket and swam back to the surface. As he surfaced, Mark looked very relieved.

"What were you doing?"

"I saw something in a cave down there. It looked like it was glowing, but it was just a rock."

"A glowing rock?"

"Yes, but it was nothing." James said without a thought as he heard a voice ringing inside his head.

"What were you doing? Did you really go look at a rock?"

James just smiled and didn't respond. He blocked his mind slightly and knew he would pay for not telling her later.

The remainder of the trip was uneventful as they climbed out the center pathway and into the presence of the remaining Sphinx waiting by the water. The reunion was sweet as they were informed they had moved into first place. All were celebrating as they ate dinner and prepared to go to bed for the night, but James just kept thinking about the rock. As he tried to push it from his mind, the light glow kept coming back. It was with this thought that he walked away from the group and headed to his tent. He would need to head to bed soon, but he wasn't in the mood to talk with anyone about the day. He just wanted to think about what had happened. They had found the second flag, but that was no longer important to him. What was the rock?

CHAPTER 33
CAMILLA'S MISTAKE

As the night progressed, James found himself sitting in his camp chair by a bright orange fire. The logs had burned down from the once large bonfire they had enjoyed after dinner and only the calcium seemed to keep the fire burning a bright orange color. The remaining chairs were packed up and put away and James sat there alone starring into the dying embers of the fire. He loved fire and was almost dazed as he starred into it. It seemed to be the only light around him as most of the tents were even dark. Bekah had just retired to bed and Gracey had excused herself encouraging everyone to get to bed. As everyone else left, James agreed to watch the fire burn down the rest of the way before going to bed, to ensure there was no fire still burning unattended.

The day had been another strange day...amazing, but strange. As he starred into the coals, he pulled a now glowing stone out of his pocket and began to imagine what it could be. Bright orange fire, dying coals and a glowing blue stone in his hand....

The fire glowed green, her favorite color of fire. She was finally alone. She was tired of everyone asking her questions, making comments and demanding she give them direction. Wouldn't it be easier if they all took personal responsibility for this? Wouldn't it be easier if she could forget about her brother James? But she couldn't help but wonder about James. Was he really Concordant, as Zoram had said? Was he progressing faster than she did? She hadn't seen him for years and could not imagine him as a 12 year-old boy. He was still a young child to her.

As she thought of James, she began to hum her favorite song and imagined holding this little baby in her arms, her baby brother when her mother was still alive. Why did Simon let her hold him? Why did he act like he cared then, when he never even acted like he cared about her before that time? She heard her mother's voice in her mind, that voice she missed so, "Your father loves you Camilla! He has always loved you. He just can't love me with me in his mind all the time." Camilla felt anger welling up insider her. Simon killed her! How could he push her away? How could he leave them both and force her mother to find a "Natural-born" with whom she would die in a car crash...

As the crash filled her mind, she remembered James laughing as they played on the floor. She loved that laugh. She missed that laugh. If only she could hold him while he slept as she had so many times before. But he is 12 years-old now and doesn't even remember who she is. Sarah didn't want him to remember her. In fact, she had forgotten that Sarah Owens was probably the reason Simon and her mother had separated. She was the cause of all these problems. WAIT! Why did she leave Sarah alone? Why was Sarah safe at home while her mother was buried under the ground. Why had she forgotten that Sarah was one of the reasons she had to leave her baby brother years ago? Yes! Sarah needs to pay. Not just Simon, but Sarah too must pay!

The plan began to formulate in her mind. She could capture Sarah without a problem using her Order. The Band of Fire is distracted teaching the students. She could sneak in, capture Sarah and ensure James wouldn't have to suffer any more. She loved James and needed to protect him from his parents.

Then a beautiful, almost haunting music filled the air. "Your feelings open will hurt you still!" Fogo sang into her mind. "Will you let others read your mind? Learned nothing have you?" Camilla shook her head in surprise at the words and realized her reminiscing had caused her to think more deeply and fail to protect her thoughts. She didn't even allow her Order to read her thoughts but thinking of James caused her to forget her protections. Thankfully, Fogo helped her right the wrong...

James eyes opened, with tears falling down. The fire was now nearly gone with barely embers glowing. The bright orange flame was gone, the stars and moon above were masked in rolling clouds, but the thoughts of Camilla rang in his mind. She was planning to attack his mother. That could not happen! He would warn her, or could he warn Master McAdams and *The Band of Fire?*

The night progressed quickly and James found himself rolling his sleeping bag at 4:00am. He didn't sleep much, but he wasn't tired. The words of Master McAdams were still ringing in his mind.

"Your mother will never be in danger. *The Band of Fire* has committed many years ago to protect the family of Percival Owens. Not even the Order of the Kraken will get to her! Stay with your patrol, as you are much safer there. We will ensure she is safe."

The words seemed almost hollow to him. How would they keep her safe? They didn't keep his dad safe! He would never forgive himself if The Order of the Kraken captured his mother too! But then the words of Bekah came back to his mind. He trusted her completely and knew she was usually right. But was this situation different? When Michael jumped in and Kari promised to help in anyway she could, he knew he couldn't let his closest friends down. But Gracey committing the Sphinx Patrol to help after getting the third flag, would be the final straw to ensure he stayed to finish the challenge. He trusted Michael, Kari and Bekah completely, but he knew that Gracey and the Sphinx Patrol could truly help protect his mom more than he could do without them. He would not let them down and they would ensure he was able to protect his family, even if *The Band of Fire* failed.

It was with this commitment that James carefully examined the map and reviewed Gracey's plan. Every patrol was racing now to the third flag. Being in first, they got a head start, but he wasn't able to get any visions to help them decide which of the three paths to take. So, Gracey decided to split into three groups with a telepath in each group. Thankfully, Bekah was with James as were Michael and Kari. In fact, Gracey let him choose and was surprised he chose the first years and Angelica as the first members of his group. He just knew he was comfortable with them, so she obliged and let him have them.

All paths were starting in the same grassy clearing, high in the Uintah Mountains and he knew they were headed to Stuteville Caves, but he didn't know where those were. Hopefully one of their groups would get there first so he could work on protecting his mother!

But mom was safe now. He knew it! And he heard a similar urgency in Bekah's voice as she called for them to begin as the horn sounded in their minds stating it was time to the first patrol (them) to start.

Their packs were on their backs as they raced up the dirt path to the east while Gracey took her group north and Ward and Nora took their group west. James knew his path was steepest, but also was well marked, while Ward would be taking the poorest marked path. As the small rocks and dirt moved under their feet, Bekah tried to almost run with her tiny pack to stay near the front. She was convinced she wouldn't be an obstacle this time.

As James hurried along with his group, he felt a definite chill in the air. A strong wind then started to pickup and midnight black clouds were filling the sky. As the sun was covered, darkness started to overtake them and then the rain started. Not a soft summer rain as might be expected, but a torrential downpour with lightning and thunder filling the air. The dirt ground was quickly transforming to a damp mud. Streams of water were running down the path in minutes and the group's movement began to slow.

With a smile on his face, James removed his pack and put the rain cover on his pack, while putting on his raincoat as well. As for his shoes, however, his boots were wet and would probably stay that way.

Bekah came bouncing over to him with a smile, and began talking quickly. "What an amazing storm! We will be playing in the mud before we know it."

James just smiled, but Bekah wasn't looking for a response and continued to run on. Then the darkened sky filled with light as lightening danced from cloud to cloud. The sound of thunder was deafening and nearly constant. And then James heard Bekah scream just as the thunder sounded simultaneously as lightening hit less than 100 yards in front of them just off the trail. The tree hit erupted into open flame and portions of the exploding tree fell all around them. Amazingly, the forest was in flames even with the rain falling.

Adam Simon came running from behind and started calling everyone together. Angelica was examining everyone for injuries, as only Judson Stratton had a slightly burnt arm as he was the closest to the exploding tree. Bekah and Kari were crying slightly from the startle they received, and Perry Smith and Michael were listening intently to Adam give directions. James just stood there as if in a daze as he looked around.

"Adam, we have four more fires ahead" James said carefully, "and we will need to cross a river about a mile ahead! If the rain continues, it will be difficult to cross."

"I think we should use Chronopathy to get to the bridge." Adam said quickly.

"I am not sure it is a good idea." Angelica said cautiously. "Are you sure you can get us all there without help?"

"James can help!" Bekah said quickly with fear still in her eyes.

"Wait!" Kari broke in, "Animals are racing this direction. There is a much bigger problem ahead according to the deer."

James began to feel lightheaded and he began to hear voices coming from all directions. What was happening?

...Doc McAdams was standing outside the Adamson home with Aimee Belle and Master Julianna. But there were 10 – 15 other

individuals, including Bekah's parents surrounding the house on all sides. Sarah Adamson was still inside but seemed to be packing a bag for a trip. There was no sign of The Order of The Kraken or Camilla.

"Doc, the kids are in trouble on the mountain!" Master Belle whispered from Master McAdams' left side. "There is a large forest fire and a lightning storm that is out of control."

"Yes, I know. I have sent Dakota, Rocky, and Amber to check on the patrols. Deborah, Adam and Mallory are on the mountain already. Camilla is trying to distract us, but that will be her greatest mistake!"

"Camilla can control the weather now?"

"It appears she has found a way." Master McAdams said with a smile. "Where is Zoram? He is supposed to be here helping."

"He has disappeared." Master Julianna said quickly. "He was here a moment ago."

"No, he has not!" Master McAdams said as he disappeared momentarily from view...

James stumbled and fell into the mud as Michael grabbed his arm.

"What's wrong?" Angelica asked quickly.

"We are under attack!" James said as he climbed back to his feet.

"Do you see who is attacking us?" Perry asked stepping forward. "I would love to fight whomever thinks they can beat us. Is it one of the other patrols?"

"No," Bekah said quickly, "It is The Order of The Kraken!" She then turned to look at James, "But how are they controlling the weather?"

"Nobody can control the weather!" Judson said quickly. "Can they?"

Lightning began to rain down around them and trees were exploding into flame, water was pouring down the path and the once slick mud became thick with water. But the problem was getting worse.

"Wolves!" Kari said quickly. "They are coming for us!"

"What about the other parts of our group?" Angelica asked as she looked around. "Are the other patrols also under attack?"

Before they could answer, James heard the wolves in the distance.

"Why do these children think we are weak? Why would they threaten our pack? They will pay for what they have done!"

"I can smell them!" another wolf barked. "They are not far ahead. I am ready to make them pay!"

James felt heat in his pocket and he remembered the stone. As he pulled it from his pocket it began to glow deep blue and James knew what it was.

"Everyone to me!" James said quickly, and he reached out his hand.

Everyone ran to his side and as they grabbed hands, they moved quickly past the wolves, past the fires, across the bridge of the river up the path to the top of the mountain. James looked at Adam, whose eyes were wide with surprise and everyone else was frozen in time. Even the fire seemed to stop flickering, the deer, the wolves, everything was suspended in time as they moved with Chronopathy at a much higher speed than either James or Adam were capable. It must be the stone in his hand.

Music then filled his mind, his favorite music and he saw the flaming red color of Helia ahead of them. Then she began to speak, "The stone you have is not just any rock, an artifact from before time. For if you trust its special gift, greater Chronopathy you shall have!"

James smiled and knew immediately that he now held an artifact that augmented his Chronopathy. As he thought about this, they found themselves at the base of small cave. It was not the final location, but was their destination so he came to a stop. There should be a clue here to help find the appropriate location.

Bekah looked up with her eyes wide. "How did you do that?"

James just smiled and pushed the stone back into his pocket. He would need to tell her at a later date, but now was not the time.

Adam broke in, "James was amazing! I have never seen a first year Chronopath do what he just did."

As everyone was congratulating James, Michael started to speak.

"The cave is only 20 feet deep and has a message at the back."

"I will go get it." Perry said and walked quickly to the cave.

"I will join him!" Judson said with his bandaged arm.

As they walked into the cave, James turned to Bekah.

"How are the other groups doing?"

"Sarah says they are under attack by wolves, but holding their own. They have not yet reached the clue…" As she continued to speak, James mind began to fade again.

"We have not threatened your family! We mean your pack no harm!" Gracey was barking at the wolves. "You are being controlled!"

"How dare you claim we are weak minded enough to be controlled." One wolf barked back as they pack circled the small group.

"Weapons down Lafeyette! We need them to trust us."

"We will never trust you! I know you have come to hurt us! I feel it in my mind!"

Lafeyette lowered his crossbow and Mark stepped closer to the wolves. The other Sphinx patrol members moved closer to these two as Gracey continued to bark to the wolves. The nerves were starting to come out in Gracey's voice as she continued to plead with the circling wolves.

"Gracey, I will not allow them to attack our patrol!" Lafeyette said as Mark nodded.

Just then, a pure white Pegasus/Unicorn mix came floating down to the center of the circle with Master Amber on her back. As she dismounted, a beautiful form of wolf flowed from her mouth. It didn't sound angry, didn't sound nervous, didn't even sound like a command, but a soft loving tone as a mother wolf would speak to her pup.

"Master Allisor, you are brave and powerful. Your courage is without compare and you do your family a great service. Know that I recognize your great knowledge and skill in leading your brothers. Know that I feel of the love and care you have for your sisters. I bow to your majesty and ask permission to allow these pups to pass

in peace. I promise you that I will not allow any harm to befall your family and you will not be disappointed in your trust in me and these young ones. I now shall abide by your wishes." and then Master Amber bowed low and remained in the bow.

At her example, all the Sphinx patrol fell to their knees in the mud and bowed low. Even Medley seemed to bow her powerful unicorn head.

The wolves all stopped circling and turned to look at the wolf that had been speaking. He inclined his head slightly and barked, "You shall pass! I place my faith in you." The wolves then turned and began to walk away. Amber then mounted Medley and was off...

"Nora has her group to the tree where the clue is supposed to be. They are currently digging. They missed the wolves similar to us through well timed Chronopathy."

As they continued to talk, Judson and Perry came walking with a white laminated sheet of paper. Judson was waving the sheet in the air.

"This is clue number 2. It says Latitude 40.75766."

"And the Longitude is -110.453796 according to Rose." Bekah chimed in.

"With those numbers we can travel. I say we go and get the final clue once we are there." Adam said with excitement. "Do you want to help James?"

James just smiled and carefully pulled the glowing blue stone from his pocket.

They were moving quickly to a new location, a location in the Uinta Mountains just west of King's Peak. They didn't know exactly what they were looking for when they got there. But the location was decided.

As they slowed to a stop, Adam again just shook his head. "The power coming from you is amazing. I haven't felt Chronopathy with such power in a student. What is going on?"

James smiled and held up the glowing blue stone.

"You have the Bridgestone?" Adam looked with surprise. "Where did you get that?"

"I found it. What is the Bridgestone?"

"There are currently five known artifacts that augment individual Titan powers." Bekah said as she walked towards James. "The Bridgestone creates a bridge from one location to another creating a more powerful Chronopathy in both speed and distance."

"Yes," Adam broke in, "and it allows individuals to travel across waters and even to different continents, a power only the most powerful Chronopaths can do."

"Exactly." Bekah said with a smile as everyone in the group looked at her in surprise. "I read it in *The Forgotten History of The Titan*."

James started to laugh. "I guess I should have asked you when I found this on Titan Task #2."

But as they were talking, Angelica, Kari and Michael came running forward.

"Do we know what we are looking for?" Michael asked quickly. "No other patrols are here and I want to be the ones that find the flag!"

"Sarah says the final clue is Stuteville Caves." Bekah chimed in again.

Michael looked around. "There is a cave 300 yards to the west, a different cave 400 yards to the north. I don't know where Stuteville Caves is."

James closed his eyes and focused on their location and the name "Stuteville Caves." His mind began to fill with pictures and a map formed. He could see King's Peak. He felt the breeze with water in the air form the North. That cave was full of water and he could now see it. The opening was 15 feet high, and the cave was dark, but extended back approximately 900 yards. The ground was covered in water, almost like an underground lake. The ceiling reached 30 – 40 feet up in various places, and no flag could be seen therein. That was not the location.

Then he turned his attention to the cave 300 yards to the west. Wait, there is a third cave, underground cave, to the south only 200 yards. The entrance was a small hole, only 2 feet in diameter. The hole went underground 50 feet before opening into a large room 50 foot X 50 foot with 25-foot ceilings. The room was unique and seemed to have crystal like walls. This was the location, but getting to the room would be tricky. But there was no doubt, he could see the words "Stuteville Caves" on the map in his mind. Amazingly it was a map he was remembering from when mom had taught him to use a compass. "Thank you, mom," he thought silently.

"Michael, it is the cave 200 yards to the south."

"Oh, the hole?" Michael said thinking. "Yes, I know where it is. Let's go!"

James began to think again. "Helia, we need you!"

As they began to walk quickly to the hole, lead by Michael, James could hear Helia moving quickly in the distance. But she wasn't alone. There was a second bird, based on the speed of travel and the sound of the wings it must be a falcon. Yes, it must be Fenwick.

Michael seemed to notice too.

"Why is Fenwick coming? I can hear her."

"I called them. The hole is too small for us to enter. We will need some help." James said quickly.

"Okay" Perry said disappointed, "I was hoping to dig the hole wider so that we could enter the cave."

"The tunnel is 50 feet long and goes down approximately 35 feet. That would be a difficult dig."

"But how did they get here so fast?" Kari asked.

"Phoenix have a special ability to teleport. It is actually a highly developed Chronopathy type ability. She must have brought Fenwick with her." Bekah said quickly, as if everyone should know. "It is in *Wildlife Studies* when they explain the traits of a phoenix."

Judson started to laugh. "Is there any book you haven't read already about *The Band of Fire?*"

Bekah's face began to turn bright red and she smiled guiltily. But before she could respond Angelica screamed with excitement. "It is here! I found the hole, but it is tiny."

As they gathered around the hole, everyone surprised at the size, Kari started singing to the birds.

"We have a flag at the bottom of the hole. We need you to retrieve it!"

Bekah turned to James and whispered, "I love when she sings to the birds. It is always so beautiful. I just wish I was able to understand."

"But how does she speak in two voices at once?" Angelica asked, "I have never seen a first year be able to accomplish that so quickly."

Kari just smiled in pride, "They have agreed!"

Fenwick swooped into the hole and Helia followed closely behind. The soft red glow of Helia radiated from the hole.

Perry, Judson and Michael were preparing a fire since they were all still really wet from the earlier storm and the sun was starting to set. The strong breeze from the south was causing many of them to shake and tremble. Within minutes the bright orange fire was dancing, and everyone was warming themselves by the fire. Everyone except James who was standing by the hole starring down into it.

She flew into the hole carefully maneuvering through the tunnel behind her friend. James could see it all through Helia's eyes. She was following a beautiful brown falcon with cream streaking to the nape and crown of the head. The hole seemed to be getting darker, but the soft red glow provided plenty of light. And then the tight quarters opened up. There it was, a beautiful 50 feet X 50 foot room with high ceilings. The walls glowed bright red and seemed to fill the entire room with a glow. Then Fenwick saw the flag and dived for it. Helia just kept observing the glowing red walls. She felt at home, but James needed the flag. She turned and stared back towards the surface, with Fenwick closely approximated to her tail feathers.

As the birds continued to fly, James was awakened with screaming. James heard two voices he recognized, Ryan was running out front and Lizzy was screaming as she raced towards them. The Minotaur patrol had arrived but were just barely too late. The Sphinx patrol was almost done with flag in hand.

James just smiled as Fenwick swooped out of the hole and handed the flag to Michael. They had won. James slumped slightly as he could hear the arrival of Master Juliana and several other Chronopaths to help in the return to normal. James was physically exhausted, but even more hungry. Hopefully the feast would be amazing back at camp. As James began to close his eyes to think about camp, he heard Elli yelling at the entire Minotaur patrol.

"How dare you allow us to lose. We keep losing to that first year James."

"You are also a first year!" Emma Johnson piped in.

"I don't care! We are supposed to win. I don't like to lose."

Lizzy and Ryan were moving away from her and just shaking their heads. James knew what the problem was, but he didn't really care.

CHAPTER 34
THE MINI-BAND OF FIRE

As they all walked into the Great Hall, James stomach was aching from hunger. It was definitely time to eat, so he raced to his seat and dropped his backpack. They were told not to return to their tents, but to come eat first. Every Titan was dirty and sweaty and many of them were covered in mud. Every patrol appeared to have had the same experience. The difference is that James' patrol had won!

As they grabbed their food, James pilling his plate high with chicken legs, turkey slices, ham, deviled eggs and a large salad. Bekah kept handing him orange slices, radishes for his salad, raspberries and a couple of slices of watermelon. This was almost like Thanksgiving, as he even crowded mashed potatoes onto his plate. Michael was actually filling two plates, as was Ryan across the way.

As they all found their way back to their seats, James notices Sarah, his mother, sitting at the head table on one end. He wasn't sure why she was there, but Master McAdams had something to say.

"Well done all of you! I always enjoy a great competition. Every patrol should be very proud. The Sphinx patrol won by near minutes. But there is a portion of this Patrol Challenge that was not scheduled, and I want to explain to each of you what happened. You need to know what happened and why you were placed in such grave danger."

Everyone started to talk, and Master McAdams just raised his hand in the Fire Sign and silence again fell on the hall.

"Many of you have heard of The Order of The Kraken. This is a counterfeit organization promising more complete training and higher status for the Titan. This is promised at the cost of all the Natural Born members of society. As you can imagine, I will not permit this to happen. The entire Band of Fire has committed to ensure The Order doesn't get power. But they chose to attack each of you, to draw us into a battle that would allow them to start to attack the world."

As he continued to talk, a picture of Zoram popped into James mind. As he looked around, Zoram was nowhere to be found. Elli was likewise gone. James turned to look at Bekah, but she was too enthralled in Master McAdams speech to notice.

"...As their leader, Camilla utilized the Klimastone, a specialized artifact that allows her to control the weather. This is a powerful device that in the wrong hands, hers, can make a dangerous storm and cause injury and even death. She commonly utilizes this stone to even hide the night sky when she prepares to attack...."

James mind began to fill with a recognizable voice, that of Doc McAdams. But the words were much different than what he was speaking to the entire hall. His mind was so full with Master McAdams voice, that he couldn't even hear what was being said to the group. James closed his eyes and he was there...

Master McAdams stepped into Sarah's bedroom with fire in his eyes. James had seen this look before in the forest, but the anger was much stronger and James could feel power pulsating through Master McAdams body. Master McAdams was truly a Herculopath and every ounce of his body was tensed to the extreme. James felt a little nervous. But then he saw a 5'6" woman, with long, stringy, black hair and a stony gaze standing on one side of Sarah. On the other was the recognizable dark skin, almost brownish-yellow eyes, long brown hair down to his back and a long brown, fluffy beard and mustache.

"Zoram" Master McAdams roared, "You will NOT touch Sarah. You will NOT break the trust you have with The Band of Fire and help this maleficent."

Katie's stony gaze grew angry, but she seemed to have almost a smirk on her face. "You dare try to command us! Don't you know who we are?"

"Yes Miss Stults, I know better than you do who you are!"

Within seconds she had a crossbow in her hand and she was firing at him.

James watched the arrow slow and Master McAdams caught it in midair and fired it back at her followed by a second one. Even at the slower speed, Master McAdams moved very quickly. As time sped up, both arrows found their mark. One in Katie's left bicep and the other in her left thigh. The crossbow hit the ground and she collapsed with a scream. Zoram jumped, but Master McAdams already had his arm behind his back and he was being pushed to the floor face down.

While Katie quickly pulled the arrow from her leg and set upon healing it, Master McAdams spoke quickly while grabbing Sarah's hand and pulling her quickly from the room.

"In case you don't know, Zoram you are fired. And you better hope that Elli acts better or she too will be expelled. And Katie, remind Camilla that the Adamson Family is under my protection. Sarah as a descendant of Percival Owens will always be under the protection of The Band of Fire. She cannot distract us, she cannot trick us and she can not hurt any decedents of our dear friend!"

The words faded, and James found himself again starring at the smiling face of Sarah Owens Adamson, his dear mother. She was safe and he knew why!

"…So now you all know that The Order of The Kraken attacked you all. Many of you were injured and some were required to return here for treatment. But you must also know that together we can defeat The Order and protect you and the world from them. But more importantly, we can help the wolves, the cougars, the coyotes and the wild dogs also become freed from the controlling power that caused them to attack. I invite you all to join together with us. Become *The Band of Fire*. As a group, you are much more powerful than you are alone. Let me tell you a story…"

"Birds commonly migrate south in the winter and north in the summer. The most distinctive migration pattern is the V that we commonly see when many types of geese migrate. I learned a longtime ago that we can learn a great deal from nature. In this case, the migration pattern of the goose is very instructive."

"Geese migrate in a V pattern to utilize the wing tip vortex of the bird in front of them, or reduce the drag and therefore reduce required energy necessary to migrate great distances by over 50%. In this pattern, the front bird will fly until tired and then fall back to one side or the other and another bird will take the front position to allow them to continue. This is a very powerful example of teamwork. This is a powerful construct that allows traveling of great distances at great speed while ensuring all members of the group are able to participate fully and reach the final goal."

"But the most powerful example happens when a goose is injured and needs to leave the V. When it lands, two other geese will likewise stop the migration and land in close proximity until the injured goose is able to continue or dies. If able to continue, they continue the migration in a small V pattern. If unable to continue, the two that stopped continue in a half V, taking turns at the front. Therefore, two additional geese stop to ensure nobody is ever forced to migrate alone. Only then is every goose protected throughout the migration process."

"May I invite each of you whether Sphinx or Centaur, Griffin or Minotaur to stand together and be one. As one takes the lead position in the V, may you use your energies and power to support and augment them. And may you likewise consider each Titan in this room your brother or your sister. As we stand as one, nobody can divide us, nothing can hurt us and we will be protected. Not even Camilla's Order will win!"

The Minotaur patrol stood first and began to cheer. The Sphinx were a close second and likewise began to cheer. The Centaur looked a little surprised but jumped up as well. Martha Jewel seemed to be almost dragging those around her to their feet. The final patrol to stand was the Griffin patrol, but they began to chant softly at first and then more loudly, "Band of Fire! Band of Fire! Band of Fire!" The other patrols joined in with excitement. Then Master McAdams raised his hand and again came silence.

With his arm to the square and the hand in The Fires Sign, Master McAdams invited all to join him in The Oath.

"I solemnly covenant my brothers and sisters of Fire to do my Duty to God, to serve others with all my heart, to stand as a witness of faith, knowledge and strength, to use my gifts to protect freedom, happiness and independence for all, to lift the weak, to comfort the sad and to befriend the friendless. That I may by so doing stand against evil in all its various forms. To this I pledge my sacred honor."

With these final words, the hall erupted again in cheers and all stepped forward to commit to protect and strengthen each other, even when competing. For they would stand against evil, even when the evil was another Titan.

James smiled as he walked towards him mom. Camilla had made a big mistake, for she underestimated *The Band of Fire* and Master McAdams. She just created a most powerful alliance among the various patrols, an alliance that makes even the young Titans very powerful. James hoped they would never need to exercise that power, but saving dad was the next task (when the time is right).

CHAPTER 35
IN GOD WE TRUST

Classes had continued as usual since the Second Patrol Challenge, but the Patrols were more friendly, even seemed to work together when possible and cheer the successes of others. The once divided camp was more together than ever before, and James really liked it. It made the classes more fun and the meal times a great opportunity to socialize. James had even become good friends with Ryan and Lizzy and was happy they were part of the Phoenixenses. The meeting tonight would include all eight, each having a different primary skill. He had been excited all day for the meeting, and now he just had to meet with Master McAdams for a moment and then would be headed to the cave. Helia was perched on his shoulder and was singing beautiful music in excitement as well.

As he approached the small log cabin with the green *Camp Master* sign over the door, he heard a voice in his mind, "Enter my boy." So he pushed the door open and walked inside and through the simply decorated entryway to the first room. There at a small table sat Master McAdams with a large smile on his face and sparkling, deep blue eyes. As James entered, Master McAdams began to speak.

"You have had a busy summer for a first year! But you have many questions that need answering. It is very important during the Camp Master Conference that I ask you some questions first. We will then allow you time to ask some of your questions."

"Camp Master Conference?"

"Yes! I see you still haven't read *The Book of Adam*." Master McAdams said with a twinkle in his eye. "You really should listen to Bekah and learn more about who you are. But no time for that now. I will explain the necessary details."

James sat in the nearby chair as Master McAdams indicated it with his hand and then turned back to Master McAdams for the explanation.

"Each summer, as part of *Campus Gaea*, we help you fulfill the basic requirements for *The Band of Fire Advancement Program*. This is a very distinct program where you learn to be a Titan, but also learn many of the necessary survival skills. It is similar to the Natural-Born Scouting Program, but there are skills only Titans can learn and master. You have become eligible for the first rank advancement of *Silver Spark*. You are on your way to earning the rank of *The Phoenix*, the highest rank in *The Band of Fire*, but you must know that not everyone progresses every year. You must master the necessary skills to make this step. Except for Elli, who has left camp, all the First years will be interviewed for this rank. Even so, I am excited to talk to you about this advancement. "

James began to fidget in his chair a little, as he was not sure he knew all the answers. But before he could continue to worry, Master McAdams continued to speak.

"You need not worry my boy, I can read your mind. Remember? I know that you already have the necessary skills. I just want to help you recognize what you have learned this summer. Shall we start with *Becoming A Titan*? What does it mean to you to be a Titan?"

James mind began to race. He remembered his birthday, that now seemed like ages ago, he remembered *The Classification* and then class after class raced through his head. What did it mean to be a Titan? How could he say it?

"Well, it means everything. My world seemed to open up. My questions and concerns over the years as my parents seemed to be limiting my experiences are all resolved. I understand my family more. I understand who I am more. I am even starting to believe that I really am *Concordant*."

Master McAdams just nodded his head. "And how can you help your fellow Titans, *The Band of Fire* and the world as a Titan?"

James just stopped and starred at the deep blue eyes. He didn't have an answer for this question. If only he could read Master McAdams mind…

Suddenly he saw a young Doc McAdams sitting on a camp chair across from an older man who was asking questions.

"Docery, how can you help your fellow Titans and the world as a Titan?"

"I don't know sir. But I promise to strive to be my best." He then stood, putting his right arm to the square and made the Fire Sign. "In fact, I solemnly covenant to do my Duty to God, to serve others with all my heart, to stand as a witness of faith, knowledge and strength, to use my gifts to protect freedom, happiness and independence for all, to lift the weak, to comfort the sad and to befriend the friendless. That I may by so doing stand against evil in all its various forms. To this I pledge my sacred honor."

The vision faded, and Master McAdams smiled wider and just sat there waiting for a response.

"Well, in The Oath I commit to do several things." James then stood, lifted his right arm to the square and while doing The Fire Sign started speaking.

"I solemnly covenant to my brothers and sisters of Fire to do my Duty to God, to serve others with all my heart, to stand as a witness of faith, knowledge and strength, to use my gifts to protect freedom, happiness and independence for all, to lift the weak, to comfort the sad and to befriend the friendless. That I may by so doing stand against evil in all its various forms. To this I pledge my sacred honor."

"Well said! Now what does it mean."

James again began to think. As he went through the words understanding came quickly.

"I am promising to serve others with all my heart. That means I must look for opportunities to serve and help others. And I need to serve whenever I get the chance without complaining.

"Yes. What else?"

"I promise to stand as a witness of faith, knowledge and strength. I must stand for truth and stand with strength against evil."

"Great. What about faith? Faith in what?"

"Faith in *The Band of Fire*, in my fellow Titans and in myself."

"Yes, that is part of it. But faith is not faith if you don't have faith in God. People all over the world believe in a God, often different ideas of God, but most individuals believe. Faith is taking that belief to the point of action. I want you to think about how you can exercise your faith through action, and then we will come back to it. Continue."

"Okay, I promise to use my gifts to protect freedom, happiness and independence for all. God has blessed me with special Titan abilities that I must use to serve others. I should strive daily to help protect others freedom, happiness and independence. I am not sure exactly what that means, but I really want to do it."

Master McAdams chuckled a little and then began to speak.

"Can I tell you a story?" Before James could answer, he continued, "Many years ago, Israel was in a battle with the Philistines. Israel always had a powerful army, but the Philistines had a champion, a giant that had never been bested in battle. They therefore challenged King Saul to provide a soldier to fight him and the winner would be the winner of the war. But King Saul didn't have a soldier willing to fight this giant, known as Goliath. That is until a young man, much smaller than most the soldiers, came to camp to check on his brothers at the request of his father. This young man, David, was a very skilled protector of his sheep. God had helped him develop the powerful ability of utilizing a sling and a stone to chase animals, and even kill them if necessary, who threatened the flock. He asked King Saul to allow him to stand with God against Goliath and ensure God's people could have the freedom, happiness and independence they desired. It was with this commitment that David walked onto the field of battle without armor or weapons, except a staff, a sling and a couple smooth stones. But with his faith in God, and the skills God has provided him, he killed Goliath with a single stone the soared perfectly to strike him between the eyes. It was with this that David helped protect freedom, happiness and independence for all Israel utilizing his special abilities."

Master McAdams then paused and looked at James again with a smile. "I invite you to stand with God and use your special Titan abilities to help individuals have freedom, independence and the opportunity for happiness, if they so choose to be happy. Know that you can't make anyone happy, it is their choice. Happiness is always a choice. Therefore, I invite you to also *Choose To Be Happy*."

"Okay. I understand. By doing this, I can also lift the weak, comfort the sad and be friendly with the people that need friends. I promise to do that also."

"Great, now we need to talk about the one part of The Oath you didn't mention, Duty to God. What does it mean to do your Duty To God? Maybe this is a good time to talk about Faith in God also."

James just stood there amazed that he had learned so much more about being a Titan in the last couple minutes than he had all summer. Being a Titan was truly more than just having some special abilities or skills. That meant that being Concordant was even a bigger deal than he had considered to this point because God had not just given him some special skills, but all the special Titan skills. But how does Duty to God apply here?

"Is it doing what God wants me to do? Or just making good choices and being a good person?"

"Being a good person and doing good things is important, but that view is too limited. What more could it mean?"

"How about trying to serve others?"

"Yes. I often think about daily working to make the world a better place. What can I do today to help somebody? What can I do to make someone's life easier? What can I do to change someone's difficulty or help someone in their trial? How can I help ensure more freedom, help stimulate greater joy and happiness, or even do something that an individual can't do for themselves? I believe that is what God would have me do, all while becoming a better man, a better friend, a better family member and an asset to society. I invite you to seek to understand this principle more completely."

James nodded his head slowly as he repeated in his mind, "a better man, a better friend, a better family member and an asset to society."

With that, Master McAdams smiled and after waiting a moment invited James to ask his questions.

At that, James mind began to race. He had so many questions that he had been waiting to ask Master McAdams, but what should he ask?

"Why did my dad and Aria break up? And how did my mom and dad get together?"

"Those are great questions, and deserve very good answers, but I am not the person who should give those answers to you. Have you ever asked your parents those questions? Don't you know how your mom and dad met and fell in love?"

"No. I guess I never asked. Besides, I didn't know that my dad was married before. Or at least I didn't remember."

Master McAdams smiled, and his deep blue eyes seemed to sparkle again.

"Why do I keep dreaming about my dad? I even had a dream about Camilla the other night."

"Oh, that was the question I was hoping you would ask. Your dreams are actually a great blessing to *The Band of Fire*. I have been monitoring your mind and received important information to help protect other members of The Band, although we couldn't protect your father."

"Where was my father when he got captured? And wasn't he with others at that time?"

"Yes, everyone was captured, but only your dad has been carried off prisoner. Many of them were tortured and even threatened. One relatively new Titan is now unwilling to work with *The Band of Fire*. He has decided to be Natural-Born and pretend he doesn't have Titan powers. Unfortunately, The Order of The Kraken are not all nice individuals. He was severely injured and worried he was going to die. But that is not what we should be focusing on... Your question was where was your father? Well, the location is not important and is actually classified at the moment, but he was on Band of Fire assignment. It is very concerning that Camilla was able to find him and track him to that location. I am sorry that we failed to protect him more completely."

James looked down at the thought of his father still captured and Master McAdams placed his right hand on his shoulder.

"But you are the secret to his safety to this point. In fact, if it weren't for you we wouldn't have been so quick to protect your mother. Know that she was always under surveillance and has been being protected her entire life, but they were quick to attack and without your information we wouldn't have been as ready."

"But you were also wondering 'Why' you are having these visions. Let me explain a very important fact. Telepathy is extremely powerful between individuals that have a close relationship, especially in someone that is a family member or other very close relationship. Intimate relationships, for example, produce a very powerful telepathic connection. Sometimes, in Titan relationships, this connection can create problems. But usually it is a great blessing, because this type of connection can not be blocked even by the most powerful Telepath."

"Telepathy, however, is only thoughts so you should understand another's thoughts or be able to communicate with others. But you are Concordant! That means you will combine multiple skills. You can combine Telepathy and Chronopathy and enter an individual's memory. It allows you to 'Dream' your father's or other friend's thoughts. And when strong feelings are involved, the 'Dream' is even more easily seen. It was those strong feelings that caused Camilla to stop blocking her mind from you and caused you to see her thoughts. That may happen again, because she has very strong feelings for you!"

"But I want to tell you something more about this power. Those same strong feelings can be a problem for you. You must learn to block your mind, even from me, so that Camilla will not have access to *The Band of Fire* through you. But, you should know that you also have the power to communicate with your father, without being detected, because of your Concordant abilities. He can't talk back, but you can know his thoughts. Likewise, for your mother."

James looked at Master McAdams with a start.

"Wait! You mean I could talk with my father?"

"If your Telepathy is developed enough than yes."

"I never considered that. I guess I will have to try."

"If you work on combining your Telepathy and Orientopathy abilities, you will also be able to localize your father at all times. Even if he hasn't determined where he is."

James just looked at him, but could tell nothing else was going to be said today. He would have to save his other questions for another time. In fact, there came a knock on the door and James was dismissed while Melvina Hoguel came in for her Camp Master Conference.

CHAPTER 36
HIPPOCRATESENSE

James could hardly believe that he could possibly talk to his father. Why hadn't he thought of that before? Why hadn't he tried to talk with him, like he talked with his mother from time to time? I guess it never really crossed his mind that he could communicate at such a great distance, since he knew dad was in Brazil.

As he continued to think with Helia perched on his right shoulder, he walked quickly toward the cave where he was sure the other Phoenixenses were already waiting. The dirt pathway was now very recognizable to him and the pathway was traveled at a rapid pace without even a thought about where he was going.

Before he knew it, he was behind the bush and preparing to enter the cave when Ryan Sampson came walking to the opening.

"Hello James. I have been following you for most the way and you didn't even notice me."

"I just had my Camp Master Conference and was thinking about what was discussed."

"Oh? Did he have you explain the Oath? That was a lot to think about!"

"Yes. Especially how he wanted us to think about our Duty to God."

"I know. Well, one of the ways to serve God more completely is through improving our skills. I am hoping Angelica can help me learn a little about Hippocratesense. I am not good with even first aid." Ryan chuckled a little and bent down almost to the ground to climb into the cave.

As Helia swooped in, James likewise crawled into the well-lit cavern with light reflecting off all the walls. James was home again! This place always felt so inviting and even exciting to him.

Bekah was already talking at her high pitched, rapid rate showing her great excitement, "...and we must work together no matter what patrol we may be from. The whole purpose of the Phoenixenses is to create more powerful Titans that can stand for freedom and righteousness. We have seen the threat the Order of the Kraken can be. It is for that reason I am so excited for Angelica's lesson. I need help wIth Hippocratesence.... Oh, hi James, do you have anything to add now that you are finally here?" She then smiled at James and everyone turned toward him.

Before he could speak, however, Phoenix song filled the cave and everyone heard Helia in their mind.

"A group you are and strength there be, but only if together as one. For danger is yet at your face, as one by one they'll try to take."

The song continued to ring through the cave, but the words stopped and everyone was silent.

When the music finally stopped, Ryan began to speak. "We are not always together. In fact, often we are separate in our tents, with our patrols and even in classes. We may even be separated and alone at times. For example, James and I arrived separate and alone tonight to the cave. What if the Order attacks us when we are alone? How will we let each other know?"

"Telepathy would be the best option, but not everyone is telepathic." Bekah said quickly.

"Is there a signal or code we could use?" Kari asked.

"Last year Master McAdams taught us about the Phoenix. They have a unique ability to telepathically talk to individuals

368 JAMES AND THE BAND OF FIRE

at great distances, telepathic or not, and may be an option."
Angelica said. "Could Helia help us with that?" she asked
turning to James.

"I don't know anything about that." James said petting
Helia's beautiful feathers.

"Yes" Bekah said with great excitement. "I have read about
that. We could call it the Phoenix Code! But how would it
work?"

James then heard a song in his mind. *"This I could do James,
and help each of you can I. All they do is think of me, and the
message receive I will. Then to you all speak can I and the message
given can be."*

"Well," James began to speak. "Helia has agreed. The Phoenix
Code will be as follows. All you have to do is think of her and
ask for help. She will get the message and distribute it appropriately. Because she is a Phoenix, the message can't be blocked
by another Titan. I agree this is the best way."

Ryan then got really excited. "That's perfect. Then we can
truly help each other."

As James began to think about this, he felt a little frustrated
that his dad didn't have such a resource to tell *The Band of Fire*
that he was in trouble before Camilla was able to kidnap him.
As he thought, his mind faded into blackness.

*He sat there quietly in the dark. His senses were aroused with
movement outside the tent where he lay. It was night, but The
Order of the Kraken were not sleeping. Camilla was in a tent 100
yards away and seemed to be very angry. But he couldn't hear her.
He could however feel everyone running around trying to do her
every command. They were preparing for something, but he didn't
know what.*

*All the sudden, as he sat focused on the surroundings, he heard
his son's voice in his head.*

"Dad, I know where you are and we are coming to help you."

*"Please don't! I couldn't stand for you or your mother to be hurt.
It is far too dangerous....Wait, how are you talking to me? How
do you know where I am?"*

"I can't answer that. I do know that they say I am Concordant and our familial connection makes it impossible to block our telepathic connection."

"Yes, that is correct. When you are telepathic, the connection is much stronger with strong feelings like love or hate. Many years ago, I was taught this personally..." he then stopped talking and James could see Aria and Simon fighting in their bedroom.

"Why can't you trust me?"

"I see your mind. I know everything you think, everything you are!"

"But I love you! I don't have interest in anyone else!"

"Have you forgotten that I know your mind?"

The vision faded as Simon realized James could see it all.

"Did you really love her?"

"Yes!"

"Why did you two separate?"

"I never stopped loving her! But I love your mother without equal. I can be me with Sarah and don't need to worry constantly..."

James knew he couldn't ask more, so he moved to a different subject."

"Tell me about the night you were captured. I had a dream about the first part, until you heard the music and laugh."

"Really? Well, not much to say. Immediately following the music, Camilla and The Order captured me, blindfolded me and knocked me out. The underestimated my ability to localize via Orientopathy, so they thought they could take me somewhere without me knowing."

"Yes. I have seen your various locations. I know exactly where you are and where you have been."

"Camilla has underestimated you also. As have I."

He then continued, "I still say, however, that you not try to come rescue me. Protect your mother."

"She is safe. Master McAdams has her because the Order tried to attack her."

The vision faded and James again found himself on his back with everyone around him.

"Are you okay?" Angelica asked concerned.

"This happens all the time." Michael said with a smile. "He has these visions and collapses." Turning back to James he asked, "What did you see?"

James carefully stood up and said, "I saw my father again."

"You know where he is?" Lizzy asked. "Why don't we go save him? I know as a group we could do it. I think we could even get help from other Titans."

"I'm in!" Ryan said we a smile, "I would love to attack them before they can attack us!"

"You know you have Kari, Michael and I!" Bekah said in a high pitched, excited voice.

"He doesn't want us to come!" James whispered quietly.

"We can talk about it more later, but maybe we should have Angelica's lesson." Emma said quickly winking at James.

James just nodded his head and Angelica stepped forward. As she talked about healing abilities, reviewing first aid discussions and some healing plants, James couldn't focus. All he could think about was his father needing someone to save him. Would *The Band of Fire* help?

Just then, Angelica said something that caught his attention, "There is a part of Hippocratesence that isn't discussed much in class. It is often only said in passing. Master McAdams last year would wander into the classes and help. One of those classes last year he talked to me about the energy all around us. Every cell of our bodies produces an electrical current. When you stress the cell, through injury for example, the cell increases the current across the injured side. This stimulates healing. Therefore, a true Hippocratesent will feel the energy and exude energy to help in healing. If done correctly, which I am still learning, you can speed the healing within the body cell by cell."

Bekah began to bounce up and down with excitement. "You mean you don't even need stuff to help someone heal? Why haven't I read that somewhere?"

"There is a paragraph in *The Book of Adam* saying that to truly master a Titan skill, one must use all your senses to hear, see, feel and understand the world around you." Lizzy said with a smile, excited she knew something Bekah didn't.

"Yes. I forgot about that paragraph." Bekah said with even more excitement, "It is in Chapter 7."

"I think we should practice it." Emma said, "But how do we do it without having an injury to heal?"

"That's a great idea." Angelica said. "Everyone needs a partner. Then you concentrate on trying to feel their heartbeat without touching them."

As they broke into partners, Kari quickly joined Ryan, Michael was with Emma and Bekah and James were together as usual. James mind began to race as he realized Hippocratesense could be used similar to Orientopathy. He could use his senses to listen to the body and encourage it to heal.

As he concentrated with his eyes closed, for the first time he felt in control of the functioning of the bodies around him. Bekah's breathing was rapid and shallow, her heart rate was quick with excitement and James could feel tingling in her fingers. He focused on her heart rate and it started to slow. As he thought about her lungs, they filled more fully with air. He saw every inch of blood vessel and saw them expand and contract with ease...

"How are you doing that?" he heard Bekah in his mind. *"I have never felt so relaxed. Now it's my turn!"*

James cleared his mind and waited. He could feel her search his mind but felt no effect on any other area of his body.

"Don't look in my mind." he thought carefully, *"Concentrate on my heart."*

Although he couldn't feel anything in his body, he felt Bekah's excitement grow.

"I've got it! I can feel your heart beating, and the speed of your breathing. I can't change anything, but I know what is going on!"

They continued for another hour and all of them could check the heart rate, breathing rate and even blood pressure without touching the individual by the time they left. Only two of them, however, seemed to have the ability to change anything. James was again surprised how easy it was for him.

CHAPTER 37
BEKAH HEARS THE MUSIC

As they entered the Great Hall for breakfast, James could feel the excitement buzzing in the hall. All the patrols were excited because today was the day they had been working towards. It was time for The Final Challenge. Bekah had warned him about this challenge after they won the last challenge, and James had been counting down the days for this opportunity to travel the world. They would be leaving Campus Gaea finally tomorrow morning. He wasn't sure he could stand going to classes one more day.

Bekah was even more animated then usual as she jumped from Sphinx patrol member to Sphinx patrol member discussing the fact that they would be first to leave tomorrow morning because they were ahead from the first two challenges. James wasn't sure how that was a great advantage with Chronopathy, but then he remembered there was still no way to really go back in time.

Master McAdams stood at the head table and with great excitement himself invited all to pay attention.

"My fellow Titans, today is your last day of classes this summer and tomorrow you will be participating in The Final Challenge. This is a special opportunity, and like the other Patrol Challenges

will require you to all work together. Your entire patrol is required to participate, so listen carefully as I give you the rules."

"Each patrol will be given a departure time. At that time, you will be given a clue to your first destination. This will be the first time you are required to move a great distance from camp. Some may even be required to cross great waters. If that is necessary, you will be given assistance to make it possible. There are only a few students capable of that level of Chronopathy at this time." Master McAdams seemed to wink at James as he continued.

"At each checkpoint you will again be given the next clue and be required to gather a flag. Return with all four flags first to Campus Gaea and you win the 'Patrol of Camp' award. This is a coveted award that every patrol wants. Each of you have a fair chance at achieving it."

James heard Bekah in his mind. "The Sphinx Patrol has not won that award for 10 years. Maybe this year we can win!" James smiled, again amazed that she knew these seemingly insignificant facts about camp.

"The Patrols have been assigned leaving times based on their scores on the first two challenges. The Sphinx Patrol is first and will leave at 6:00am. The Minotaur Patrol will depart next at 7:00am. The Griffin Patrol is next at 7:30am and Centaur Patrol at 8:00am. Please be on time for your departure! We will not hold up any other Patrols if you fail to all leave."

"Although this is a competition, we remind you that The Order of The Kraken is still out there and we must stick together...."

As the vision faded, James could hardly keep his eyes open. "I guess the long summer with little sleep is finally catching up to me. I thought Herculopathy would keep me from getting tired!" he thought as he pulled his pajamas on and climbed into his bed. Tomorrow was the day. The Final Challenge. As he closed his eyes, he drifted off to sleep...

She felt a little sad as she sat on her cot. This has been the greatest summer of her life. She wasn't sure she even wanted it to end. She looked at Tom asleep in his shell and noticed Kari already bundled in her bed asleep as well. She wasn't ready to sleep. In fact, she wasn't even sure if she would sleep this night. Her excitement for

The Final Challenge was too much. And the good news is that James would be with her again in this challenge. She enjoyed seeing him gain power and understanding as a Concordant. She just liked him even more as she watched him come into his own. He was probably the greatest Titan to ever come to Campus Gaea.

Just then she heard a noise outside her tent. Was James out again wandering at night? She would need to check. But wait, she couldn't even hear the wolf walking around. It was completely silent outside. How could that be?

As she stood and walked toward the door of the tent, the hair started to stand up on the back of her neck. Something was wrong. She would have to be very careful. As she reached the door of the tent and opened the door, music started to fill her mind. Strange music, music she almost recognized but didn't. Why did she think she knew this music? And then a laugh and everything went black...

James woke in a cold sweat. His mind was screaming! "Bekah! Not Bekah! Camila how could you!"

And then Helia was standing on his chest, singing rapidly as his mind was filled. "*To take her quick were they. Already gone they are! Rescue her you must!*"

Within moments Kari and Angelica could be heard on the path. James sensed the other Phoenixenses running to them.

"They have her!" Ryan was yelling as he ran up.

Tent after tent opened and Sphinx patrol members came running out. Ryan and Lizzy stood there with Emma Johnson. Gracey Smith, however, was the fastest one to James side.

"Who has whom?" she asked.

"The Order of The Kraken have Bekah!" Ryan blurted out.

"How do you know?" Gracey asked looking at him suspiciously. "Aren't you in the wrong camp Minotaur?"

"She's our friend too! We will help you find her!" Lizzy said adamantly.

Sarah came walking up. "They are telling the truth Gracey!"

"Then The Final Task is out!" Lafeyette said strapping on his crossbow. "Where are they and how do we get her back?"

"We can't have all of us go. It is too dangerous." James said. "They will know we are coming in such a large group."

"You are probably right. According to what I have been told in the Camp Council, they have been monitoring camp all summer. What do you propose?"

"The Sphinx Patrol must compete, or at least appear to be competing since we are the first patrol to leave, or all will be lost!" James said.

"Okay. Here is my proposition. Why don't you take a few Sphinx with you and we will start the competition? Sarah will stay with me and then we will determine how best to help you instead of truly competing."

"Emma, Lizzy and I will be going with James!" Ryan said with his arms crossed.

"Perfect." Gracey said looking at him with a smile. "We will let Jon, your patrol leader, know in the morning. It would cause too much of a stir tonight."

"We also need to cover for our patrol. They will know if James is not with us!" Ward said quickly. "Can we fake it?"

"Helia will stay with you. That will be enough of a distraction. Then she will join me after you leave camp."

"Hopefully that works."

"Whatever, I am leaving." James walked back to his tent and grabbed his already packed bag. Michael was right behind him. Kari and the other Phoenixenses already had theirs.

They walked from the patrol camp as the other Sphinx patrol members continued to talk. Fenwick, Jack, Fleur, Randy and Beliza were all with them. Helia, however, was sitting on Ward's shoulder as their only hope. James knew where they were going and for the first time all summer, he was not worried about whether he could get them there. Chronopathy would not be a problem this night…and he won't even need his stone!

CHAPTER 38
FREE AT LAST

Although she was small, she put up a big fight as they pulled her from her tent. While blindfolded, she could feel they were traveling, but since she didn't have the orientopathy abilities, she wasn't exactly sure where she was. The music was still ringing in her ears, and the laugh, that horrible laugh made her skin crawl. What is happening? Is this Camilla and her Order?

As they came to a stop, they removed the blindfold and a beautiful, slender girl with long curly brown hair (like her mother), dark blue eyes, a small nose and a slightly round face with a grin on her face. Her dark blue eyes seemed to sparkle as she spoke.

"You are Rebekah, right? I was told by Elli that you are James best friend." Elli stepped forward, partially hiding her face. "And I have captured you! The Band of Fire was unable to protect one of their students from inside their very camp. They celebrated too early for protecting that natural-born Sarah. I will get at Doc McAdams and The Band of Fire!!" The smile was now an angry scowl and Bekah heard the quiver in her voice.

"You underestimate us Camilla! Nobody fears you! You know so little about The Band of Fire and the true powers of a Titan.

Did you know your brother is Concordant?" Bekah spoke slow and very meticulous.

"And you think a first year Concordant should scare me? Doc McAdams couldn't protect you. We are much more powerful than any of your little Band of Fire!"

"I think you should let me kill her!" a white woman with long, stringy black hair and deep green eyes with a terrifying stony gaze stepped forward. A slight smile seemed to cross her lips, but only made her more scary. "That little thing would almost not be worth the trouble."

Zoram stepped forward, "Killing her will not help us get James here. We need to get him away from The Band of Fire and Doc McAdams. He could be very powerful in our hands. Isn't that what our plan was Camilla?"

"Exactly. I will let you kill her after we capture James!" Camilla turned and walked away.

Bekah felt fear start to creep into her body and she remembered the Phoenix Sign and she began to think about Helia. Hopefully it will work. James and the Phoenixenses need to know where she is.

Zoram began to speak again, "Ensure we are blocking her mind. She is a powerful Telepath for a first year!"

"I have been blocking her since we left Campus Gaea. I will let James see what I want him to see when I am ready. Right now we need to prepare for him to come."

The vision ended as anger pulsed through every ounce of James body keeping him still on his feet. Camilla had gone too far this time and would not get away with it. The Phoenixenses were over talking about a plan as James stepped forward to the bank of the incredible waterfall. Iguazu was amazing, but the power of the waterfall seemed miniscule to the current power he felt flowing through his body. The Order of the Kraken didn't yet know they were there, but they would soon know and feel his wrath!

The sky was still pitch black, except for the light from the moon, but James knew where the camp was, knew where Bekah was being held, and even knew where Dad was. The Phoenixenses were anxious to get moving, but James wasn't sure he wanted to enter camp without a plan. He knew that Sarah, Gracey and the Sphinx Patrol would not be able to contact them there because he could feel the block hanging over the land, but Helia would be with them as soon as The Final Challenge was initiated.

As the mist from the waterfall bathed his face, he knew they required more information. He reached out to Dad, but he was sleeping. He reached out to Bekah and the vision was opened again...

"You know Elli, James and I considered you a friend."

"Nobody considered me a friend."

"We were always kind to you. I also know that Ryan and Lizzy were as well."

"They had to be because I was in their patrol. But they never allowed me to help us win the competitions."

"Why are you doing this?"

"Zoram and The Order of the Kraken are my family. I will do whatever I can to help them. James would be a great asset to us."

"You know he will never join you!"

"He will have no choice!" a cold voice came from behind her and the girl with the stony green eyes stepped forward. "Elli, I need you to leave the prisoner. She's trying to confuse you!"

"Thank you, Katie. I will leave her with you!" and Elli slowly walked away.

"You try to act tough little Rebekah!"

"God is on my side! And the Phoenixenses."

"The what?" she said with a laugh. "There is no Phoenix patrol!"

Katie drew a small knife. I know they don't want you dead, but I can at least cut out your tongue, so you can't keep talking back to me.

"I am a Telepath! Do you really think I need a tongue to talk back to you?"

"I still say it would be very rewarding to see you really squirm."

Bekah closed her mouth and began to speak telepathically to Katie, "So, what does your grandma think of threatening to cut out a 12 year-old girls tongue? Would she be proud of you as you wanted her to be?"

"Stay out of my mind. How dare you talk about that woman who tried to keep me from becoming a powerful Titan!"

She thought further, "Powerful? Still threatened by a 12 year-old?" Bekah then started to laugh, a little forced at first and then stronger. "The Order must truly be pathetic to have you as a member."

Katie stepped forward brandishing the knife with fire behind those stony green eyes. "Camilla will have to be okay with me killing you!"

As she stepped forward to stab Bekah, however, a pure white hoof came out of the darkness and connected to Katie's skull. Katie fell to the ground unconscious and Medley, the beautiful, pure white Pegasus/unicorn mix stepped over her to Bekah. Bekah bent down and using the knife cut the ties around her wrists and legs and pulled herself onto Medley's back. As Medley started to fly, Bekah looked back to see Camilla and others running towards her.

"Katie!" Camilla yelled. "What have you done! The Titan Protection was invoked when you tried to kill her! Don't you know anything?" And Bekah was gone...

James finished walking and turned back to the other Phoenixenses. "Bekah is safe, but my father is still here!"

"Let's get him free too." Ryan said with a smile.

"How did Bekah get free?" Kari asked with excitement.

"Katie Circe tried to kill her?"

"She what?" Angelica said with fear in her eyes

"Yes, but she was protected by The Titan Protection. Medley appeared and took her away. What is The Titan Protection?"

"It is talked about in *The Book of Adam* James." Lizzy said. "As young Titans, we are protected from adult Titans that try to kill us if we aren't doing anything wrong."

"Bekah was protected, but we will not be." Emma said quickly. "We have broken a number of rules to be here."

"Then let's not get caught." Michael said with a smile. "I believe Simon is only 150 yards to the east.

"Yes, but he is surrounded now. We will have to fight him out!" James said quietly. "And Camilla is here!"

Music could be heard by all as clouds filled the sky. The once bright moon was now covered and James could feel individuals moving forward. As James concentrated, time slowed down and seemed to stop. Even the movement around them had stopped. James quickly removed his pack, pulled out the crossbow and an arrow and lit it on fire. The white emergency fire burned large and James shot it into the ground 10 feet in front of them. The fire exploded as James quickly added wood and then allowed time to start again.

A large 8-foot-high fire burned and individuals were seen moving towards them. James recognized them all and knew they were coming. Within minutes Zoram was lying face down, bleeding from his nose, unconscious with Ryan standing over him. Elli was running forward, but Ryan was defiant. Fenwick was flying overhead, Jack was growling standing next to Kari and Fleur had just sprayed Minnie who was coughing and chocking. Emma and Angelica had both stepped forward next to James as Angelica yelled, "You shall not touch any of our friends!"

Camilla began to laugh as Fogo flew from her shoulder and captured Fenwick with her powerful claws and broke his wing. Fenwick fell from the sky with a scream from Michael. He then ran forward, knife in hand and plunged it into John's shoulder. This black man with short, curly black hair began to laugh and punched him between the eyes. Michael collapsed in a heap. John pulled the knife from his shoulder and turned on Lizzy who had just stepped forward with Beliza by her side.

Just then James saw him, Adam, a broad shouldered large man with white blond hair, shoulder length, dark brown eyes, tan skin and a large pointy nose stepped into the light. Emma and Angelica quivered a bit, especially as he lifted his walking stick, removed the handle and had a large M15 in his right hand.

Camilla began to speak, "You have one choice my young Titans. We want James. You will give us him and you can take everyone else back home."

"We will NOT give you anything." Kari said with a slight tremor in her voice.

"Oh, you are the young lady whose dad was killed by a gang of natural-born."

"And you are the woman whose mother died in a car wreck." James said as he saw Kari start to tremble.

"How dare you!"

"You stole my dad!"

"He was my dad once too!"

"You attacked my mom!"

"She's the reason my mother is dead!"

"You are truly an idiot!" Lizzy said. "Don't you know that Aria was killed in a natural-born car crash according to the newspaper articles."

"Yes. But Sarah was the reason they got divorced. If they hadn't gotten divorced she wouldn't have been riding in a natural-born car."

Adam stepped forward. "Can I kill them?"

"Yes." Camilla said without hesitation, "Except James. He is my brother after all!"

As Adam raised the M15 portion of his walking stick, Simon came with chains dangling from his wrists and ankles and tackled him to the ground.

"You shall not hurt any of these young people." Simon said as he hit and punched Adam over and over again. The walking stick lay on the ground next to them.

Camilla, surprised by the sudden appearance of Simon, was momentarily distracted and then Fogo started singing a horrible, fight song as a lava red bird attacked him.

Just then, Doc McAdams stepped out of the shadows with a smile on his face and a twinkle in his blue eyes.

"You never learn do you Camilla? You have assumed you could capture any of my students without my knowledge?"

"I did capture her."

"Is she still here?"

"No, but that is because of a mistake made by Katie."

"Medley was sent by me. All of these Titans will be going free! Even Simon!"

Medley came walking out of the shadows with Bekah on her back and moved toward the Phoenixenses.

"All of you go. Including you James." Master McAdams nodded to Medley.

"I will not leave without my father."

"He is to go also."

"You think you can command in my camp?"

"You lost control of your camp when you captured Simon. James has known the entire time about all your plans." Master McAdams smiled at James and then continued. "And I have been monitoring his mind the entire summer. He even saw your plans to attack his mother, but that was from your mind!"

Camilla's eyes flashed anger and she stepped towards the walking stick on the ground.

"I will not fight you now!" Master McAdams said. "Not until everyone is free."

In a flash, lightning fell from the sky and separated Medley from Master McAdams, Camilla and James.

Simon was closer to Medley than James and began to scream, "Don't hurt my son! Don't hurt my son!"

Master McAdams began to laugh. "So you found the stone. Well fire needs oxygen."

James saw Master McAdams move at an amazing speed and all the fires were out, covered with dirt. James felt himself lifted to Medley's back and they were all gone.

Camilla screamed in anger and echoed through James mind. He could see that her anger was unsupressed as she punished Adam.

"Why didn't you leave Simon in the camp?"

"I did! I swear I left him in the camp!"

"Then how did he escape?"

"I don't know. Please, I did my best."

"I am surrounded by incompetence."

The vision faded as they all landed back near the Great Hall.

"James," Master McAdams started, "You need to know that the Sphinx Patrol has been disqualified for not using their entire patrol for The Final Challenge. And it appears we didn't realize the Minotaur Patrol should also be. Sorry. That is the rules."

Dakota Ironhorse stepped from the shadows holding Fenwick. "Your friends and their animal companions will all be okay. No injury is too serious, but they could have been much worse.

"James, I asked you not to come." Simon said with anger in his voice as he hugged his son.

Just then Sarah came running from Master McAdams cabin.

"Simon!" she screamed with tears running down her face. "I was afraid I had lost you forever."

James felt Simon and Sarah collapse together as they pulled him to them. He might be in trouble later, but for now he was home with his family. Daddy's free!! James felt as if time had once again stopped.

CHAPTER 39
THE FIRE CEREMONY

The summer had been somewhat predictable where routine days seemed to be unnoticeable and went from sleep to food, to class, to food and back to sleep. For this reason, anything different seemed to stick out. Today was one of those days. Today was the Fire Ceremony and the buzz around camp was palpable. James had been told this was an amazing ceremony and many of the students considered it a highlight, especially now that classes had come to an end. With everything that had happened already this summer, James was wondering how it could be better. Bekah, chattering on with excitement as they walked, was sure it was going to be amazing. They hadn't talked about the kidnap or rescue, and James felt Bekah wanted it that way. Everyone else had fully recovered thanks to Master Ironhorse, even Fenwick's wing.

As they entered a large open-air pavilion, where they hadn't been before, James was amazed at the large semicircle of raised benches and the four distinct areas with each patrol flag. Even the benches were painted in the patrol colors. The Sphinx Patrol was to the far right and James joined Bekah, Michael and Kari near the front.

Each section of benches lined up behind a large round firepit, making up four firepits surrounding a large central firepit. All had wood in a pyramid centered in each pit. As the students all filed in, James watched Master McAdams walk to the very front, behind the large firepit. Then he watched Master Belle move to the Sphinx patrol firepit, Master Lindsley to the Centaur patrol firepit, Master Walker to the Griffin patrol firepit and Master Savage to the Minotaur patrol firepit. All other professors were at the back of the benches. There was no big staff table or benches up front.

Master McAdams began to speak, "Welcome to all of Campus Gaea tonight. We are so happy to have all the patrol members here. May I welcome the Sphinx Patrol." He paused and the fire in front of Master Belle lit with a bright orange flame. It immediately engulfed the wood and was burning two to three feet above the firepit. James could feel the excitement welling up inside him.

"Welcome to the Centaur Patrol." Master Lindsley stepped forward and the Centaur fire burst into a dark red flame of similar magnitude.

Master McAdams just nodded his head and continued. "Welcome to the Griffin Patrol." And the fire before Master Walker erupted into a large purple flame.

"Welcome to the Minotaur Patrol." Master Savage lit the final fire, a large blue flame.

As the flames continued to burn in their radiant colored flames, Master McAdams continued. "Let me make a simple observation. We utilize rope on a regular basis. Ropes can be made to carry and support very heavy objects. The strength of the rope is not in a single strand, but in the combination of multiple strands. I think of a simple thread that can be easily broken combined with 100s of other threads to make a small rope. Then you combine 100s or small ropes to make a larger rope. This large rope can support great weights and is not easily cut even. As *The Band of Fire*, we can likewise be stronger if we continue to come together. To combine into one."

As Master McAdams finished the final phrase, the bright orange flame, dark red flame, purple flame and blue flame disappeared from the firepits and a large silver-white fire erupted with 4-5 feet flames in the large central firepit. "I am excited to celebrate each of you as members of *The Band of Fire*."

James was amazed as he looked from firepit to firepit and noticed all the fires were out except the one. It was as if the central fire was lit by the four. Before James could figure out what had happened, Master McAdams continued.

"We will begin with the Champion Patrol award. This goes to the patrol that completed The Final Patrol Challenge first. This award goes to the Griffin Patrol!"

The Griffin Patrol section erupted with excitement and the Patrol Leader walked forward to receive the Gold Cup that would remain in their camp until the end of next summer. Bekah smiling leaned over to James and whispered, "The Griffin Patrol has never won this award!"

"Congratulations to all for the great summer and the stiff competition on all three Patrol Challenges."

As the clapping subsided, Marcus and Martha took their places next to Master McAdams. He then continued, "We now invite all the First Year Titans forward. For only the third year in a row, all the First Years still here at camp have earned the first rank of Silver Spark."

As James, Bekah, Michael and Kari walked forward, they were joined by the first years from each patrol. Each had an 8-pointed silver star pinned on their shirt. James looked down and was excited to have his first Titan award, especially when he looked up to see Mom and Dad both in attendance. Bekah was beaming from ear to ear.

As they returned to their seats, each year was recognized for those that earned the rank advancement for the year. It was interesting, but as they moved to later years fewer and fewer individuals were involved enough to get the next award. Only 3 individuals stood for the final year, one of them being Marcus, the Senior Patrol Leader and the other Gracey from the Sphinx Patrol.

"This award is the greatest award that can be earned as a Titan. It is The Phoenix." Master McAdams then help up a beautiful red, white and blue ribbon from a pin with a rose gold bird with its wings spread handing from the end of the ribbon. The bird was decorated with a golden flame on its left breast, an 8-pointed star (The Silver Spark) behind its head and a midnight black rock in its left talon and lightning in its right talon. James was very impressed and wanted to ensure he earned that award in the future.

As the clapping subsided and pictures were taken, Master McAdams stood next to the fire again as the fire started to die down. As his blue eyes twinkled in the firelight, he began to speak.

"A native American chief watched eight braves playing in the open field and realized they were now old enough to become men. As was the tradition of their forefathers, he invited all the braves to his tent the next morning to make the final trek from boyhood to manhood. It was a trip they would have to make alone, a trip that would determine who they were to be. His invitation to them was therefore very carefully worded."

"He started, 'You are all great young men, braves your parents can be proud of, but will be making decisions now that will determine who you become.' He paused carefully looking at each one. 'I, therefore, will be challenging each of you to make a trek to manhood this day. It is a simple trip, one that you can go only as far as you desire. Your progress and growth is yours to determine.'"

"The braves all looked excited at the challenge, even as they stood in the dark before the sun was yet to rise. 'Each of you will leave this camp and head to the mountain in the distance. Climb as far as you can and then bring me a twig of the tree at the point where you turn back. Then I can know to what heights you have climbed. You will receive your reward based on the heights to which you have climbed.'"

"The excitement in the group began to grow. Many were sure they would reach the top and bring back proof of their arrival and get the greatest reward. As the eight prepared, the chief was pleased with them preparing food and drink for the trip and several of them preparing backpacks. But one brave was unique and seemed to be more carefully preparing. As he released the group, two ran ahead, wanting to be the first to arrive at the top. Two were moving more slowly but were likewise in a hurry. Two more grabbed their backpacks and started to drink water even before they left. The second to last was very meticulous and left a few minutes later than the rest. The one that really caught the chief's attention, however, was the final brave who packed and unpacked his bag several times ensuring sufficient preparation. When he finally left, the other braves were already well on their way."

"Several hours later, one of the first to leave running came hobbling back exhausted but carrying only a cactus leaf. 'Son,' the chief started, 'you didn't even make it across the desert. You didn't even get to see the great mountain.' The brave walked away with his head slightly down."

"An hour later, another brave returned with a branch from a pale-gray shrub with yellow flowers and silvery-grey foliage. 'My son,' the chief said after examining the branch, 'you bring a branch of the Big Sagebrush, a plant located at the base of the mountain. You have seen the great mountain and saw its great beauty but failed to even start to climb. You therefore have your reward.' The brave nodded his head and walked away wondering if he should have gone further."

"The next young brave returned carrying a branch with 2-5 inch long and wide, veined dark green leaves with reddish leaf stems. He looked excited and exhausted. 'You, my son,' the chief said after examining the branch. 'You have brought me the beautiful branch of a Rocky Mountain Maple. This is the tree of the first forest as you climb the mountain. You made a good climb but missed much of the rewards of the climb.'"

"Within moments another brave returned carrying a branch with a dark green leaf with doubly-serrated and pinnate venation. Leaves 2-5 inches long. The chief gathered the branch from him and smiled. 'You, my son, climbed past the base of the mountain and through the first forest to the beautiful Thinleaf

Alder trees. The beauty you were privileged to see was missed by any that didn't climb to your same height. Well done.'"

"The fifth brave returned later in the day carrying an evergreen branch with 1 inch long green needles with bracts at the base. 'You crossed the great river and entered the beautiful Douglas Fir groves. The smell and wildlife you saw were amazing. You reached halfway up the great mountain.'"

"The next returned with a branch with a broad-leaf rounded foliage saw-toothed on the edges and pointed at the tip. 'The Quaking Aspen is at the base of the second forest. By reaching that level, you 2/3 of the way to the top. The view from there is amazing. Well done, my son.'"

"As the sun began to set, the 7th brave came walking into camp. He was tired, but excited as he discussed reaching the highest trees. In his hands he was carrying an evergreen branch with 1-inch light green, extremely sharp needles. 'Well done, my son, you have reached the highest trees as you have brought me the Blue Spruce branch. Where is the last brave?' As they all looked around, they just smiled. 'He probably got lost!' they said in unison."

"As the moon rose into the sky, a brave came walking quickly into camp. There was a bounce in his step, a large smile on his face and nothing in his hands. As he entered the camp the other braves started to laugh thinking he didn't even reach the mountain and had truly gotten lost. 'I could not bring back a branch dear chief,' he said with a song in his voice. 'There were no branches at the height where I had climbed. But I saw the valleys to the other side. I saw the mountain goats jumping from rock to rock. I saw the rivers and the forests and felt the cool breeze come from the caves round about. I reached the top of the mountain and need no reward.' The chief smiled and turned to the others who were now quiet. 'He couldn't bring a branch, because no trees grow on the top of the mountain, but the glow in his face, the smile on his lips, the song in his voice and the bounce in his step all show proof that he was where he says. Well done my son, for you have reached the greatest heights and will continue to do anything you desire to do.'"

"So now as we come to the end of camp, I am inviting all of you to go back into the world similar to this final brave. What new heights can you reach? What new learning and service will you participate in? You are now a Titan and a member of *The Band of Fire* and therefore must act accordingly. What you do from now on will not just affect you, but will be an indication of who you really are and who we all are. Are you ready?"

The benches started to buzz with noise as Master McAdams paused. "And now for the rules. 1) You cannot tell Natural-Born individuals about your skills or Campus Gaea. You were here for a 'Summer Camp', not a special educational opportunity. 2) You cannot use your skills in ways that will draw attention to you. If any Natural-Born questions your abilities, because of something you have done that doesn't make sense, you will be reprimanded by *The Band of Fire*. 3) You are to participate as much as possible in normal life. Therefore, plan on attending school, participating in your church and other responsibilities. Only then can you truly get integrated into society and be a valuable member of *The Band of Fire*. 4) I was told not to give this rule, but I feel you need it. Be careful with The Order of the Kraken. They don't want to make you better! They are only worried about themselves. "

James turned to look at Bekah as her fists clenched. She just winked at him and said nothing.

CHAPTER 40
CONCORDANT I AM

He lay quietly on his cot and all the night sounds were quiet. The fires had been out for hours and the August wind that had been blowing through the trees since midnight was now calm. Helia had failed to return to the tent that night and even Michael's heavy breathing at night was absent. Not a sound could be heard and James felt like he was again having a dream. But this time there was no music and no laugh.

He crawled carefully from his sleeping bag and off his cot, slipped off his pajamas and back into his clothes. When he slipped on his shoes and prepared to leave his tent, he noticed that even Jacques' usual noise while patrolling the path was absent. Where was he?

As he walked to the tent door, everything came into focus and he knew at once what was going on. The Order of the Kraken were not attacking, but instead there was someone outside. He stood 15 feet from James' tent door and Jacques was silent, standing in the center of the path at attention. Helia was on one shoulder and Feliciity was on the other. Master Doc McAdams was standing outside.

"Are you coming out, or should I just continue my walk without you?" came the voice in his head. *"Just you and I are awake in camp."*

James walked from the tent to see Master McAdams standing in the darkness in all black with only the glow of two phoenix from his direction.

No words were spoken as James approached him, and they both turned and walked away.

"You have done well this summer. Your parents and I are very proud of you. But you must remember that although you are Concordant, you are not yet well skilled at these various abilities. Camilla, however, is! Please be careful to not put yourself or your friends in grave danger by challenging The Order. There will come a time when you will be ready to face her, but now is not that time. Please don't seek her out. Please don't engage them. We need you to develop into a true Concordant!"

James didn't speak, but just nodded his head.

"When you entered camp, we found you to be Concordant, but you didn't believe us. We took you through tasks, and you still didn't believe us. I sense now that you are still worried and not sure that you truly are Concordant. Do you truly believe?"

James saw the first trip in the bus, when he recognized the bus traveling through Chronopathy. He saw *The Classification,* when he travelled with Master McAdams to Iguazu Falls where he would later return to rescue Bekah and Dad. He saw each class with highlights from learning to row a boat in Herculopathy, learning to orient without a map in Orientopathy, learning to understand health more completely in Hippocratesense. Then his mind started racing more quickly from Patrol Task to Patrol Task.

...He looked around and everything changed...

He wasn't standing next to Michael anymore, but was standing by a large tree. The willow tree had a large, straight branch that he easily removed with his pocketknife. As he was cutting the branch, some of the bark fell to the ground, and he placed it into his backpack. With minimal effort, he formed the branch into a bow. He then quickly formed a string using a combination of roots and willow stems he was able to find around him. He also quickly cut three additional arrows and sharpened them to a point. If he was going to fight, he was going to be prepared. He looked around again and noticed a large fallen tree to his left and quickly shaped a portion of it to a club and another portion into a shield. The shield when complete was about 4 feet wide and 4 feet tall. This would be perfect to protect the girls as they continued to dig. He also quickly formed a second shovel and decided it was time to return.

Moments later he was standing next to Michael again and he noticed everyone was still stopped. He wasn't exactly sure how it all happened, but he was excited to see he was now ready for the battle. So, he placed the shield covering the girls and placed the second shovel next to them. Everything then started to return to normal speed.

He had forgotten about that part of Patrol Challenge 1.

…James felt a unique desire to breath. But breathing underwater didn't make any sense. But his mind was calm and clear and without hesitation, he knew he could breathe. So, he took a deep breath and his lungs filled with water.

As he took a deep breath, Mark was shaking his head vigorously with his eyes wide open. He grabbed at James, but it was too late. He was drowning as his lungs filled completely with water and then James felt his chest tighten and he saw every alveolus of the lung contract in great strength, almost like a grape being squeezed for juice, but instead of juice oxygen was released into the blood stream from the water. He was breathing without difficulty under the water…

James turned back to Master McAdams. Yes, he knew he was Concordant! Master McAdams just smiled and continued to speak directly to James mind.

"Now that you understand and know, your training can really begin. Too bad the summer is over, but there is yet much to come."

They didn't talk the rest of the walk, but James knew this was the most important instruction of the summer. He was Concordant and now even he believed it. Next summer can't come quick enough, but at least in the meantime he will have Bekah just down the street and Mom and Dad at home that he can talk to.

ABOUT THE AUTHOR

Dr Brandt R Gibson is the father of 11 children and husband of an amazing woman, the two roles he enjoys the most. He is also a podiatric physician (specializing in foot and ankle care) and has revolutionized the care of Peripheral Neuropathy for his patients. He also thrives on service to his community, state and his church, including serving a church mission to Brazil for two years, coaching many soccer teams over the years and working in the Boy Scouts of America for over 21 years. As an Eagle Scout and now Scoutmaster for 8 years (this time), he has learned to love "God's beautiful world" and enjoys taking youth out into the wilderness to camp and hike. He feels it is one of God's secret training grounds that is underutilized today. These trips are still some of his most beloved experiences.

One of his great goals as father, as soccer coach, and as scouter is to help kids and youth grow into better individuals, stronger community members, better servants of God and ultimately individuals that help create miracles throughout the world. He wants them to touch the world through their own lives and even the lives of their future children. He has watched many boys and girls become men and women that make the world a better place. He hopes to continue to make these changes as he touches the lives of youth and adults alike around the world.

BECOMING CONCORDANT:
Using Balance and Knowledge to Become The Ideal You

If you could join *The Band of Fire* and learn and grow as James and his friends are, would you do it?

If you could learn how to use your talents, strengths and even weakness to make a difference in your own life and the world around, would you?

Maybe you have found that you are often distracted from making the progress you desire and improving your life or the lives of others.

The truth is, although you aren't a Titan in the sense of *The Band of Fire Chronicles,* you are unique and can *Become Concordant* in your life!

Dr Brandt R Gibson, through years of working with his children, patients, scouts, teams and even adults in his community has found seven proven steps to becoming The Ideal You and A Leader in Life.

Join Dr Gibson for this Journey
TheBandOfFire.com

Do You Have Children or Youth That Would Benefit From This Story?

Master storyteller Dr Brandt R Gibson, in hopes of making this book available to a larger audience, decided to read his own book in audio format. This Story is now available in multiple formats including audio version on iTunes, Audible.com and other locations. Now you can join James and Bekah on their journey of growth and adventures at home, in the park, while exercising or even in the car.

Get your audiobook copy today.

CPSIA information can be obtained
at www.ICGtesting.com
Printed in the USA
BVHW07s0727040918
526010BV00004B/5/P